THE BETWEEN

RYAN LESLIE

Edited by Celeste Hawkins, Megan Hultberg

Cover Illustration by James Hutton

Parliament House Press

www.parliamenthousepress.com

CHAPTER 1
BE HUMAN, PAUL PRENTICE

Paul's shovel hit something hard, something that shouldn't have been there in the clay soil of his suburban backyard, and the jolt from the impact shook him out of the robotic work-trance he had been in all morning. He frowned at the shovel like it had failed him and wiped his brow with a sleeve that was already soaked with sweat from the Texas summer sun.

When he had told Julie that he planned on doing the landscaping work himself, she gave him an amused look that said, *oh you silly creature who never learns*. It was a look he had grown quite familiar with over the five years of their marriage. You would think, with Julie's track record of being right, Paul would recognize that look as a signal to rethink the ill-considered plan he had enthusiastically described to her. Instead, even with his history of failures, he took that look of hers as a challenge, an opportunity to prove her wrong. And so, each time, her look became a little more amused, he became a little more determined, and the failure became a little more spectacular.

This time was proving to be no different.

Mounds and mounds of dirt surrounded him, and yet he had only cleared away about a third of the dirt on the slope leading down to his kitchen door. After the hard rain in May when water ran from an overflowing spring two blocks to the north, the water had cascaded down his backyard like a waterpark ride, pooling outside the kitchen, rising inch after inch, threatening catastrophic damage to their non-flood-insured home.

Min-woo Kim, their neighbor across the street, said they needed a retaining wall and a channel to clear the water to the side of the house. Paul put a quick estimate of the materials at about a grand, give or take. The first contractor came back with a quote of $4,500, and the second doubled that, including a rainwater collection system Paul neither asked for nor wanted.

He convinced himself that the work would be, if not fun exactly, rewarding in an evolutionary psychology kind of way, releasing the primal drive to build shelter, to homestead. Or something like that. And maybe Julie would be impressed. Those good spirits lasted about an hour and a half into the actual digging, when the morning clouds had been burned away and the temperature crept toward triple digits.

And now he had hit something solid with his shovel. Probably a limestone boulder he'd have to unearth, and then he'd need Jay's truck to pull it loose. Saturday would end with little to show for it, and tonight Julie would ask, "How's it going out there, sweetie?" and he'd say, "Just super. Everything according to plan. Pass the bourbon."

He should've hired the work done. He and Julie had the money after all, but Paul was still trying to recover financially from the statue incident back in the spring. He wasn't being cheap. There was a difference between being cheap and being *a good steward of family resources*.

He'd actually said those words out loud in April when Julie deleted the household budget spreadsheet he'd spent an entire weekend setting up, complete with electronic feeds of their bank transactions, credit card purchases, and brokerage data. She even nuked the cloud backup of the file.

"Normal people don't use phrases like *good steward of family resources*, Paul. This is a marriage, not a corporate cost center, capeesh?" she said. "To make up for budgeting me *discretionary spending* of $200 a month—a fucking allowance!—I need to see an act of unadulterated frivolity. For penance, you must buy something irrationally expensive. On a whim. I know you can do it. I've seen you drop a couple hundred bucks on an old, stinky book."

"I've collected rare books as long as you've known me."

"Oh, yes. Collecting. Investing. Every purchase rationalized away and properly accounted for. But I want to see if you're capable of letting loose, Mr. Accountant. So no books, got it? Un-a-dul-ter-a-ted fri-vol-i-ty." She emphasized every syllable of his lexical kryptonite. "It should feel like getting a tattoo. If some part of your brain isn't screaming *this is a bad idea!* while another part is screaming *do it do it do it!* then you've failed. Be human, Paul Prentice."

It was the *be human* comment that really got to him.

I'll show her unadulterated frivolity, he thought. A week later, at the Wayland Gallery on West Sixth, a short walk from their house, he spent almost five thousand dollars on a wooden statue called *First Mother*. A six-foot-tall, buffalo-headed, pregnant nude carved in American basswood. The gallery owner claimed it was a feminist, Native American re-spinning of the Greek minotaur figure. Or something like that.

Julie had seemed quite taken by the statue when they saw it in the gallery together. When she encountered it unexpectedly standing in the corner of their living room, on the other hand, it nearly gave her a heart attack.

First Mother stared out the living room window at Paul with her accusatory animal eyes, arms crossed on her distended, pregnant belly. How fitting was it that he had a shovel in his hand, with the figurative hole he was digging himself out of with Julie, and the statue-shaped hole in their bank account?

He gave the statue a half-hearted smile that looked more like a wince and then put his focus back on the problem at hand. The rock in the ground. He moved about a foot to the left of where he'd been digging and jammed the shovel down into the clay. *Boom!* He hit the rock again, but this time it echoed, almost like a great bell had rung.

"Are you kidding me?" he muttered and tried again another foot over.

Boom!

Confused, he looked to the left and right. It did sound like a bell, or at least something metal, and the sound seemed to come from all around him. He began scraping away at the top of the soil.

Ten minutes later, he had uncovered a rusty iron door.

Over the next several hours, Paul avoided the door as if he had never seen it, as if it weren't a persistent void on the edge of his periphery. When Julie came home around 6, sweaty herself from a 90-minute hot yoga session (why anyone would pay for 100 degree studio time when the Texas summer supplied it for free, Paul had no idea), he saw her through the kitchen window and ran inside to meet her. He rambled on a bit about hitting some snags here and there, rocks in the soil, one big rock really but nothing he couldn't handle, and the unforeseen time it was taking to get the angles right. Without the right angles—the correct angles, he should say--what was the point? She didn't need to go back there. Stuff to trip on. Hard to gauge progress without understanding his master plan. Would she like to see his master plan?

He didn't tell her about the door, because telling her about the door meant worrying her needlessly, and anyway, he had stopped acknowledging the existence of the door, so there was really nothing to tell her.

Julie gave him an arched right eyebrow. "I'm sure your master plan is quite masterful, but I'm taking a shower. Will you be done before Jay and Min-woo get here? Aren't they coming over to watch a boxing match or something?"

The boxing match! He had almost forgotten! The backyard would have to wait. Paul turned on the television, set the DVR to record—in case Min-woo was late, as usual—and went out to sit on his front porch in the still-100-degree early evening. Not thinking about the door.

An hour or so later Jay pulled up in an old pickup truck that had recently developed the same, strange gurgling exhaust note that all of Jay's previous automobiles eventually produced. *Gugguta-gugguta-gugguta.* Jay stepped out onto the curb and held in his outstretched right hand a six-pack of *Carta Blanca* longnecks like he was Perseus proudly displaying the head of Medusa. The beer's cardboard carrier box chose that moment to give out. In the Greek myth, which Paul knew well, two drops of Medusa's blood dripped from her severed head, forming the winged horse Pegasus and the winged boar Chrysaor. Instead of drops of blood, however, two beer bottles fell from the carrier box and exploded on the concrete curb, soaking Jay's jeans. No winged animals appeared.

"Uh. Two of the three beers I brought for you just exploded," Jay said.

Paul laughed so hard he started choking. Jay scowled and cursed, but soon wore the crooked, dopey grin Paul had seen almost daily since they had met in elementary school over twenty years ago. Jay seemed to have changed less during that time than anyone else Paul knew. He had the same curly hair that always ended up going every which direction. The same way of walking without swinging his arms, strides a bit too long, his whole body bobbing up and down like a boat on rough water. Or better yet, with his gaunt frame and exaggerated features, like a big marionette. Of course, now there was the receding hairline, perpetual scruff, and an almost imperceptible sadness in his eyes that hadn't always been there. But otherwise, Jay was the same gangly kid he'd always been, just in manchild form.

"Oh, those were my beers that broke, were they?" Paul jumped down from the porch and met him on the sidewalk. He still found it strange to shake Jay's hand. Not that handshakes, in general, were strange. Okay, maybe a bit, with the weird masculine display of hand strength, where you have to look strong without looking like you're trying to look strong, grasping the opposing hand somewhere in a Goldilocks Zone of firmness. Other men seemed to approach handshakes naturally, but Paul always became self-conscious, which sometimes ended up with an incomplete latch, his fingers getting squeezed, and both parties pretending like this social failure hadn't just happened.

Second-grade Paul hadn't started by shaking second-grade Jay's hand after the incident at the swing-set during recess. It must've been college before they switched from non-hand-shakers to hand-shakers. Jay surely extended that first palm, having picked up the habit from all that hanging out in bars he did. And still did. Lots of hand-shaking between tipsy men in bars.

They shook hands (successfully), and Jay pulled him in for a half-hug. The hugging was a newer phenomenon than the hand-shaking and usually meant Jay had been drinking. But Jay pulled back after encountering a cocktail of sweat, mosquito repellent, and spray-on sunscreen from Paul's shoulder.

"Is the big fight on, or are we still in the undercard?" Jay asked, and then, with a step back and a look like he'd smelled something wretched, added, "What the hell are you doing out here, anyway? It's hotter than the devil's asshole. You're all sweaty and stinky."

What had Paul been doing for the last hour? Not thinking about the door—that was for sure. "I was, uh, working in the backyard. Lost track of time. Don't worry about the fight. I'm recording it. Min-woo's always late, anyway, and we should wait for him before we start watching. Maybe I should go get cleaned up. De-stink. You mind?"

"No, I prefer you stinky and sweaty." Jay narrowed his eyes and then added, "You're acting weird. What's going on?"

"Nothing's going on," Paul said before he could catch himself. Besides his wife Julie, the other person he couldn't lie to was Jay. Jay had a sixth sense about people and lies. One of Jay's bizarre talents which worked especially well on Paul. All the air seemed to rush out from him, and he sat hard on the porch step.

Jay sat down next to him and used the step's edge to bang off the caps of two of the beers. "Here you go. Now, whatever it is, out with it."

"I found something, and it's got me a little freaked out," Paul said.

6

Jay nodded solemnly, took a deep breath, and asked, deadpan, "Is it a lump on one of your nuts?" He folded his arms and shook his head. "It's all that sitting on a bicycle you do. I told you that can't be good for the boys. But we'll get through it. Same thing happened to Lance Armstrong, and with one ball he still won all those bicycle races. Of course, he was blasting steroids up his ass the entire time. All I'm saying is there's hope."

Paul took a long pull on the beer and said, "Are you quite done?"

"Done? Me? Never." It was true. If you gave Jay empty space, he tended to fill it, Robin Williams style. The best way to keep Jay from descending into manic zaniness was to keep him occupied.

"I found a door," Paul started, and before he knew it, he was unloading all these fears he had surrounding the door that hadn't even cohered yet in his own mind. What the hell was under his yard, maybe even under his house? Could the whole house fall in, like what happens with sinkholes sometimes, and would his insurance even cover that? What if it happened when they were sleeping? What if the door led to a secret torture room or a burial chamber full of bodies? Austin had its own Jack the Ripper back around the turn of the twentieth century. Maybe this was the killer's hideout. It's why the city built the moontowers around here a century ago, to try to make this area safer at night. It had happened right here! And what about Julie? What would Julie think with a crypt or something just feet from where they slept?

Jay listened without interrupting, without smiling when Paul's rambling grew more and more absurd.

"You're free to tell me I'm being an idiot," Paul finally said after running out of horror story scenarios involving the door.

Jay shrugged and opened a second beer for himself. He offered the last one to Paul, but Paul's was still mostly full. "So ... you're being an idiot."

"Thanks. You're a fucking pal."

Jay winked and jumped to his feet. "I don't see why a crypt full of dead bodies has to be creepy. You didn't even have to pay extra for it. Free square footage, man! And if it is a secret torture chamber, think of how much fun you can have terrorizing the neighbor kids during Halloween. You could even charge for admission, with a royalty coming back to me for giving you the idea."

"Is this supposed to make me feel better?" Paul asked.

"Laughter is the best medicine. That's what they say, right?"

"I'm not laughing."

Jay squinted at Paul and slowly nodded his head. "Hmm. You aren't laughing. Maybe you're failing to see the ridiculousness of the situation. Is that a word? Ridiculousness? Or is it ridiculosity?" He didn't wait for an answer and grabbed Paul by the forearm, yanking him to stand up.

Paul pulled his arm away. "What the hell are you doing?"

"We're trading places," Jay said. He sat on the porch, where Paul had been sitting. "I'm Paul now, and you're me. I mean, you're Jay. Now ask me why I look like someone stuck a booger in my peanut butter sandwich."

Paul rolled his eyes. "This is stupid." But Jay kept giving him that crooked grin, and Paul knew damn well that Jay would keep at it until Paul played along. "Fine. Okay, I'm Jay. Look at me being Jay." Paul walked in circles in his front yard without swinging his arms, taking overly-long strides, and bobbing his head. "I'm walking around being Jay, looking like a doofus."

"Very funny," Jay said. "Now ask me about the door."

Paul curled his lip and asked, Elvis-like, "What's the deal with the door?"

"I'm sitting here overthinking things, as usual, you know, being Paul," Jay said, voice raised a half-octave, face contorted like he was constipated. "I got all worked up about a door I found buried in my backyard, but it's probably just something a construction crew buried, but I'm gonna worry about it anyway until my handsome and much smarter friend Jay, who by the way has a much bigger penis, comes and checks it out for me."

"I don't talk like that," Paul said. "And anyway, what the hell is the purpose of this?"

"I have no idea," Jay said, springing to his feet. "You think I'm Dr. Phil or something? It's time to go check out this door of yours."

Their back-and-forth imitations had lightened Paul's mood, but when Jay started walking toward the side of the house, Paul's sense of dread returned. "What about the fight?"

Jay looked back over his shoulder, grin wider than ever. "Paused, mofo. Like you said. Now let's go!" And with that, he skipped toward the backyard like they were on their way to second-grade recess.

CHAPTER 2
THE CALL OF THE VOID

With the sun finally set, the main light source near the iron door was a bug zapper hanging from the lone pecan tree, casting an orange glow that flared and crackled every few seconds as a winged insect met its demise. The orange cast made the door look like it had been heated to near melting by a magma-filled cavern below, as though it opened directly to a fiery hell. That image pushed Paul over his limit —time to call the whole thing off, come back one morning, possibly with a cement truck and trained professionals who could fill up any sinkhole, or crypt, or gateway to Hell that sat under his backyard.

But Jay had already seen the door. Paul's heart caught in his throat as he watched Jay run straight toward it, jump, and land hard right in the door's center with both feet. The door boomed with the impact but held.

"Jesus, man! You're gonna get yourself killed!"

Jay dropped to his hands and knees so he could examine the door up close. Without looking back, he said, "You're always saying I'm gonna get myself killed, and how many times has it happened so far?"

"It only takes once." A montage of near-Jay-deaths played through Paul's head. The fall from the tree with the rope swing freshman year. The rollover of Jay's old Isuzu Trooper in the high school parking lot. The water moccasins in Lake Austin when they were jumping off the rocks back in middle school, or maybe fifth grade. And the first near-death experience, the one they never spoke of. But that wasn't Jay's near-death. That was Paul's.

Jay traced the edges of the door like an archaeologist who had discovered the entrance to a secret Egyptian tomb, brushing aside dirt, nodding his head knowingly. "There's a chamber of some kind here," he said. "No doubt about it. See how it's set into concrete? Look at the size of these hinges. I bet this door weighs a hundred pounds." He hopped off and grabbed the door's handle. He yanked twice, creating more reverberating booms, but the door didn't open.

Paul shifted his weight from one foot to the other and waved off the mosquitos that had started orbiting his head. "It's too dark to see anything. Min-woo's coming over to watch the fight also, remember? He's probably at the front door wondering where the hell we are. We can fuck with this tomorrow."

"Julie can let Min-woo in," Jay said, fishing his cell phone out of his pocket. After a few taps on the phone's screen, the door and its surrounding few feet shone under the phone's piercing little LED flashlight. "Ah! Here's the problem. A padlock. Numbers are all rusted off, but it looks like one of those old standard kinds like we used to have on our lockers."

A wave of relief washed through Paul. If the door was locked, they'd need a locksmith or maybe some bolt cutters. Can you cut through a padlock with bolt cutters? He didn't know, and it didn't matter, because he didn't own any. The door would have to wait for another day. He told Jay as much, but his single-minded friend remained hunched over, ass in the air, ear pressed against the back of the padlock, twisting the lock's dial slowly.

Jay held a long, bony finger up to his lips, balancing in the world's worst yoga pose. "Shhhhhh. I'm demonstrating my lock-picking skills. Did you know I have lock-picking skills?"

"You should add that to your online dating profile," Paul said. "Proficient in lock-picking and masturbation." He expected some sort of response, but Jay was focused on the lock. The longer Jay kept twirling the dial back and forth, the more Paul's anxiety returned.

"We'll mess with it next weekend. We could be inside right now watching boxing and drinking beer. Oh, and I've got some new bourbon you need to try. Cask strength, eighteen years old. Knockout stuff." He cringed at that last bit, hearing himself encouraging Jay's drinking.

"Quit the chitter-chatter," Jay said, not taking the bait. "I need silence for this to work." Jay twisted the dial slowly to the right for two or three full rotations and then nodded. He adjusted it slightly to the left. Nodded again. Ninety or so degrees back to the right.

"You have no idea what you're doing," Paul said.

"Is that so? Witness my excellence," Jay said, and with a *SNAP!* the lock popped open.

The door was heavy and took both of them to pull it open. Paul almost fell in, and when Jay grabbed his shirt, he almost fell in as well, as if the yard suddenly sloped down and toward the hole.

"Mother of God," Paul said, backing away from the open black hole in the middle of his yard.

Jay wasn't smiling anymore. "Mother o' God indeed, man. That's a serious goddamn hole." He got down on his knees and knee-walked until he was a foot away from its edge. "Feel that? Come closer, Paul. Careful, though, I can't see the bottom. Feel how cold it is?"

The cold air reached Paul's ankles first and then ran up his body like little spiders. Worse than the cold was the smell. Damp. Bitter, aggressive mold. An earthy smell so strong that he could taste it in his mouth when he inhaled. A smell that dug up memories Paul had kept buried deep in his mind. When the memories came loose, they flooded into him, filthy water pushing through his nose and into his sinuses, pushing down his throat, filling him with that rotten smell, that feeling of being taken over by something alive and alien.

A look of alarmed confusion came over Jay. "Dude. You need to sit down or something. You look like you're about to pass out."

"I don't know what you're talking about," Paul spat. "I'm fine."

Jay eyed him suspiciously.

Paul walked forward two steps, even though every part of him wanted to turn and run. "I'm fine," he repeated. He could hear the unsteady tone of his voice.

Jay stared at him for several seconds and then shrugged and pointed his phone's light down into the hole. "There's a ladder. Room doesn't look very big, but it's hard to tell without going down."

"So go down, then," Paul said. "Or don't." Now he was getting reckless. The ladder could disintegrate under Jay's weight. But when Jay started lowering himself down, Paul didn't protest.

A black mass slid across the moon. Where had the cloud come from? Hadn't it been wide open sky all day? All the stars seemed to have gone out. Even with the city's light pollution, Paul could always see a few stars. So maybe more clouds had rolled in. A toad near the edge of the fence started croaking, like a squeaky door hinge opening and closing. All that came from the moontower, somewhere beyond the trees, was the hint of a dying sun setting for the final time. So much for casting out the hiding places of serial killers.

A thudding came from the hole, getting louder and louder until Jay's head re-emerged.

"You have to come down here, man," Jay said, crooked grin illuminated by the phone in his hand. "We've got ourselves a cool little hangout. There's a sofa and all these bookshelves full of old books. I think we may have hit the Paul Prentice jackpot! Could be some rare stuff down here!"

The crescent moon reappeared, and its light seemed to push away the musty smell coming out of the hole—either that or Paul had gone nose-blind to the smell. Had a menacing darkness really come over the backyard, or had he been about to pass out? What had Jay said about books? Rare books? Paul took a deep breath and said, "Let me run inside and get a real flashlight. And make sure Min-woo isn't waiting on us."

Jay gave him an amused nod as if he could see the mental hand-wringing going on inside his friend's head. Jay didn't protest or rush him, but Paul still hustled. He grabbed the big, aluminum Maglite from under the kitchen sink and then almost had a heart attack when he walked into the living room and saw *First Mother* standing there in the corner like a monster hiding in the shadows.

No sign of Min-woo. As he jogged back toward the kitchen, he noticed that the light in the study was on. Julie sat with her back toward the door, framed by the light of her laptop. She had her big headphones on and was bopping her head to music only she could hear. He had a sudden urge to tell her about the hole and let her be the one to ruin Jay's fun. *You're not exploring this thing at night. No fucking way,* she'd say. That would be that. Jay wouldn't argue with Julie.

But Paul couldn't let Julie do his dirty work, so he gave himself a brief second to watch her and to breathe in the Julie-ness of the moment before he went back outside.

The Maglite, with its four D batteries, put out a cone of light like a magic wand. Jay's eyes glimmered in reflection before he threw his hand up. "Are you trying to blind me or something?" he said before he ducked back into the darkness.

"Sorry," Paul said, too quiet for Jay to hear. He stared at the hole. Everything in the world ceased to be, except for Paul and the square of black directly in front of him. The emptiness pulled at him. It grabbed a hold of the part of him that couldn't resist peering into the void.

Come down here with me, Paul Prentice. Come.

He walked to its edge and looked down. With Jay flashing his phone around the room below, there was no void for Paul to see. He felt cheated, and at the same time horrified at himself for feeling cheated. He let out a deep breath and shined the Maglight down.

A room, like Jay had said. A 1970's worn, plaid sofa sat against one of the concrete walls, and bookshelves lined the others, with one tall bookshelf directly across from the sofa that stretched almost from the floor to the ceiling. From above, the room seemed small, but it must've been fifteen by fifteen, and at least ten feet high—or, he supposed, ten feet deep.

He descended carefully, the flashlight in his left hand, the side of the metal ladder gripped tightly in his right. Some part of his brain was already doing math: maybe twenty-five books per shelf, times 1-2-3-4-5-6-7-8-9 shelves. Two-hundred twenty-five books, give or take. A nice little library. What the hell was it doing down here?

"Hold this," he said, handing the flashlight to Jay. If it hadn't been for the books, he would've wondered about the temperature; cold enough to make them both shiver, too cold to be explained by simply being underground. Bookshelves were Paul's catnip. Any time he went into a new house—friends, colleagues, etc.—and he passed by a bookshelf, he found himself compelled to stop. You could tell a lot about a person by what books they kept. Which ones looked old and worn, read and reread. Which were new and untouched. Lots of non-fiction showed a hunger for learning. The classics showed a person was thorough and patient (unless the books all had aging college bookstore stickers on them). Self-help books showed a healthy intro-spection, unless there were too many, or heaven forbid the only books on the shelves. He loved knowing a person's *home genre*, so to speak.

Someone had built this underground library. What did the books say about them? He pulled one at random from the shelf and imme-diately recognized it. "Jay," he said. "Jay! You have to see this."

"It's a book," Jay said.

"Not just a book. It's the first US printing of *The Stranger*. Probably from '46 or '47. I shouldn't even be handling it without gloves." He shivered, either from the cold or from the exhilaration of finding a first edition he had dreamed of owning. He started to open it but imagined his unsteady hands tearing the 70-year-old pages, and instead held it tightly shut.

The whole room seemed to quiver as Jay walked up next to him with the flashlight. "Never heard of it. Is it valuable?"

"Is it valuable? You've never heard of *The Stranger*? Albert Camus? Maybe the most famous work of twentieth-century French litera-ture?" Paul heard himself—particularly the way he said *al-BER cah-MYOOO*—and winced. "My lord that sounded pretentious. Sorry."

"Oh, I'm quite used to it."

Their breath was condensing into a hazy fog. Paul waved the air clear so he could see Jay's face. "Sorry," he repeated. "I'm excited."

"I'm excited for you," Jay said in his high-pitched, Paul-impression voice. Jay winked and then shivered, jostling the flashlight, making the room again seem to shake. "But I think I'm ready for that whiskey, now. It's like we're in a meat locker down here, and I can't see anything. I'll help you do a complete inventory tomorrow. When the sun's up and I'm wearing a parka."

It did feel like they were in a meat locker. Paul nodded and started to turn back toward the ladder, but the bookshelves called to him. "Just a couple more."

Next to *The Stranger* was a book bound in black leather with inlaid patches of what looked like ostrich skin. On its spine were the words *La Nausee*. Paul slid the book out gently. The light shone on the rough gilt edges of the pages.

"I think this may be Sartre's first novel. The title is *Nausea* in English." Paul's heart was beating fast, and his quick breaths were creating so much fog that he could barely see the book in his hands. "It could be the original French edition, or an early limited version, or something. I think I've seen this exact version before, and if I recall correctly, it's worth more than my car."

"People pay that much for books?" Jay said, stepping up next to Paul and peering over his shoulder. "Shit, if I could find a secret chamber of antique books in my backyard, all my money problems would be solved. Are they all French? Who's this guy Nabokov over here?" Jay pointed at a book two shelves higher.

Paul put the Sartre back. "Vladimir Nabokov. *Despair.* Don't tell me this is the original British version from before World War Two. That's almost impossible. They were all destroyed in the bombings of the war. This has got to be worth a fortune."

Jay reached past him for the Nabokov and Paul had to almost physically restrain himself to keep from grabbing it out of Jay's hands. "Careful with that," Paul said, regretting it as soon as the words left his mouth.

Jay acted like the book was about to slip out of his hands—

"Whoa! Whoa!"—and then shot Paul a snarl. "I'm not an idiot, dumbass."

"Sorry. I mistook you for the guy who just exploded a couple beers on the street up there."

For the next few minutes, Paul mentally cataloged the contents on the tallest bookshelf, taking deep breaths each time Jay pulled one out and handled it. He counted several Graham Greenes, including *Our Man in Havana*, his favorite. Again, probably first edition. He wasn't about to open the books and risk tearing the pages with his shaking hands. *Ficciones* by Jorge Luis Borges. Everything Kafka ever wrote. Hermann Hesse. *A Clockwork Orange*, by Anthony Burgess. *The Catcher in the Rye*. And, oddly, an assortment of early, pulp detective novels by Hammett and Chandler.

If he had taught a college-level course on twentieth-century literature, as he often imagined doing instead of managing hospital cost centers, the list of books he would've assigned could all have been found on this very shelf.

Something about that was unsettling. A little too coincidental.

"Paul!" Jay was shaking his shoulder. "Paul!"

"What?"

Jay shoved a book at him. *The Stranger*.

"Whoa. Careful, man."

"Open it." Jay's pupils were wide dark holes.

Paul turned the book over in his hands. Pristine, considering its age. Almost like the chamber down here had preserved it. He ran his fingers along the edges of the pages. All smooth, no dog ears, no creases from being pressed against other books. He steadied his hands as best he could and then opened the book to a random page. His heart skipped a beat. Another random page. Then he dropped the book on the ground and picked another from the shelf. After again turning to a random page, he dropped that book as well.

"The pages are all blank."

"All of them," Jay said.

"Those books, too?"

"Each and every one."

Paul's next breath tasted of mold and slime, of black, stinking water flooding into his sinuses, down his throat, into his lungs. His whole body clenched, doubling him over, trying to expel the water, but what came up instead was a mix of bile and beer.

Jay must've thought Paul was about to pass out, and so went to catch Paul just as Paul flailed backward with his arms in a panicked effort to grab the ladder, to get out, and then the flashlight was knocked loose, light spinning around the concrete walls, flashes of the door in the ceiling, the metal ladder, the old plaid sofa, their eyes wide seeing the flashlight in flight, until it hit the ground and all went dark.

The darkness boomed.

"Goddamn!" one or both of them yelled, the black air seeming to intensify the sounds of their voices, their increasingly frantic breathing.

"Jesus, where's the flashlight?"

"What was that noise?"

They banged and bumped into each other. Paul heard a flat scraping on the ground but realized it was only the sound of his own hands sliding across the floor searching for the flashlight.

"Fuck, fuck, fuck! I want to get out of here!" Paul said.

"Calm down, man. I got the light."

"Is it broken? Why isn't it turning on?!"

"Calm down. Here."

The light came on directly in Paul's face, from blinding darkness to blinding light. He turned away but orange-purple after-images filled his vision. "I can't see! I can't see!"

Jay grabbed him by the shoulder and steadied him. "No big deal, we're fine. Okay? Now let's go watch the fight and drink half the bottle of that bourbon. Maybe the whole bottle."

Paul could just make out the light shining this way and that, while Jay said, "Uhhh..."

"What's wrong?"

Jay's hand left Paul's shoulder. After a long exhale, Jay said, "We seem to be missing the ladder."

Paul blinked until he could make out the colored splotches of the book spines on the shelf in front of him. He turned toward where the ladder should have been and then realized he had instead ended up facing the wrong direction. He grabbed the flashlight out of Jay's hand and slowly spun all the way around.

"Shine it over there," Jay said.

"I did. See! Look, no ladder." Paul knelt down and put one hand to the ground to stabilize himself. "That sound was the door shutting, wasn't it?"

Jay had his arms out wide, palms up, like he was questioning the universe, or simply reaching his hands where the ladder should be in case their eyes were playing tricks on them. "I don't get it, man. What happened to the ladder?"

They both turned their gaze upward to where the hatch should have been. Instead of the underside of the iron door, what they saw was uninterrupted concrete.

When the flashlight went out for good, Paul's mind closed in on him, his whole body closed in on him. The air thickened and became heavy with the smell of earth, earth and rot and death, a smell that reached deep into the locked-away recesses of his memories and pried something loose. His lungs tightened up, refusing to take in more of the sour darkness, but it was already inside. It had *always* been inside, waiting.

He felt the uncontrollable urge to tear himself free *from himself*, not knowing what that even meant, but he couldn't act on the urge because he couldn't move his arms. He couldn't stand back up. When did he even fall down? If the sofa weren't pressing into his back, he'd be flat on the floor, his own weight crushing his lungs, making it impossible to breathe.

Needles prickled every inch of his skin. He had a certainty that the prickling was oxygen deprivation and his whole body was dying. That thought came with waves upon waves of urgency.

The world began to shrink around him, compressing in from every direction. The concrete room with the books and the sofa had changed—he couldn't see, but he knew it had changed—into a stone cylinder with him at the center. The ground below him became soft sludge, wet and stinking of death.

He was at the bottom of a well.

The well.

Water rose around him, seeping up from the ground until it ran into his ears, poured into his mouth and nose, burning his sinuses with its rancid stench. It covered his face in an oily film and pushed its way around his eyes and into his skull. He could feel its devouring black presence entering his mind.

Somewhere in the darkness, in the well with him, a figure emerged, a part of the darkness both living and dead. He saw its ruined canine maw, bone stained brown, flesh turned green and black with mold. Its empty sockets staring into his own eyes.

He couldn't turn his head. He couldn't move as the well's stone walls compressed tighter around him and the rotting dog carcass, pushing it toward him. The collapsing world would crush it into him until it became a part of him, or he became a part of it.

Just like before.

And like before its void eyes stared into him until the darkness smothered his entire being.

Another June night, eighteen years before.

Paul and Jay were in the ranch truck, the torn vinyl bench seat biting into young flesh with every bump in the field.

Jay was driving, despite being only 14, despite the lack of adults for miles.

Jay's older brothers were off somewhere, killing something with Jay's dad, who everybody called Big Cal.

Just the two of them. Paul and Jay.

The guns rattled on the rack behind their heads. The .22 they were allowed to shoot, and the big one—the *serious* one—they weren't.

The headlamps punched through the night, stirring insects like stars against the darkness. Windows down. Hot night air in their hair.

Paul looked over at his best friend who seemed to gain a decade of maturity whenever they came to the Lightsey family ranch. Earlier, Jay had taught Paul to shoot the .22. He said it was the gun to learn with because it didn't kick. Jay shot the big one, the one they weren't supposed to shoot, the one that sounded like a cannon, and they had to put on those hard plastic ear muff things, so they didn't go deaf from the blasts.

Jay talked like he'd been handling guns all of his life. Out here on his family's ranch, Jay talked with the confidence that only adults have.

Big Cal, with his menthol cigarette hanging out of his mouth and the sun glaring off his gold-rimmed aviators, never said Jay could take the truck out on the dirt roads and across the fields where there were no roads and across the stream where the water goes over the tires. But he didn't say not to.

Paul's parents never would've let him come to the Lightsey ranch if they knew about the truck or the guns or the four-wheelers or the rattlesnakes, or if they knew about the swarming Africanized bees that lived in the corner of the bunk-house just feet from where he and Jay slept. "Ignore 'em and they'll leave you alone," Jay had said, and it turned out they did.

Jay hit the turn signal and then cranked a hard right on the steering wheel. Paul laughed so hard he snorted. For some reason, nothing right then could be funnier than turn signals in an empty field.

Another turn, to the left this time, again preceded by the clicking signal, and then Jay slammed hard on the brakes, carving ruts into the grass. Paul barely caught himself before smashing into the dashboard. Before Paul could say anything, Jay opened the door and jumped out, .22 rifle in his right hand.

Paul walked around the truck, through the heat and gray exhaust pumping out of the tailpipe, *gugguta-gugguta-gugguta*, and Jay handed him the gun. "You see," Jay said, pointing in the path of one of the headlights. Paul didn't see, so Jay held his arm in front of him, finger pointed out like an arrow.

"Jackrabbit," Jay said. "They dig holes, break cows' legs. Cause problems." He set the rifle in the crook of the truck's open door and motioned for Paul to grab the gun and line up the shot like he had learned how earlier.

"Dumb fucker'll stay there all night if I keep the lights on him," Jay said.

The rifle's wood stock slipped in Paul's hand, gaining a frown of disappointment from Jay. Paul had never shot anything living before, never killed anything more than an insect. Shooting the cans earlier was different, right? Or maybe it wasn't. It wasn't different to Jay.

Paul leaned in like Jay taught him and placed his finger against the trigger, feeling the curve of cold metal give with the slightest pressure. He lined up the rabbit and a certainty came over him, like the rabbit was already dead, like he'd killed it and pulling the trigger was just snapping his fingers and waking from a dream where the rabbit still lived.

And since the rabbit was already dead, he couldn't keep looking at it, standing there, eyes shining, looking back at him. The dead rabbit staring back at the boy who snuffed it out. Paul looked everywhere except for the rabbit, ignoring Jay's impatient exhale. He looked and he saw a line of stone. "Hey, what's that?" Paul asked, looking for a way out, always a way out. "Those stones?"

Jay frowned and took the gun away. Instead of putting it on its rack strapped to the truck's rear window, Jay walked around the side of the door, held the forestock steady with his left hand, and put his right eye to the sight.

Crack.

The rabbit dropped like it had never really been there. Lost in the grass and never thought of again. If Paul fell in the grass and vanished, would the world even notice? Who would say he had ever existed in the first place?

He kept his eyes away from where the rabbit fell, as if there were a void there waiting to pull him in also.

They got back in the truck and were about to drive on back to the bunk-house, but then Jay asked what Paul saw.

That's how they ended up standing in front of the well.

Rough-hewn limestone blocks, worn and mottled with green-black mold. A ring, three rows high, up to their knees, missing a stone here and there. A ring surrounding a dark abyss.

The boys stood there, silent, goosebumps on their legs from the cold air of the well. An intense smell of earth, of death, and of the life that feeds on death.

The light of the truck's headlamps behind them created two black stripes on the ground and across the well, the boys' towering shadows stretching until they became part of the night sky.

If they weren't looking in the well, they might've noticed their shadows changing, growing bigger, blocking out more and more of the light. But they didn't notice. They only looked into the darkness of the well.

The truck behind them, engine off but left in drive without the parking brake engaged, crept forward.

To Paul, the well looked almost like a dead eye staring up from the ground. He had this urge to lean over it, to look it right in the eye, to stare down death, but he knew it would pull him in with its gaze. And yet he still wanted to put his weight on the crumbling old wall and lean over.

It was this desire—*l'appel du vide*, the call of the void—that still haunted him two decades later, more so than what happened next, because it was like he asked to be devoured by the well. He chose to keep standing there knowing what would happen.

Jay broke the silence, saying something about how Little Cal talked about an abandoned well once, the last time they were out at the ranch, and how they threw *Cadejo*, the old black Labrador Retriever, down there after he died instead of burying him. And maybe if Jay hadn't started talking, they would've heard the grass crackling under the tires rolling toward them. Maybe if Paul hadn't had his hands on the top ring of stone, if he hadn't been leaned over, entranced by the darkness, he might've moved, or at least been knocked clear, like Jay was knocked clear when the truck rolled into them.

Instead, the driverless truck came up behind Paul and pushed him.

Over the stone ring and down into the black depths of the well.

And then the truck rolled over the stone ring and high-centered itself.

Cutting out the light of the moon.

Leaving Paul, battered from the fall, in the wet, stinking darkness.

CHAPTER 3

THE FRUIT OF TANTALUS

When Paul came to, the darkness still covered him, but it was a leeching darkness and not the clinging, oily black of the well. His body shivered and shook. He was against the ground, both arms over his head, moving backward, being pulled. He frantically tried to free himself, but whoever or whatever had his wrists was gripping too hard, and he had no strength at all.

He tried to talk, to address the thing pulling him, but all that came from him was, "Wha-wha-wha-"

"Fuckin' A, man, I thought I'd lost you." Jay's voice responded, resonant and echoing. Jay stopped and propped Paul against the wall. "After the flashlight went out and you, uh, passed out," Jay said, the cold causing his voice to quiver, "I searched the room. By feel, you know? I moved the big bookshelf, thinking I'd use it as a ladder, and I felt the air moving where it had been against the wall. There was another door hidden behind it. A smaller door, and it led into this here passageway. I didn't know what else to do but drag you. Can you stand? I think I see a light up ahead."

"I'm okay," Paul said. When breath after breath pulled in air—cold and clean air and not the well water—his body came back into his control. "I'm okay," he repeated, as much for himself to hear as for Jay.

Jay gave a half-snicker. "For once, I get to be the one to bail you out."

Paul leaned forward, taking his back off the cold wall. His body didn't collapse, so he put his hands on the ground and tried to stand. Jay helped steady him, clumsy in the dark, and even when Paul finally felt secure on his feet, Jay still kept both hands clutched against his ribs.

"I think I can take it from here," Paul said, unsure that was the truth.

Jay let go with one hand but kept the other bracing the small of Paul's back.

"Really, I'm good," Paul said. The steadiness had returned to his voice enough to almost sound convincing. He'd had panic attacks before, but never anything this intense. The residue of the attack still clung to him, the residue of doom.

You're in control of your body, he told himself. He imagined a river flowing through his mind, and every time the well entered his thoughts, the dark water washed into the river and was swept away. Over and over again, the bloated dog carcass washed down the river.

He kept one hand against the rough stone wall next to him and took a cautious step. When his leg didn't collapse under his weight, he took another step. Bit by bit, the black of the passageway became an almost-black gray that brightened as they reached the passageway's end.

Paul could finally see the light source, and it gave him something real to focus his attention on—a small flame in a metal bowl on a three-legged stand next to a plain white door. Even though the tunnel wasn't nearly as cold as the false library they had come from, Paul had the sudden urge to wrap his arms around the metal bowl and absorb as much of the heat as he could.

He staggered toward the flame. The bowl at its top, about waist high, was etched with a complex pattern, swirls within swirls, and lighter edges overlaying deeper ones.

"Who cares about the thing with the fire," Jay said. "There's a door, and I say we use it to get the hell out of here. I'm putting on a

26

good show of looking not scared, you know, for your benefit, but the truth is I'm pretty damn creeped out myself." Jay reached for the door, but Paul told him to wait.

"Something isn't right," Paul said, and as the words left his mouth, he recognized what it was. "There's no smoke coming from this flame. The passageway here slopes up toward where we came from, so we should've been able to smell whatever it's burning for a while." He reached his palm tentatively toward the flame. Feeling no heat, he prodded, sticking his hand in a little deeper each time, until he left it in the flame, turning it palm-side up and then palm-side down, over and over again.

"It's not hot?" Jay asked.

"Not at all," Paul said. "It's like it's not even there. Except for the light coming off it. Really strange."

"Stranger than a disappearing door or a bookshelf full of fake books?" In the false-flame's dim light, Jay's face looked gaunt, drained of blood. He looked exhausted as well.

"Enough of this shit," Paul said. He felt a sudden rush of strength and used it to walk by Jay and grab the door handle.

As Paul swung the door open, both men sighed in relief. Beyond the door was a square room, about the size of the concrete bunker behind them, but richly adorned in French antique furniture. A sofa with silk floral cushions and intricately carved wooden legs took up the center of the room. A tall, golden floor lamp, with several inches of fringe hanging from its cloth shade, illuminated the room. Purple-and-gold damask wallpaper covered each of the walls. The floors were a deep mahogany covered partly by a footworn Persian rug.

Jay stepped in. Paul followed. The room greeted them with the layered smells of linseed oil and old-house mildew.

"We're in your neighbor's basement or something!" Jay exclaimed, causing Paul to raise a finger to his lips, worrying briefly that they'd alarm the house's owner. Which neighbor's house would it be? He'd gotten all turned around, and the panic attack had left his mind rattled.

As far as he knew, none of the houses in his neighborhood had basements. The clay soil and high water table wreaked havoc on foundations, as Paul and Julie had already discovered. Building a basement in Central Texas would cost a small fortune.

The room had plain, white doors at each of the other three walls, just like the door that had led from the stone passageway to this room.

"Which way you want to go, boss?" Jay asked.

"You pick." Anxiety began itching at Paul's insides again. The mildew smell here was too close to the smell of the well water. In his mind, the river kept washing away the thoughts of the well, but the river water was starting to turn black. The dead dog, *Cadejo*, bobbed up and down in the water, its missing eyes staring at Paul from inside his head. "Pick, man."

Jay bounced a pointed finger at each, mouthing *eeny, meeny, miny, moe*. If it weren't for Paul's exhaustion, he would've screamed at his friend. *Move! MOVE!*

With *moe* pointing to the door on the left, Jay circled around the sofa, grabbed the knob of the left door, and swung the door open.

"Uh..." Jay turned back to Paul, confused. As if Jay were watching a tennis match, he looked through the doorway, then back into the room, through the doorway, then back into the room. "Is this some kind of sick joke? It ain't fucking funny."

Paul dragged himself around the sofa, and, standing next to Jay, looked through the open door. It led directly to a room that appeared identical to the one they were standing in. He pushed his way past Jay into the next room, where he ran his fingers over the sofa's carved wooden arm, passing over a little crack. He returned to the first room and repeated the process on the other sofa. "Absolutely identical. Even with the same imperfection."

Jay shook his head and said, "Follow me. I'm pretty sure I already know, but I need to confirm something." He walked through the door into the identical, second room, and Paul followed. Jay opened the new room's left door, and it, too, led to another identical room.

"What in the hell is going on here?" Paul asked.

"Wish I knew, buddy," Jay said. "Look on the bright side. Once we figure out how to get out of here, we come back with some moving vans and start loading up an endless supply of these sofas. Think of it like a sofa-ATM, where we just keep withdrawing tidy profits. Leave the entrepreneurial shit to me, my man. You handle the accounting."

Despite everything, Paul laughed. "You're taking this awfully well."

Jay's smile slipped a bit. "This ain't so different than my everyday life. I keep trying to move forward and I keep finding myself right back where I started." Jay flopped down on the second room's sofa, arms folded behind his head, feet propped on the sofa's wooden arm. He closed his eyes.

Paul sat on the sofa's arm next to Jay's dirt-crusted Redwing boots. He opened his mouth to say something consoling, but he found nothing. In a sense, Jay's life hadn't changed since childhood, aside from his little house in East Austin. Jay had never really been employed but somehow made ends meet with his clever but never fully realized internet start-up companies. His latest used crypto-wallets to allow charities to provide funds directly to individuals in developing nations where personal bank accounts weren't practical. Jay had been working on it for three years, backed financially by Big Cal, who had sold the mineral rights on the Lightsey Ranch to fund the ordeal, thinking the family might hit it big on Jay's entrepreneurial talents.

But Big Cal's money had almost run dry and Jay's big break-through was like the fruit hanging before Tantalus, always beyond reach.

Paul's opportunity to say something reassuring had passed. He sighed, stood back up, and wandered around the room, examining the furniture in detail. It all looked real—real as in authentic—but he had the feeling that everything here was as empty as the books in the false-library. Seemingly real, but somehow vacant of substance.

A shiver rose up his spine. "I need to piss," he said. "I don't suppose any of these doors leads to a bathroom." Opening the two remaining doors confirmed what they already knew.

"More of this shit?" Jay, eyes still closed, asked.

"Yeah. No bathrooms."

"Then I suggest we use one of these rooms as the shitter. One room always has to be the shitter. That may be some deep metaphorical, quotable shit I just said. Feel free to quote me on that if you want."

Paul gave a soft laugh and then picked one of the rooms at random. He positioned himself in a corner, unzipped, and readied himself. Something about the elegant texture of the wallpaper threw him off. Velvet and gold leaf? He closed his eyes, tried pushing, tried not pushing, tried not thinking about pushing or not pushing. But it didn't work. His bladder strained with its full load, but it was like standing at a piss-trough at the football stadium, surrounded by strangers, feeling more and more awkward as absolutely nothing happened.

He zipped up and walked back into the room with Jay.

"Shy bladder?" Jay asked, eyes still closed.

"Yes. Fuck off. I'm going back to the stone passageway. Something more natural about pissing on dirt than on fancy wallpaper and wood floors. It would probably splash back on me, anyway."

"You should piss on the flame in the brazier."

"Why would I do that?"

Jay opened one eye and grinned. "Science!"

Paul walked back into the first room. Had they shut the door to the passageway? He vaguely remembered shutting it himself, but the more he thought about it, the less convinced he was. He shook his head and marched purposefully to the door. Opening it, he discovered that it led not back to the passageway but to yet another identical room, with the same sofa, lamp, rug, and wallpaper.

Was it a different door? No, he had the right door. A wave of relief came over him as he realized he was still one room away. But after stepping into the next room, he knew that was wrong. He checked its far door just in case it led to the passageway, but it, too, led to another of these sitting rooms.

At this point his bladder really did feel like it was going to explode. He looked from corner to corner and then decided to piss directly into the crease between cushions on the sofa.

Walking back toward the room with Jay, he loudly recounted his experience soiling such a fine piece of furniture, knowing Jay would appreciate it. As he entered the room with Jay, he found that it wasn't, in fact, the room with Jay, as there was no Jay with his eyes closed on the sofa.

He ran from room to room, randomly choosing doors. Five, ten, twenty rooms, all the same, heart pounding in his chest and darkness creeping into the corners of his vision. As he was about to collapse and ball up on the ground, he found himself three feet away from Jay, still on the sofa as if nothing had happened.

"You say something?" Jay asked.

"We can't get separated!" Paul said, breathing so heavily that the words barely came out.

"Whoa, man. Calm down. Pissing on the brazier was a bad idea?"

"I didn't piss on the brazier! We can't get back to the brazier even if we wanted to. The door to the passageway leads to another one of these rooms. When I came back, this room wasn't this room. It was a different room! I've been running through, I don't know, at least fifty before I randomly found you again. And I bet that was luck."

Jay sat up and opened his eyes. "That's all kinds of fucked up, man." He frowned. "I didn't come up with anything brilliant while lying here. At least the sofa is pretty damn comfortable. When it comes time to sleep, we'll be set."

"One of us, anyway. We can't stay in separate rooms. And I don't even want to think of being here through the night. Where will we get water? Food?"

"Beer!" Jay said, and then he stood, mouth open as if he'd just been struck by brilliance. "That's it! You know how a beer bottle can be made into a weapon by holding the neck and smashing the bottom against the edge of a table?"

"Uh. I haven't spent nearly as much time in Mexico as you, buddy."

Jay nodded and grabbed the lamp, frowning for a second as he noticed it lacked an electrical cord. Then he shrugged and said, "We're going to walk into the next room, and I'm going to take this with us. Then I'm going to break the pole here and use the rough edge to carve into the wallpaper. We'll start numbering the rooms."

"Mapping our way. Good thinking," Paul said. "Wasn't sure where you were going, but you got to a good place. Let's do it."

Jay declared that their current room would be *Room 1*. He tossed the broken lamp pole to Paul and said, "Write a *1* on the wall. I'd do it myself, but my handwriting is terrible."

Paul looked down at the pole and then back at Jay. "Handwriting?" By then, Jay was already describing his room naming convention.

"We go through the door on the left first, and that room becomes *Room L*, since it's from the left door of *Room 1*. Then we come back and go through the center door and name that one *Room C*, for center. The next is *Room R*, for rectum."

While Paul scratched a large *1* into the wallpaper, he said, "You know, your sense of humor hasn't changed since second grade"

"No time for humor," Jay said. "Each room thereafter will keep the name of the room we came from plus the letter of the door we used. Brilliant, eh?"

"Truly."

They began systematically working their way through rooms but discovered a fatal flaw to Jay's system before getting very far. While they could reliably return to the room they came from, they couldn't go back beyond that without finding themselves in a random room, sometimes with a scratched-in name that no longer fit.

"I have this feeling that the rooms are also repairing themselves," Paul said. "Scratches in the wallpaper disappearing like they were never there. I bet if we tried to get back to the room missing the lamp that the lamp would be there. And we haven't seen the sofa I pissed on."

"Or the one I took a dump on," Jay added.

Paul backed a few steps away from Jay. "What'd you use for toilet paper?"

"The fucking cushions, man. Most luxurious wipe I ever had. If I get rich one day—I mean, richer than I am now—"

"You're a regular thousandaire."

"Ha ha. But accurate. If I get really rich, French silk cushion ass wipes. I'm not sure how disposal will work, but I'll figure that out. Maybe that's my next business. Maybe that's how I become mega-rich."

Paul started to sit on the sofa in the room labeled *LCC*—although that label probably meant nothing and would soon disappear—checking the cushions for piss, or worse, and then sank, exhausted, into the purple floral print.

"What are we gonna do, Jay?"

"About my cushion-ass-wiping business?"

"I'm being serious. I'm already pretty thirsty. I imagine we can go a couple days more, but... I don't understand. What is this? Why is this happening?"

Jay dropped cross-legged to sit on the rug. His near-constant goofy expression softened, and his eyes took on that far-off look he sometimes got when he drank too much and let his shield of humor down, when he talked about his fears of always being alone, of his business failing when Big Cal ran out of *investment support*.

"I don't know, Paul. The more I think about it, the scarier it is. So I don't think we can think about it. That's how I get through every fucking day, man. Try not to think about everything that's wrong and just keep putting one foot in front of the other."

"Worked so far, I guess."

"If by *worked* you mean I'm not dead yet, then sure."

Paul took a breath to respond but then let it out. He closed his eyes and leaned back into the sofa.

"Enough serious shit," Jay said. "I have a new plan."

Paul opened one eye.

"We start walking."

"We just start walking?" Paul repeated.

Jay jumped to his feet. "Yep. No scratching into wallpaper. No trying to make sense out of anything. We pick a new door each time and keep going. Eventually we have to run into something new, right?"

"I, uh... Sure. Let's go." Paul stood. Jay held an upturned hand out, presenting the available doors for Paul to choose. "Right, because I'm right-handed," Paul said, dragging the lamp pole behind him to the door on the right.

"As good a reason as any."

They both had walked through the doorway and into the adjacent room before realizing that it wasn't another clone of the sitting room. It was like a chapel but with writing scratched into its stone walls as if by hand. And an altar, upon which laid a man's body, with a blue-handled knife buried into his chest.

CHAPTER 4
COMINGS AND GOINGS

With its bare stone walls and floor, and the rough-hewn altar, the room looked like it predated the adjacent sitting room by a thousand years or more. Even the air pouring out of the room felt somehow different—warmer, heavier, and with greater humidity. Paul had the feeling that a step across the threshold would also be a step into a bygone era, and maybe from continent to continent as well. With no windows or other doors, there was no way to tell if this was just a feeling or a part of the underlying nature of this place.

"I'm not liking this one bit," Jay said, immediately backing away from the door.

A numbness spread throughout Paul that was more than exhaustion. He stepped into the room and circled its walls, keeping his distance from the altar and the body, examining the letters scratched into the stone.

NSEWE

"The room looks ancient, but these letters look like they were carved recently," Paul said. "See how white the stone is here? I have no idea what NSEWE means."

"Who cares what it means," Jay said. He had backed all the way to the sofa in the adjoining room. "That's a fucking dead body, man!

Now get out of there before it sits up or comes back to life or something."

Until then, the only dead body Paul had ever seen had been at the open-casket funeral for his grandfather. The overly fleshy makeup and uncharacteristic suit-and-tie made his grandfather's body look like a shell, like something artificial that had never really housed life. This body, on the other hand, hadn't been preserved or adorned with false color. Its skin had tightened and shrunk. The eyes at some point had decomposed or been removed. The jaw hung broken and gaping with yellow-brown teeth. Unlike *Cadejo*, the Labrador carcass that had become living again with the scum of the black well water, the corpse here just looked empty, vacant, like the human equivalent of a hollow cicada shell. Its right hand, mostly visible bone, clutched at the strange, blue blade stabbed through its chest.

Jay tiptoed into the room, enough to get a full look around. "This room doesn't lead anywhere," he said. To the body: "Sorry to disturb you, dead guy. My buddy and I were leaving."

"You were the one so quick to go down into the hole in my backyard."

"Dead body puts things in a different category. Now let's go. If we can find one new room by random chance, maybe we can find more."

"Maybe," Paul said. He expected the dead body to bother him, or to call back *Cadejo* from its hiding place in the deep recesses of his mind, but instead, he felt a tired calm. At least a dead body was something physical, something in front of him that he could deal with, unlike an endless maze of repeating rooms.

He reached the lamp pole toward the body and prodded, as much out of curiosity as out of a desire to prove to himself that he could do something brave. At the first touch of the pole, most of the body turned to dust, clothing sinking to the stone altar like a deflated balloon.

"You just released a bunch of dead guy powder. You're breathing dead guy, now. You're probably cursed." Jay had his shirt pulled over his nose.

"I think we're already cursed," Paul said. "Come over here. This knife is something else. Check it out. It looks like even the blade is blue. Maybe it's ceramic or something. The handle part looks like a bunch of sapphires fused together. I've never seen anything like it."

At the word *sapphires*, Jay's eyebrows perked up. His eyes darted between the knife and the body's eyeless head, staring it down as if it were likely to come to life at any minute. "That thing might be valuable," he said.

"Like the antique furniture and rug?" Paul had let the lamp pole's jagged tip rest on the ground and had moved in closer to look at the knife.

"Easier to carry a knife than a sofa."

"You're welcome to grab it," Paul said. "Something creepy about touching a knife still embedded in this poor guy's heart. Or what's left of his heart."

"Since this poor sack of shit ain't using it anymore I guess I—" Jay started, but a scraping sound at the door behind him caused them both to jump back. "What the fuck is that?!"

A dog-like creature stood in the doorway, eyes glaring, teeth bared in a silent snarl. Instead of fur, it had mottled skin of black carbon and ash, like scorched wood. It looked burned alive.

"Ugh. Some kind of zombie dog?" Paul said, pointing the pole at the creature like a fencing foil.

Jay slid behind Paul. "Fuck outta here, zombie dog! Shoo!" He jabbed Paul in the ribs. "Go stick it. Chase it away. Maybe it'll get lost in those rooms."

A deep rumble came from the dog-creature, more like grinding gears than a growl. It entered and slowly followed the room's perimeter, circling toward them. Long claws clicked and scraped on the stone floor. A trail of soot followed behind it.

Using the altar as a barrier, Paul and Jay matched the creature's circling. For two whole rotations, it kept the same, slow deliberate pace. Paul glanced to the door, about to suggest that they jump through and slam it shut as they passed, and saw another of the ash-covered dog-creatures enter, circling the opposite direction.

Both creatures let out a metal-scraping-on-metal howl and pounced.

Paul caught one square in the chest with the pole and a cloud of soot burst from the creature. The thin pole bent on impact, but it hit solidly enough to make the dog miss its strike. Jay slid toreador-like, hands over his head, and his creature smashed into the altar. In the brief daze of the collision, Jay kicked with all his might, the tip of his boot crunching into ribs, creating another plume of black char and sending the beast sprawling into the wall.

The other dog leapt again at Paul and knocked him down. Paul gripped it by the neck, but its squirming head and thrashing legs were loosening his grip and covering him in ash and char. It broke free and snapped at his face before Paul could get his arm up to block, but it stopped as if suddenly frozen, teeth less than an inch away, fetid breath burning his eyes. Paul scrambled back and saw Jay's hand gripping the knife, plunged through the dog's neck so that several inches of the blue blade emerged from the other side.

Jay pushed the dog off the blade with his left foot, and in two quick motions, cut the throat of the injured creature against the wall and stabbed a third that Paul hadn't seen enter.

Neither could do more than breathe heavily for the next several seconds, shirts pulled over their noses to mask out the black cloud hanging in the air. Where each dog had died now sat a pile of ash and charred bone.

After it thoroughly sunk in that this *did just happen* and that he was somehow still alive, Paul used the altar to push himself up, wincing at the scratches and tears on his stomach, at the burning sensation on his palms and forearms where he had grabbed the dog-thing. He tried to wipe the soot from his face, but the sleeves of his shirt were as covered as the rest of him.

"That thing would've gotten me if you hadn't stabbed it. I don't know how you did all that, but thanks, man," he said.

Jay didn't seem to hear. He was muttering "*stelisto... stelisto... stelisto...*" while wiping the blade on the tattered remains of the dead man's shirt. With a far-away look in his eyes, he asked Paul, "How long have we been in this room?"

Paul frowned. "What kind of question is that? A few minutes, I guess? What was that you were saying, *stelisto*? What does that mean?"

"No idea, man. I just had this weird daydream thing, and that word is what's left in my mouth, like an aftertaste of the dream." He looked at Paul and shook his head. "I feel like a lifetime just passed, but at the same time, just a few minutes, like you said. I grabbed the knife. Reflexes, you know? I grabbed it, and then I was somewhere else. I was some*one* else."

Paul rubbed at the scratches on his forearm, deep enough that they should've bled, but the wounds looked cauterized. "I don't get what you mean, Jay. Somewhere else? Someone else?"

"I don't either. You know how sometimes you're in that twilight state between being awake and being asleep? Where dream elements are superimposed on the real world? It was like that, but more of the dream world than the real thing. A lifetime worth of dreams—somebody else's dreams—compressed into a second, that second when I grabbed the knife." He swiveled the knife in his right hand so that he held it upside down by its blade between his thumb and middle finger. For a man who had recently butterfingered a couple beer bottles, the knife twirl looked unreasonably dexterous and casual. He stared at the knife's grip, peering through the sapphire gem cluster.

"Somebody else's dream?" Paul said. "Whose?"

Instead of answering, Jay brought the knife closer, squinting his eyes. "There's a thread-like thing in here. It's hard to see, but if you turn it in the light... Yeah. There it is. A frayed bit of string suspended in the middle like the filament in an incandescent light bulb. It almost looks like it's glowing."

"Let me see," Paul said, stepping over a pile of ash.

Jay pulled the knife in close to him and eyed Paul suspiciously. "The knife is mine, got it?"

"What's wrong with you? I wanted to see the filament thing, not to take it from you. Are you suddenly 3 years old or something?"

Jay laughed but the coldness in his eyes remained. "Sorry. I don't know what came over me." He took a leather shoulder harness from the corpse, taking care to disturb the remains as little as possible. He fastened the harness over the plain white t-shirt he wore, slid the knife into the sheath, and said, "Let's get out of here."

Back in one of the sitting rooms, Paul sunk into the sofa and closed his eyes.

"I keep waiting for all of this to make sense, but it keeps getting more and more fucked up. Instead of a panic attack back there in the false-library, maybe I passed out and I'm dreaming this whole thing. Maybe it's all a hallucination."

Jay's boots thudded against the wooden floor as he paced back and forth. "How are we both hallucinating the same thing?"

"Who's to say we are? Maybe I'm just hallucinating the entire thing, you included. Maybe I had an aneurysm working in the yard while waiting for you to come over, and now I'm in a coma in a hospital. Or maybe I died and this is purgatory or hell or limbo or whatever." Paul's eyes shot open as the sofa shook from being kicked by Jay's boot.

"World's always revolving around ol' Paul, ain't it? Jay here's nothing but a figment of his imagination? Here for comic relief, like usual." Jay flashed him a crooked grin, but Paul felt the sting of accusation and the weight of history in Jay's words. Before Paul had the chance to apologize, Jay said, "You used the term *panic attack* a second ago. Is that what that was back there?"

Paul's natural response was to wave it off, to deflect. To blame it on low blood sugar, or even heat stroke from working under the hot sun all day. Even though he'd really spent half the day inside. More angrily than he intended, he said, "Just because I don't turn a night with friends into a therapy session after I've had too many beers doesn't mean I don't have my own issues."

"Whoa," Jay said, backing up two steps, arms crossed. The grin had left Jay's face, and his eyes shimmered with anger. "I thought I was the one with the knife, but look at you stabbing away." He shook his head. "But you know what? I'm gonna let that comment slide right on by. Was that the first time this has happened? I'm betting it wasn't, because you knew what to call it."

The sofa felt like it was sucking Paul down into it. Especially right now, this was the last thing Paul wanted to discuss, but after what he'd just said to Jay, he felt he owed him a little honesty. Maybe he owed himself a little honesty, also. "Ever since I fell in that damn well out at your ranch, I've had an issue with claustrophobia, or maybe it's agoraphobia. I don't know. Sometimes I get this intense feeling of being trapped and everything closing in on me. The first time was at that awful firm, right out of school. I honestly don't remember what set it off, but I was sitting in this partner's office, and he'd asked me something, and everything felt wrong, you know? Like the room became warped, and I couldn't answer. I couldn't make a sound come out of my mouth if my life depended on it. And the whole time I remember him staring at me. It was fucking humiliating."

As he spoke, his heart rate quickened. The feeling of that moment, almost ten years ago, began to return as if it had been hidden under the memory and released once he gave the memory new life. "I can feel my face turning red. This is why I don't talk about this shit."

Jay's face had softened, and he was leaning against the wall, rubbing at the unshaven gruff on his chin. "You have to talk about this stuff man. Otherwise, it eats you up inside. But you're not one for therapists."

"Neither are you," Paul said.

Jay gave a humorless laugh and shook his head. "That's because I can't afford shit like that. I don't even have health insurance." He took the knife out of its sheath and began rolling in his palm. Without looking up from the knife, he said, "You could've talked to me. You never said anything about the well after. How the hell was I supposed to know it's been bothering you all this time?"

Paul stood and grabbed at his hair, pulling, wanting to pull Jay apart. Never said anything about the well?! What the hell was wrong with Jay? "It was your fucking idiot dad that made us promise not to talk about the well."

"My dad's not an idiot."

Anger built within Paul, pushing away the panic. "Your dad is a fucking narcissistic bastard, and you know it. Do you remember what he said after he and your worthless brother finally pulled me out of that hellhole? After they almost killed me when they knocked all those stones down trying to dislodge the truck?" Now it was Paul's turn to pace, behind the sofa, needing that physical barrier to separate him from Jay. "Your dad said to me—you were sitting there—he said, 'I'm gonna have to tell your parents.' Remember? He terrified me, both of us, with the trouble we'd be in, and how my parents would never let me go to the ranch with you again, or even hang out with you. And then he manipulated me into pleading with him not to tell. We promised not to talk about it—not because Big Cal was being magnanimous. Not because he was doing me a favor, but because he was worried about being sued. Then and now, your dad has only ever cared about himself." Part of his mind was screaming at him to stop, but a dam had broken and the words poured out. "He manipulated me, like he's been manipulating you, keeping you from doing anything that doesn't in some way vicariously redeem him for his own failures. Right? He never wanted you to get a real job, because if you got a real job then he'd be the only one sitting on his ass. And if you created a successful business, then he'd claim it as his success. His fucking brilliance. Way to go, Big Cal. Instead, he's pulling you down with him. You're a hundred times smarter than him, but the more you listen to him, the more he turns you into him."

Jay looked up from the knife. For once, Paul had no idea what was going on behind Jay's eyes.

"You gonna say anything?" Paul said.

Jay shrugged. "I'm waiting for you to finish. See what else you've been keeping up in that head of yours." He gripped the knife so hard his knuckles turned white. "Real job," he said, each word like the cut of a blade. "Like what I do every day ain't a real job. You don't believe in me either. Nobody else does, so what's one more person? It was just a matter of time, I guess, before you abandoned me, too."

"Don't turn this into a big fucking thing," Paul said. "Nobody's abandoning anybody. I'm exhausted, and none of this makes any goddamn sense." He looked at Jay and, as matter-of-factly as he could, said, "I've always believed in you, okay? Always. And I still do."

The lie hung in the silence, and for what seemed like minutes neither man spoke. Finally, Jay turned and walked to the door behind him. He swung it open like he didn't have a care in the world what was behind it. Paul thought Jay was walking off, leaving him. But Jay grabbed the arm of the sofa in the neighboring room and pulled it back to the room with Paul.

"Pull the others in," Jay said.

Paul hesitated and then realized what Jay had planned. They soon had five sofas pulled together, one in the middle of the room, and a sofa wedged against each of the four doors. With their solid wooden frames, the sofas were much heavier than they looked.

"We need some rest, even if it's just an hour or two," Jay said. Without any acknowledgment of their past conversation, Jay walked over to the lamp and tilted his head to look under the shade. "Get comfortable. I'm turning this off." He looked back at Paul. "Unless that's gonna bother you."

"I'm fine," Paul said. Another lie. But he was so tired that it might as well have been the truth.

With a *click*, the room went pitch black except for a dim blue line in the air. Another *click* and the light returned. "The damn thing glows," Jay said, turning the knife this way and that. He slid it back into its sheath. "Sweet dreams."

Click.

Paul sat at a wooden table that had been scratched and gouged by the countless prior occupants of his seat. Names overlapped names. Below the blue cloud of cigarette smoke, he used his apartment key to carve his own name atop the name dogpile.

PAUL.

The woman across the table set her pint glass down so hard it sloshed beer onto his hand and filled in the letters of his name. She was saying something about the fragility of masculinity and how vandalism and war and rape were expressions of the male fear of being irrelevant. The male scarring of the world. Something like that. He couldn't make out the words. But he knew the words because he'd lived this moment once and replayed it in his head a thousand times. This is a dream, he thought, but the thought disintegrated into the dream-ether.

Others sat around the table, all with scratched-out features like someone had scribbled up the air in front of their faces. All scribbled over and unimportant but Jay and Julie. Julie, holding her half-empty pint glass, gray-blue eyes fixed on Paul's handiwork.

Paul's mind slipped out of the moment to take in his surroundings—the familiar features of The Crow's Nest, a bar just north of the University of Texas campus, with its lacquered brown walls crowded full of nautical miscellanea and rusty metal advertisements of products that had sunk to the bottom of time's ocean. A single ship's lamp illuminated their table and only their table, leaving the rest of the bar behind a dark, smokey curtain.

His awareness settled back into his body right as his eyes looked up at Julie, right as his chest swelled, taking her in with a single deep breath. Her brown hair had been buzzed short the night before, something she had wanted to do since high school, since running her fingers against her then-boyfriend's prickly-soft head and wanting to be the recipient of that touch. The Paul in the bar that night shouldn't have known any of this. Sitting across the table, she told him the buzz-cut was her way of protesting societal expectations of women.

The rest of the room dissolved around her. She'd been sitting across from him every Thursday night for the whole fall semester, pulled in from a neighboring table by Jay, like Jay pulled in the others. Jay, the gas giant whose gravity attracted comets—comets that circled and then rocketed away, never to be seen again.

She'd been sitting there, night after night, but had Paul really looked at her before? Had he ever noticed that her cheekbones, chin, and nose were all sharp angles that wanted to cut into him? Had he seen the broadness of her shoulders and how the tendons of her neck looked like the tight strings of a musical instrument? The only makeup she wore was dark liner around her eyes and a paintbrush smear of purple across each eyelid.

She leaned over to Jay and whispered something, conspiratorial eyes darting back every second or two toward Paul. Jay nodded and flashed his crooked grin at Julie before getting up and walking to the bar. When he returned, he had a beer for himself and a beer for Paul, which he placed in the middle of the table. Paul reached for the beer. Julie reached for it as well. When their hands intercepted, the pint glass tumbled. The beer cascaded in a single, foaming tan sheet over the carved wood of the table and onto Julie, darkening her gray shirt and spilling into her lap.

She stood, wet, exasperated, throwing words like little knives at Paul. He tried to hand her the wet-circled napkins that sat under the pint glasses, but she knocked them out of his hand. She grabbed his wrist and pulled him into the darkness, and when the light returned, he was standing in the women's restroom, in front of three sinks with three mirrors side by side that all watched her point at the paper towel dispenser.

Clean up your mess, Paul Prentice.

He tugged each sheet from the dispenser. Click-click-click. He tried to hand her a wadded up mass of the paper towels, but she pulled her own hands back, raised them up as if to say that she had meant the words that still echoed off the stained tiles lining the walls and floor.

The restroom seemed to shrink around them. She stepped into his outstretched hand, still clutching the paper towels. His semi-drunk mind tried to comply, began trying to dry her off, and then the room shrank again until it was a tight space just big enough for the two of them, and his hand froze, wet with the beer that had wicked through the paper towel, hand still pressed against her, against her wet tank top and the swell of her breasts underneath, and all at once, as he looked up into her gray-blue eyes, he knew she had orchestrated everything so that he would be here, alone with her, completely under her power, his hand petting down her chest, his entire body electrified.

Get another paper towel.

Click-click-click.

The room tightened even further, darkness crowding in, a darkness that shouldn't have been there. He looked into her eyes, and instead of seeing the source of the electricity filling him, like he had when this moment really happened, he saw instead the reflection of the creeping darkness closing in on him.

Click-click-click.

His eyes opened to the darkness. Clicking sounds filled the room all around him. Not the clicking of the paper towel dispenser from all those years back. A clicking of little claws on a wood floor.

He jumped up and felt something small and hard scurry away when he reached to steady himself against the arm of the sofa.

"Jay!" he yelled.

A thud. Jay rolling off his sofa, hitting the floor. The clicking sounds went into a sudden frenzy, as though they were bees in a disturbed hive. Paul took two steps toward where he thought the lamp was but hit the back of one of the sofas and doubled over it. Something ran across his back with claws like needles.

Jay cursed and thrashed, and the clicking grew louder.

"Goddamnit! Something bit me!"

Paul flailed his arms in the darkness and hopped from his left foot to his right. "Turn the light on! Turn the fucking light on!"

He heard Jay tumble again right as his flailing hand hit the velvet wallpaper. With his right hand tracing the wall, Paul made his way around the room as quickly as he could, scrambling over sofa after sofa lodged against the doors. He stepped on something that moved and almost turned his ankle.

Where the hell was the lamp?!

Suddenly the room was filled with blue light. Jay stood in the center with the sapphire-handled knife raised above him, flooding the room with its glow. All around the room, little shadows the size of rats darted in a clicking frenzy away from the light. Paul vaulted a sofa to stand next to Jay. Dozens of little eyes stared back at them.

They looked like roach-sized rats or rats with roach-like chitinous shells.

Jay made for one of the doors, and the roach-rats on its barricade sofa fled as the knife's blue light came closer. Paul shoved the sofa aside, and then they were through the door, with the door slammed shut behind them. Another sitting room, lamp on, sofa present even though they had pulled in the sofas from each of the neighboring rooms before they slept.

"I hate this fucking place," Paul said.

Jay still had the knife out, and it still glowed blue, making Jay's skin look pale and gray. "I guess nap time is over. What the hell were those things? Looked like evil armadillos."

"I have no idea, and I don't care. Let's keep moving. No more rest until we find a way out."

They resumed their random walk through the sitting rooms. If there was one positive thing that came from nearly being eaten alive in their sleep by roach-rats, it was that Jay had seemed to forget their conversation from before. Paul hadn't forgotten, though, and to him it felt like an invisible presence, following them from room to room.

Paul tried to push all other thoughts aside and focus on looking for patterns. He absently reached for his phone in his left front pocket, where he normally kept it, but it was probably sitting on the coffee table in his living room. When he never returned from going outside, Julie would've called the phone, only to hear it ring in the neighboring room.

Julie. His mind recalled the last image from the dream, with the enclosing darkness reflected in her eyes. This place had gotten into his head and was poisoning his memories. He couldn't think of Julie now without exposing her memories to the corrupting force around him. The only thing to do was to push on and find a way back as quickly as possible.

In each room, Jay used the knife to do some unique form of damage. A slice through a cushion, a line through the lampshade, a corner cut off the rug, the letters J-A-Y scratched into a door. All with an edge of malice that Paul hadn't before seen in his friend. They never encountered any of Jay's vandalism as they continued. Either each room was new or the little wounds were being healed.

Regarding wounds, Paul's stomach and arm showed only the faintest traces of the scratches and tears from the ash dog. The ash itself was gone as well, but he could feel little welts where the roach-rat claws had pricked his back.

"Here we go!" Jay exclaimed, arresting Paul out of his thoughts. "Another new room."

In many ways, the new room was identical to the altar room—surfaces of rough stone, air heavy and warm—but it lacked the scrawled letters on the walls, and in the center was a ladder, extending to a hatch in the ceiling high above.

"That's gotta be the way out," Paul said. "Finally."

He stepped around Jay and began climbing two rungs with each step. Jay followed. At the top, Paul inspected the hatch. Just a slide latch and he should be able to push it open.

"You two have any idea where that leads?" came a voice from below.

A skull-faced woman in a black robe stood in the doorway leading back to the sitting room maze. Paul almost lost his grip and fell off the ladder. For a split second, the woman appeared to be a walking skeleton straight out of a horror movie, but the knot of blonde hair atop her head didn't look at all skeleton-like. The skull was just face paint in the style Paul recognized from *Dia de los Muertos*, the Mexican Day of the Dead.

Jay jumped to the floor and started walking toward her, knife raised with his elbow cocked.

From within her robe, she pulled out a dull gray rod about the length of her forearm and pointed it directly at Jay.

"I wouldn't come any closer," she said, with a hint of familiar Texas drawl.

"Or what?" Jay said, still moving toward her, his voice as harsh as Paul had ever heard it.

"Or you'll be splattered all over the wall."

Jay stopped and glared at the nondescript rod in her hands. Paul slid down the ladder as quickly as possible, saying, "Whoa. Hang on. No harm meant. We had a bad run-in with some zombie dog things and some roach-rats. We don't really trust anything here."

The woman pointed the rod at Jay's knife. "You shouldn't have picked that up. Did you kill anything with that?" Without waiting for them to answer, she said, "You don't know what things can do here. You need to be more careful."

"More careful?" Paul said. "Who are you?"

"A prisoner like you," she said.

Jay finally lowered the blade. "A prisoner like us, you say. If that's true, it's nice to have company. Even if you do look like a creepshow."

"It *is* nice," Paul interrupted. "I'm Paul, by the way. Paul Prentice. This is Jay Lightsey. Normally he's a little more easygoing. This place has us a little high-strung. And your name is..."

She put the rod back into her robe. "I don't know if my real name means anything anymore. The others called me Skull Girl. You can call me that."

"The others?" Paul said. "There are more of us?"

"All dead or lost. More come and they die, too."

Paul groaned. It was like a sick joke. Every time they found something new, every time their hopes rose, they rose only to be crushed. Like a snare that tightens the more you struggle to get loose.

"What's with the creepy costume?" Jay asked. "It ain't Halloween, Skull Girl."

After staring at each of them in turn, her hard expression softened a bit, her shoulders sagged. "It's a long story that I don't feel like telling. The short answer is: I was wearing a costume when I came here. If I wash off the makeup, it comes back. I guess this is how I look while I'm stuck here."

"Stuck here like us," Paul said to himself. The more he focused on her makeup, the more intricate it appeared. Her eyes were piercing white in contrast to the black circles surrounding them, which were in turn surrounded by little painted rose petals. Her nose was a black spade, and lines across her lips formed the teeth of the skull. The rest of her face was covered by flowering vines atop a white powder base. Paul was about to ask *Where is here, anyway?* when Jay blurted out:

"Isn't it cultural appropriation for a caucasian lady to wear costumes like that?"

Paul shoved Jay's shoulder. "What the hell is wrong with you?"

Any softness in Skull Girl's demeanor vanished. With a glare, she said, "I'm not staying near you any longer, not as long as Jay has that knife. Look at his eyes, Paul. Do you see that?"

"What's wrong with my eyes?" Jay asked, turning to Paul.

If Paul had to answer, he couldn't. Somehow Jay's eyes, usually so lighthearted, had become cold and intense. And the color was wrong, just barely. The blue of his irises had become muddy, maybe even red.

"Don't try to follow me," she said. She pointed at Jay. "And if I see you again and you still have that knife, you're dead."

"We'll see who's dead..." Jay muttered as the door shut behind her.

"Are you happy, now, you idiot? You ran off our only source of information." Paul pointed at the blue knife in Jay's hand. "Maybe you should get rid of that thing. There's something, I don't know, *off* about it and about you now also."

"Off? Well, you can *piss off*. How about that? She only said that shit about the knife because she wants it."

Paul jogged to the door, cracked it softly, and turned back to Jay. "We can't let her go."

"Then follow her. I'll stay here."

Paul started through the doorway but hesitated. "I'm not leaving you."

Jay pointed past Paul and snarled, "Stop treating me like a child and go before you lose her. She's our only hope at understanding what the hell is going on." His eyes flared, and Paul could see the red clearly, like Skull Girl had said. "Go, dumbass!"

Paul turned just in time to see a door in the neighboring room click closed. He ran, leaped over the sofa, and grasped the doorknob while Jay's accusation from last night echoed in his head. *It was just a matter of time, I guess, before you abandoned me, too.* All Paul could do was keep moving. He counted one-two and pushed the door open as quietly as he could, in time to catch the next door—again directly ahead—closing. He left each door open as he passed through, hoping in vain that would keep the room sequence in place.

The next time, she took the door to the right, but when Paul—still trying to time things perfectly—entered the room, all the doors were already shut. In a panic, he quickly opened each of the three remaining doors, worried less about being seen than of losing her, but each adjacent room was empty.

He retraced his steps, opening doors that should've stayed open, knowing full well it wouldn't lead back to the ladder room. When he opened the door that should've led back to Jay, he found yet another empty sitting room.

He was lost. Worse, he had done exactly what he said he wouldn't do. Paul had abandoned his friend.

CHAPTER 5
THE GRAVEYARD

Jay kicked the heel of his boot into the loose dirt on the floor over and over again until his knee and hip hurt and a dirty fog hung in the air. *Your dad is a fucking narcissistic bastard, and you know it*, Paul had said. Jay kicked the ground again and felt a sharp twinge in his lower back. That just made him madder. It was the *and you know it* part that pissed Jay off most because Jay did know it, and every time Jay looked in a mirror he saw more and more of Big Cal and less and less of himself.

Paul could be such a sanctimonious motherfucker sometimes. Normally he acted like he was giving friendly advice. *Hey, you should check out this programmer job that opened up down at the hospital.* Yeah, like Jay wasn't already working around the clock trying to get a business off the ground. Like everybody should just live their life like Paul. Work their way up a corporate ladder doing a job they fucking hate. Abandoning their dreams, getting a mortgage, keeping the hamster wheel spinning. No thanks.

And now this shit about Jay needing to get a real job? "Straight through the fucking heart," Jay muttered.

He was glad Paul had run off after that creepshow woman. Everybody else had given up on Jay, why not Paul also? He started to kick the ground again, but all the energy seemed to leave him at once. His shoulders sagged, and he sat back heavily against the third rung of the ladder.

Paul wouldn't have left if Jay hadn't yelled at him and told him to go. He could be irritating and a know-it-all, but Paul was as loyal as a Labrador.

Labrador. Jay winced at the word, remembering Little Cal, probably only 17 at the time, leaning back and carrying *Cadejo*'s dead body from the bed of the truck to the old well. He remembered *Cadejo*'s limp form spinning down into the darkness and the echoing splash a second or two later. A splash in water he couldn't see, or maybe the sound had been the rupture and explosion of the dog's carcass, spraying maggots and rotten death-fluid on the well's stone walls.

Paul had been down there, in the dead muck, with what was left of the dead dog. How the hell had Paul gone so long without talking about it? So long that Jay had forgotten. Like he had forgotten to put the truck in park, and had forgotten to use the parking brake on an incline like his dad had told him to, time and time again.

He stood and was about to rub his eyes, but the knife was in his right hand despite him having no recollection of taking it back out of its sheath. He tried to push aside his guilt about the well and his anger at Paul over everything Paul had said. There'd be time to be guilty and angry later. Or maybe not.

He looked up at the hatch above the ladder. Skull Girl didn't say *not* to go up there. She just asked if they knew where it led. It led out of the sitting room maze—this, Jay knew with certainty. If Paul was off trying to discover things with that costumed whackjob, Jay could do some discovering on his own instead of sitting around here feeling sorry for himself and pissed off at his friend.

He rubbed the knife's sapphire handle between the palms of his hands, and in doing so noticed a slight pain in his left forearm. Three even lines had been cut into his skin about two inches in length and a quarter-inch apart. Three. The number of ash dogs he had killed.

Had he been keeping a kill tally without realizing it? The thought made his stomach quiver, but an alternate thought of his arm carved full of tally marks gave him a cool jolt of adrenaline. Maybe Skull Girl knew a thing or two about this knife after all. Maybe that's why she wanted it for herself.

"I think you're a naughty little knife, aren't you?" Jay said. "Let's go exploring, you and me. Maybe we'll come up in Paul's neighbor's basement. We'll buy the house and start selling French sofas and zombie fire dogs. No guarantees on dog training. Keep away from combustible material."

The hatch was heavier than it looked, and as Jay strained to lift it, he felt the ladder creak and crack under the weight. He pushed harder, climbing up a rung to get leverage so he could use his legs. Damn the thing was heavy. If Paul were here, he'd be saying some shit about Jay needing to hit the weight room. As far as Jay was concerned, exercise was for suckers with nothing better to do with their time. Jay could eat anything he wanted and still stay skinny as a rail. Or, at least he could until about age 30, and then either age or the five or six (or, maybe seven) beers a day had started to catch up to him.

He pressed his shoulders into the underside of the hatch, knife handle clutched between his teeth, and gave it all he had. The ladder shuddered and his jaw burned with the intense effort of making sure the knife didn't fall. He should've put the knife back in its sheath, but he wanted it as close at hand as possible.

A little cloud of dust exploded out as the hatch broke its seal to the above. He expected light to pour in, but the open space was cold and dark. Two more steps up the ladder and he had the hatch perpendicular. He realized, too late, that once it started to fall away, it would be too heavy to catch, but thin chains attached to the enclosure kept the hatch resting open. Open, but precariously ready to crash shut.

It took a while for his eyes to adjust to the darkness above, so he waited at the top of the ladder until the new room took shape. He wished the knife weren't glowing in his hand. Seemingly with that thought, the cold blue glow vanished.

Once his eyes had adjusted to the darkness, he saw that the room above wasn't a room at all. It was a giant cavern, illuminated like a nineteenth-century city at night with what looked like gas street-lamps. All around him, circling him, were strange dark stones, like the teeth of a great, decaying mouth. Amazed, he climbed the rest of the way up.

Tombstones. He had emerged into an underground cemetery. Seeing the hatch from the other side, he realized he, himself, had just climbed out of a grave. The cemetery extended a couple hundred feet in each direction, with the cavern walls bordering it on two sides. To his right, a path led away into the dark punctuated too infrequently by streetlamps. To his left, up a hill was a massive two-story colonial house, windows glowing. It looked like a dark corner of a town had been surgically removed and placed in the cavern. He had never seen anything like it.

The sound of water running—and his sudden intense thirst—drove his attention elsewhere. He scoured the cemetery looking for its source, keeping low and quiet as he walked. Rather than a garden fountain, as he expected, the running water instead came from the mouth of a shrouded frieze figure carved into the side of a tomb wall. He leaned and put his mouth under the stream, the water as cold and pure as any he had ever tasted. Above him, releasing the flow, was a skull, the face of death.

He nearly coughed the water up, but his fear and revulsion were no match for his thirst. After drinking his fill, he sat back on his heels, looked around, and wondered what the fuck he had gotten himself into.

Without realizing it, he had moved into one of the darkest parts of the cemetery. The hatch, about fifty feet away, glowed with the light coming from below. It stood out conspicuously, drawing attention to itself. Jay had seen enough and was ready to go back down, to find Paul and figure out what to do next. But that meant stepping into the light, exposing himself to anything waiting in the shadows behind the stones and tombs.

So, he waited, back pressed against the cold stone of the tomb. His knees ached, prodding him to stand, but a tickling sensation in the back of his mind kept him still.

Something had his spidey sense going.

Another several minutes and his knees couldn't take any more. Before he knew what he was doing, he stood and stretched, right leg and then left and then—and then he froze. A shadow near the hatch had moved.

There, again! The shadow had gone still, but now that he knew where to look, he could see the silhouette of a human-like form, crouching behind a gravestone. Maybe it was the angle, the foreshortening of the shadow, but it looked disproportioned—too thin, too gangly to be human. Another movement, a twitch. Something was waiting. Was it waiting for him? Had it seen him come up from the hatch?

Did it see him now?

Just then a brighter light came from the cavern wall behind the hiding form. A slit widened into a glowing square. Elevator doors. Two women stood in the elevator, eyes wide, stunned. They looked to be in their mid- to late 20s, and, judging by their matching spandex uniforms and muscular bodies, they were athletes of some kind on the way to a competition. Both of their left legs, below the knee, were prosthetics.

"What the hell?" the shorter woman said. "Is this under the stadium?" She looked to be around five-foot even, if that, and had pale, almost white skin and short, gelled-up hair. Her thighs looked like they had been hastily carved from stone.

"Is that a graveyard?! What the ever-loving hell, Frankie?!" her much taller companion exclaimed, strong Indian accent matching her brown skin. A knot of jet-black hair wobbled atop her head with every movement. She backed away from the elevator's opening and then jumped forward to push buttons frantically.

The door stayed open.

"This is amazing!" the one called Frankie said, stepping into the cavern with a slight favoring of her leg of flesh. "You have to come see this, Supriya."

Supriya was having none of it, still mashing on the uncooperative elevator buttons. "Why won't this work? It's not working!"

Who the hell were these two, with their missing legs and beefy bodies? And where did that elevator come from? Jay had the sudden, almost overwhelming urge to sprint to the elevator. But he knew—like he knew something else lurked behind the stones—that the buttons would never work. Like with the hole in Paul's yard and whatever must've trapped Skull Girl, this elevator was a one-way path here. Running to the elevator also meant running by the thing hiding in the shadows.

The knife quivered in his hand, and before Jay knew it, he was stalking the thing. He was the one creeping from shadow to shadow.

"Oh my god, there's a house! You have to see this!" Frankie said. "Supriya?"

"I want to see nothing but this door closing!"

As Jay drew nearer, the thing began to move too, hunting its own prey. It slipped from behind a crooked gravestone and slid up against the cavern wall. Its oversized rib cage rose and fell in deep, anticipatory breaths, but despite its breathing, it looked to Jay more like a machine made out of ill-fitting parts than a creature of flesh.

He had a window of a second or two to blindside it before it attacked the unsuspecting duo. Jay took off in a run, but his first step kicked a rock back as if it had been slingshotted into a tomb behind him. The crack echoed through the cavern, and all eyes turned to him.

Something crashed into him from the side. His leg caught a low headstone, and his body cartwheeled, the cavern spinning before his eyes until he landed upside down on the ground. And then it was straddled on top of him. Another of those machine things. One arm was much bigger than the other, with a rusty street sign—*SPEED LIMIT 55*—screwed into it. It used the sign like a cleaver, hacking downward at his head, narrowly missing once to the right and then to the left.

He tried to push it off, but the damn thing was all scrap metal and heavy as hell.

Its little arm backhanded him, and he felt a tooth come loose in his mouth. He slashed up with the knife—somehow still in his hand—and felt it slice through the little arm as easily as through paper.

The machine turned its head, made out of a car's headlamp, to look at its missing limb. In its second of confusion, Jay grabbed the dismembered arm with his left hand and smashed the machine in its head.

"How you like gettin' beat with your own fucking arm!" he yelled.

In his right hand, the knife slashed out as if it had a mind of its own, cutting through metal, through wires and rubber hoses. He cut through something that looked like a serpentine belt in a car, running and twisting throughout the body of the machine, and as it snapped, every part of the machine fell apart at once, leaving Jay covered in random automotive junk.

He pushed himself up, body bruised from the tackle and the fall, and saw the first machine pinning the short one, Frankie, on the ground, bringing its street sign down over and over and over. By the time Jay got there, her head looked like a dropped watermelon on the cavern floor. He made a swift cut to the machine's inner belt, and it collapsed into a pile of parts.

Jay turned to Supriya, expecting her to be huddled in the corner of the elevator or frantically jabbing at its buttons, but instead she stood in its center, chin raised defiantly, fists on her hips. A one-legged, Indian Valkyrie.

"Are you going to kill me now?" she asked, despite looking like she could tear Jay limb from limb if she wanted to.

"Kill you? I'm the guy who saved you!"

Without looking her companion on the ground, she said, voice starting to quiver, "Frankie's dead, then?"

Jay glanced at the headless body near his feet and then at her. She was doing her best to look strong, to keep from looking anywhere but straight ahead.

"Yeah. Sorry I couldn't save your, uh, friend there."

"Frankie was my partner," she said and then quickly added, "my business partner."

He could see the strength leaving her as she started blinking faster, weight shifting unsteadily between her black prosthetic and her one leg of flesh. "Supriya, is it?"

"Yeah."

"Well, Supriya, the time for grieving ain't now. Whatever sport you two were playing at, you're in a new sport now. It's called let's-get-the-fuck-out-of-here-before-we're-next. Like it or not, you've got a new partner. The name's Jay."

CHAPTER 6
WINDOWS OF SUNLIGHT AND DARKNESS

Paul walked room to room, randomly opening doors, wishing he hadn't chased after Skull Girl, wishing he hadn't left Jay behind, wishing he had kept his mouth shut. He was too exhausted to feel dread, but dread's insidious cousin, hopelessness, thrived in his exhaustion.

The hopelessness clung to him like the stench of the water from the well. Even hours after he had washed it off, he still smelled it. Through all the years since, when he felt the right mix of exhaustion and fear, the water's oily film began to cover him again and burn his sinuses.

The identical rooms with their identical furniture made time seem to stand still. He tried counting rooms, to prove to himself that he was, in fact, moving, but upon hitting one hundred, he stopped and sat on the floor, head between his knees, eyes closed.

At least the ash dogs and the roach rats had been physical challenges—not that he wanted to encounter either, but physical challenges were something he could meet head on. The endless maze of rooms, on the other hand, was breaking him down mentally.

He took a deep breath and tried to clear his head. Brute force and reason. The two Paul Prentice approaches to a challenge. The former was getting him nowhere. Time to try the latter.

He ran through what he knew. So far, the sitting rooms had led to at least three non-sitting-room locations: the altar room, the ladder room, and the pathway from the false library buried in his backyard. Skull Girl, as she called herself, clearly knew how to navigate the sitting rooms, which suggested that they led to more locations. How many more? It could be one or one thousand. In the case of the latter, who knew if he'd ever find his way back to Jay?

Following Skull Girl had been a mistake, but that was a sunk cost, to use an accounting term. He couldn't let himself waste more time and energy on the past. He thought instead about Theseus, who had overcome the Minotaur and escaped from Daedalus's labyrinth. Theseus had used a rope or something, tied to the entrance, to lead himself back out. Paul looked over the contents of the sitting room. Maybe if he had a knife, he could tear apart the Persian rug and make a wool rope. But since the rope wouldn't be tied to the entrance, it didn't seem that useful. And besides, the only knife was the one with the sapphire handle that Jay had, and something about the knife seemed off to Paul. Poisonous.

Forget Theseus. What about the letters carved into the stone wall of the altar room? *NSEWE*. Was it a word? He tried saying it out loud. Phonetically it sounded like *ensue*, to follow or succeed.

What if the letters stood for north, south, east, and west, with each direction corresponding to one of the sitting room doors? With that thought, energy and hope surged back into him. He jumped to his feet. Which way was north? He closed his mind and tried to recreate the first glimpse he'd had of the sitting room after he and Jay entered from the tunnel with the smokeless brazier.

The sofa had been facing them. Did that mean north was directly behind the sofa? It was worth a try. He walked through the corresponding door to a neighboring sitting room and then froze. Going north and then south meant walking directly back into the room he had just left. And that would be true for the east-west-east portion of *NSEWE*. Had he and Jay really done that? Only one way to tell. He shut the door behind him, opened it back up, and continued following the *NSEWE* sequence, no matter how senseless it felt.

When he opened the final door, he felt the heavy, wet air of the stone altar room before he had the door open far enough to see the room for himself. The sequence had worked! Before him sat the altar with the decaying body. On the walls, he saw the letters carved into the stone, but they seemed fainter than before, like the room had begun healing or reverting back to some type of starting state.

Could that be possible? He shook his head and shut the door to the altar room. He'd wonder about the fundamental nature of this place later. All that mattered now was that he'd proven the maze did follow some form of order. He had no way of knowing if all of the patterns had five elements, but it gave him a starting point. Five elements, with four options each, meant how many possible sequences? He tried to do the math in his head. Did he need to use factorials? No. It was simpler than that. Four to the fifth power, which was ... one thousand and twenty-four.

Shit. A thousand possible sequences.

<hr />

But now he needed to piss, despite the hours without drinking anything, despite his thirst. He positioned himself in a corner, unzipped, and let out a few bursts of deep, almost brownish-yellow.

A *thud* caught his attention. As he looked up, a streak of light flashed before him. Another thud. Two small, silver knives stuck into the purple wall just inches from his head.

He spun around. Skull Girl stood in the doorway in front of the sofa, the same doorway he used to enter the room. In her hand, she held a third knife.

"I said I didn't want you two around me."

Paul raised both hands in the air. "It's just me. Jay's back at the ladder." As he heard his own words, he knew they were wrong. Jay probably lasted two minutes maximum before wandering off.

Skull Girl's black-outlined eyes narrowed and then lowered their focus.

"You might want to tuck that in," she said.

Paul looked down. "Oh, shit. Sorry about that." He turned his hips back toward the wall, put everything in its proper place, and zipped up his pants.

"You're like a lost dog that's gonna get run over, you know that? Let me give you some free advice," she said. "If you see a woman in a white dress with gold eyes, make sure you—"

She was interrupted by a bell ringing. It sounded far away, but it carried with it a deep tremor that Paul felt in his bones, echoing in his head. He put his hands to his ears, but that did nothing to lessen the feeling of a hand reaching into his chest, shaking him by the spine. As the reverberations faded, he struggled to catch his breath.

"What the hell was that?" he asked.

She held a hand up and looked around the room, eyes narrowed in their painted black sockets. She dropped her hand and said, "It was nothing you need to worry about. Like I was saying, if you see a woman in a white dress with gold eyes—"

The right side of the room seemed to become ... *loose* ... the space jittering and unsteady, the wall flashing between alternate states, as if each second that passed recalled a different history, first torn and ragged, then back to the velvet wallpapered form, then burned, then blood-splattered, then normal again. The floor and the furniture flickered likewise through alternative versions of now. Smashed and then whole again, and every possibility in between. The *loose* portion of the room expanded toward them, bringing more and more of the room into the stutter-shifting chaos.

For a brief second, Skull Girl's steely exterior broke, and Paul saw fear in her eyes. Then her wall went back up. "We have to run! Now!"

She sped through doors, through more clones of the sitting room, and Paul followed, not knowing what he was running from but his heart almost beat out of his chest nevertheless. Twice she hesitated before a door, as if working up the courage to open it. Each time the door led only to another empty room.

And then she opened a door and sunlight flooded in. Paul's eyes watered and burned with the light's intensity. After so many hours, after perhaps a day or more enclosed in this bizarre, dark place, the sudden sight of a field of golden grass, of the outside world, brought tears to Paul's eyes.

Skull Girl turned to make sure he was still following. She shook her head as if she knew what he was thinking—that she'd led him back to the outside world. "We have to keep moving."

"But we're free, aren't we?" Paul asked as he stepped into the grass and felt the heat of the noonday sun on the bare skin of his face and forearms.

The field seemed to extend off forever in front of them, a small stream ahead and a giant gray boulder, the only interruptions. Skull Girl ran through the stream and crouched behind the boulder. He followed. He opened his mouth to ask what they were hiding from. It was then that Paul saw the statue. The door to the field was at the base of a giant, ruined statue, its collapsed and broken parts strewn across the field for as far as he could see. The boulder they were hiding behind looked like it may have been part of the statue's hand. All that remained, still standing on the base, was a single leg up to a knee. The sandaled foot, by itself, was as big as Paul's university football stadium. The whole statue would've been incomprehensibly tall, bigger than any skyscraper built by man. Its scale took his breath away.

Even though there were no clouds in the sky, the day suddenly grew dim. The door began to open.

"Turn away," Skull Girl whispered. "Stay quiet and don't look at it."

"Don't look at what?" Paul asked. She elbowed him hard in the ribs.

The sky's blue turned to red and then a dull, diseased brown, growing darker by the second. He pressed his back into the boulder and fought the urge to peer around it at the door. The bell rang again, this time seeming like it came from within Paul's head. He pulled at his hair, wanting to open himself up so he could let the sound out.

His teeth pressed together so hard his jaw burned. The reverberations made him feel like he was liquefying from the inside out.

Whispers. Thousands of voices tickling at him like a swarm of insects.

The whispers grew louder. Something was getting closer. He could feel the heat being pulled out of him, back through the boulder, toward whatever it was that had followed them through the door. To his left, Skull Girl had her hands over her eyes. The world around him had become *loose* like it had before, everything unstuck from its rightful three-dimensional position. His legs in front of him seemed to overlap with hundreds of copies. His hand, held in front of his face, was a hundred hands, layered on top of one another.

Without realizing what he was doing, he turned to his right. Somehow he could see *it* through the boulder: a towering silhouette of darkness, vaguely human-shaped but with limbs a bit too long and hands like giant spider crabs. *It* looked right back at him, and the thousands of whispering voices took him...

...someplace else with a brown, diseased sky. An oil-black sea lapping at a rocky coast. A great bell tower standing before the shore, the source of the echoing rings, a tower made of stone like scales on a living thing. The tower reached up like a crooked finger scratching at the sky, trying to scratch out the light of the dying sun. Thousands of iron statues stood on the rocky shore, a silent army fanning out from the tower. From each statue's agonized face, a voice cried out. The voice of a soul trapped within. One statue among them was quiet, a statue that looked like Paul, a statue made for him, waiting, waiting to contain him, to become his eternal prison...

She turned his head and pressed her hands over his eyes, screaming over the pounding echoes of the bell, "YOU CAN'T LOOK AT IT!" In the split second before her hands blocked out the world, he saw in her eyes something familiar, so reassuringly familiar that it pulled him back. He grabbed onto that familiarity and it kept pulling, holding him tight. But the *thing*, the towering creature was in his head now, too. Somehow, he could still see it. Despite cowering behind the boulder, with his head turned away and her hands covering his eyes, even though it should have been impossible, he could still see the thing walking closer, as though its image were tunneling through stone and flesh and bone, tunneling directly into his mind. With each of the thing's steps came another echo of the bell.

It stopped, eyes burning. Some core part of Paul had been sucked out of his physical body, pulled through the boulder, almost to the thing. If it took another step... If Paul opened his eyes... If it reached out its dark hand... It would consume him. Consume his soul. And he'd be trapped forever in the statue made for him on the shore in front of the black sea.

Paul's eyes were closed, but he could see all of this as if laid out before him.

And then the bell's echoes drained out of his skull like water leaking through a cracked vessel. The sickness in the sky faded away, the brown reverting to red and then back to painfully bright blue.

The door slammed shut.

He felt like his body had been pulled apart and hastily stitched back together.

"I told you not to look at it." Skull Girl stood, a hand rested on the boulder to keep her balance.

"Is it gone?" he asked. He tried to stand, but the ground seemed to shift a foot to the right as he stood, and he slumped back down against the boulder.

She looked off somewhere beyond the door, beyond the broken colossus, and said, "For now."

"What the hell was that thing?"

She returned her attention to Paul, really looking at him with those strangely familiar eyes, studying him like a stray dog at the pound she was considering adopting. She frowned and shook her head, as if unsatisfied or maybe disappointed in what she saw. "I've heard it called the *Košmaro*," she said. "But I don't know if that's its real name. Or if it has a name. I don't know what it is. Only that it comes for the souls of the dead. It takes them back—"

"To the statues by the bell tower?" Paul interrupted.

"You looked deep into it, didn't you?"

"I couldn't help it. It was pulling me in, somehow." Thinking about being locked in its gaze made him sick to his stomach. Somewhere in the pit of his mind, the rotted Labrador, *Cadejo*, was laughing at him. It had the same void-eyes as the thing Skull Girl called the *Košmaro*, eyes of darkness that bored deep inside him. *If you had stayed down in the well, I would've taken you to your statue myself, Cadejo said. You're coming anyway, Paul Prentice. You're coming to be with me forever.*

The mold-and-death taste of the well water filled his mouth. The taste of doom. Even with the sun's flooding light, darkness began closing around him, like he was being pulled backward into a tunnel. He turned to Skull Girl to apologize—for what, he had no idea—and saw in her eyes the familiarity, making the darkness stutter enough for him to grab hold again. If she understood what had happened, she made no outward sign.

When he felt his voice had returned, he asked, "Was that a real place I saw? The black sea? The statues and the tower?" He wanted her to turn back toward him, but she didn't.

After a few seconds, she said, "Is it a real place? I don't know how to answer that. Is where we are now a real place?"

How could this not be real? He looked around at the sky, the field, and the trickling stream. It all looked and felt as real as anything he'd ever experienced. But he had seen it jitter and threaten to come apart when that thing, the *Košmaro*, had come through the door behind them. "You said the *Kos*—" he choked on the thing's name.

"*Košmaro*," she said.

"Right. You said the *Košmaro* comes for the souls of the dead. Does that mean someone recently died?"

A small splash came from the stream, but she didn't seem to notice. "Yes. Someone died. That's why it was here, and it must've sensed us close by and followed us." She looked down at him, but the sun was just over her shoulder, so he could barely see her face. Her voice became matter-of-fact again. "You're thinking of your friend, right? Jay? I don't know if it came for him. There are always more of us getting pulled here, so it could've been anyone. One way or another, Jay is doomed. Sorry. If he's not dead yet, he will be soon."

She shook her head and then squatted down next to him. "You're shaking. Probably dehydrated. Come on." She grabbed him by the forearm and pulled him to his feet with unexpected strength. His legs barely supported his weight. It was all he could do to keep up as she walked him back down to the edge of the stream. Her grip tightened on his arm as they stepped across waterworn gray stones. "Get a drink. Cool off."

She let go and he fell to his knees. He drank the cold water from his own cupped hands, and it tasted better than anything he could recall, with the possible exception of the Old Fashioneds Julie liked to make on Thursdays with rye and those Italian cherries that cost like a dollar each. He splashed water on his face and poured it over his head. Where was this place? It reminded him of northern Idaho and Wyoming. How did they travel so far so quickly?

"We're not," Skull Girl said, behind him, sitting on a large rock above the stream. She had removed her black robe and was unbuckling glassy brown shin guards that looked like they were made from the chitinous exoskeleton of a large insect or crustacean.

"Not what?"

She took off the rest of her shell-like armor and boots before standing and responding. "You're thinking we're outside. And I guess maybe we are, but it's not the outside back home. We're still in the Between." She walked down next to him, now wearing a tank top and jeans. Unlike the painted white skin of her face, her shoulders and arms looked almost as sun-gold as the tall grass of the field where they weren't covered with scars and tattoos.

She stepped into the stream, kneeled down, and submerged her head completely underwater. She sat back and twisted her hair, pushing its remaining water out, running down her face, shoulders, and shirt. The paint on her face had smeared and run, making her look for a second like a vampire melting in the direct light of the sun. With a few more splashes of water, she scrubbed off the remaining paint and became human again.

Paul started to say something, but it slipped away as if carried off by the stream. The Between. Outside but not outside. Jay and the knife that was somehow *wrong*. The sickening bell. The creature with the burning empty eyes and the whispering voices. And, almost as strange, the transformation of the woman next to him. Guarded and severe before, even deadly. Now, the extreme opposite. He found himself staring. She looked about his age, early 30s or so, but her eyes were sunken in, cheeks hollow, like those years had been rough. She was thin, painfully thin, with the musculature of someone who compulsively exercises until the body starts eating itself. And the tattoos, scars, and bruises...

She looked strong and brittle at the same time. And maybe even beautiful in the way a dried flower can be. He turned his head to keep from staring, and the sudden movement seemed to shake loose a memory.

He knew her.

"Corinne," he said. "Corinne Pelletier."

She looked at him in surprise, and the familiarity was so intense he wondered how he hadn't known it was her. He saw recognition in her eyes as well.

"I know you, but I don't know where from," she said.

Without the costume and makeup, her face—despite the dozen years since he had last seen it, despite all the changes and everything she had been through—her face was almost as familiar to him as Julie's. He threw his hands up.

"How did you not recognize me?" He jumped up and bent down to hug her, but she pushed him back, and suddenly the cold armor of her costumed persona returned. "But it's me! Paul Prentice! When I said my name earlier... When you saw me, how come you... I was your boyfriend in high school for three years! Until you went off to—"

"To Oklahoma?" she said. Her shoulders slumped and her wall

69

dropped, replaced by sadness. "But in my past, we shared a couple classes together. Nothing more."

"Oklahoma? Nothing more than classmates? We lost our virginity together! The hour between when school let out and your mom got home, every single day, was... In your room, with the poster of that ladypunk band, what was their name... Apoca Lypstick! Yeah, the Apoca Lypstick poster on the back of your door!"

The more she shook her head, the more he redoubled his efforts. "You were going to study biology and then go to vet school. You had every type of pet imaginable. Dog was Kiko, right? You rescued him from a shelter. He had been abused—and hit by a car. Yeah? That's why he always limped. And guinea pigs. Your mom—"

"Hated them, yes," she said. "Please stop."

"Your younger sister... What was her name? Katheryn! Katie! She loved me, remember? She'd always be hanging around and—"

"Stop, Paul."

"And what about Jay? I can't believe you didn't recognize him either! The three of us used to—"

"STOP. I don't know you. I never knew you other than as some kid in a few of my classes. Jay seemed vaguely familiar. I think. Maybe. But that's it. I was never friends with either of you, and certainly nothing more."

Paul shook his head, but before he could go on, she held her hand up.

"You're not wrong. But your Corinne from your past isn't me. The others before me figured out that we've all come from different pasts."

"Different pasts?"

"More than just different pasts. Different versions of the world. That's why they call this place the Between. It's between all of our worlds somehow. Some of those worlds have different rules, and so you'll see things here that could never exist in your world." She sighed. "But I never thought the difference would be something so personal."

He wanted to keep talking about the past, to force her memories and his to come together. To make sense somehow. But as much as he wanted answers, he got the sense that his questions about the past were hurting her, picking at a deep, old wound.

"Do you know how to get out of here?" he asked.

She sighed, and without looking at him, said, "I don't know a way out for me. But for you it's simple. The *gardistaro* will come to you soon, and she can send you home. Or trap you here forever, if you don't know what to say to her. I can help with that."

"*Gardistaro*? Why are you stuck but I can still get out? And what about Jay? He's my best friend. I'm not leaving him by himself."

She began walking away, toward a makeshift tent at the statue's base that must've been her home. Without turning back, she said, "If Jay's still alive, he's lost from you forever. If you try to save him, you'll die or lose yourself as well."

He wearily pushed himself to his feet and began following her. "What do you mean Jay's lost and that I would lose myself? Lose how?"

She stopped, and he thought she was about to turn around, but after a deep breath, she walked on until she reached the little tent she had constructed with sheets, poles, and other odds and ends. From a small chest within the tent, she retrieved a brown suede bag, which she handed to Paul.

"Take this and don't hesitate to use it," she said.

The bag was heavier than it looked. Inside was a dull gray revolver and a smaller bag, filled with what felt like bullets. Seeing the gun made the bag feel somehow heavier. He hadn't fired a gun since that night at the Lightsey ranch, the night of the well. He couldn't bring himself to shoot that rabbit, standing in the dark field in the light of the truck's headlights. But he wouldn't hesitate here if he ran into more ash dogs or something worse, would he?

"Everything here is part of a story that's playing out over and over again," she said. "New people, like you and Jay, come in, but soon you start playing roles, and you become those roles, the roles play out, and you're replaced by someone else. Wash, rinse, repeat. Got it? That knife Jay has? Did you notice how he started changing after picking it up? You noticed his eyes, the irises turning redder and redder?"

"Yeah."

"Each role has a triggering artifact. If you possess it, you start playing the role. The Knife of Undoing is the artifact of the *stelisto*, one of the nastier roles here in the Between. Your friend will lose himself to the role. He'll become the *stelisto* and kill everything around him. When he runs out of enemies, he'll kill his friends. When he runs out of friends, he'll kill himself. He won't be able to stop killing unless something or someone kills him first. Those who play the *stelisto* never last long."

"That's the word he was saying. *Stelisto*." Paul frowned. "Look, I know you're saying I can't help him. I hear you. I really do. But he's like my brother and I have to go back for him."

"That's why I gave you the gun. It'll take care of most anything you'll find in the first world of the Between, provided you don't miss. If you hear the bell ring again and it sounds close by, run. A thousand guns won't help you with the *Kosmaro*. If Jay went up the ladder, don't follow him. You'll need more than this." She jabbed a pointed finger at him with each instruction. "If you accidentally find the stairway leading down, don't go near it. Whatever you do, don't go down any deeper. Don't go to the Between's other worlds. Got it?"

Down? Why would he want to go further down? Other worlds of the Between? "How do I get back to the ladder?" he asked.

Something about the frustrated, little shake of her head triggered memory after memory of Paul's high school afternoons with her, particularly right near the end, when they were arguing about college and going their separate ways. The Corinne standing in front of him now wouldn't remember how cold she'd been when she told him she wanted to leave everything in Austin behind, including him.

"I'll get to that. Be patient," she said, snapping him back to the present. "You'll eventually run into a woman in a white dress with gold eyes. She's the *gardistaro*. She's your only hope of escape. Don't threaten her and pay attention to everything she says. She'll ask you if you want to stay. You have to answer no."

"Why would anyone answer yes?"

"Because they don't realize what she's asking. Here's the sequence through the maze that leads to the ladder. Don't forget it or you'll be lost, and I'm not coming to find you again. Okay? Always start with the sofa facing you, and then the sequence is: right, right, center, back, center, back. Got that?"

Paul started to say that he preferred thinking in terms of north-south-east-west rather than center-back-right-left, but the impatient look on her face suggested he let that go. He ran the sequence through his head several times before repeating it. He created a mnemonic device: *really rotten cantaloupe breeds creepy bugs*. Not eloquent, but hopefully effective.

"Good," she said. "Now go." The paint on her face was coming back, as if washing it off had only been temporary.

He started to ask about the paint and her strange costume, but he knew it would lead to more questions. The coldness in her eyes said that the time for questions had passed. And anyway, he had to get back to Jay, to make up for leaving him. He grabbed the door handle, took a deep breath, and was about to say goodbye when she said:

"Did we love each other?"

Her question blindsided him, as much as if she'd punched him in the gut.

"Yeah," he said without turning back to look at her. "We loved each other. We were young. Didn't understand what we had. Wanted new experiences in college, and neither of us were willing to compromise. But we loved each other as much as two high school kids could. It feels like a hole ripped out of me to hear you say you never experienced it. Like it threatens how real my memory is. Goodbye Corinne-not-my-Corinne."

CHAPTER 7
THE WOMAN IN THE WHITE GOWN

After pulling the door closed behind him, he slid six bullets into the revolver's cylinder and tried pointing the gun toward the sitting room sofa. It occurred to him that, without Jay to show him, he had no idea how to hold a pistol. With one hand, arm extended, the gun felt surprisingly heavy, and it wanted to wander around. Did he need to pull the hammer back, like they did in Western movies? What if his thumb slipped while pulling the hammer back? Would the gun go off?

He started to put it back in the bag, but then he imagined fumbling for it with fire-breathing creatures leaping toward him. It wouldn't fit in his pocket, and stuffing it in the waist of his shorts, the back or, even worse, the front—that just seemed like asking to accidentally blow off an appendage.

So he kept it in his right hand, with his index finger pointing straight forward above the trigger. Something wasn't right about a tool that dealt death with the barest twitch of a finger.

He moved quickly, wanting to avoid more ash dogs or anything else that could cause him to need the gun.

Really — right, or what he thought of as East.

Rotten — right, again.

Cantaloupe — center.

74

Breeds — back.

Creepy — center.

Bugs — back, again—but he hesitated. He put his ear to the door, not knowing what he expected, but feeling that something was waiting on the other side. No sound at all except for the echoes of his own pulsing blood.

As he pulled the door open, he felt the hot, humid air reach around it, almost like a creature's tentacles. He knew the sequence worked before the door was open enough to see the stone walls and the ladder. And like he sensed, there was a presence in the room, but it wasn't Jay.

A woman stood next to the ladder, hands at her side, chin elevated slightly as if she were looking down at him. She wore a white, almost translucent dress that hung still to her feet. On the one hand, she didn't look at all like a threat: she carried nothing, no sense of malice in her expression. But on the other hand, something about her entire presence seemed artificial, as if she'd be completely without human warmth if Paul were to touch her.

He lowered the gun but traced the trigger guard with his finger.

"I am the *gardistaro*," she said, taking a step toward him. Her dress didn't seem to move, and neither did her dark hair hanging straight, almost to her waist.

"Where's Jay?" he asked. "Where's my friend?"

"Do you wish to have the answers?" she said, her voice like the rest of her: another aesthetically beautiful part that came together as an empty whole.

Of course I want answers, he was about to say before catching himself. *They don't realize what she's asking*, Corinne had said. Is she asking him to stay in the Between right now?

"I need to know where my friend is."

"Do you wish to have the answers?" she repeated.

He waited to see if she'd say anything else, and he quickly got the sense that she'd stand there looking at him, with that same question hanging forever.

"What if I say no?"

Again, she repeated, "Do you wish to have the answers?"

He looked to the top of the ladder. The hatch was open to darkness above. Jay must have gone up there, where Corinne told Paul not to follow. Where she said the gun wouldn't be enough.

He swallowed and took two steps toward the ladder, toward the *gardistaro*. She took two equal steps backward, and her stare became somehow colder.

Would she let him leave without answering? Or worse, would walking toward her provoke her? With a deep breath, he took another step. This time, instead of stepping backward, she widened her stance and turned her palms slightly outward, fingers spread and extended. Her eyes narrowed.

"Are you challenging me for the role of the *gardistaro*?" she hissed.

Paul stepped backward until he reached the door. He carefully slid the gun back into its brown bag and held his hands up.

"Lady, I'm not challenging anyone for anything. I just want to find my friend and get the hell out of here."

Her empty expression returned, hands again at her side.

"Do you wish to have the answers?"

He was stuck. No way to move forward without answering. Did he wish to have the answers? Based on what Corinne said, a yes answer meant losing the way home. If you want the answers, you have to stay. But would answering no mean leaving Jay behind? Is this how the others Corinne mentioned—whoever they were—is this how they got stuck here?

He looked again at the ladder. If Paul stayed, could he find Jay? If Jay was even still alive... But as Jay's lifelong friend, wasn't it Paul's obligation to try?

After a deep breath, he opened his mouth to say yes. Yes, he wanted the answers. Yes, he'd go to hell and back to find Jay. But the word seemed trapped in his mouth, and the harder he tried to say it, the more his thoughts turned to Julie, panicked at his sudden disappearance. By now, he knew she had called the police, his parents, everyone they knew. Since the night of the spilled beer, they'd scarcely been apart. As frightening as the Between had been for Paul, Julie had been someplace even darker and scarier.

His heart tore as he heard himself say, "I do *not* wish to have the answers." The words were like a knife in Jay's back, a repudiation of two decades of friendship.

"Then you may leave," the *gardistaro* said. She walked past him, never fully letting him leave her sight until she reached the door back to the sitting room. She shut the door and traced its outline with both hands, leaving a blurry trail around the door's perimeter. When she opened the door, the sitting room had been replaced by the flame-lit stone tunnel that led up to the false library.

"Thanks," he said.

For a brief moment, her robotic persona dropped, like an actor breaking character, and with a look and voice that chilled him to the bone, she said, "Get out, and never, ever, come back here."

He ran past her, past the brazier with the false flame, through the ascending passageway until the brazier's light faded to nothing. With one hand forward, and one brushing the low ceiling overhead, he kept pushing onward.

He found the small door Jay had described, leading to the library, or bomb shelter, or crypt, or whatever it was. Kicked aside books, felt the bookshelf where it had been moved toward the center of the room. Next to it was the ladder. He started to climb, but the weight of the revolver in its brown suede bag felt like an anchor pulling him down. He didn't want the gun coming back home with him, so he placed the bag on the ground next to the ladder.

At the top of the ladder, with the heavy door pushed open and the heat of the Texas night beckoning with the safety of home, he hesitated. Once he crossed the line, once he set foot in his backyard, in the real world, Jay was truly on his own. In all their years of friendship, how many times had they picked each other up after a nasty fall?

As he prepared himself to step up into the night and to leave Jay behind, he found himself staring at the neighbor's swingset just visible over the fence. The chains of the nearest swing shined in the moonlight. It was like the swingset had been put there, with the ground cut out and its legs set into concrete years ago, in waiting for this one moment tonight. To remind Paul.

It had all begun with the swings, after all, that day in second-grade recess.

CHAPTER 8
SWINGSET ICARUS

Second-grade Paul Prentice sprinted through the Cedar Creek Elementary School hallways, his Nike trainers screeching on the vinyl flooring. Normally running inside the school was a good way to get a lecture, or even worse a *white slip*, which was pretty much the worst thing that Paul's eight-year-old mind could imagine. But it was recess time, so the hallways were empty. The no-running rule probably still stood, but Paul was missing recess soccer, the highlight of his school day. So a little rule-breaking, given the context, was in order.

He knew he missed the team selection, and that stung a bit because last Friday he was chosen first—first!—and after scoring two goals, he knew he'd be picked first again. His mom signed him up to be room helper this week, which meant that instead of going out to recess, he had to stay in the classroom to help Ms. Ells do things like organize her bookshelf and move the chairs into a circle for reading time.

Ms. Ells had given him the list of chores. Thirty minutes worth, but he was done in five, jabbering the entire time about how he thought the ball curved a little on his second goal, and how that curve put the ball just past Nate Garner's fingertips, and how Nate was the best goalie in the school but maybe no goalie could stop a ball that's curving, right Ms. Ells?

Ms. Ells had told him he might catch the second half of the game if he hurried. She didn't exactly say run in the halls, but come on.

When Paul got to the field, it was empty. He thought for a moment with his heart pounding in his little chest that maybe he missed the bell and recess had already ended. But he heard the voices of children playing at recess-like volumes, so he followed their sound, past the empty field and down to the playscape in the trees.

Every second grader and even several of the third graders were gathered around the swings. He considered climbing on top of the monkey bars to see over the crowd of children, but seven or eight kids were already up there. Too tight quarters for Paul. He might fall off.

What could possibly cause all the kids—practically the whole world to his young mind—to gather around the swings, of all things?

"Why aren't we playing soccer?" he yelled up to Mikey Townsend, perched at the top of the monkey bars.

"Because Jay is flying!" Mikey yelled in return.

Jay? Paul didn't know any Jay, except the strange new kid in Ms. Vasquez's class who always wore the clothes that were two sizes too big and full of holes. The kid that talked nonstop and had, according to Stacey Klutz, gotten three *white slips* already this year.

Paul worked his way through the crowd until he reached a crepe myrtle tree that he could shimmy up to get a better view. What he saw filled him with what he later described as vicarious existential dread. The new kid, Jay, was indeed flying.

Now Paul had jumped out of the swings before. It was practically something you had to master before turning8. He knew well that prickly feeling that covered your skin when you let go and your stomach lifted up within you. The thud of both feet hitting the dirt simultaneously, the jolt that carried up all the way to your teeth.

What Jay was doing could hardly be considered the same thing. Jay was wearing a huge hooded sweatshirt with the front pocket half torn and dangling over jeans rolled up past his knees. The sweatshirt's hood and its loose black ties fluttered behind Jay as the swing rocketed down from its nearly parallel-to-the-ground backswing and arched upwards, like the swing intended to go all the way around. Before it reached its apex, Jay launched himself forward, pushing with both hands against the edges of the black rubber seat where it connected to the chains.

For a split second, Jay defied gravity. His sweatshirt billowed up, a mini parachute trying to arrest his fall, and his curly brown hair waved almost like he was underwater. His eyebrows curved to the top of his head as if even they were doing what they could to keep him there hanging above the ground.

And then he landed, arms out wide like a hawk's wings as it touched the ground. His look of intense concentration softened, and the corner of his mouth curved upward into the grin that Paul would get to know so well.

The children cheered and turned their heads looking for adults. Surely a teacher would run in any minute and put an end to Jay's flying. But no adults came running, and so, for now, Jay was the lord of the playground. Instead of basking in the adoration of his school-mates, Jay caught and steadied the swing, and said, "I think I can go higher."

The swing's chain squealed each time Jay threw his weight forward and then back, pumping with his legs and then snapping straight as a board to sail higher with every iteration. Paul felt a sudden pain in his hands and realized he was gripping a tree branch so tightly that his knuckles had turned white, as if it were his fingers wrapped around the cold chains of the swing. Each time Jay swung up, Paul expected him to jump, but Jay kept pushing higher and higher. He finally reached the point that all young playground pilots knew and feared: where the chain started to go slack and its rider began experiencing slivers of weightlessness.

Paul held on even tighter, and his own stomach tightened into a knot. Jay was going too high. Paul wanted to yell, took several deep breaths that should've turned into warnings, but before he made a sound two things happened at exactly the same time.

The red, bowl-shaped bell on the brick wall facing the playground rang in unison with its counterparts scattered around the exterior of the school, sending a wave of Pavlovian command through the children. At that very moment, Jay tried to push off from the swing, but it entered that window of weightlessness high above the ground, and rather than pushing himself up and out of the seat, Jay instead pushed his torso forward, out and past his legs.

Jay hit the dirt flat on his front, a perfectly executed belly flop from the high dive, only without the swimming pool there to catch him. The noise Jay made on impact sounded like an accordion being crushed, letting out a final, sharp cry.

Some of the kids hesitated for a second or two. But the bell had rung. The bell! You had to mind the bell! A girl in pigtails and a ketchup-splotched yellow dress even took a step toward Jay before running back toward the school. Mikey Townsend and the gang on the monkey bars all dropped down and ran without so much as a glance back over their shoulders.

They all ran back toward their classrooms, leaving Jay there on the ground, encircled by a settling halo of dirt. His body still, deathly still.

Paul wanted to run back to class also, and maybe he could've if he'd been among the first to run because others might've stayed. But there were no others, now. Only Paul.

Paul's feet touched the ground and a clock in his head ticked away the seconds remaining before the next ringing of the bell, the ringing that separated the on-time students from the tardy. A sweat broke out on his forehead.

"I'm going to get a teacher!" Paul yelled to Jay, trying not to look directly at him, in case Jay was dead. If he saw someone who was dead he'd never be able to sleep again. He would've run, then, if not for the sound, every second or so, the sound like a little hiss of air being let out of a tire, only softer, so soft Paul could barely hear it.

The clock in Paul's head ticked louder, but he walked instead toward Jay, still unmoving on the ground. The little hisses got louder the closer Paul came.

They were coming from Jay.

Paul bent down and brushed Jay's curly hair out of his face. Jay's eyes were wide in frozen panic like he'd been turned to stone. With each second, his body made the tiniest of quivers and he sucked in a little hiss of air. *Hiss. Hiss. Hiss.*

Before he knew what he was doing, Paul grabbed Jay's hand with his own, and with his free hand began to rub Jay's shoulder. "You got the wind knocked out of you, that's all," Paul said. "It happened to me last week when a soccer ball hit me in the stomach, and everyone circled around me, and I couldn't breathe and I couldn't stand up, and they just stood there and I thought I was dying while they just stood there." A tear began to roll down Paul's cheek. "But I wasn't dying. I had the wind knocked out of me. That's what happened to you, and you're scared because maybe it's never happened to you. And everybody left, or I mean, everyone didn't leave, because I'm still here." Over and over he rubbed Jay's shoulder.

Jay's wide eyes turned to meet Paul's, even though the rest of his body couldn't. And Jay's eyes, too, were filled with tears. The hisses became longer until they grew into the recognizable sounds of breaths.

After a couple minutes, Jay stood. Without a word, he began walking back toward the school, dirt covering the front of his jeans and sweatshirt. Dried blood on his left knee and crusting the corner of his mouth. He didn't say anything to Paul, but he kept Paul's hand in his until they reached the double doors leading into the empty hallway of the school.

Finally, Jay spoke. "Don't tell on me, okay? My dad said that if I get in trouble again..." He took a deep breath and shook his head. "Thank you for staying with me."

Before Paul could respond, Jay had let go of his hand and was walking back toward Ms. Vasquez's class. Paul waited until Jay turned the corner, out of sight, and then he, too, walked to his classroom.

When Ms. Ells asked why he was so late, Paul just shrugged. He never regretted, for a minute, getting that *white slip*, because every day at recess for the rest of the year Jay was there leaning on the soccer goal post waiting for him, crooked grin on his face.

CHAPTER 9
THE GRAVEYARD MANSION

Jay grabbed Supriya's hand and, without any regard for her prosthetic leg and her ability to keep up, yanked her to follow him toward the hatch in the center of the graveyard. She crashed into him from behind, before they had made it three steps, and they both fell sprawling into the dirt.

Before he even knew which way was up, she was back on her feet, brushing off the dirt. The glare in her eyes looked so ferocious that he found himself spitting out apologies and curses. But then she froze.

Jay turned and saw the shadows of more junk creatures rising from within the graveyard like the dead coming up from their graves. Some moved toward the hatch and created a wall of defenders, undulating with that strange false breathing, rising and falling metal ribs. Others walked toward them, spreading out their attack. They moved with a swaying, off-kilter gait as if their legs were uneven lengths. Each step came with a chalkboard-scraping whirr.

"Fucking junklings," Jay muttered under his breath, unsure where the name had come from. It fit, so he went with it. "Goddamn ugly junklings."

"What now, Jay?" Supriya asked.

"I can tell you what we aren't doing, and that's going to the hatch. Or staying here." Jay looked at the colonial mansion up the hill, glowing windows like eyes watching them. The house's age and style reminded him of the sitting room maze. He had a bad feeling about that house. The only other option was the path leading deeper into the dark of the cavern. Although more streetlamps followed that path, their light faded into darkness long before giving any hint of the path's destination.

"We gotta get to the house up there," he said. "Are you able to—"

Before he finished his question, Supriya took off toward the mansion, moving in uneven bursts, frequently hopping twice on her good right leg before her prosthetic left foot hit the ground. "Well, come on, then!" she yelled back over her shoulder.

Jay spent a half-second surprised at her speed but motion to his right brought him back to the situation at hand. The junklings had changed direction, too, moving to reach the mansion before them.

He sprinted, quickly catching up to Supriya on the grassy hill leading up to the mansion. Two of the junklings had also reached the hill, with another half dozen close behind.

"We're not going to make it!" Supriya said through gritted teeth as they reached the gate of the wrought-iron fence surrounding the house.

Jay struggled with the latch, losing valuable seconds, but then it was open and they headed down a hedge-flanked path leading to the mansion's front door. He could see in the pain on Supriya's face that she was pushing herself to move as fast as possible, but it wouldn't be fast enough. The junklings tumbled over the fence to their right, slowed only for a second or two before their pursuit continued.

About fifty yards remained to the door, but it might as well have been fifty thousand. Two junklings had broken away from the pack, their whirring gears shrieking like banshee cries.

"Get inside! I'll be right behind you!" He took out the knife, felt a wave of cold confidence flow through him, and then launched himself toward the loping metal creatures. The junklings tried to stop, clumsily reaching out as if the air could help slow them down. Jay ducked under the outreached arms of the lead junkling and stabbed up into its rusty ribcage. The blue blade found the serpentine belt, and the metal creature collapsed into a pile of automotive garbage.

Jay snickered and turned to face the second junkling right as an Alaska license plate caught him flush on the face. He spun from the backhand blow, crashing into the mansion's brick exterior. He pushed himself up, but a kick to the stomach sent him back down again. Behind his attacker, he could see more junklings climbing and falling over the fence. A hundred or more, like insects swarming toward them. Where the hell had they all come from?

Another kick, but this time Jay caught it inches from his face. He rolled under the creature and sliced at the piston that served as its calf. The knife cut through metal almost like cutting through the air. Another slice took out the junkling's other leg.

He jumped to his feet as the junkling collapsed and gave it a solid kick to the head.

"Ow! Fuck!" he yelled, hopping, holding his foot. The kick had done little to the metal creature, which was dragging itself toward Jay. And now Jay was angrier than ever. He wanted to cut out each of the junkling's gears and springs and pistons, leaving the serpentine belt intact until the very end.

A screaming Supriya and the roiling horde of junklings now halfway across the lawn convinced him otherwise.

"Get in here, Jay!"

He jumped through the opening into a room of dark mahogany and stained glass, illuminated by a chandelier of candles. She slammed the door and latched its four separate locks.

"How'd you get the door open?" he said.

"It was unlocked."

Jay took a deep breath and worked his jaw up and down, pain coursing up through his temple. Then he noticed the large glass windows flanking the door, windows that would offer no resistance whatsoever to the metal creatures intent on coming inside.

He looked at Supriya and her eyes told him she had made the same realization. The house offered little, if any, protection.

When the junklings arrived at the mansion, they only stared

through the window with their headlamp faces. Twitching nervously, jockeying for position nearest the window, they made no attempt to break through.

"Why aren't they coming after us?" Supriya said. She stood like a coiled spring next to him, arms out and ready, like a linebacker about to slam into an approaching running back. Her cheek twitched, maybe in pain, as she shifted her weight back and forth between her good leg and her prosthetic.

Jay stole a quick glance away from the junklings in the window and took in the entryway and the rooms beyond. Dark. Overly ornate. Too pristine. Inviting them deeper in. He didn't like it one fucking bit. "Maybe they're waiting out there, because something else, something worse, is waiting for us in here."

Jay tried not to stare as Supriya made adjustments to her prosthesis.

"My leg has a processor in it that adapts to what I'm doing," she said without looking up. "But unfortunately, I have it locked in the settings I use for powerlifting, so the run up the hill was ... not fun. I can adjust it with an app on my phone, but my phone is ... conveniently ... in my workout bag back in the elevator." A tear dropped off her cheek and onto the carbon fiber sleeve covering her upper thigh. She hurriedly brushed it off and wiped at her eye with her shoulder.

Jay turned away and acted like he hadn't seen the tear. "Powerlifting? So are you, uh, part of, what is it, the Special Olympics or something?" he asked, trying to take her mind off the recent dismemberment of her friend.

Supriya stood and put her fists on her hips. Her lat muscles flared out like wings. Her eyes glistened, eyes so brown Jay could barely tell where the pupils stopped and the irises started. "You're thinking of the PARA-lympics! Paralympics, you bozo!"

"Bozo?! Hey, keep your voice down!" Jay said, louder than he intended, louder than Supriya had been. "This *bozo* just fought off a bunch of damn junklings on your behalf!"

Supriya tugged the bottom of her singlet-shorts over the prosthesis sleeve. "Junkling? What the hell is a junkling?"

"That's the name I gave those robot bastards. Junklings. You gotta call 'em something. *Junk robots* doesn't quite fit. *Junk creatures*? That's too many syllables."

Her coiled spring seemed to relax a bit, and she might've given him the hint of a smile. Maybe. "You are a strange man, Jay. It seems we're stuck in this—whatever it is—together. I suggest we go deeper into the house before your junklings decide to break the window and come in after us."

Jay rubbed his jaw and nodded toward her prosthesis. "You okay?"

"No, Jay, I'm not okay," she said, and as Jay felt a heavy weight descend on him, she really did smile—a beautiful, the-world-can-go-fuck-itself smile—and added, "But if I have to tear a new leg off a junkling to keep going, that's what I'll do."

Jay gave her his signature grin. "I think we're gonna make a good team, Supriya. Let's go."

From the outside, atop the hill, the mansion looked massive. Two stories with a rooftop balcony, most of a football field wide. But inside, it felt cramped and small. A study connected to the entryway and led to another room beyond. With all of the junklings swaying in the study's window, Jay thought another way might be better. Three doors were ahead, thankfully none of them closed. He'd had enough mystery doors in the sitting room maze.

Through the doorway on the far wall, he saw shelves of books that reminded him of the blank books in the false library, the trap that led here—wherever *here* was. He wondered what kind of books they were. Old? New? Real? Full of blank pages?

"Let's go this way," he said, walking across a worn but expensive-looking rug, dragging his finger across the entry table. He looked at his finger. No dust. Not that he was expecting any.

Supriya followed behind, silent on the floor's series of interconnected rugs, despite her wedge-soled weightlifting shoes.

The room with the bookshelf was, as Jay suspected, a library, with more bookshelves lining two of the walls. A series of golden arches led up from the bookshelves and met in a point atop the room's vaulted ceiling. The spaces between the arches were alternatingly painted white and green. Jay thought it looked like the underside of a high-end circus tent.

Moonlight, impossible as it seemed, filtered through the arched window on the far wall, tinted red and blue from the stained glass. The only other light came from a silver candelabra atop a desk. On a hunch, Jay held his hand above one of the flames. Although the flame danced and flickered as a flame should, and although a thin black line of smoke lifted from its yellow tip, the flame produced no heat. Just like the brazier in the old stone hallway leading to the sitting room maze.

When Jay finally moved his hand and walked toward one of the bookshelves, Supriya tried it herself. When her hand didn't burn, she lowered it directly into the flame, and when it still didn't burn, she tried to blow the flame out. Nothing happened.

"What does this mean?" she said.

"I wish I knew," Jay said.

Jay pulled a book at random from the shelves and flipped through the pages. Blank. He didn't need to look at any more to know they'd all be this way. The books, the flames—what else about this place was a thin veneer over emptiness? He rubbed his jaw again. Certainly some things—like the license plate that smacked him in the face— were real enough to hurt.

He pulled open a drawer in the desk. Inside were pens, paper, and a crystal decanter of a brownish liquid. He took out the decanter and removed the stopper. The liquid inside smelled spicy, with the sinus-burning heat of a strong whiskey or brandy. Supriya gave him a disappointed frown as he tilted the decanter back and took a big swig.

"That's the real deal, honey. We're taking this with us."

"I don't think getting drunk is high on our priority list."

"Alcohol is the Swiss Army Knife of fluids. It'll clean shit, disinfect shit, and if worse comes to worst, light it on fire and burn shit, Molotov Cocktail style." Jay put the stopper back in the bottle and looked around for a satchel, bag, or anything to carry around the various treasures, like this bottle of fine whatever-it-was, but of course, unlike your typical department store, bags weren't conveniently located to help uninvited guests loot the place. "Nothing else to see here. Let's keep moving."

He started walking toward a door to their right, but Supriya held out her hand and physically stopped him by pushing on his chest.

"We should be quieter," she whispered.

Jay censored the various responses that sprang to mind ("But I like my women loud") and nodded. Supriya had a point. Suddenly he felt reckless carrying the decanter and placed it on the desk.

"We'll come back for it when the coast is clear," he whispered in return. He drew his knife and motioned for her to get behind him. He leaned into the next room, a dining room with a long table set for twelve. Bone china, crystal, silver. The whole shebang. Three candelabra, all lit with their false flames. Through the wall of windows, he could see a moonlit lawn leading to a forest, with no sign of the cavern.

He signaled for Supriya to wait while he checked the shadowed area next to the china cabinet—for what, he wasn't sure. Finding the room vacant, he nodded for her to enter and then pointed to the moon visible through the windows.

"Is that outside?" she whispered.

Jay shrugged. He grabbed a cloth napkin from the table, unfolded it, and pressed it to one of the small, six-by-six panes of glass. With a tap of the tip of his knife, the pane shattered, making twice as much noise as he had hoped for. He looked at Supriya expecting to be scolded or at least frowned at, but the now missing window pane had her eyes wide with attention.

Where there had been the dim light of the moon, now was darkness. A square of near pitch black, surrounded by panes that still maintained their outdoor night image. Jay squatted down and looked through the empty square. A few inches out was the smooth cavern wall.

Supriya closed her eyes and bit her lip so hard that a tear rolled down her cheek and dropped onto the rug below.

Jay tried to think of something to say to console her, to console them both, really, but nothing came to mind. He instead placed his hand on her shoulder, too unsure of himself to be firm, to be comforting, and so it felt awkward.

Supriya didn't flinch away, as he expected, and took a deep breath and opened her eyes. She started to say something, hesitating once and then twice, another tear rolling down her cheek.

Heavy footsteps came from above. Someone, or something, had walked from one side of a room to another.

Jay's hand tightened around the knife, and he felt a warm energy flow up his arm and through the rest of his body. He moved quickly, and she followed, going through the door ahead and into a breakfast area attached to a kitchen and other rooms beyond. A wooden block of knives sat atop the counter near a series of white ceramic jars. He pointed, and Supriya grabbed a long-bladed silver carving knife. And then they were moving again.

A long hallway full of portraits led to a set of stairs that doubled back above them.

Supriya gave Jay a look that seemed to ask if this was such a good idea. He nodded coldly. The knife pulled him toward the stairs, onward for the hunt. A single wall sconce gave its faint illumination to the stairs' landing one flight up, but other than that, they were surrounded by darkness. Once they reached the landing, they could see nothing of the second floor, whether the stairs led to another hallway or a great room covering the entire floor.

Jay lifted the glass cover from the sconce and set it on the wood landing, making the slightest of noises but one that nevertheless echoed through the otherwise silent space. He muttered, "Shit," without meaning to, and Supriya backhanded him in the ribs, almost making him call out *shit* that much louder. Instead, he gave her an angry look that paled in comparison to the one she was giving him.

He grabbed the candle from the sconce and began taking the remaining stairs, one every several seconds until he could see into the floor above. It was indeed another hallway, with a dim light coming from a cracked door at its end. That room would roughly line up above the dining room, where they had heard the footsteps. Or thereabouts. Hopefully.

Behind him, Supriya was still making her way up the stairs, strong muscles in her arm flexing as she pulled against the banister, lifting her prosthesis up stair after stair. Not for the first time, Jay felt a flash of intimidation. Intimidation with a tinge of lust.

As they crept down the second-floor hall, Jay tried to ignore the fact that the darkness obscured everything to their sides. The candle did almost nothing but illuminate his left arm reached out in front of him. Doors could be open next to them with towering creatures waiting for them to pass by, and they'd never know until the claws sank into their flesh. Jay couldn't even tell if Supriya was still behind him.

Noises came from the lit room ahead. Little clinks and clanks, metal on metal, followed by footsteps. Jay wondered if the sounds belonged to a junkling, but the footsteps had been too regular, too human-like. He stopped and then reached back to keep Supriya from running into him, and put his palm flat into the sponginess that was one of her lycra-compressed breasts. A quick slap stung his forearm, and the sounds ahead became silent.

He cursed in his head, thinking that maybe now he should sprint wildly through the door, preserving whatever element of surprise might still be left, but before he could do anything so rash, the noises started up again. Tinkering noises, like someone using tools.

Three more steps and he reached the doorway. He tried to blow out the candle, worried that its flicker might call attention to the otherwise dark hallway, but of course, the false flame remained lit no matter what he did. He didn't want to set it on the ground, false flame or not, because the whole damn house looked like an inferno-in-waiting. Holding the candle far away from the cracked-open doorway, he peered in.

A man sat hunched over a desk with a series of leafed monocles over his eyes, a soldering iron trailing smoke in his right hand. The source of his attention was a brass forearm and hand, with a panel open exposing its mechanical viscera. In addition to the strange set of monocles, the man wore on his head what looked like a cross between a king's crown and a device for electrostimulation of the brain. He had wavy black hair with shocks of gray and a similarly gray Van Dyke beard. His clothes had the same ornate, Victorian look of the mansion.

Jay pulled back and let Supriya look, and then they exchanged blank expressions in the candle's glow. Now what? If the man were piecing together a mechanical creature of some kind, it was conceivable, and perhaps likely, that he had made the junklings. And since the junklings had attacked Jay and killed Supriya's buddy—Frankie or whatever the hell the little woman's name was—wasn't that reason enough to suspect this guy was also bad news? Reason enough to run in, stab first, and ask questions later?

Even with the pull of the blue knife in his right hand, it was one thing to kill one of those goddamn ash dogs or a junkling when it was attacking. It was something else entirely to murder a man working at his desk, especially before knowing if the man really was an evil, death-bot-building scientist. Besides, maybe the man knew how to get back home. A lot of good it would do them to kill him and still be surrounded by a horde of junklings with no idea what to do next.

That settled it.

Jay opened the door and ran at the man, planning to knock him down and scare him into giving answers, or something to that effect. But from the moment he swung the door open wide, everything went wrong. The man looked up from his work, startled eyes magnified across the dozens of circular lenses like the many eyes of a spider. The door ricocheted off the wall and hit Jay just as he had taken his first running step into the room, and now he was off balance crashing atop the desk to the man's right instead of diving across it directly into him.

The man jumped back from the desk and threw the monocles off, cursing in an unfamiliar language, as Jay slid from one side of the desk to the other, carrying gears and gadgets, including a painfully hot soldering iron, with him in a crash on the ground.

The man grabbed a little bronze orb off a nearby shelf and pointed it at Jay, who was getting to his feet. A blinding flash exploded out from the orb, and to Jay, the world vanished.

CHAPTER 10
LORD OF THE GRAVEYARD MANSION

Supriya threw the knife a half-second too late, but it found its mark. The man screamed in agony as the knife embedded itself in his shoulder. The orb fell from his hand and landed with a hard bounce on the wooden floor. The man fell backward, the wall's bookshelf keeping him on his feet. With a series of yells, he pulled the knife out.

Jay, meanwhile, was staggering, almost falling as he kept stepping on the various mechanical parts on the floor, shouting, "I can't see anything! I can't see anything!"

Supriya grabbed him and pulled him back toward the door as the man regained his composure and grabbed another device from the bookshelf.

"Run you idiot!" Supriya screamed, yanking Jay behind her. The man held what looked like a thick tablet covered in knobs and dials with long bunny-ear-style antennas. Through the man's pain-wracked face she could see an angry determination. He punched at buttons and adjusted knobs on the tablet and then glared at them.

"<other language cursing>!"

Supriya pulled Jay hard enough that he almost knocked her down. "Keep moving!" she screamed.

The two of them burst into the hallway. Jay crashed into the wall next to them, and Supriya's prosthetic foot caught on the rug, sending her headlong into Jay's stomach. She pushed him forward and tried to follow behind, but something was off with the rebound-swing of her prosthesis—it was snapping forward too slowly, and the sleeve binding was biting into the stump of her left leg with every stiff-legged step.

They had made it halfway toward the stairs when she felt the floor shudder.

"What the hell is going on?! I can't see shit!" Jay yelled.

"Just keep going!" she said.

The shudder turned into a rocking wave. It was like they were on the surface of the ocean, wood planks rolling underneath them. Supriya tried to keep her balance and might have done so if Jay's foot hadn't caught on the rippling current of wood. He tumbled sideways, clipping her good leg and sending her down with him.

The floor seemed to punch up at them through the rug. She tried to regain her balance and stand, but wherever she put her weight, the floor shifted and sent her crashing this way and that.

The man now stood in the doorway to his workroom, its light haloed around him. In his injured left arm, he cradled the control tablet. In his right, he held a tube, which he pointed directly at them.

Supriya turned to Jay and saw him get to his knees only to be thrown forward onto his side. All she could think to do was to grab the nearby edge of the rug and roll backward, holding it as a makeshift shield between the two of them and the man.

Dozens of needle-sharp darts thumped into the rug, catching and stopping inches from Supriya's face like the nails of an iron maiden. She threw the rug down and with her left hand grabbed a nearby doorknob and pulled herself back onto her feet. She reached for Jay, but one of the hallway doors swung open and caught him in the face, knocking him back to the floor.

The hallway's other doors were now swinging open and shut as well. Supriya dragged Jay toward the stairs and looked back at their pursuer. The man had thrown the tube on the ground, where it bounced and rolled with the shifting floor. He twisted a knob back and forth, and the hallway responded in synchronized waves.

Jay managed to get to his feet, but instead of heading for the stairs, he stumbled toward the man, knife in hand.

"You're blurry, but I can see you, motherfucker," he said.

The man kept looking at his control panel and then back at Jay. When it was clear that the rippling floor and opening and shutting doors weren't going to stop Jay, the man calmly set down the control panel and pulled the sleeve back on his right arm. A bronze bracer covered his forearm. With the press of a button, part of the bracer unfolded and curled over the man's hand, forming a metal fist.

"Look out, Jay!" Supriya yelled.

The man waited until Jay reached his end of the hallway and watched without movement as Jay slashed the air harmlessly a few feet in front of him.

Then he snarled something in his bizarre language, ducked down, and punched Jay in the chest. Upon impact, the bronze fist boomed, and Jay went flying backward like he'd been shot out of a cannon.

The floor stopped its crazed movement. Supriya hobbled to Jay who was now lying on his back near the top of the steps. The man had picked his control panel up and was walking toward them.

"I can't breathe," Jay whispered through staccato coughs.

Supriya didn't know what else to do, so she started pulling him down the steps, one hand gripping into the meat of Jay's left arm, the other tight on the banister. Every part of her body screamed in exhaustion, and no matter how hard she tried, she couldn't move fast enough to get away.

The man stopped at the top of the stairs, only feet above them, and flipped a series of switches on the control panel. The wall of the stairs' landing beneath them shook and then a set of long, black spikes extended out of its lower portion. The stairs underneath them rotated with a snap and became a slick ramp, sending them tumbling toward the spikes.

There was no way to control the fall. Jay had slipped from her grasp and hit the wall first, somehow missing the spikes through dumb luck. Supriya almost slid directly into a spike, but a last-second twist kept it from impaling her chest, and she skidded along its length into the wall behind it. She felt an abrupt jolt of metal hitting metal. A spike had broken through the false calf of her prosthesis and stabbed into its microprocessor controller. With a sizzle and a puff of smoke, the prosthetic knee went completely limp.

The ramp clicked back into stairs, and the man descended toward them.

Through the tears in her eyes, she made eye contact with him. He spat a litany of what could've been curses or insults or just about anything else, holding his bronze fist in the air. The fist made a low-pitched hum that grew louder and higher pitched until the walls vibrated with its buzz.

"Go," Jay said, pushing her toward the lower set of stairs. Jay had gotten to his knees. His face was pale and his eyes looked glassy. He still somehow had the blue-bladed knife in his hand.

Halfway down the first set of stairs, the man stopped and touched the crown on his head with a finger from his left hand. He spoke in his unfamiliar language, but after a second's delay, a metallic voice said in English, "Stay still and I will kill you quickly."

Supriya's blood went cold. She limped to the lower stairs and started down, having to hop from stair to stair on her right leg.

"Come on, Jay," she said, but Jay hadn't turned his attention from the approaching man.

"Go, Supriya. Go and hide. I'll be fine."

With every step down she hated herself more and more for leaving Jay behind.

Each breath was a chore, taking more effort than Jay had to give. His head still rang like a bell from its collision with the wall, and the license plate before that. His chest felt like an elephant was sitting on it. But he stood tall and tried to look as calm as possible. The knife in his hand sent waves of warmth through his arm, almost, but not quite, making up for his exhaustion and pain. At least his vision had more or less returned.

"You're not getting through me, Inspector Gadget," he said.

The man stopped a few steps above him and gave a silent laugh at the blade in Jay's hand. Again his voice came in its foreign tongue, overlaid by the mechanical translation.

"Where is your black costume, *stelisto*? You don't even know what you are. Or how to use the Knife of Undoing. The *stelistos* always die early. I've killed four, myself. About to be five."

The words, the names—his name, *stelisto*—all felt so familiar and foreign at the same time. It was like Jay was playing a game but didn't know the rules, the tricks, the tactics. Inspector Gadget, here, clearly did. If there was one thing Jay did know it was never to play a game where your opponent knows how to win and you don't. He had no intention of making a stand here. He just needed to give Supriya a few extra seconds to get away.

"I know more than you think," Jay bluffed.

The bronze fist unfolded back onto the bracer on the man's forearm and a two-foot blade snapped together in its place.

"Do you, now?" he said through the mechanized voice.

Jay slashed out at the man's feet, causing him to jump back a step.

"You know what they say about knife fights," Jay said. "The loser dies on the street. The winner dies in the hospital."

The man glared and made two cautious slashes as he stepped down toward Jay.

Jay could almost feel the wall's spikes pressing into his legs behind him, so he feinted left and then shuffled to the open area of the landing above the steps leading down. His breathing was coming easier now, and his headache was only a mild jackhammering.

The man glanced down at the control panel in his left hand, and with the touch of his thumb, the lower set of stairs retracted into a ramp, and the floor at the bottom dropped away, revealing a pit of darkness.

Maybe the man hoped to force Jay to stay and fight, but Jay did the opposite, sliding legs-first down toward the pit and at the last instant catching the heels of his Redwings and catapulting himself forward. In the air, Jay recognized two things: 1) if there was such a thing as a bottomless pit, he had found it, and 2) his downward momentum had utterly ruined any hopes of making it all the way to the other side.

He slammed into the edge of the pit with his waist, knocking the wind out of him once again. If the knife hadn't jabbed through the rug and wooden floor beyond the pit, he'd be falling into darkness. As it was, he had both hands clutching the knife's increasingly slick, jeweled grip. He lacked the breath and energy to pull himself up, and the barest effort threatened to loosen the knife and send him plummeting.

Behind him, the ramp clicked back into stairs, and the man descended. He set the control panel down, and with his left hand grabbed under the blade connected to his right arm. The blade snapped off, and what looked like a long, snaking metal hose came with it, emerging from the man's sleeve. He held the blade in front of him, and the bronze hose stiffened into a six-foot handle for the blade.

You've got to be fucking kidding me, Jay thought. He would've said it out loud, but it was all he could do to keep breathing. Inspector Gadget had a spear up his sleeve.

Before the man could use the spear, Supriya limped around the corner from the kitchen. Cradled under her arm she had the wooden block full of knives. One after another she let them fly.

None came within five feet of the man, but it was enough of a distraction to give Jay the chance to put all of his remaining energy to pull himself up and out of the pit. Before the man could retrieve the control panel and restore the floor below, Jay and Supriya had vanished back into the kitchen.

As soon as they entered the kitchen, Jay grabbed Supriya and pulled her to a stop.

"Go back to the library, and make a lot of noise on the way there," he said.

Her eyes widened as she realized Jay planned to wait and fight. Again. "But—," she started.

"But nothing," he said. "We'll never escape from him in his own house with all his tricks and traps. We need a trap of our own! It's our only chance, Supes."

A booming echo came from the hall—the floor snapping back into place, covering the pit.

"Now go!"

Supriya gave him one last look, a look that communicated more than every word they'd spoken to each other so far, and then she hopped and limped into the dining room, using every piece of furniture for support along the way. Jay recognized the sound of chairs falling over and plateware knocked to the floor. Well done, Supes.

Supes? Where did that nickname come from? He felt a sudden weight settle onto his shoulders. Any other man or woman would've recognized the weight of responsibility, but Jay had thus far orchestrated his life to avoid responsibility of any kind. And so he mistook the feeling for another, equally unfamiliar. Love.

He pressed his back against the wall next to the door and rolled the knife in his right hand. His mind raced through countless permutations of the next several seconds. What if he failed? Supriya would be alone. At least Jay had a weapon. She had nothing, and it looked like that mechanical leg of hers wasn't working at all. What if the man knew Jay was waiting? What if he came through the door across the kitchen instead?

And then an even scarier thought. What if the man cut through the house another way, to get ahead of them? He'd find Supriya, alone, while Jay waited here. For nothing.

Was that a footstep?

The harder Jay strained to hear, the louder the ringing in his ears became. All those years of blaring AC/DC in his pickup truck. If it *had* been a footstep, that could mean one of two things: either the man suspected Jay might be waiting for him, or the man had, indeed, chosen not to follow them directly. The life drained out of Jay in a single, pathetic breath. Every second that passed left Jay feeling like he was falling deeper into the man's trap and that he was failing Supriya. He looked at the three doors leading out from the kitchen, wondering which way he should go, becoming increasingly sure that he was wasting time hiding next to the hallway door.

He was so lost in indecision that he didn't realize the man had walked through the door next to him and toward the dining room. The man himself was so focused on the control panel in his hand that he also hadn't realized the room had another occupant.

Jay lunged forward, almost pulled by the knife. The blade hit true, square in the man's back.

The man tried to spin around, losing his balance in the process. The control panel fell to the ground with a loud crack, knobs and gears spilling out of it like the guts of a smashed insect. The man stumbled to the counter and looked at Jay, not with eyes of anger or hatred, but with fear and confusion. Like Jay had done the unthinkable.

For a second Jay thought that maybe he had done something wrong. But the man did say he was going to kill Jay, right? And what about the spikes and the bottomless pit!? It's okay to stab someone trying to kill you and the woman you've known for all of thirty minutes and may be in love with, isn't it?

After that second, the remorse was replaced by a bloodlust that cascaded from the knife, up through Jay's arm, through his heart and into his mind.

"I don't have to kill you," Jay said, although now he wanted to so much that he didn't know if he could stop himself. "We came in here to escape."

"You don't know anything," came the mechanized translation over the man's voice. "If I let you live, you'll still try to kill me, like you'll eventually kill the woman."

Kill the woman? Why would he kill Supriya?

The man's eyes narrowed. "But I won't let you." He touched the crown on his head with two fingers and began to blink rapidly.

"What the hell are you doing? Stop that!"

The man stopped and smiled. "You won't get out of here alive."

Jay took a step toward him and said, "We'll see about that."

Then the windows in the dining room and in the nearby break-fast room exploded, and junklings started climbing in.

CHAPTER 11
THE MASINISTO

Supriya moved as fast as she could through the dining room and hallway. As fast as she could, unfortunately, meant barely faster than her old, two-able-legged walking pace. The hydraulic unit in her prosthetic was completely shot, and the knee joint swung freely. If she put her weight on it before it hit full extension, it would collapse. Her right leg burned with lactic acid, the muscles built strong for bursts of power, not playing double-duty while being chased by killer junk-robots and a mad scientist.

The images of Frankie's death kept flashing into her mind. The license plate crashing down like a cleaver... The way Frankie's head opened up like it had a second mouth under her ear... A second mouth that vomited blood...

Supriya stumbled as a part of her mind wanted to succumb to the pain, the exhaustion, the terror, but another part of her mind, reflexively, countered:

...the heart to conquer...
...the heart to conquer...
...the heart to conquer...

The phrase came from a litany that Nani, her grandmother, recited over and over while bedridden, bone cancer spreading throughout her body. *Let me not beg for the stilling of my pain but for the heart to conquer it.*

It was a line from a Rabindranath Tagore prayer. Supriya had forgotten the line, or maybe her mind had locked away the entire memory, until it flooded back years later, in the same hospital, perhaps even the same room. The same cancer. *Osteogenic sarcoma.* Only this time, Supriya lay in the bed, left leg freshly amputated. As the anesthesia wore off and the room and her parents beside her bed came into focus, she began to hear Nani's voice, speaking the words from beyond the grave. *Let me not beg for the stilling of my pain but for the heart to conquer it.* Louder, each time Nani's voice repeated it. Louder, until Supriya's parents grimaced and tried to calm her, calling for the doctor, for the nurses, for anyone to help. Nani's voice caught, then, like a record skipping and replaying the same few seconds...

...the heart to conquer...

...the heart to conquer...

...THE HEART TO CONQUER...

...until Supriya coughed and gagged for air and realized she had been hearing her own voice.

Since then, the phrase had acted as an involuntary response, transmuting her pain into energy. She had gotten into powerlifting to channel that energy, using it to do things with her body that her pre-cancer, secondary-school self never would've imagined possible.

And so, staggering through the mansion, broken prosthetic threatening to sheer apart at any moment, the words filled her mind —*THE HEART TO CONQUER!*—and no amount of pain or exhaustion could have slowed her down. Jay told her to make noise, so she channeled her pain into furniture-smashing energy, knocking everything within reach to the floor.

She smashed her way through the mansion until she found herself back in the entry hall where they had started. She considered hiding in the adjacent study behind a large chair in the corner, but the junklings staring in through the windows with their headlamp eyes looked too much like an audience gathered to watch her die.

The nearby small washroom was a dead end, and with its floral wallpaper above wainscot, it looked like a burial plot in a garden. The only other door led back to the stairway. Fortunately, the man with the strange crown had left. Had he gone back up the stairs, followed them into the kitchen, or sneaked off somewhere else to hide?

Jay wanted her to hide, but even one-legged, she couldn't leave him to fight the man alone. If she hadn't doubled back once already, the man would've surely stabbed Jay with the bronze spear-thing and sent Jay down into that pit. The kitchen knives she had thrown were still littered near the stairs.

She hobbled to the knives and picked up the longest one. It was just a plain kitchen knife with a wooden handle and a heavy, curved blade---an altogether different species than Jay's menacing weapon, but a weapon nonetheless. The litany repeating in her mind increased in volume and speed.

the-heart-to-conquer-the-heart-to-conquer-the-heart-to-conquer

She started for the kitchen, hoping she wasn't too late, but before taking her third step, the kitchen door swung open and the man stumbled through, his side covered in blood. He had the bronze spear but used it to aid his lopsided run. Supriya held the knife toward him, her body tense and ready for the fight, but he didn't even look at her when he passed by. The man was halfway up the stairs before Supriya noticed the crashing sounds coming from the kitchen.

The kitchen door swung open again, and this time Jay emerged, eyes wide in terror. He slammed the door shut and pushed his weight against it.

"Slide that table over here!" he yelled. "We need something to brace this door shut!"

"Shut against what?"

The door shook as something struck it from the other side.

"The damn junklings! They came through the window!"

Supriya grabbed the nearby table and tried to pull it toward Jay without falling over in the process. "What about that door?!" she yelled, pointing at the door leading to the dining room.

The wood next to Jay's head splintered and split, the corner of a rusted yellow license plate disappeared only to break through another spot even closer to Jay.

"Shit! You're right."

She heard more glass shattering. The study next to the entry hall. They were coming from every direction. "We have to go up the stairs!"

No sooner had she said the words then the door to the entryway crashed off its hinges. Several junklings tried to go through the doorway at once and got jammed, giving Jay and Supriya a few precious seconds to make it to the stairway. They lost those seconds when Jay manhandled her and tried to drag her up the stairs. She had to slap his hand away twice before he let go.

The kitchen door tore open next, right as Supriya and Jay turned to take the second flight of steps. Junklings filled the room below, the closest now on the lower steps. Supriya expected the man with the crown to be waiting at the stairway's top with his spear, but all that was ahead of them when they reached the top was the dark hallway. The man's door at the end was shut. He had retreated to his work-room safe haven to let the junklings finish the house's invaders.

The lead junkling had taken the stairs two at a time and reached the top right behind them. Jay slashed at it with his knife. The junkling raised its license-plate-clad forearm to block the blade, but Jay's knife cut through the metal like it was paper, and half of the machine's arm fell to the floor. A second slash shattered the thing's curved glass face, and it reacted like it had been blinded, flailing wildly until it fell backward down the steps, taking two other junklings down with it.

In a second, the downed junklings were on their feet again and climbing, with more right behind them. Supriya backed away down the hallway, watching as Jay somehow seemed to find their every weakness with that knife of his. Where had he learned to fight that way? Or did it have more to do with the strange blue knife itself?

Whatever Jay's advantage, it wasn't enough to hold them off for long. Supriya pulled open a door next to her, looking for anything that would buy them a few more seconds. The door led to a bedroom.

A dead end. Worse than that, a junkling had climbed halfway through the window. Despite its faceless gaze, she could feel it staring right through her.

―――――――――

There's music in killing, Jay thought to himself. A strange thought to be had while fighting for one's life, but as he somehow kept four—and now five—of the mechanical creatures at bay, it fit. If the blue knife had been a musical instrument, it would've been a player piano, rising and falling in its own melody. It cut through metal, plastic, and rubber like they were little more than air. One strike barely complete before it yanked Jay's arm toward its next target.

Unlike someone sitting, uselessly, in front of a player piano, Jay in some way conducted the music, if not the melody itself. As he looked from one target to the next, the knife translated. It understood. Threats that needed to be extinguished. He felt like the actions, the decisions, were his, but he'd never learned to fight like this. However it worked, the knife made it possible.

Junklings whirred and died, and still more came, climbing over their fallen brethren. The knife struck true into the neck-space of the nearest junkling, severing its serpentine belt, and then another strike, this time to deflect a license-plate-clad arm swung like a headsman's axe toward Jay's own neck. The blade hit its mark, but his margin of victory was growing smaller and smaller every second. Pushed back into the hallway, he had little room to move. It didn't matter how accurate he was. The junklings could keep pressing forward; it was like trying to fight against a bulldozer.

"I can't hold them much longer," he screamed back to Supriya. He glanced her direction and saw her hopping backward from an open door before a junkling's foot caught him in the stomach. He fell, but Supriya, balanced on her one leg, caught him and shoved him back upright with astonishing strength.

"More coming through the windows!" she yelled.

The fucking windows? They were about to be surrounded. A

license plate whistled through the air inches from Jay's nose and embedded itself in the hallway's wall. He thrust the knife at the approaching mass of metal, and in the split second the mass recoiled, he turned and ran toward the door at the end of the hallway.

He rammed the door at full speed and simultaneously slammed the knife into the door's lock, the tip of the blade catching the bolt dead-center. The door burst open, but the momentum carried Jay into and over Inspector Gadget's desk once again.

By pushing off the hallway wall with her left hand every time her prosthetic foot hit the floor, Supriya managed to limp-run fast enough to stay ahead of the junklings. When Jay hit the door, she already had her kitchen knife raised, and the second she entered the room, she let it fly with every bit of anger and strength she had. The man with the mechanical crown stood hunched over, shirt covered in blood, near his bookshelf. He had another device, a silvery rod of some kind, pointed in their direction, but before he could make use of it, Supriya's knife hit him square in the forehead.

Unfortunately, it was the knife's wooden handle that struck the man and not the blade. But it was enough. He dropped the rod and staggered backward, the strange, geared crown falling off his head and onto the floor.

She sprang toward him, a one-legged jump that took her the entire distance. With the litany roaring in her head, she brought her fist down into his nose. She had never in her life punched anything or anyone, never channeled all of her energy, her anger, her fear, into another human being. The moment her fist struck, as the bridge of his nose exploded, so too, did something break within her, and her body flooded with hate.

The man's head snapped sideways so violently that his body twisted after it, like an air-twirling ice skater who missed the landing and pirouetted hard into the ground. She would've jumped on top of him, then, and kept smashing her fists down until she did to him what the junklings had done to Freddie, or her fist would disintegrate in the trying, but a junkling grabbed her by the neck and another by her right arm.

Jay's knife severed both junkling arms in a single blow, and she fell backward into the room's corner. She tried to stand but her hands and the floor were slick with blood, and she fell back down.

The wall of junklings pressed tighter in, stepping over their bloody and broken leader, who was trying to crawl back to the hallway. Jay fought off a junkling that tried to climb over the desk, but his slashes had slowed, and his shoulders drooped in exhaustion.

They were cornered. The man had escaped, and the junklings were inching unstoppably closer. Jay's blue knife wasn't enough. The litany in her head had gone silent. It all was coming to an end.

She looked to the floor for her own knife, an act of instinctual, doomed last hope, and found the knife under the man's crown. Something in the crown pulled at her, like it had latched on to the hate and anger within her, forcing her hand to reach out and grab it instead of the knife. With the crown in hand, she stood straight up, as if the floor and her shoes weren't slick with blood, as if her right leg weren't numb with fatigue. As she moved to place the crown on her own head, she saw, in silent slow-motion, a junkling backhand Jay, and more, like metal spiders, crawl over the desk, climbing atop him, arms raised like guillotine blades.

All feeling left her body, even the hate and the pain, and the crown, raised over her head, slipped from her fingers so that it fell, fell, fell, and...

...*The world was replaced by a million dreams, a million flashes of another life, where her own hands built machines of metal and glass, where she focused giant lenses that made worlds overlap, where she created the Patchwork World connecting the outworlds and the Between, the entry point for those she lured inside ... filling the machine with fresh blood, fresh souls... She dreamed of a word, a name—masinisto--that tied together all the dreams...*

...and a lifetime and a split second later, the junklings were frozen, killing blows cocked but not released. Then their bodies slacked, and they turned away, their attention back in the hallway, where the man had crawled. They had turned against him. She felt it through the crown. They wanted to kill him, now. Now that he didn't wear the crown. And she could feel their questioning come to her.

Do we kill him, masinisto? *Is it your wish?*

With a thought, she answered.

A scream, and then silence.

CHAPTER 12
THE LITTLE YELLOW STAIN ON SUPRIYA'S SOUL

From atop the rooftop terrace, Supriya stared down at the two freshly dug graves at the edge of the cemetery. At the last minute, she had changed her mind, and now, following her thoughts, several junklings were refilling the holes. Even in death, Frankie shouldn't be trapped here.

Frankie. She had described her to Jay as her business partner, as if they happened to work together. As if her entire life hadn't changed that day when Frankie told that anesthesiologist to go to hell.

Supriya had been pre-med, then, and volunteering at the children's hospital. She'd never thought of any career outside of medicine. At the time, her oldest sister was a third-year general surgery resident, and her middle sister had just gotten accepted to Tennessee Health Science Center's program in pediatrics. When Supriya imagined herself wearing the physician's white coat, it was at a hospital bedside, and she was talking to patients about pain, and about how she'd help them overcome their pain.

She imagined herself in anesthesiology, helping others of course, but implicit in the daydream was the eradication of her own pain. The phantom pain that came from a limb that had been removed years before.

Until that day in the hospital when she met Frankie, she had never spoken to an actual anesthesiologist, and she didn't know that anesthesiology wasn't even the right specialty if she wanted to help others (and herself) deal with long-term, chronic pain. Over the year or so that she'd volunteered at the children's hospital, she'd memorized almost everyone's names by stealing glances at their identity badges.

Kara Edmondson, RN, PICU.

Rishi Ramanathan, MD, Orthopaedics.

Lauren Sylvestre, CA.

Robert Sandoval, MD, Anesthesiology.

She'd passed Dr. Sandoval dozens of times in the halls, each time tensing up in anticipation of his Caribbean-blue eyes focused on her. He always seemed to be in mid-conversation with another physician, or flipping through pages in a chart, or talking (presumably to a patient in need) on his cell phone, or... Or he was alone and she let him walk right by.

When those eyes finally turned to her, it wasn't with the recognition she'd imagined ("Oh, of course! I recognized your familiar face! We're always passing each other in the halls, aren't we?") but with confusion, and a touch of disdain. *Why are you occupying my time?* those eyes said. *And who are you again?*

She hadn't gotten more than a sentence or two out, when he said, "You do a lot of standing up in anesthesia, kid." He pointed to her prosthetic leg. "You might want to look into psychiatry, or, hell, computer programming."

His words had taken her completely off guard, and as she stared at those blue eyes, those piercing, scornful blue eyes, she moved her mouth, and sounds came out, but nothing that resembled words.

"Don't listen to him. If your dream is to be an anesthesiologist, don't let that leg stop you."

Supriya turned and saw an unfamiliar woman with short-cropped hair and bone-white skin. The woman was 30 or so, and almost a foot shorter than Supriya but with a presence that made the hallway feel smaller somehow. The woman wore tan chinos and a polo shirt that strained more from the wide muscles of her back than from her small breasts. She had a hospital badge on a lanyard around her neck, but the badge's surface was turned away, so Supriya couldn't catch the woman's name or position.

Dr. Sandoval scoffed. "Are you a physician? You know what it's like to work hundred-hour weeks during residency? No? Then why don't you stick to what you know, kid."

The woman flashed Supriya a smile and then pulled up the left leg of her pants. The fluorescent hallway light gleamed off the metal rod where her ankle should be. "Stick to what I know? You're in my lane now, shitbag, so I have a better idea. You can go to hell, and my new friend and I are gonna talk about all the ass she's gonna kick, doing whatever she wants to do. Mmkay?"

Dr. Sandoval turned and stormed away, almost knocking down a nurse who was sliding her badge through a timekeeping kiosk attached to the wall. Supriya could barely believe what she'd seen. "Aren't you worried about getting fired, talking to him like that?" she asked.

Frankie waved her fear away like it was a gnat and nothing more. "This"—she tapped the hard plastic sleeve of her prosthesis through her pants—"puts me in a protected class of employee. It's Federal law. He's not gonna complain to anyone, and if he does, Human Resources will send him to sensitivity training."

Supriya's life, at that moment, took a sharp turn down a road she hadn't seen coming. The chance hallway encounter with Frankie led to a fast friendship. She saw how Frankie, a physical therapist, inspired her young patients by showing them how powerlifting had made her stronger with one leg than she'd ever been with two. Soon Supriya was in the gym with Frankie, and only a year later, obtained a personal trainer certification and was training the newly disabled herself.

Then one afternoon, Frankie took *the picture*: Supriya on the powerlifting platform at full deadlift extension, 315 pounds making the barbell sag at each end, straining oversized quadriceps of her right leg in stark contrast to the machinery of her left. Two of

Supriya's clients cheered her on in the picture's background, both of them with visible prosthetics as well.

Frankie put the picture on her Instagram account and added as the caption the words she'd heard Supriya say time and time again. *Let me not beg for the stilling of my pain but for the heart to conquer it.*

The picture became a social media phenomenon, and before Supriya knew it, she had a following. She never went to medical school and never became an anesthesiologist—much to her parents' chagrin. Instead, she found her own path, or more accurately, her own path found her.

Without Frankie, none of it would've happened.

Now Frankie lay dead in a strange cavern, somewhere outside of the world she had known. Supriya wished she could grieve for Frankie, but the role of the *masinisto* pushed her own emotions to a back corner of her mind. The best she could do, maybe, was to give Frankie an exit from this place through flame.

The graveyard cavern had no trees to cut down to build a funeral pyre, so Supriya had the junklings tear apart furniture from some of the mansion's upstairs bedrooms, along with the table and chairs of the dining room.

A junkling with a crack in its headlight that looked a bit like a mustache, whom she had named Reginald after a loyal Dalmation she'd grown up with back in New Delhi, looked back up at her wondering if the pile was to her liking. That's what it felt like, the communication from it through the crown and to Supriya. She knew Reginald didn't really wonder about anything or have its own individual thoughts. It was just interconnected metal parts, gears, and belts. The personification was an extension of her, projected out into all the machines that she controlled, like parts of her own body. Appendages that could function at her direction or involuntarily. Like the human body's lungs.

Make it bigger, she directed Reginald with a thought.

The initial awareness—if that was the right word—the awareness of the machines was overwhelming, but soon they slipped to her subconscious, only reemerging when her focus was needed.

As Reginald retreated back to the mansion to drag out yet another wardrobe to become kindling, Supriya ran her mind's fingers over her new, machine-extended psyche. The junklings down by the cemetery all, in turn, stood stiff expecting instructions until her touch moved on to the next machines. The mansion, itself a machine of sorts, felt like a living extension of her, its hallways like veins, and torture apparatuses deep underground as its bowels. Up here, on the rooftop terrace behind her, was the most important of all the machines: a twisting array of lenses, gears, and mirrors that attached this place to the outworlds. The World Lens. Her tool to pull more here, like she, Frankie, and Jay had been pulled...

Pulling more innocent people here was now her purpose, her role as the *masinisto*.

Like Jay had a role. She had only known him for, what, two hours? Maybe three? But they already had an unspoken bond through their roles, unlike anything she had experienced with another person. Jay's knife was like her crown. The irises of his blue eyes were streaked with red like hers had become streaked with gold. He was sleeping now, as if none of this was a big deal, but before he went to the bedroom, she asked him about his role. And he knew what she meant.

"That guy called me the *stelisto*. The same word came to me in a daydream earlier today, but it feels as right as an old pair of boots. What does it mean to me? What's my role as the *stelisto*? Just killing, plain and simple," he had said.

His response should've terrified her, but it didn't.

Again, Reginald looked up at her, requesting further instruction. The pile of torn furniture sat eight, maybe ten feet high, and at least that wide. She touched her crown and nodded. Below, the junklings dragged the bodies and placed them atop the pile.

Now it was her turn. She walked across the rooftop toward the stairs leading down to her workroom. After taking care of the bodies, she'd repair her prosthetic knee or replace it altogether, stripping parts from other devices in the workroom. Maybe the knee would be better than before. All of the *masinisto*'s machines—even those that appeared crude and made of junk--were imbued with a power beyond electricity that she was still trying to understand, a power that made all the machines from her outworld home feel limited in comparison.

For now, she had the broken knee tied so that the prosthetic leg stayed locked in full extension. Along with a cane she had found in one of the bedrooms, it made walking awkward but at least predictable.

In her workroom, she grabbed a smooth, red rod from a display on the bookshelf. The rod was warm to the touch. A foreign memory told her something of how it worked: using focal stones to rub together the surfaces of nearby worlds, the friction creating heat that could be projected. A fire wand, built by one of her *masinisto* forebears.

Inside the house, the junklings had already cleared all of the debris from their battle with her predecessor, but some of the house's scars would take longer to heal. Rugs torn by the feet of the junklings. Windows smashed. Doors torn from their hinges.

Outside she walked past the hedges and through the iron gate, cane in one hand, fire-rod in the other. Despite her injuries, she felt stronger than she ever had.

Then a booming sound from the dark passageway knocked her to the ground, both the fire-rod and cane slipping from her hands as she grabbed to hold onto her crown. Another boom, metallic and resonant, the ringing of a great bell.

The streetlamps in the cavern began to flicker, and their light shifted from sulfur yellow to red and then to a diseased brown. Whispers came from the cavern like bats flying toward her.

She pressed her hands against her ears, but she couldn't keep the bell's echoes out. The junklings backed away from the dark path's opening, away from the piles of broken furniture and the bodies.

Through the crown, she felt their familiarity with the bell, with the thing emerging from the darkness.

It stepped into the dim brown light, and Supriya's head felt like it was going to explode.

She tried to turn away, but even with her arms covering her face, even turned into the dirt and grass, she could still see it. Walking on two legs, human-like in shape, every part of it an absence darker than black, especially the burning void where its eyes should be. Around it, reality buckled and warped. The names on nearby tombstones blurred with overlapping permutations, and then the stones themselves seemed to come loose from their three-dimensional positions as if jittered on the axis of another dimension.

With each of the creature's steps, the cavern throbbed as if it were the inside of a great, black heart. The creature approached the bodies on the pile and reached out to them as if it were twenty feet tall. And it was twenty feet tall, but also the height of a normal man and every size in between. A dim lantern hung in its left hand.

It reached a black finger to Frankie's forehead and drew a spiral in the dead flesh with its claw-like fingernail. It pushed its finger through the center of the spiral, deep into Frankie's skull, and then pulled out an iridescent, ghostly copy of Frankie, silently screaming, trying to free itself from the touch of the thing's hand. The creature held Frankie's *soul* (that was the only word that made sense to Supriya). It pulled Frankie's soul close, examining it, twisting and turning it, before stuffing it into the lantern, like a bird into a much-too-small cage. The lantern's glow brightened. The creature reached out to the former *masinisto*'s body and repeated the soul-extraction process. With a second soul locked away, the lantern's glow pulsed like a heartbeat.

The creature looked at the remaining shriveled husks of the bodies, and then it slowly turned its head toward Supriya. Despite every part of her body fighting against it, she found herself pulled into that gaze, pulled to...

...a shore beyond a river black as oil, the great bell tower looming ahead like a gnarled gray finger scratching out the light of the dying sun, statues

all around, silently screaming, a statue now of Frankie, eyes of stone somehow still seeing, face wracked in permanent fear, and a nearby statue with her own face waiting for her...

...and beyond the statues and the tower, something greater, a machine like the World Lens atop the mansion but the size of a city, using the cries of the statues to connect the outworlds, to pull the outworlds themselves closer and closer and closer until they eventually smash together as one...

The bell's echoes faded to silence. The creature had gone, but her mind kept ringing.

In her workroom within the mansion, Supriya tried to ignore the burning smell in the air from the pyre and the bodies. She tried to ignore the visions that kept flashing back into her mind, of the creature that warped everything around it, of the great bell tower and its statue-prisons. Of a doomed fate that seemed to be waiting for her.

She sorted through the past *masinisto's* gadgets and books, through memorabilia and gruesome trophies of past battles won, but nothing kept the visions from her mind until she found a worn, leather-bound journal thousands of pages long, full of undated entries made with the same foreign, ornate script. Without realizing what she was doing, she spun down a pair of monocles from her crown and twisted their focus until the script became, somehow, not translated exactly but comprehensible.

For hours, she read through the journal's entries, through tales of discovery and rediscovery, of experimentation and creation. It read like the words of a single person who lost and then had to re-find her memories, like a tide that over and over again became full and then receded to leave its shoreline bare.

She read three different accounts of the workings of the World Lens, each tale describing the machine's function in a different but complementary way. The World Lens could focus on an *outworlder*—a word she kept encountering but didn't fully understand—and its focus could create a path here, to what the journal called the

Between. The elevator that had taken her and Frankie from the outside world to the cavern—it had been a creation of the World Lens. An overlapping of elements of other worlds, lined up by the lenses to connect distant worlds and places.

She read about staircases leading to other worlds, about artifacts and roles, but the journal entries contradicted themselves, and for every statement written as fact there were dozens of questions without answers.

Two-thirds of the way through, the journal entries stopped, with blank pages from thereon. If she wanted answers, she'd have to discover most of them for herself. She pushed away from the desk and started to stand, but a fountain pen resting in the eye of a skull caught her attention. She picked it up and twisted its end, releasing the flow of ink. On the next blank page, she began...

The hand that writes these words belongs to Supriya Reddy (age 27, daughter of Raj Kumar and Geeta), but this is not my handwriting. I like to make little circles for the dots on my i's. But look: i i i i !!!! No circles!!!! No matter how hard I try, my hand only writes in this crazy script. It's beautiful, but it isn't mine!

When I look at this house, the cavern, the graveyard, and all these machines, they trigger memories that aren't mine, either. Something happened when I put on the crown. Something entered me and became part of me, or maybe I became part of it. Like a mitochondria within a human cell???

A foreign invader has taken residence within me. Or am I the foreign invader? (Not a pleasant thought!!)

Am I the foreign invader? ...I remember asking this question countless times before. I don't remember it ever being answered.

These are not my memories.

I put on the crown and became the masinisto. I know my role is tied to the machine atop this house. I'm sickened by the idea of pulling more, like me, to this place, but I have a sense that I will do just that.

The masinistos *always do their job. Why did I just write that?!?!*
These are not my words.
I AM SUPRIYA REDDY, DAUGHTER OF RAJ KUMAR AND GEETA!

I've spent two nights, now, in the mansion. I say nights, but I really have no sense of day or night here in the cavern. The windows with false moonlight never switch to false daylight, so, while time passes, I feel like I'm living in perpetual midnight.

The junklings, as Jay calls them, are not frightening to me at all, despite what they did to Frankie and what they tried to do to me and Jay. As soon as I put the crown on my head, they felt like... I don't know ... like my fingers, I guess. A part of my body, but not capable of right or wrong on their own. If I should fear or hate anything or anyone, it should be my predecessor. If not for him, I would be home, and Frankie would still be alive.

Why is it, then, that I'm so fascinated by the machine that ensnared me? Half the time I walk through the mansion's halls, I end up on the rooftop standing before the World Lens. This morning (when I woke up, anyway, whatever time that was) I walked toward the kitchen, to have one of those strange, green grapefruit-like citruses in the bowl near the sink. (Don't ask me how, but there seems to be an endless supply. I should know, I've eaten like 50. They are delicious!) Instead of the kitchen, I found myself on the rooftop again, staring at the machine.

It was cold, and I was wearing only the thin robe I found hanging in the dressing room attached to the master suite, but the cold didn't seem to touch me while I stood there. Everything in the world (worlds?) had stopped except for me and the machine.

Its great pendulum swung back and forth, and the clicking gears made the rooftop vibrate. The vibration ran up my prosthetic leg and seemed to grab ahold of my hip and make all of my bones tremble. It sounds awful, the way I'm describing it, but it was just part of the connection with the machine. It didn't feel good or bad.

If the junklings resemble humans in form, the World Lens looks like a giant sea anemone, with telescoping metal tentacles waving and extending. Each tentacle with lenses running up and down its length. The lenses line up and twist as if they're focusing, and then they shift and line up a new way that wouldn't have seemed possible until I saw it happen.

I made the mistake of looking too deeply in one of the lenses, and instead of seeing a warped version of what lay beyond, I felt like I was slipping into a swirling space with too many dimensions.

At the World Lens's center (which was hard to get to! I had to duck and dodge all the moving arms!) was an open area, with a platform, where I knew I was supposed to stand. There in the center, all the vibration stopped. I would describe it like being in the eye of a hurricane, but instead of feeling disconnected from the swirling storm around me, I felt as if the lenses had become my eyes, allowing my mind to see into a space perpendicular to what we normally perceive.

I know that doesn't make sense, but I'm not sure how else to explain it.

I saw a lattice, a giant multidimensional web. Some of the nodes were dim, while others glowed so brightly it hurt to look directly at them. I don't know why, but when I found a node that looked hazy and stained yellow, I felt the pang of a dopamine reward. This is what I was looking for.

The lenses focused, the machine's arms aligned, and the yellow-stained node grew before me until it wasn't just a single node anymore, but a swarm of little yellow nodes like fireflies. I kept working the machine until each of the little fireflies lined up perfectly with the others. Little solar eclipses, all lined up at the intersection of a dimension beyond the one they inhabited.

It sounds so simple, my explanation of a few sentences, but it took hours working the machine and, by the end, I was exhausted and the robe was soaked by my sweat.

Shortly after the machine got the fireflies into alignment, their combined yellow light vanished. I had moved it somehow out of its space.

The node had been a person, hadn't it? The many expressions of an individual, its light stained yellow by ... by what? One of the foreign memories in my head tells me that it's pain. Deep, repressed emotional pain.

The pain, when put into pure focus, gives the machine something to connect with.

To ensnare the person behind the pain and pull them outside of their world.

To pull them into the Between.

Oh God, what have I done?

They don't all come that easy.

(...said the whore with her new wad of cash.)

(I should have been a comedian. Comedienne?)

Through the World Lens, I can't see who I'm targeting. Only what they hide. What stains the souls of all their outworld incarnations. What makes them vulnerable in life makes them vulnerable to me, the masinisto.

I told Jay a little about what I've seen, what I've done, and what I know. He plays dumb, but he's a clever one. Dangerous, too, beyond his role as stelisto. *Jay came through to the Between with his friend, Paul. I don't know which of them my predecessor targeted. If Jay has repressed vulnerabilities, he hasn't shared them yet. Maybe when he gets more comfortable with me he'll open up...*

(his wallet ... said the whore. That was supposed to be funny, but I keep looking at the word whore and it looks three times as large as the words around it, even though it isn't. I'm the one who wrote it, but I feel skewered. If I'm a whore, what of myself have I sold? And who is my pimp?)

(enough of this)

I don't think the World Lens was focused on Jay. He was in the wrong place, at the wrong time, with the wrong friend.

Like Frankie.

Frankie.

I should be crying when I write that name. I said it out loud, and still my eyes are dry. I want to cry. For Frankie. And also for myself, to prove that the woman I think of as Supriya Reddy isn't gone. Hasn't been replaced.

(whore)

(fuck you)

The World Lens focused in on my hidden fear. Of course it did, that's why I'm here.

So what is this fear of mine?

With the masinisto *role detaching me from who I am, who I should still be, I can say the things I couldn't have before. I can see the things I couldn't have before. I know what the World Lens focused on within me.*

I'm going to write the words that I've tried not to think for nine years.

(deep breath)

The cancer will come back.

It doesn't matter how strong I make myself.

The cancer will come back.

(There. Are you happy now?)

I strain my muscles until I tear them down and force them to grow back harder and stronger. My ligaments thicken. My bones harden.

Still, I am only flesh. And my body aches and hurts.

I stand before crowds, in person and on online streams, and I speak until I can speak without my hands shaking.

Still, I am only flesh. And my mind is plagued by doubt.

I hunt down every fear and try to burn it away.

Still, the fears return, and new ones emerge. But no fear so deep, no fear so pure...

As my fear...

The cancer will come back.

Have I been living my life or building a false life?

This is the yellow stain on my soul, a stain that I'm sure glowed, bright as the sun, when the past masinisto *saw it.*

Here's the worst of it. For the first time in nine years, I'm not scared about the cancer returning. But I am scared. I'm scared that I'm going to use what I've learned about my own fear to pull more into the Between.

And get that jolt of dopamine each time it happens.

(Just like a good little whore.)

I am Supriya Reddy, daughter of Raj Kumar and Geeta.

I am Supriya Reddy, masinisto.

CHAPTER 13
A VISIT FROM THE GARDISTARO

Weeks later, Jay scowled at the battlefield in front of him. His army had been cut in half, and the invaders' noose tightened around his neck. He lifted his black bishop and moved it to guard his last pawn, his last remaining hope.

"Are you sure you want to do that?" Supriya asked. She stood looming over the chessboard, wearing a long, dark green Victorian military coat tailored to trace the lines of her broad shoulders and back, her narrow waist and wide hips. It hadn't really been tailored for her, had it? The coat fit her perfectly when she found it hanging in the bedroom wardrobe. Like the white, ruffled blouse, the matching green corset, the corduroy trousers, and the knee-high polished black boots that all made her look like a general surveying imminent victory. A queen-general wearing a mechanical crown.

"What's wrong with this move?" he said, scanning the board, looking for one of Supriya's traps. "Oh, and have Reginald grab another bottle of that whiskey or brandy or whatever it is." He glared at the junkling standing in the corner of the study. Even wearing a butler's coat, with a top hat tied to its headlamp, even given the name Reginald, the junkling still looked like it buzzed with nervous energy, waiting for the opportunity to pay him back for the deaths of its siblings. The fact that the junklings were now under Supriya's control only gave him the barest sense of comfort.

Without a word or even a glance from Supriya, the junkling named Reginald left the room. From the chessboard, Supriya picked up her remaining knight, kissed it atop its alabaster head, and placed it so that it attacked Jay's bishop.

When he reached to move his piece to safety, she tsked and shook her head. "You're in check. You can't move the bishop."

"Ah, hell. A damn knight fork. You forked me, ya forkin' forker."

Supriya patted him on the cheek. "Once again, I'm on top." As she said the words, a memory of the previous night filled her mind—Jay, wrists and ankles tied to the four posts of the giant bed in the upstairs master suite; she, sitting atop him, rolling her hips, wearing only the crown, the unbuttoned military coat, and the polished black boots. Her prosthetic knee made a clicking sound ever since she rebuilt it, and as she rocked back and forth it sounded like she was a wind-up toy with a coil inside her tightening and tightening.

In the outworld she thought of as home, she'd never left her prosthetic on during sex. Here, with the knee joint rebuilt using her *masinisto* knowledge, the prosthetic felt like part of her, and she didn't like taking it off, even when it hurt. Taking it off would be losing control and, as the *masinisto*, she wanted to control everything. Even Jay. *Especially* Jay, her black-hearted killer. Her *stelisto*.

Whenever Jay, lying beneath her, had tried to speak, she slapped him on the cheek. Harder each time, to make sure he minded. She had scratched her nails across his chest, leaving intersecting trails of welted flesh and a few scatterings of blood. She had even bitten him, hard on the inner thigh, hard enough that he cried out and his dick began to soften. "Did I say you can go limp?" she had demanded, hand now wrapped around it, gripped tightly to show she owned it, owned him.

Where had all this come from? She knew the term S&M, the words sadism, masochism. She knew about domination fetishes but never had so much as fantasized about participating. Some of it, undoubtedly, came with the role of the *masinisto*, but the role only intensified something that already lived deep within her.

On the one hand, the feelings were exhilarating. But they terrified her as well. The clothes, this place, and now even her personality. The scariest part wasn't how foreign and strange it all was. The scariest part was that, in going along with it, in turning off her fears and her attempts to rationalize or explain all of this, it had begun to feel normal. She had used the World Lens to bring more people here —to what the journal called the Between—to bring them to their deaths, and that thought didn't bother her at all.

What had happened to the Supriya Reddy who tried to inspire her thousands of YouTube subscribers and Instagram followers? If she ever made it back home, if she could relinquish the *masinisto* role, could she be that Supriya again? Or would all of her followers just be, to her, another legion to command?

"You've gone along with all of this," she said.

"All of what?" Jay said, looking at the chessboard.

"This." She pointed at the room, pointed at her crown, and then twirled around with her arms up to indicate everything else.

Jay slouched deeper in the chair and hung his left arm over its back. He could make any piece of furniture, no matter how upright and rigid, look like it had been built for lounging. "Like I said before, if you want to redecorate, knock your socks off, Supes. That said, from a resale standpoint, I think most Realtors would've advised against turning the formal dining room into a weight room, but liftin' heavy shit and puttin' it back down again makes you happy, so what the hell. This house will take a special type of buyer anyway."

She picked up a white pawn, rolled it between her fingers and thumb, and then flicked it at Jay, who squawked when it hit him right between the eyes. "I don't mean the house. I mean us, you idiot. We've been feeding the machine. We're not prisoners anymore. We're the jailors. We're the executioners."

Jay picked up the pawn, and for a second Supriya thought he was going to throw it back at her, but with the hard press of his thumb he snapped its head clean off. "I'm the executioner," he said coldly. "Don't take on my guilt."

"Do you have any guilt left, *stelisto*? I haven't asked you where you disappear off to sometimes, even when you come back covered in blood. It should terrify me, but it doesn't. I drag the lambs to the slaughter. What difference does it make who holds the blade?"

"We talked about this, Supes. What choice do we have but to keep on keepin' on? You say we're not prisoners, but we've tried to leave twice already, and nearly died both times. Staying here's gonna eventually end badly, like it did for Inspector Gadget. We've had, what, six or seven uninvited guests to the cavern? Mostly unlucky bastards who don't know what the hell is going on, but that last duo, a few days ago... That was a planned attack." He rubbed at the dozens of hash-marks carved into the skin of his left forearm.

Reginald handed him a tumbler a quarter full of the noxious-smelling liquor, and Jay threw it back in a single gulp. "Even with the threat of invasion and death, I'm enjoying just accepting things without asking questions for a little while," Jay said. "Thinking of it like a vacation from reality. So, yeah, I've gone along with all of this, like you said. What other choice do we have?"

"And what about me?" she asked.

"What do you mean, what about you?"

"You've just gone along with me?"

He raised his left eyebrow. "A little more than *gone along with you*, wouldn't you say? Look. I'm trapped in a strange place that seems bent on either killing me or driving me insane, but with me is the most gorgeous woman who has ever given me the time of day, and who's smarter and stronger and a hell of a lot tougher than I'll ever be, and who's already saved my life, what is it, five times? I'll *go along with that* any day of the fucking week."

She could see the love in his eyes and wondered if she felt anything like that for him. He would do anything she asked, and he never asked for anything in return. Maybe she loved the role he was playing, irrespective of who played it. "You've noticed how I've changed since we've been down here," she said, telling, not asking.

"How could I not? Some of what you did last night will probably leave scars."

"Why do you let me? Have you always been into submission?"

"I let you because I like it. Not the submission part. I like that you like it."

"I want to hurt you, Jay. And I don't know where that feeling is coming from. I've never had any of these desires before, and now they keep getting stronger and stronger."

He gave her his crooked grin. "You can hurt me, Supes. I'm tough. I can take it."

"I don't think you understand what I mean. A week ago it was rough sex. Last night I drew blood. Now I want to carve my name in your back. In the trunk by the bed, where I got the bindings, there are other things I want to use. A gag. Clamps. Whips."

Jay winced. "Not sure about having your name carved into my back, babe."

"A strap-on dildo I want to wear and fuck you in the ass."

Jay's feet slipped off the table, catapulting the chessboard and its remaining pieces across the room. "Yeah, wherever the line is, that's quite a bit past it."

"While I choke you right to the edge of death and see if I can keep myself from pushing you over that edge."

Jay's eyes never left hers, and she only recognized that something had changed when Reginald stepped between them. At some point, Jay had taken out that blue knife of his, what the mansion's previous occupant had called the Knife of Undoing, and Jay now rolled it back and forth casually in his palm, maybe not even realizing himself that he was doing it.

"Get back, Reggie," she said.

The junkling turned its headlamp face toward her and buzzed and whirred. Then it looked back at Jay.

"Feeling lucky, Reginald?" Jay said.

"Now, Reggie!" Supriya said, and the junkling complied. To Jay, she said, "Something is changing in me, and I don't like where it's leading. Or maybe I like it so much that it scares me. I've seen you change, also, and when I see you holding that knife, like right now, I see a bloodlust that will eventually focus on me. Do you ever want to throw that knife away? Can you?"

"I'm sure I could if I wanted to, but I don't."

"You sound like an alcoholic, which incidentally you might be as well, but let's focus on one addiction at a time. I think the same way about this crown. Like if I take it off I'll lose a part of me. But it's the crown that's devouring me, just like it's the knife devouring you. We need to get out of here before we kill each other. Leave all of this—this whole place, the crown, the knife—leave it all behind."

"Agreed. How about one more night in the mansion, and we'll take off tomorrow morning?" He put the knife back in its sheath and smiled. "I've never been with a woman who wanted to kill me."

"Yes, you have. Last night."

Jay inspected the chest of supplies that Supriya had assembled. Canteens of water, dried meats and cheeses, bread so hard it needed to be soaked in water to be edible, knives, more knives, strange clock-work gadgets including a magnet-powered rod that shot mini darts. Also that fucking strobe light thing Inspector Gadget used to nearly blind him. And clothes. Weeks worth of clothes.

He made the mistake, a while back, of asking where all this shit came from. Supriya waved her hands around while spouting mumbo-jumbo like *superpermutation* and *confluence of outworlds*. The whole thing sounded a bit made up, if you asked Jay.

Supriya had laid out a change of clothes for him as well, flat on the bed like someone had been wearing them and then vanished, leaving the clothes behind. The outfit resembled hers: Victorian, overly ornate, ruffle-ridden shit that looked smothering. He looked at himself in the mirror. White t-shirt, untucked, a few stains. Jeans, worn through on the knees. Red Wing boots.

Fuck those frilly clothes. He wasn't changing.

Fuck the whole chest and the three hundred pounds of shit

Supriya put in here, he thought. How'd she think they'd get the chest down the hatch's ladder, even with the junklings' help? Weapons, a little food, and some water. Nothing else needed. Including the damn junklings.

Jay looked at the bedroom door, expecting Reginald to be standing there twitching, but of course Reggie, as Supriya called him —called *it*—was somewhere downstairs with her. Watching over her. Keeping guard.

He thought about Inspector Gadget's last moments, as the man was torn apart by the machines that had previously kept guard over him. And maybe over countless more wearing that crown before him. Inspector Gadget, like Supriya now, was playing a role that had been played time and time again before. *The* stelistos *always die early. I've killed four myself*, the man had said. *Stelistos*, plural. Like Jay, with his Knife of Undoing, was playing a role, too, that had been played before.

Maybe all of the Inspector Gadgets—Jay liked his term better than the *masinisto*—all eventually get torn apart by their creations. And now Supriya was the new Inspector Gadget. Or would the title be Inspectress? Inspectrix?

Jay wadded up the clothes laid out for him and threw them back in the wardrobe. None of this shit should be coming back with them, including the junklings. He paced back and forth, trying to think of how he'd convince Supriya to leave the crown in the dirt of the grave-yard when they closed the hatch behind them.

A flash of light came through the window. He cupped his hands around his eyes and pressed against the window, looking out on the always-night of the mansion lawn and the graveyard down below. Junklings were scurrying up the hill, toward the source of the flash, toward the house.

A figure in a white dress walked from the gate down the path leading to the house's front door. Jay felt the fire of bloodlust growing within him, and he rolled the knife back and forth in his hand. He had seen this woman before. Supriya had as well, referring to her as the *gardistaro*, a name she had apparently picked up from that giant journal she was always either reading or writing in. Three times in as many recent days, the *gardistaro* woman had walked close to the house and said their names. And when the junklings got near, she vanished in one of those flashes of light.

"Jay," the woman said, looking up at him through the window. She didn't yell, and he shouldn't have been able to hear her, but her voice came through as clearly as if she'd been standing only feet away. "Jay Lightsey. Supriya Reddy."

Behind him, he heard Supriya's distinctive footstep cadence and the loping pattern of Reginald.

"Her again?" she asked.

"Yeah. Same shit. And she's about to do her disappearing act when your goons get to her. I wish I knew how she did it."

"I don't know how, but I think I know where," Supriya said. "She doesn't just vanish. She always goes through a door. Like right now. Watch. She's standing next to the gate. I'm assuming the gate will work."

"What do you mean, you're assuming the gate will work?"

"Watch."

The woman in the white dress called their names two more times before the junklings were within feet of her. Without any sign of hurry, she opened the gate, but as the gate swiveled on its iron hinges, a column of light appeared and spread to form a rectangle filling the gate's threshold. The woman walked into the light, pulling the gate closed behind her, and the light vanished.

When the junklings reached the gate, they pulled it open and shut, peering with their headlamps in vain attempts to find their prey. Supriya touched the side of her crown and the junklings abandoned their search and waddled back down to their hidings spots within the graveyard.

"That's a hell of a trick," Jay said.

"Last time she did it with a door to that crypt up on that hill by the cavern wall. I didn't see her come out, but I saw her go in. Not to the crypt. The door she used led someplace else. Someplace bright."

She looked up at him. "The past *masinistos* didn't trust her, and I don't either. What do you think she wants?"

He traced his finger down Supriya's temple, across her cheek, and down the middle of her lips. "I don't know, Supes. But I have this feeling that we're not going to get too far tomorrow before we find out."

CHAPTER 14
LEAVING THE MANSION

Jay slept little that night. He wasn't even sure it had been night, just like he wasn't sure that the last month hadn't really been three weeks, or five, or seven. His usual means of telling time, beyond the rise and fall of the sun, had been his phone, which had run out of batteries on their first day here. He had never gotten accustomed to wearing a watch.

On his eighteenth birthday, his grandfather gave him a fancy watch. It was supposed to be symbolic or something. Self-winding, stainless steel. Take care of it, and it would last Jay the rest of his life. That's what his grandfather said. On his first attempt, Jay wore it a grand total of about three hours. By then the metal band had pinched and pulled out most of the hairs on his wrist. Every time he moved his hand it yanked out another one. A little jolt. Zap. And then a minute later another one. Zap. He took it off and set it on the dresser in his bedroom, where the face stared back at him every morning.

The fucking thing was symbolic, all right. Adulthood, responsibility, obligation, and all that shit. By not wearing the watch, Jay felt not only that he was letting his grandfather's gift go to waste, but also that he was failing to cross the threshold into becoming a man. It's a serious word: *man*. Not guy. Not dude. Nor even, in his grandfather's west Texas drawl, fella. Man. The three-letter root of the foundational words of the species laid bare. The word that separates us from the apes, from the rest of the animals. Hairy and smelly and strong, yes, but upright, too. By design—or by evolution, anyway. Upright not in a temporary, lumbering gorilla way, but stable and ludicrously precise. A double-layered word, man. A pinnacle category of creature, and then layered on top, the creature's strongest and most serious form. Man.

He made the decision one morning to be a man and put the watch back on and wear it until every goddamn hair got pulled out and then got pulled out again and again until his left wrist wouldn't grow hair anymore, if such a thing were even possible, even if it took years. But the fucking watch had stopped, and although it was supposed to wind itself, Jay's limited arm movement while wearing it foiled the little self-winding mechanism, causing it to lose a few minutes here and a few minutes there. The lost minutes led to late arrivals at classes and finally to him unintentionally standing up the cute girl who worked at the bowling alley who he had finally worked up the nerve to ask out, who decided, after sitting alone at that coffee shop on the Drag for forty minutes, that what she had taken for a dreamy-eyed charm was in fact just run-of-the-mill laziness. When he finally arrived at the coffee shop, the girl behind the counter asked if he was Jay, and when he nodded, she said she'd been told to give him a message. The message was, simply, *Fuck you.*

He took the watch off, put it in his dresser, under a stack of sweaters he never wore, and decided that responsibility and adulthood—being a man—was overrated. His grandfather died a month or two later, leaving Jay an inheritance just big enough to support a low cost, low responsibility lifestyle until at some vague point in middle age. The universe supported his decision regarding the watch and the overratedness of being a wristwatch-wearing, certified man.

Supriya didn't wear a watch, either. With all of the gear-filled gadgetry throughout the house, he would've thought there'd be a clock or two or three in every room, but there wasn't a single one anywhere—they had looked.

Whether it was morning-time or not, they were standing in the entryway with the chest full of supplies suspended between the arms of two of the junklings, one of which was Reginald, the only junkling that had a name. Through the window, Jay could see the horde of junklings gathered by the gate, ready to escort them to the hatch and beyond.

Too bad Supriya's elevator had vanished. He wished she could use that octopus machine on the roof to smash together another way out, but Supriya said it didn't work that way. Something about it all being kind of random, and the more you tried to force something specific, the less *real* it was, and you ended up with books with blank pages and flames without heat. The *masinisto*'s gadgetry and rules were too complicated for him. I've got a knife and I stab people with it, he thought with a chuckle.

Jay opened the door, and the junklings waddled through with the chest. He looked at Supriya standing there dead serious, arms crossed below her breasts, surveying her troops before battle. He said, "I'm going to miss our little house of torture devices and killer robots. What about you?"

She stared through him for several seconds and then said, "I'm having second thoughts. I have a feeling like this is my home and I need to stay and defend it."

"That's the crown talking. You said it yourself last night. If you did stay here—if *we* stayed here—eventually one of the invaders is gonna be successful, like we were successful. Or we'll eventually kill each other. No matter what, staying here doesn't lead to a happy ending." He tried to find a hint of feeling behind her steel expression. "I didn't want to bring this up yet, but you're gonna have to take that crown off at some point soon and leave your fan club behind."

"I know. When we find the way out. And you'll leave your knife behind, too, right?"

Jay watched as Reginald and his fellow luggage carrier reached the other junklings by the gate. The rusty machines let out various *whirr*s and percussive *thonk*s, headlamps swiveling in focus from one junkling to the next. Greeting each other? They did seem to communicate with their mechanical parts, although he didn't see how that was possible. The only thing for certain was that they creeped him out.

"Maybe for your crown, it should be sooner than that, Supes."

"How much sooner?"

He acted like he was giving the question deep thought. The sooner she was without the crown, with the damn junklings left far behind, the better. "Like when we reach the hatch," he said.

"I thought you said there were fire dogs and stuff like that."

"I did. But we can handle them. Together, I think the two of us can handle anything." He hoped she'd agree with him, or at least nod, but she instead stared out toward the gate. "Also, I don't think the trunk will fit through the hatch."

That got her attention and finally caused some emotion to return. Unfortunately, that emotion was anger, manifested in a glare that could've burned holes right through him. "Why'd you let me pack the whole thing if you knew it wouldn't fit?" she said.

"I didn't. I mean, I don't know it won't fit. It's possible that it, uh, might not. The hatch isn't that big. Anyway, even if it does fit, that trunk's gotta weigh five-hundred pounds. How are the junklings going to get it down the ladder? Have you ever looked at their feet? I don't think they were built for, uh, ladder navigation."

"We'll see," she said and turned back to the gate. "If that strange woman shows up, I need you to be ready."

"I'm always ready," he said, although he had no idea what she meant by it.

"She somehow repurposes closed doors and makes them lead someplace else. We saw her use the gate last night, so I have twenty junklings guarding it. I have another two at each crypt door in the graveyard, and then four at the crypt on the hill. Am I missing anything?"

Jay saw one of the shadows on the hill move. "Don't think so. Looks like you have them all covered."

"Be on your guard just in case."

He nodded and they stood in awkward silence. When she didn't show any signs of breaking it, he said, "Ladies first."

For a second, Jay thought he saw her face soften, thought he glimpsed the Supriya that had slipped farther and farther away, but before anything came of it, she turned and strode out the door, her mechanical left knee clicking with every step.

"Well. Off we go, I guess." He pulled the front door shut behind him as he left the house and took two quick steps to catch up with Supriya before he realized what had happened. He had just closed the mansion's front door. Supriya had each door guarded except the one they had exited. As he turned, he already had the blue knife in hand, was already starting his strike.

He met her right as the mansion's door opened, before she had a chance to speak, before drawing a single breath, and he was on her, eyes now only inches apart, the woman in the white dress, who he had seen only through the window, from far away, whose pale skin at that distance looked as white and featureless as the dress she wore, but up close he saw the freckles on her cheeks, the shocks of green among the gold of her eyes, eyes wide with the surprise of Jay's knife plunged dead into her heart.

She fell, and as the light behind her poured, near blinding, into Jay, he felt the shock deep in his chest, as if he had been the one stabbed instead. In less than a second the certainty of his action—to protect Supriya—turned into certainty of a mistake, and already he felt his forearm sting with the fresh new tally mark of his latest kill.

He looked at the fallen woman, on what looked like a white marble floor, blood running down her chest, down her neck, and he had the sudden urge to pick her up and cradle her. To push his hand over the wound and keep the blood inside her. But he knew his strike had been perfect.

Supriya ran up behind him.

"Good," she said. "The bitch is dead."

Supriya looked around within the strange, white marble room they had entered through the door that should have led them back into the mansion. With the door open, she could still see into the perpetual night of the cavern. Around the door, the air crackled and blurred.

The room was octagonal, with a small fountain in the center and teardrop-shaped alcoves in each wall. Roman-style statues of the same white marble stared down at them from every alcove, save one which was empty. The dead woman on the floor with her pale skin and white silk dress could've passed for the missing statue if not for the pool of blood growing around her and the color coming back into her skin, her face. Why would she become less pale in death? Maybe the woman had been playing a role, like Supriya and her *masinisto* persona and Jay as the *stelisto*. Now that role had ended, and the woman was becoming her past self.

This woman was like them. Another trapped person who had found a way to survive. And they killed her.

The thought should've saddened Supriya, or at least made her feel something, but more and more her thinking had become like that of a clockmaker-god, like the components of the world existed solely for her to manipulate.

The woman in white was a curious machine, but just a machine. Unlike the junklings, Supriya had no idea how this machine worked, so she began examining the woman's belongings.

"Don't we need to get going?" Jay asked. "I don't want to be around that body any longer than I have to. I think I'm having killer's remorse with this one."

"Go wait outside, then," Supriya said. She heard his boots on the hard floor walk to the door and back out into the cavern.

Aside from the white dress, the woman was dressed simply. Two bracelets and a pair of thin sandals. No other possessions. She saw nothing special about the bracelets or the sandals. So the dress must be the artifact, she thought.

Prior *masinistos* had theorized about artifacts in the journal, and based on those entries, Supriya had a vague idea of how they worked and what to look for. The word *artifact* had a usual, literal meaning: an object of historical significance made by a person. But that's not what the word meant in the journal. *Artifact* had a second meaning: something that looked real but was only the result of your perspective. A false result in a statistical analysis, or a shape resulting from the noise in a video compression algorithm.

According to the journal, the artifacts somehow existed as across all worlds without really existing in the worlds themselves, individually. The key was the filament incorporated into the object: in the sapphire handle of Jay's knife and in the mesh cap of the *masinisto* crown. The woman's role must be connected to her white dress. Supriya searched the dress until she found the peculiar filaments woven into its fabric.

"I think I want to be you," she whispered to the corpse. The bracelets loosened when she pinched together their interlocking prongs. She rinsed the blood off them in the fountain. The water turned pink for a few seconds and then became clear again. The sandals looked as if they were made of a single, leather strap, looped and interwoven from the soles all the way above the ankle, but after a few minutes of examination, she found that the single, rectangular jewel over the toes could be twisted to tighten or loosen the strap without untying and dismantling the entire thing.

Ingenious, she thought, and before she knew it, her *masinisto* attributes took control and she became lost in a moment of considering all the various potential uses for such a mechanism.

Jay's voice, calling out to her from somewhere outside, brought her back to the present.

"One more minute!" she yelled.

She tried to keep from looking at the woman's face, and in particular from looking into her still open, no-longer-gold eyes, while examining the dress. Even though the knife must've plunged through the dress's bodice, she saw no indication of a cut or tear in the fabric. In fact, the blood still leaking from the wound in the woman's chest somehow didn't stain the dress at all. The blood seemed to run off it like water on a lotus petal.

The dress is calling to me, she thought, and before she knew it, she was removing her own clothes in anticipation of putting it on.

"Why is it that women always take forever?" Jay grumbled while weighing a small stone in his hand. When Reginald turned and began lumbering toward another of its siblings, Jay lobbed the stone in the air. It landed with a clank on top of Reginald's headlamp, and the junkling spun around, looking for the rock's source.

Jay whistled innocently, picking at the dirt beneath his nails. "Need somethin', Reggie?"

The junkling whirred and sputtered angrily before returning its attention elsewhere.

Jay snorted and then cursed. "Quit looking at the goddamn statues, Supriya, and let's get a move on!" He marched toward the door, with an arsenal of complaints and frustrations ready, but when he got there he saw Supriya, naked and blood-covered, rolling around the half-naked dead body like it was a ragdoll, tugging at the dress at this angle and that. The jiggling flesh, dead and alive, along with Supriya's grunting and sudden almost rhythmic yanking spasms, and the sight of blood everywhere, especially the blood all over her Frankenstein-reconstructed left leg—it all came together in an image of a necrophilic nightmare that burned deep into Jay's brain.

He turned away and dry heaved. After catching his breath and giving himself a few seconds to ensure his convulsions were done, he walked over to the Reginald and the junklings gathered by the gate.

"Well, I think she's gone full-on crazy, Reggie. Which means I'm pretty much fucked."

Reginald stared with its hazy automotive lens and then turned its attention to the door.

"I wouldn't go over there. You might barf up a sprocket."

He really was fucked. In some ways, the last month had been the best days of his life, but as the role of the *masinisto* settled on Supirya, her infectious optimism had been slowly replaced by a controlling—no, domineering—demeanor and a growing sadism.

"I think your lady lord may have gone off the deep end," he said.

Reginald looked back at him and then shot toward him, swinging its license-plate-clad arm at Jay like an angry butcher.

"Whoa," Jay exclaimed, tripping and rolling in a clumsy backward somersault. "I take it back. She's as sweet as a blood-covered angel!"

The other junklings had turned and were doing their fast hobble-walk toward him.

"Can't you fuckers take a joke?"

He tried to dodge Reginald's attacks—the junklings were supposed to be escorting them on their escape, for fuck's sake—but as the others joined the attack, Jay found himself running in circles, juking this way and that. The junklings tripped with every feint and change of direction, but they kept coming. Jay's heart threatened to pound out of his chest. He had about another thirty seconds, maybe less, of this type of frantic scrambling before he'd be gassed and on his back on the mansion's lawn.

He took a few steps toward the mansion's door and the blood-filled marble room, but that couldn't be an exit. And crazy, naked Supriya might be even more dangerous than her band of junkyard henchmen. His only hope, then, was to leave Supriya and the whole scene behind and make it to the hatch. He gave another feint, hard to the left, so hard his left leg almost gave out on him, and then sped around the junklings toward the gate.

Two steps before he got to the gate, a shimmer appeared around its perimeter, and the gate became a door swinging wide, revealing the bloody marble room. His momentum carried him through the door, and Supriya slammed it shut behind him.

CHAPTER 15
NEW POWERS AND NEW COSTUMES

Jay's feet slipped out from under him as he hit the marble floor, slick with blood, and slid into a statue at the other end of the room. A Zeus-like, bearded statue looked down at him with contempt. Jay scrambled to get to his feet, but slipped, tried, and then slipped again. He grabbed onto the statue to pull himself up, but his hands were blood-slick now, too, and so was the lower part of the statue. The more frantically he moved, the more he found himself slipping and sliding. He rolled to his back, expecting Supriya to—to what? To do something. To hit him with something. But the Supriya he saw didn't resemble any Supriya he had been with before.

She stood over him in a pristine, white dress that fit her like it had been painted on her body. Her jet-black hair was wet and slicked back, and her skin shined like milky coffee. On the floor nearby was a pile of the *masinisto*'s Victorian battle clothes, and atop the pile was the crown.

"Oh, I like this so much better. Don't you think this role suits me?" she said, her voice like a cat's purr. "I'm the *gardistaro*, now."

Behind her, the door bulged and rang out with the sounds of the junklings trying to get inside.

"I had to take off the crown to put the dress on. I couldn't wear both. Sorry, I forgot you were out there."

Jay reached up to rub at a bump forming on his head, but seeing the blood on his hand, he thought better of it. "Uh. Apology accepted, I guess."

"Use the fountain to wash yourself off. It doesn't matter how dirty the water gets, it becomes clear again in a few seconds."

"What about your former death squad? They'll get through the door soon. It's just wood."

"You're right, of course. Let me try this again." She held up her hands so that her palms were facing the door. At first, nothing happened, and the pounding continued. Then the fuzzy air around the door's perimeter began to pop and become staticky before it reverted back to its previous fuzziness. "I think we're good now. The door leads somewhere else now."

"Somewhere where?"

"I'm not sure. I'm new to this role."

Jay scrubbed the blood off his hands in the fountain and thought about trying to clean off his jeans and shirt, but all he really wanted was to leave this room.

"Wherever it leads," he said, "it's got to be better than this shithole. Let's go."

With that, he opened the door and found a familiar sight: the sofa, rug, and ornate wallpaper of the sitting room.

Jay crashed on the sofa and stretched out his legs, wanting to let his exhaustion take him into oblivion, but his mind was still replaying the bloody scene in the marble room just minutes ago. He watched as Supriya walked through the room, inspecting a wall or piece of furniture and then parts of herself in turn, and occasionally looking up at nothing, or at something only she could see.

"I feel like in another life I made this room, but the memory is fading," Supriya said in a voice, that while still hers, had exchanged all of its previous hardness for the softness of a morning breeze. It even sounded like her voice surrounded him.

"Well, I sure as hell remember it. It's the damn maze where the doors keep leading back to the same room. Paul and I tore up several copies of this room. We marked up the walls, moved the sofas. And we even..." His eyes opened wide and a look of alarm took his face. He jumped up and started inspecting the crevices of the sofa, neck craned away like he expected to find something awful.

"What the hell are you doing?" Supriya asked.

Jay exhaled and sat back down, making space for her next to him, patting on the cushion several times to entice her to sit.

"We had to turn a few of these sofas into, uh, facilities of relief, if you know what I mean." He frowned. "By facilities of relief, I mean, like, toilet facilities. Hey, hey, hey. Don't look so disgusted. It wasn't this particular sofa. That's what I was checking. Not that you seemed too worried about getting covered with bodily fluids a few minutes ago. Sit. It's fine. I promise."

She sat and crossed her metal leg over her leg of flesh. Even her posture had changed, softened. She kept looking off at something beyond the walls and the ceiling. He waited for an explanation, but none seemed to be coming.

"What do you think of this sofa? Nice, isn't it?" he asked.

She nodded absently and then stood back up. She walked to one of the doors and slowly waved her right hand around its frame.

"Hey, now," Jay said. "Let's hang on a minute and get our bearings before we start adventuring off. I want your thoughts on this sofa. What would you think a sofa like this would fetch in the, uh, sofa marketplace?"

Her hand stopped mid-wave and she turned to him. "How much would the sofa cost? What kind of crazy question is that?"

"Humor me, Supes. Paul and I were thinking that we could make a fortune selling these things on account of this room spontaneously generating an endless supply. We were arguing about the price and..."

"I can feel someone," she interrupted. "I don't know how, but I feel a woman, wearing a painted mask of some kind. She's nearby. In a field by a broken statue. A giant statue, bigger than anything possible before it fell."

"Paul and I ran into a woman wearing a black robe with a creepy *Dia de los Muertos* skull painted on her face. Called herself Skull Girl. Threatened to kill me. Is that who you're talking about?"

"Yes. She's alone. I can feel her."

"Feel?"

"As soon as I put the dress on, it was like I had another sense. An awareness of this world and the people in it."

"This world? What the hell are you talking about, Supes?"

She frowned. "I don't know if I can explain it. I understood it as the *masinisto*, but those memories are slipping away. We're in the Patchwork World right now, and I can feel all of it. This room, and all the neighboring rooms and spaces... I can feel it all. There's a room with a ladder leading up to the cavern where we just came from. I can feel that room, almost like part of me is in it, and I can feel the cavern, also. That's how the woman before me, the past *gardistaro*, knew we were there. She could feel us. The cavern and the mansion are all part of the Patchwork World, but the Patchwork World is only the beginning. It's like we're in a parking garage below ground, and I can see everything on this level but nothing above or below. I can feel another room with stairs leading down, but I can't feel what's down there. I remember some of the entries in the *masinisto*'s journal referring to stairs that led to other worlds within the Between."

"That's among the strangest things I've ever heard," Jay said. "But for the last month I had a butler made out of old car parts, so at this point, I'll believe anything. If you can feel Skull Girl, what about Paul? Can you feel him?" Suddenly a wave of guilt overcame Jay. At first, after they had been separated, Jay had thought of Paul often, had worried about what had happened to him, but with each passing day, he had lost track of everything except Supriya and the mansion. Even, for a bit, the outside world, or what he thought of as the real world.

Supriya closed her eyes and took several deep breaths. "Tell me more about Paul," she said. "Uptight? A little quiet? A rule-follower?

Always doing what he thinks he's supposed to do, but feels trapped by the obligation to be responsible?"

Jay sat up and crossed his arms. "Trapped by obligation... Yeah, that's Paul. Exactly. The responsible older brother. Always the designated driver. You know he dreamed about being a literature professor, from the time we were little, but when the time came, he majored in accounting instead. Fucking accounting. I love him—you know, friend-ways, nothing gay—but it's exhausting to see him build all these walls, to imprison himself with responsibility that no one's asking him for. That said, if you need something, Paul's the one you call." He eyed her suspiciously. "I haven't told you any of this stuff. Where are you getting it?"

"I can feel a residue of him, if that's the right word. He was here, but now he's not. He's gone. I think I would know if he died. He could've gone down the stairs, to the next world. Or maybe he found a way back home."

"Paul sure as hell didn't go down a mysterious set of stairs. He doesn't have an adventurous bone in his body. The fucker got the chance to escape and took it. We gotta follow him. Can you feel the exit? We came in through a phony-library-bomb-shelter. Do you feel that place?"

"No. But I do feel what may be your room."

"My room?"

She walked to the door directly in front of the sofa and waved her hands around its frame. The frame became hazy, like a fog had appeared, limited to the door's outline. She opened the door, and it led to the room of stone with the altar where Jay had found the knife.

He jumped to his feet, knife in hand, expecting more of those ash dogs, but, walking into the room, all he found was the familiar corpse on the altar, only now all the flesh had vanished, leaving only a skeleton behind in a black outfit and boots.

"I think you need those clothes. I didn't have to wear the Victorian military suit when I was the *masinisto*, but it made me feel so much more complete when I had them on. Like I embraced the role, and it embraced me." She looked him up and down with a half frown. "The knife is your artifact, but the stained white t-shirt and blue jeans kill the whole *stelisto* persona. Plus, you're still covered in the past *gardistaro's* blood. Embrace your role. Put those on." She pointed at the altar.

Jay grumbled and poked at the skeleton. He started to argue, but Supriya had that look in her eyes that he'd seen over and over again during the past few weeks. Ultimately, she'd get her way. The only question was how much pain he caused himself between now and then.

He yanked on the skull, and it popped off in his hand. For a second he felt like he was holding his own skull, but the expected nausea and revulsion never came. The corpse had made him squeamish when he'd first encountered it with Paul, but now the sight of death had become commonplace, almost comforting in a morbid kind of way. He threw the skull into the corner of the room, snickering at the hollow *thonk* it made hitting the stone floor, and proceeded with the rest of the skeleton. The shirt and pants were all black, aside from stitched red, white, and yellow flowers. The black boots had flowers stitched on them as well.

"I'm gonna look like a mariachi. What's with the fucking flowers?"

"Just put it on."

He followed her instructions. The shirt fit a little tighter than he would've preferred, and he had to suck in his gut to keep the lower buttons from looking like they were about to burst. The pants fit like a glove, as did the boots. But those flowers...

"I feel ridiculous," he said.

"Now when I look at you, I see the *stelisto*. Although you do look a bit like a mariachi. A particularly sinister mariachi. Who likes very fitted clothing." She wiggled a finger at him. "Turn around. Fits nice in the butt."

He glared. "Fucking mariachi... Sinister, I'll take. You have to be a little sinister to survive this place. Enough of this clothing chitter-chatter. Let's figure out how to use your new powers to get the hell out of here. You said you couldn't sense a bomb shelter, or a concrete bunker full of bookshelves, right?"

"Right. The Patchwork World has hundreds of rooms, but I sense none like you're describing. What about the field with Skull Girl? Maybe we should go see her. Maybe she can help us."

"Remember, I said she threatened to kill me. I could probably talk her out of that. Probably. If not, I'm a lot tougher now than I was when we last met. And I have you. But I don't think we should be looking for more fights. We have no source of water or food. It's gonna get ugly real quick."

"What do you propose, then?"

Jay paced the stone floor of the *stelisto*'s chamber. "How about a tight passageway, like a cave passageway, and a door with a brazier next to it? Can you sense that?"

"A brassiere? There's a brassiere next to a door, like on the floor or something?"

Jay smirked. "No, Supes. Not a bra. A BRAY-ZEUR. A metal bowl that holds a flame. Like a torch that stays put."

Supriya got that far-away look again and then her eyes lit up with recognition. "I see a door with a metal torch thing next to it, and a hall that winds and leads into the darkness."

"That's it! Do that hand-wavy thing to the door here and let's go!" He ran to the door and pulled it shut, with one last look at the work-manship on the sofa's wooden legs—if Supriya could get them in and out easily, he and Paul could make the sofa business a reality. First thing's first, though. He jumped away from the door, nervous energy sending him back into his pacing of the room.

Supriya once again made the air around the door crackle, and then when she reopened the door, Jay saw the familiar sight of the brazier and the rough, narrow hallway.

"Follow me," he said. He grabbed the brazier and headed toward the false-library. The bouncing flame made the hallway seem to wobble. As they came through the passage that had been hidden behind the bookshelf, Jay worried that they'd find the metal door above gone, replaced by uninterrupted concrete, like before. Not only was the door there, it was open, and with the ladder back like they first had found it.

"Hallefuckinglujah," Jay exclaimed and ran to the ladder. "Ladies first."

"Hang on," she said. "I made false places like this as the *masinisto*. I want to look at it."

"False places? What the hell are you talking about?"

Supriya walked around the room, moonlight pouring in from the open hatch above. She touched the couch and then the bookshelf. She picked a book up off the floor and flipped through its blank pages. "I can't believe how real it feels, but it's all empty. It's a projection of the World Lens, like the elevator Frankie and I took down to the cavern. Overlapping pieces of other worlds, meant to draw us in." She dropped the book and looked up. "The night sky looks a bit fuzzy, doesn't it?" Supriya asked.

Overlapping pieces of other worlds? Fuzzy sky? Half the time he had no idea what Supriya was talking about.

She continued without waiting for his answer. "The World Lens needs to be adjusted periodically, or it gets out of alignment. Without a new *masinisto*, this will all collapse."

"Well then let's get the hell out of here. Paul probably thinks I'm dead, and I'm about to show up in his backyard with a superpowered girlfriend."

Supriya raised an eyebrow. "I'm your girlfriend?"

Jay stepped back and crossed his arms, the knife handle pressing into his left biceps as if reminding him of its presence, as if he might need it. "Well, shit. I don't know what the right label is, but we did live together for a month in the mansion like a married couple. A married couple where the wife likes to tie up her husband and..."

"Okay, okay. Enough of the married couple and husband stuff. I'm your magical-goddess-girlfriend. It's official. That makes you my evil-assassin-boyfriend. We're not telling my parents any time soon. Probably not my sisters, either. We'll see."

"I'm pretty good assassin boyfriend material," Jay said. "Fathers love me."

"Not fathers with the last name Reddy. But let's talk about this outside, tomorrow."

Jay held his hand out toward the ladder. "Be my guest." As she neared the top, he began to climb. "I see your costume didn't come with underwear."

"Pay attention to the ladder so you don't fall and kill yourself, you perv."

CHAPTER 16
KNOCKOUT OF THE YEAR

It took all of his strength for Paul to hold back tears as he saw the night sky and breathed in the warm air of home. Through the window of his kitchen he saw Julie, headphones on, bopping her head while washing dishes.

It was like he hadn't been gone at all. He ran to the backdoor, opening it with such force that it ricocheted off the kitchen wall.

"Look out there, Hercules," Julie said, glancing up with a smirk.

He took her in as if it had been years since he had seen her, as if he were taking his first breath of air after swimming up from the depths of a cold, dark sea. She still had her hair buzzed short, like in the dream, like the real night when those blue-gray eyes pierced right through him for the first time. He found himself unable to speak. He wanted to run to her, grab her, and hold her tight. Tell her how terrified he had been of never seeing her again.

She looked back down and dried off a knife with a dishtowel, oblivious that she had just gutted him with her eyes. "I think Minwoo's waiting on you to start the fight." She slid her headphones down so that they collared her neck. "Look. He poured me a glass of fancy champagne. Where's Jay? I thought I saw him walk into the backyard with you." She looked up at him, and again her eyes stared right through all of his layers. "Paul. Paul? Is something wrong? Why are your eyes so red?"

He swallowed and forced himself to take a breath. "Allergies. Must be the grass outside." A lump was growing in his throat, and the more he looked into Julie's eyes, the harder it was getting to swallow. So he hugged her.

Julie's arms splayed out, gloved hands covered with soap suds. "Okay there, loverboy. Something's wrong."

He tightened his hug and pressed his cheek into hers. There was no hiding his feelings from Julie. It didn't matter what excuse he made. But he couldn't tell her he'd really been gone for days, that he'd been attacked by an undead pack of dogs, that Jay might be lost forever. Fortunately, Julie gave him the out he couldn't make for himself.

"You'll tell me when you're ready. Unless it's about that intern at work with the big tits who gets all moon-eyed around you. Is this about little miss yoga instructor?"

Paul laughed and kissed her, hands cradling her face. "I have no eyes for any woman but you," he said. "Forever and ever. By the way, I love it when you taste like champagne."

With her index finger, she put a dollop of suds on the tip of his nose. "I always taste like champagne. It's a curse to be so delicious," she said. "So is it work, then? Your parents? My parents?"

"I thought you said I could tell you when I'm ready."

She responded with a classic Julie gesture: head cocked, eyes looking up, rapid faux-innocent blinks. "You know I'd never pry."

"Yeah, sure."

"Well, Min-woo is in there waiting, so you better move along, mister. But first, how about another of those champagne kisses?"

He put his forehead against hers and looked into her eyes. As he kissed her again, their eyes stayed open. It should've been a quiet, intimate moment where a thousand little thoughts and emotions flowed between them wordlessly, but movement in Paul's periphery caught his attention. Caught Julie's as well.

"Is that Jay?" she said, looking at the bearded, black-clad figure walking from their backyard around the side of their house. "And when did he grow a beard? And who is that stunning creature with him?"

Paul rubbed his eyes but the strange sight didn't change. It was Jay, all right, or at least it looked like Jay, but somehow the two-day unshaven gruff he'd had when they got separated had turned into a full beard. And the outfit? Black coat and pants with ... were those embroidered flowers? The woman was the biggest mystery. She was Indian or Pakistani, almost as tall as Jay, and built like an athlete. Her left leg was mechanical but unlike any prosthetic he'd ever seen. It had a fantastical, impossible look to it, with gears and a cluster of pistons where the muscles of her calf should be. The white dress she wore was more astonishing, still, seemingly both reflective and translucent. Like the dress the *gardistaro* had been wearing.

"The beard is new," Paul said. "Relatively. I have no idea about the woman. With Jay, there's no knowing."

"Why are you still friends with him again?"

"Hey, now. Without Jay, there'd be no me and you. I know he can be a little, what's the word, exasperating at times, but..." He waved his hands around a bit, waiting for his mouth to finish the sentence, but nothing else came to him.

Julie rolled her eyes and went back to the dishes. "At least it looks like he's found some female attention, although I probably owe it to my gender to warn her."

"You'll do no such thing. And leave the dishes. I'll do them after the boxing match."

"You won't. You'll have a bunch of drinks and then fall asleep."

"That's a definite possibility. Then I'll do them in the morning."

"The roaches will have a buffet all night. Nope. I can't sleep with dirty dishes sitting out. And you spent all day landscaping, so I'm guilted into doing something domestic." Without looking back at him she motioned toward the living room door. "Now get out of here."

Paul had a moment of terror when he entered his living room and found a horned, buffalo-headed woman standing, waiting for him, but it was the stupid *First Mother* statue. After catching his breath, he said, "How goes it, Min-woo?"

Like usual, Min-woo had chosen to sit in their reproduction Eames plywood chair with his legs crossed underneath him. With his heavily starched shirt—purple paisley this evening—and rigid posture, it should've looked uncomfortable. It would've been uncomfortable had it been anyone else, but Min-woo operated with his own brand of effortless precision.

"You were taking too long, *dongsaeng*, so I unpaused it," Min-woo said with his over-emphasized southern accent. He often called Paul *dongsaeng*, which was the familiar term for little brother in Korean. "It's one of the undercard fights. A mismatch designed to highlight this little Peruvian boy's skills, but he's looking a little sloppy if you ask me, and you didn't, but I did, so there you are. I also started the champagne without you. As I poured a glass for Julie, we discussed just how out of your league she is. Charitable, really, that a creature as wonderful as she would give herself to you." Min-woo's eyes went wide. "Did you see how he set up that uppercut? Maybe the boy has skills after all. Have a drink. And wipe the whipped cream or whatever it is off your nose."

"Thanks a million, Min-woo," Paul said, running the back of his hand across his face.

Min-woo had brought his black iron champagne bucket (with attached stand; probably custom-made), including several crystal flutes which hung underneath. With the champagne and ice, it must've weighed fifty pounds or more, and Paul chuckled at the image of the diminutive Min-woo lugging it across the street. Paul picked up the open bottle—French, unrecognizable to any of them but Min-woo—and poured himself a glass while staring at the door, waiting for Jay and his mystery guest to knock while Min-woo continued filling the air with a blow-by-blow recount of the action on the television screen.

Jay's signature shave-and-a-haircut knock came from the door.

Paul opened the door, stepped onto the porch, and closed the door behind him.

Jay looked almost unrecognizable, as much because of the outfit and beard as the relaxed confidence in the way he stood. No stooped shoulders. No awkward thumbs in his pockets.

"Now that was a fucking adventure, not that you'd really know seeing as you left me," Jay said with a crooked smirk that didn't match the hard stare from his eyes. "Meet Supriya."

The woman at Jay's side stepped toward Paul and brought her hand up. He reached out to shake her hand, but she turned the gesture into a little wave, and so Paul was left with his hand hanging in the air awkwardly for a few seconds.

"Good evening," she said in a voice that had the same eerie smoothness as the *gardistaro*'s, despite the heavy accent.

"Nice to meet you, Supriya," Paul said. "You look just like the *gardistaro*. Except for the bionic leg and numerous other physical differences that it's probably not socially acceptable to list."

"That's 'cuz she is the fucking *gardistaro*," Jay said. "The new *gardistaro*, anyway. Don't ask what happened to the old one."

"He stabbed her in the heart," Supriya said matter-of-factly, as if the death was a minor detail.

Jay shrugged his shoulders. "Yeah, Supes and I had to learn to play by a different set of rules down there." Jay looked up at the crescent moon and then back at Paul. "It looks like it's the same night we left."

"It's not just the same night, it's only minutes later," Paul said. "I'd guess it was maybe two days for me, but judging by that beard, it looks like it was longer for you."

"A few weeks," Supriya said. "We lost track of the days. Do you mind if I borrow your phone? I need to call my roommate and tell her I'm not coming home tonight, or she'll be worried."

"Uh, sure," Paul said. "But before we go inside... I haven't told Julie anything. Min-woo's watching boxing in the living room, and I haven't told him anything either. Do we tell the media? The police? The FBI? NASA? What's the protocol here?"

"Hell if I know," Jay said. "But we're not going to figure it out here on the porch. I say we have a few drinks, get a real-world night's sleep under our belts, and talk it through in the morning. Deal?"

"Deal, I guess?" Paul said.

Min-woo did a double take as they came in the front door. After pausing the action, he said, "That's quite a new look for you, Jay. A pansy pistolero? A buttercup bandolero? Whichever, you're giving off this old-west-assassin-loverboy vibe. I appreciate a man who feels no obligation whatsoever to conform to any predefined style. I didn't know you had it in you." Min-woo hopped from his perch on the chair and walked up to Supriya, who towered over him by almost a foot. "You boys and these ladies you don't deserve..." He examined Supriya from head to toe, giving a surprised "How marvelous!" at the sight of her mechanical leg. "I'm Min-woo Kim from across the street. If you tell me you're a goddess come down from the heavens, I just might believe you."

"I am, indeed, a goddess," Supriya said with a wry smile. "But not from the heavens. New Delhi by way of Brooklyn. I'm Supriya Reddy."

Min-woo poured the last of the champagne bottle into a crystal flute and handed it to Supriya. With a wink, he said, "Cheers, Goddess Supriya."

"I'll take one while you're at it," Jay said, flopping into the middle of the sofa, directly in front of the television.

"By all means, make yourself at home," Paul said.

Jay, ignoring Paul's comment, waved Supriya toward the spot next to him, and said, "Min-woo, here, is a nut when it comes to boxing. And he always brings his fancy French stuff. I'm more of a Mexican beer guy, myself, but if he's gonna bring it, I feel obligated to drink it."

Min-woo toweled off the empty bottle and popped the cork of the second, which was buried neck-deep in the ice.

"Another for you, Paul?" he said.

Paul shook his head. "It was delicious, but a little straight whiskey is what I need right now."

They watched the next fight in silence, aside from Min-woo's commentary. Paul looked at his second (or was it third?) whiskey sitting on the coffee table and then at Jay and Supriya next to him on the couch. After the reality-defying experience they shared, how could they all sit there and not talk about it? His mind began to flip through scenes: the sitting room maze, the altar, the field with the broken colossus, Corinne, or an alternate Corinne with her Skull Girl costume over armor. She had called that place *the Between*.

His eyelids drooped, and the modern, clean-lined sofa he sat on became the sitting room's antique sofa. The television dissolved, all the room's features dissolved, and identical doors appeared on each of the room's four walls. He tried to turn his head toward Jay, but his neck wouldn't move. Behind him, he heard a door open, something scratching and clicking on the floor, but he couldn't stand. His body was locked in an immovable state as the scratches, the footsteps, grew closer, until they were right behind him, hot breath on the back of his neck, and then a voice that came with the stench of mold and death.

You haven't escaped, Paul Prentice. Come back down and be with me forever.

He jolted awake. Jay and Supriya glanced over at him and then turned back to watch the boxing match. Min-woo seemed not to notice, leaning toward the action on the screen.

"I can't not talk about this," Paul said. "It's too fucking big. I started to fall asleep, and then I'm back in the damn sitting room maze. The stupid sofa and the doors and then..." He let the words trail off. The worst of it all wasn't what he'd seen in the Between; it was what the Between had reawakened in Paul's mind.

"The sitting room maze was nothing, which you'd know if you hadn't run off after that crazy lady," Jay said. "Ain't that right, Supes?"

"I wouldn't say the maze was nothing, but it wasn't the mansion in the cave," she said.

Paul tried to sound calmer than he felt. "What's this mansion? Cave? And you told me to go after Skull Girl, Jay," Paul said.

They all looked toward Min-woo, but Min-woo seemed only to have attention for the fight. His commentary continued, "Do you see how when Jimenez retreats, he goes straight back with his chin high? He may be able to get away with it against scrubs like whatever-his-name-is, but that's going to bite him down the road if his coaches don't train it out of him."

"He's a bottle in and oblivious," Paul said.

Over the next half hour, they traded stories—most of them coming from Jay and Supriya. At first, they all kept looking over at Min-woo and being careful with their words, but it became clear that Paul was right. Min-woo was off in his own little world, recounting the action like he was part of the broadcast team.

The strangest thing to Paul, hearing Jay and Supriya's stories, wasn't the stories themselves. It was the transformation in Jay—and presumably Supriya—and the confidence with which they talked about their "roles" in the mystery world they had found. Instead of feeling trapped, like Paul had, Jay and Supriya talked like conquerors retelling their conquest of a new land.

When Julie walked in, all the stories stopped.

"I'm a little perplexed by the new look, Jay," she said.

"I told him he looked like a prissy pistolero," Min-woo said without turning from the television, making Paul wonder just how oblivious he had been to their prior discussion. "Or, maybe I used the word pansy."

Julie and Supriya exchanged smiles and names, and then Julie said, "That is an astonishing dress. What's the material? It's heavenly. A little sheer. Your nipples are staring at me, dear. Would you like a scarf or something?"

Paul shot Julie a frown. A single glass of wine was all it took to obliterate Julie's limited verbal filter. If she thought it, she said it.

Min-woo refilled Julie's glass, looked at Supriya, and took a dramatic, deep breath like he was inhaling the experience of viewing Supriya. "It would be a crime to cover that dress, nipples or not. We all have nipples, my Julie. I'm sure yours are wonderful as well. Drink some more champagne and join us."

"Main event's on," Paul said as he pulled a startled Julie next to him on the cramped sofa. He drained his whiskey in a single gulp, and right as the opening round's bell sounded, fell fast asleep.

Paul awoke to Min-woo and Julie jumping around the living room, cheering a spectacular, come-from-behind knockout. Or, at least, to Paul's groggy eyes, that's what Min-woo was cheering about. Julie, on the other hand, seemed to be cheering on Min-woo's dancing jubilation, a giddy tap dance routine.

"We just saw the knockout of the year!" Min-woo exclaimed and then danced over to the sofa and started slapping Paul's knee. "Get up and celebrate! You slept through the knockout of the year! Here it is in slow-motion!"

Paul shooed Min-woo's hand away and looked around for, but didn't find, a glass of water. The television screen crawled frame-by-frame, a looping overhand right nearing an unsuspecting chin. The impact was like hitting the power button on a machine and having it shut instantly off. No stumbling, staggering, et cetera. No catching the fall before the head bounced off the canvas.

"That's brain damage," Paul said, suddenly queasy. "You're cheering about that guy getting brain damage."

Min-woo didn't seem to listen. Julie giggled again at Min-woo and then sighed.

"That's it for me. I'm going to bed," she said.

Paul started to grab the empty glasses off the coffee table, but the first one slipped from his hand and rolled onto the rug. At least it didn't break. "What happened to Jay and, uh, what's-her-name?"

"They went home," Julie said. "I'll get the glasses. You're drunk. Say goodnight to Min-woo."

"I'm not drunk," Paul said. He'd only had the champagne and a little whiskey, but he was so exhausted that he might as well have had twice as much.

Julie hugged Min-woo and kissed him on the cheek. "Thanks for the champagne," she said to him.

Min-woo said, "I'm adopting you as my sister. Is that okay with you? Can you adopt a sister?"

"Enough of the love fest," Paul said. "Need help with your giant, iron chalice, Min-woo?"

"I never turn down offers of free manual labor."

Julie gave a final goodnight, grabbed the empty glasses, and left through the kitchen.

Paul picked up the champagne bucket and propped its stand on his shoulder as if he were carrying an oversized musket.

When they walked out the front door, Min-woo said, "I overheard you talking about the Between. I lost two years to it during undergrad and would recommend staying away, but if you kids want, I can provide some hints and save you some time and frustration."

Paul stumbled over his own feet, spilling ice water down the front of him. "The Between? You know about the Between?"

Min-woo stopped in the middle of the street and stared up at the moon. "A fellow student introduced me to the Between during undergrad, and I became so obsessed by it that I nearly flunked out." He shivered and closed his eyes.

Paul set the iron champagne bucket on the street and rubbed his shoulder.

"This was back when I was trying to discover who I really was," Min-woo said. He opened his eyes and looked at Paul. "The Between was like an addictive, psychedelic drug. An escape from a world that didn't seem right to a hidden world where I could step into heroic and villainous roles at will."

"I can't believe we're talking about the Between so matter-of-factly," Paul said. "What about—" He started rambling questions one after another, interrupting himself before Min-woo could answer. A wave of vertigo swept over him, and he sat down in the middle of the street. He had discovered the entrance to an alternative, fantasy world in his backyard, and immediately after returning, his neighbor said he'd known about it for years. To Paul, it was like the laws of Newtonian physics had suddenly failed to hold and the reaction of the world was, yeah we've had another set of rules all along—did nobody tell you?

"Up off the street, *dongsaeng*," Min-woo said. "You've had too much whiskey. We can talk about the Between tomorrow. It's not going anywhere." He pointed at the champagne bucket. "Now finish this last chore and crawl into bed with that beautiful wife of yours."

"But..."

"But, nothing. We'll talk tomorrow. I have some errands to do during the day, but my evening is open. I'll escort you into the Between and dazzle you with my knowledge."

CHAPTER 17
JAY'S LATE NIGHT PHONE CALL

The buzzing phone on his nightstand jolted Paul out of a dreamless sleep.

"We've gotta go back!" Jay exclaimed and started talking so loudly through the phone that Paul had to hold it several inches away from his ear. Julie rolled over and pulled a pillow over her head.

Paul squinted at the bright display on his phone. 2 a.m. Only two hours or so since they left. He trudged into the walk-in closet and shut the door behind him.

"Slow down, Jay. What's going on?"

"Supriya talked to her roommate."

"I know. She called on my phone."

"No, man. She got her roommate's voicemail when she called from your phone. I mean she just talked to her five minutes ago."

"Talked to who?"

"Supriya's roommate."

"Why are you telling me about Supriya's roommate?"

"If you'd quit interrupting, you'd already know."

Paul sat hard on the closet floor and dropped his forehead into his hand. "It's 2 in the morning, Jay."

"I know damn well what time it is. Now fucking listen to me.

We're over at my house, and Supriya finally gets ahold of her roommate. Apparently Anika—that's her roommate's name—apparently Anika was at some dance club and couldn't hear her phone ringing. So Supriya finally gets through, you know, to tell her not to worry that she's not coming home tonight. And, this is the fucked up part. Anika says that Supriya's standing right next to her. She thinks it's a fucking prank or something. So Supriya—the Supriya at my house—says to put this other Supriya on the phone, and holy fucking shit it's another goddamn Supriya. I listened to the whole thing. The other Supriya was laughing like it was a crazy joke, and then they started quizzing each other with facts only the real Supriya would know, and they both fucking knew them. They started talking faster and faster, jumping between English and Indian."

"Hindi."

"Whatever. They were speed talking in Indian and both freaking out until Supriya—my Supriya—hung up. I had to block Anika's number because she kept trying to call back. What the fuck, man? What the actual fuck?"

"Hold on," Paul said, sitting up. One of Julie's dresses hung into his face. He batted it away like it was an attacking mosquito and said, "There are two Supriyas now?"

"Yes. Two goddamn Supriyas! I think we took my Supriya out the wrong exit. That's why we've gotta go back. You gotta come with me. You owe it to me for abandoning me."

"Like hell I'm going back there. And I didn't abandon you. Shit. Maybe I did. Anyway. Calm down. We have to think this through." Two Supriyas? The wrong exit? "Maybe you're right about the wrong exit, Jay. Remember what I was saying earlier tonight about Corinne not remembering being my girlfriend? You spent almost as much time with her back in high school as I did, but she didn't remember being friends with you either. She said we've all come from different pasts. That the others—presumably the others like us who she had met in the Between—that they all came from different pasts. Meaning they came from other versions of the world. Or something like that."

Jay gave a little growl. "I still can't believe that damn Skull Girl is Corinne. If she doesn't remember me, there's got to be some crazy parallel world shit going on, because I'm one memorable mother-fucker. But that ain't what's important. What's important is that our world now has two Supriyas. That's one too many goddamn Supriyas! I've gotta take her back."

"I hear you, but don't do anything until tomorrow evening. Min-woo overheard us, and after you left he told me he knows all about the Between. He said he knows it like the back of his hand."

"You're shitting me."

"No. He said he'd tell us all its secrets. Let's wait and see what he knows."

"What's his number? I'll call him right now."

"No, Jay. Get some rest and we'll figure it out tomorrow. We're all exhausted and need the sleep. Don't do anything rash. Min-woo's coming over tomorrow evening. We'll sort it out then, and if we need to call in the military, we'll do it."

"We can't call in the fucking military. We're on our own. Supes and I are going back now."

"Tomorrow evening."

Jay's voice took on a far-off sound as if he were holding the phone away from his face. "It may just be us, Supes."

"What, Jay? Hello? Come on, don't do any—"

"We'll wait for you in the *stelisto*'s chamber. The stone room with the altar in the middle, remember? I'm assuming Min-woo will know how to get there. We'll wait for a bit, and if you don't show, we're going back up to the cavern. Maybe with Supriya's *gardistaro* powers she can open a door into her elevator." Jay cleared his throat, or maybe it was a growl. "If you weasel out, maybe I'll see you in the next life."

"Weasel out? Goddamnit, Jay! What do you mean the next life?"

The line went dead.

Paul leaned back and was surrounded by Julie's dresses, elimi-nating what little light was in the closet. His mind spun, incoherently trying to make sense of everything, trying to think of what to do next.

But his exhaustion overcame him, and on the floor of the closet, he fell asleep again.

CHAPTER 18
HIDING SOMETHING MORE INSIDE

Supriya paced back and forth in Jay's kitchen, trying not to think about the call with Anika and the conversation with the other Supriya, the *wrong* Supriya. She tried not to wonder why her *gardistaro* dress had begun losing its luster, or why her prosthetic knee's *click-click-clicking* was now accompanied by a sandpaper grinding sound. "Can you hear that?" she had asked Jay, but he was fiddling with one of his boots, trying to cut out the embroidery with that blue knife of his.

"I don't hear anything."

She could hear it, and she could feel it, too, like a hesitation in each step. She had taken the leg off and tried to diagnose the problem, but the more she looked at the knee, the more foreign its machinery appeared. She remembered the act of building it, back in her workroom, the *masinisto's* workroom, but she no longer remembered how she built it or how it worked. The memories of the past *masinistos* were no help, either, because they had faded from her mind almost completely.

Even the *gardistaro's* memories, which had been force-inserted into her head only hours before, had grown hazy. The longer she had been out of the Between, the more its effects on her seemed to slide away.

Which would have been fine—welcomed, even—if not for the horrors knocking at her door, eager to fill the empty space within her.

Death

Frankie had been the beginning, when she was innocent.

Guilt

Then she became *not* innocent.

Shame

She had killed people.

Deathguiltshame

She had *killed* people!

DEATHGUILTSHAME

Her body started to shake. She grabbed at the counter to keep her balance. The full weight of it hadn't really settled in yet, but she could feel it probing within, deciding where it would take up residence.

"We have to go," she said. "Now! I don't want to be in this wrong world any longer than I have to!"

It will follow you, from the wrong world to the right.

She dug her fingernails into her scalp until it hurt.

Jay looked up from his seat at the cluttered kitchen table. He wasn't wearing his *stelisto* attire. In fact, he wasn't wearing much at all: chalky white boxer shorts and a stained undershirt. His left arm was covered with hash-mark scars. He dropped the boot onto the table and let out an exasperated sigh.

"Five more minutes, Supes," Jay said. "I've gotta fix these goddamn boots. The stitching irritates my calves. There's about a four-inch region between where my socks end and the top of the boots. Whoever made these boots didn't consider the damn sock gap. Look at this." He tried to show her the inside of a boot and continued on talking as if he were oblivious of the incredulous glare she was giving him. "I thought about using duct tape—you know, you can fix anything with duct tape—but I think the tape's lack of breathability will make me sweat more, which in turn will ruin the adhesive quality of the tape, and before long, my boots will be full of sticky, duct-tape spaghetti and duct-tape residue."

She stormed out of the kitchen and made her way to his

bedroom, the grinding of her knee like an angry bee trailing her from the previous room. In a drawer in his closet, she found what she was looking for.

When she re-entered the kitchen, Jay had the knife inside a boot, holding the blade pencil-wise, performing surgery. She slapped the wadded up ball of fabric down on the table, making him miss the little red loop of thread he was going for.

"Longer socks," she said with a growl that was all Supriya and not the least bit *gardistaro*. "Problem solved. Now get your ass dressed and let's go."

As Jay changed into his costume in his kitchen—changed in his kitchen of all places!—Supriya tried to keep her mind distracted by examining Jay's house. When they had pulled up in his truck, she thought he was playing a joke on her. One of those groan-worthy Jay-jokes that wasn't funny to anyone but Jay.

The neighborhood, somewhere deep east of downtown, looked like it had been put into a giant oven and left to bake for, oh, a couple decades. None of the lawns had any living grass, and what few trees stood before the houses looked like they had rained down most of their leaves as tears of misery. The houses, themselves, showed all ranges of disrepair, and every set of windows sat behind rusting jail-cell bars.

Jay had opened the chain-link gate with a bowed head and a wink as if he were presenting her with his grand manor, something on par with the graveyard mansion they had left behind. For the umpteenth time in the last few weeks, she wondered what her parents would think upon meeting this peculiar, gangly, non-Indian man of uncertain employment with whom she had become intimately involved. They'd think she was the one playing the joke. Her father would refuse to shake Jay's hand, and her mother would do what her mother did any time she encountered something about the world she couldn't tolerate: she'd act as if Jay didn't exist. Even if he stood right in front of her.

No amount of explanation could prepare them for Jay.

Could she even explain the match to herself?

When Jay had opened his front door, she saw that he had, indeed, been playing a joke. Just not the one she suspected. The house's interior differed so completely from its appearance on the outside that it felt like she had walked through a *gardistaro* gateway into a completely different house. But of course, only she could've made that possible.

The entrance led directly into an open space, divided by a bar into a kitchen and a living area. The floors were covered by wide, gray slats of wood that looked like they had lived an earlier part of their life in another building, before being sanded, stained, and polished. The bar and the kitchen countertops were made of rough-hewn concrete, and the wood of the vaulted ceiling was painted black with exposed ductwork and a big, metal i-beam stretching across its length. The furniture and the kitchen appliances looked old but thoughtfully chosen and restored.

She had given Jay a perplexed look, standing there with the front door open, and he had pushed her—actually shoved her—inside.

"Don't want the local riff-raff getting a glimpse of my pride and joy, here." He shrugged and took on a kind of embarrassed look. "I know it ain't as fancy as Paul's place, but I'm working on it. This neighborhood's gonna be top dollar in five years or so, mark my word. Maybe ten."

"You did all this? It's..." She hadn't known how to describe it. The house was like Jay himself, rough around the edges but hiding something more inside.

Jay, now in the black outfit of the *stelisto*, caught her eye and gave her that crooked grin of his. The grin, an acknowledgment of an inside joke. Only this joke was the size of the whole world. No, bigger. The size of all of the outworlds and the Between, too. The shared joke, the secret in Jay's expression, just for her, was that none of it could touch them. Not the monsters of the Between, not the death of

Frankie, not the presence of her dopplegänger. Not as long as they stuck together.

She looked at him standing there, all in black, leaning against a metal column at the end of the counter like it had been built to serve only the purpose of supporting him. She looked at him and didn't care whether her parents understood—or if she even understood, for that matter. She wondered if, maybe, before risking life and limb again, maybe another ten or fifteen minutes of pleasure wouldn't hurt. Show this *wrong world* a thing or two.

"You gonna stand there looking at the merchandise, or you gonna open one of your magic doorways?" he asked with a wink.

She answered in her smooth as silk *gardistaro* voice, "Now who's in the hurry, Mr. Jay-the-*stelisto*?"

"That's Mr. Jay-the-*stelisto*-Esquire, baby."

"Esquire? I didn't know you were an attorney."

"Attorney? Is that what esquire means?"

All thoughts of a quick rendezvous in his bedroom vanished. "Nevermind. I'll open a gateway." Supriya crossed her arms and stared at the closed pantry door, waiting for the familiar moment when the door seemed to split into thousands of copies, all layered atop one another. As *gardistaro*, she could see the alternative paths through doors that others couldn't see and choose which path would remain real. She hadn't figured out all the strange rules of this ability, but connecting two existing doors was second nature.

At least, it had been in the Between. In the real world—if this was, in fact, a real-world—there were too many potential destinations. It all became a bowl full of noodles in her head. She tried to make the connections, to make a direct link between the pantry's doorway and Paul's front door, or at least to something in the vicinity.

Did it work? Did she even make a connection? She twisted the pantry doorknob and pulled it open. Jay's scattered assortment of tuna fish cans and half-empty cereal boxes stared back at her.

"It's not working," she said, closing the door. She tried again, concentrating so hard she could feel her face turning red, but trying harder caused the noodles in her head to multiply until she became so disoriented that she had to grab a chair to keep from falling. "I can't connect this door to anything," she said. "Too many possibilities. It's all a mess."

Jay examined the pantry door, knocked a few times on its surface, moved it back and forth on the hinges. "Too many possibilities, eh? Do you have to start with a door, or can you do that hand-wavy thing and make an opening right next to the kitchen table?"

Supriya considered this for a second and shook her head. "I have to start with a real door, and connect to another real door." She let go of the chair, stood tall, and took a deep breath. "At least I think so. Let's see if I can do it without using real doors." She traced a rectangle in the air. When nothing happened, she scowled and glared at the empty space next to the table, and then drew another rectangle, an angry rectangle.

A fuzzy-edged gateway appeared in the air—two gateways, really —but only a few inches across and connecting space just a few feet apart. A wave of exhaustion flowed through her. So much effort for so little. Creating gateways in the Between, from real door to real door, connecting long distances, had been much easier.

"That's all I can do," she said. "It's not going to get us back. I might be able to make them bigger, but they'd have to be pretty close together. It's exhausting without using real doors."

Jay gave a flippant shrug and said, "You're right, it's worthless."

She glared at him and made another of the *worthless* mini-gateways, connecting the space above Jay's head with a space above his kitchen counter. Half of Jay's salt shaker, cleaved clean through by the gateway, fell on Jay's head, exploding in a plume of salt.

"Worthless? I didn't say it was worthless," she said. "You're worthless!" Tears flooded her eyes, more out of frustration at her suddenly limited ability than anger toward Jay. It was as if the great clarity of purpose had suddenly left, leaving her empty and weak, smaller than she had been before finding the Between in the first place, vulnerable to the guilt waiting for its opportunity to fill her and take over.

Jay rubbed his hand back and forth in his hair, sending salt all over the floor. "A salt scrub is good for your hair, right?" he said with a smirk. When she didn't laugh, his face softened. He reached his hand out and wiped a tear from each of her cheeks, using a flick of his thumb, like flicking a switch. "No time for tears, beautiful. It'll all come back." He grabbed his truck keys from the counter next to the bottom half of the salt shaker. "We'll go down in Paul's backyard the old fashioned way, and be back to ass-kickin' before you know it. We'll get back to your elevator, and your magic will work, and we'll be in Supriyaville in no time."

"How do you know it will work if it didn't before?"

"A hunch. The door to Paul's backyard didn't work until we came back in our roles, or for Paul, when the old *gardistaro* got him back there. Maybe you have to play the game, babe."

She breathed in the smell of smoldering wood that seemed to surround him when he wore the *stelisto*'s costume. "Let's do it," she said. As he stepped toward the door, she said, "Hang on. You're forgetting something." She opened the refrigerator and took out two beers, tossing one to him.

———

Beer splashed out of the can in Supriya's hand as Jay accelerated hard, breaking loose the truck's rear end into a sweeping fishtail. "You're going to get us killed!" she exclaimed and smacked him in the shoulder with the back of her left hand. "Look at the mess you've made. No, don't look. Watch the road. This is a residential area! What the hell are you trying to do!"

Thump-thump. A shudder ran through the truck.

"I think I crushed some kid's Big Wheel. That'll teach 'em not to leave it in the street. Life lesson." Jay chuckled, but there was no humor in his voice. The closer they got to Paul's house, and the entrance to the Between, the more Supriya could see the *stelisto*'s malevolence return in Jay's eyes.

She could feel a change in herself, too. A growing perception, like a sixth sense, of the interconnections of the places in this world, this outworld. The *gardistaro* sense, not yet strong enough to turn those interconnections into a physical gateway, but growing stronger the closer they got to the entrance of the Between. The bigger change was the return of the *gardistaro*'s emotional detachment. The guilt of everything they'd done, the pain of Frankie's death, even her initial fear of going back—the feelings were all still there, but external somehow, separated from her by a thickening skin of calm.

Jay looked at her out of the corner of his eye and his lips curled into the hint of a grin. She felt herself grin back. This connection between them, was it love between the real Jay and the real Supriya, or was it a scripted partnership between their roles? Whatever the answer, she could feel it now and hold onto it.

"I've been meaning to ask you something," he said, and she could feel in the tone of his voice that he felt it, too. "It's something that came to me back in the cavern."

She put her hand on his arm. "What is it?"

He looked off and nodded, finally slowing the truck down to a slightly less unreasonable 45 miles per hour. Then he said, "When you were the *masinisto*, did you ever think..." He cocked his head a bit like he was searching for the right words. "Did you ever think about having, like, oh ... eight or ten junklings combine together to make a mega-junkling? Like in those old Japanese robot cartoons?"

Anger broke through her wall of calm. "Japanese robot cartoons?! What the hell are you talking about?!"

"You didn't watch those?" Jay cut a corner through someone's yard, smashing a row of bushes. "A missed opportunity, that's what. If I'm ever the *masinisto*, I'm making a mega-junkling. I'm making my own Voltron!"

With a screech, Jay slid the truck into an abrupt stop in front of Paul's house, causing Supriya's beer to splash onto the windshield, the dash, and her dress.

So much for that moment of connection.

"At first I worried about how much you drink, but I've found that you spill at least as much as makes it down your throat," she said. "I just prefer you not spill my drinks."

"No time for chit-chat, Supes," Jay said as he jumped out and slammed the door behind him. Supriya crossed her arms and watched as he jogged past her door and kept going toward Paul's backyard without once looking over his shoulder.

"And they say chivalry is dead," Supriya said, pushing her door open so hard it bounced back and almost hit her in the face. With a snarl that pierced through the *gardistaro* calm, she jumped out and slammed the door, and then opened and slammed it again when the noise failed to get Jay's attention. Who cared if it was 3 in the morning? "Oh, my parents are going to love him."

CHAPTER 19
TRUST, BUT VERIFY

Paul sat up straight at hearing a dull thud from outside. Something grabbed his face and wrapped around his neck. He reached up, yanked, and found himself covered in a pile of clothing. Julie's dresses. Had he fallen asleep in the closet? He stood and banged his head against the hanging rod, sending wire hangers spilling to the wooden floor.

When he walked out of the closet, Julie said, "What in the hell were you doing in there? I'm going to sleep on the living room couch. You're making too much noise."

He kissed her on the forehead. "No, I'll go to the couch. Sorry."

In the living room, he pushed apart the blinds and saw Jay's truck once again parked on the street in front of his house. The thud had been the hatch in the backyard. He had the sudden urge to run into the backyard, throw open the hatch ... and then what? Go back in? Alone?

He looked back at the couch and then at *First Mother* watching him from the corner. No chance he was going to sleep again. So he poured a bowl of cereal and milk and sat at the kitchen table, pushing the little barrels of frosted wheat around with a spoon until they disintegrated into a grayish muck. He wasn't in the mood for coffee, either, but he made some anyway.

Julie trudged in wearing bunny slippers and a bathrobe she had stolen from a swanky New York City hotel several years ago when they were dating. "Are you trying to wake up the neighborhood, or just me?" she asked.

"I have to tell you something."

She poured two cups of coffee, placed one in front of Paul, and sat down in the chair on the opposite side of the table. "Is this about what upset you earlier?"

"Yes," he said. "But you won't believe any of it. I'm not sure I believe it, myself, which is the scariest part. The only explanation that makes sense is that I'm losing my mind."

"I don't know that you ever had a full mind, dear." She smirked playfully, but then reached out and grabbed both of his hands. "Oh, honey. You're shaking."

"I'm not shaking. Or maybe I am. Shit. I don't know how to explain any of this."

"Don't worry about how it sounds. Just talk."

Paul let go of her hands, stood, and walked to the sink. He pointed out the window. "Over there, near the bug zapper, I found a door in the ground that leads to, like, some other world, or something. That's where Jay found Supriya. We got split up, and I was down there for a couple days, but he was there for like a month. But no time passed when we came back. No time here. We both experienced all the time down there."

Julie blinked several times but otherwise made no expression.

He continued. "And now Jay and Supriya are back down there because there are too many Supriyas, and he has to get her to the world where she came from and not this one, and I abandoned him once already, and I didn't go with him again, and I feel like I should've gone with them because of how long we've been friends. He wouldn't have let me go down again by myself. He wouldn't have abandoned me. But I don't want to go back. The thought of it is terrifying, and so I'm fucking abandoning him yet again, but he's too goddamn impulsive, and it was like a choice between supporting him or staying with you. And I couldn't leave you, right?"

Julie took a long sip from her coffee. She tilted her head slightly to the right and stared at him with her left eye. That was her poker look. Her I'm-dissecting-you-like-a-frog-in-high-school-science-class look. "I'm not sure what I expected," she finally said. "But it wasn't that."

"See. I'm probably losing my mind."

"I only married you for your body, so it's not a big loss."

"I'm serious, Jules."

"I know when you're lying to me. I'm not telling you how, but I know. And I know you're not lying now, so..." She stood up and began rummaging around in a drawer by the sink. "Ahah," she said, holding a flashlight. "If there's a door to the shadow realm in my backyard, I'd like to see it."

"The shadow realm?"

"What else should we call it?"

Paul frowned. "A person down there said it was called the Between. Min-woo heard us talking about it and also called it the Between."

"Min-woo knows about this, too?"

"Yeah. He acted really familiar with it. Said he spent a lot of time there in college. Or maybe it was in grad school." He slumped his shoulders. "I don't remember. Too much whiskey, too little sleep."

Julie crossed her arms and shook her head.

"You don't believe me," Paul said.

"I'm required by our marital vows to believe you. But as Ronald Reagan once said, *Trust, but verify*. So let's go see it, and I'll be calling our good neighbor friend Min-woo when the sun comes up."

"When did you of all people start quoting Ronald Reagan?"

"Shortly after you started claiming the entrance to Never Never Land is in our backyard."

Under the gaze of Julie's flashlight and the orange glow of the bug zapper, Paul heaved at the door until he had it balanced upright.

"Shine the flashlight down there, but don't get too close. It's a long way down. And hurry. This thing is heavy."

Julie walked up next to him, pointing the light at the large square of dirt uncovered by the door. "I see worms and various creepy-crawlies. Lots of dirt. But no hole." She stepped out onto the patch of night-black dirt, dodging as Paul tried to reach out his free hand to stop her. The bunny slippers sunk down an inch, enough to cover the buck teeth on the fronts.

"Don't stand there. Get back. Please!" Paul yelled.

She looked at him with sad eyes and stepped back into the grass. "Let's go back inside," she said.

CHAPTER 20
ASCII DREAMS

The next evening, Julie came out of the bedroom in full charity gala attire, wearing heels and a 50's Audrey Hepburn style black mini dress, firetruck red lipstick and heavy black eyeliner. She carried the Pinot Grigio Paul poured for her at least forty-five minutes ago, before she retreated to *throw something on*. The wine, untouched until now, vanished in a single swallow.

"I really don't want to leave you here after last night," she said.

"Nah. You've got thousands of dollars to raise tonight and a women's clinic that's counting on you. I'm sorry I'm not up for it tonight. You know how I love watching you work the room."

It was true. At these events, Julie effortlessly floated from little group to little group, breaking in with a smile and maybe a laugh, a well-placed hand on a forearm, a hug and a nod. She always remembered everyone's name and could jump right into the last conversation they'd had, even if it had been two years prior. Every bit of it was alien to Paul, who hated large gatherings and sometimes forgot the names of people he'd worked with for years. In truth, it was better for Julie to be unencumbered. Better for everyone.

"And don't worry about me," he continued. "I think it's just work stress. The hospital is going to miss budget for the fourth month in a row, and I don't see it getting better anytime soon. I might have to let some people go, including that new kid I was telling you about." He wished that were the real explanation. The corporate world and his job seemed so distant and artificial. Like the two-dimensional characters in the nineteenth-century novel *Flatland*, he had discovered another dimension and now his own world felt thin and empty. He tried to give her a playful smile. "I'm getting my midlife crisis out of the way early. Does that mean I get to buy a Porsche? Ha. That was supposed to be a joke, but you're not laughing. You look beautiful, by the way. You'll knock 'em dead."

Julie put her empty wine glass next to the sink and crossed her arms, weighing and measuring him in a look. "Where are you, Paul?"

He stared blankly, looking for a clue as to what she meant by that, and then it all hit him like a knockout punch that would've had Min-woo cheering. He hadn't needed an iron door in the ground to take him to a different world. *Are you off in your own world again?* How many times had she asked him that, recently, while his mind worked through the latest accounting problem? And had it only been recent?

"This weird thing with the door last night," she said, "it worries me, but the worry has been there for a while. You go to the gym before I wake up, you work all day, and then you're asleep by 9. And on the weekends, you spend hours on the internet looking for deals for your book collection. Hours, Paul Prentice." She stepped closer until she was about a foot away from him and put her hands on his shoulders. "It's nice that Min-woo and Jay come by most weeks, although I could do with a little less of Jay, to be honest. But that's it for your social life. You need to get out of the house. Have new experiences. Take me out on dates. You have a wife that adores you, but that wife is feeling neglected."

He started to respond, but she put a finger on his lip.

"The joke about the Porsche?" She shook her head and pointed at the house around them. "You think I need all of this? Don't be absent from life and think you're doing it for us, like you're some sort of martyr."

His shoulders slumped. "I'm sorry."

She kissed him on the cheek, letting her kiss linger about three times longer than usual. "I know you are, honey, but I don't want words. I want action."

The sound of a car horn came from in front of the house.

"That's Trish," Julie said. "I forgot she's picking me up."

They walked together through the kitchen and held hands for the five or six steps it took to make it to the front door in the living room. He opened his mouth to make a promise about being more present, more active, or something like that, but she stopped his words with raised eyebrows. He did it again, but this time with an exaggerated *Eureka!* gesture, finger pointed up like an illuminated light bulb. She responded with a *Psycho* knife-stabbing action. For the next minute, they continued their pantomime improv duel, Paul beginning to speak and Julie shutting him down, until an impatient triple honk from Trish out front brought the game to an end.

They shared one final kiss, lips tired from all the crazy expressions, and she left through the front door. Paul was about to shut the door when he saw Min-woo walking toward the house carrying a backpack over his right arm.

Sweat beaded up on Paul's forehead, as much from the outside heat as from seeing Min-woo. After Julie's reality-check-gut-punch, he had momentarily forgotten that Min-woo was coming over this evening to show Paul the Between. Min-woo, who hadn't responded to any of Julie's calls or texts so far today. Min-woo, who was now deep in conversation with Julie, while an impatient Trish looked on from her white, overly large SUV.

Now Julie was laughing, and Min-woo, too. She leaned over to let him kiss her cheek and then threatened to tousle his precision-sculpted hair. After she left, Min-woo sauntered down the walkway and greeted Paul with the slightest of bows.

"Apparently your bride has been trying to contact me all day. Sometimes you have to turn all electronics off for a while to reclaim your humanity, am I right? Little annoying devices constantly seeking your attention. We're all becoming neurotic slaves to our own creations."

Paul was about to tell him to come inside, but Min-woo walked past him like he owned the place, back through the living room and into the kitchen, where he set his backpack on the table and pulled from it a bottle of nice Japanese whiskey.

"I think I had enough last night," Paul said.

Min-woo was already grabbing tumblers from the cabinet. "Nonsense. The Between requires some dulling of the senses." He put the glasses on the table next to the bottle of whiskey and from his backpack pulled a thick binder filled with a ream of paper and dozens of colored tabs. The binder looked like it had survived a war zone, with Min-woo's graffiti-like doodles tattooing every inch of the cover and overlapping layers of duct tape holding it all together.

"What the hell is that?" Paul asked. "And also, what did you and Julie say to each other that was so funny?"

"She asked me about the Between. Apparently it gave you nightmares. Understandable. I've had my share. But I reassured her. With me as your guide, what could go wrong?" He held up the binder. "This here is my pride and joy, the culmination of years of neglected schoolwork. It's the original printout of the Between's FAQ I've had since 1994, complete with my handwritten notes. You have to remember, this was in the days before hyperlinked wikis translated into every language. Big text file FAQs got unwieldy, and there were version issues and all kinds of other problems. I had to translate this thing from Esperanto." He batted away Paul's hand. "Careful with it, thunder-mitts. It's a one of a kind, limited edition." Min-woo flashed his eyebrows and poured two fingers of whiskey for each of them. "In case you're wondering, I don't consider using my notebook here cheating. It's incomplete, of course, but what fun would it be if we had all the answers? Whiskey and my magic notebook. That's all we need to make the Between our bitch."

FAQ? Frequently Asked Questions? The Between had an FAQ? It hadn't even occurred to Paul to check the web. How could an interdimensional mystery world be common knowledge without causing the entire breakdown of modern society, of religion, of sanity? And what the hell did Esperanto have to do with it? Wasn't Esperanto the made-up language that Eastern Europeans used to think would sweep the globe?

Paul pushed the whiskey away from him. "Let's get really clear about this, Min-woo."

"Clear about what?"

"The Between. Your nonchalance is a bit unsettling, if you want to know the truth. I could've died, and Jay and Supriya already went back, so who the hell knows what's happened to them. Jay suggested we meet in the *stelisto*'s chamber, but there's not a chance in hell I'm going back there."

"Ah, yes. Jay's get-up from last night. The *stelisto*. Piss-poor role, but it suits him. Those two are really getting into it, with the cosplay outfits and everything." He pushed the whiskey back in front of Paul, leaned back in his chair, and folded his arms. "Hang on, *dongsaeng*. When you said that you could've died, it sounded like you meant it literally."

"I did mean it literally. Dead as in *dead*. How else could I have meant it?"

"Character permadeath. Dozens, maybe hundreds of hours gloriously wasted."

"Character permadeath? What does that even mean? Hours wasted? You're talking about the Between like it's a game, Min-woo."

"And you're talking about the Between as if it's real life, Paul. Of course it's a game. A computer game. My favorite of all time."

"A computer game?"

"Of course, silly boy. It's an ascii terminal game. Just text. Beautiful text. The first game to combine procedurally generated content in a multi-user environment. No extra lives, no takebacks. If you die, you start over. You lose everything! The Between was way ahead of its time in the early 80s, but since the whole game was in Esperanto, only a handful of Hungarians played it before someone coded the first language filters in the late-80s and it began to spread. I encountered it back in my undergraduate days."

"The Between is a computer game?" Paul repeated.

"Did you recently get hit on the head, Paul? What are you talking about? If you didn't think it was a computer game, what exactly did you think it was?"

Paul threw back the whiskey in a single gulp. "We're gonna need another drink or two. The Between isn't just a game. It's real, and the entrance was in my backyard."

CHAPTER 21

LEARNING HOW TO PLAY THE GAME IS
THE GAME

Over the next hour, Paul told Min-woo the story of the previous days. The sitting room maze, the ash dogs, the execution chamber, Skull Girl and the giant field, the *Kosmaro*, and finally his interaction with the *gardistaro* leading to his escape.

Min-woo listened, interrupting only occasionally to ask about minor details. He knew about the broken stone colossus in the field. He asked about rooms attached to the maze that Paul never saw. He asked about obsidian staircases winding down to other levels, other worlds.

"It's quite a fabulous story, Mr. Prentice," Min-woo said. "Not remotely believable, mind you, but fabulous nonetheless."

"It really happened."

"And now the door is gone, so you can't show me? Sounds a bit convenient, *dongsaeng*. Any recent experimentation with LSD or strange mushrooms? Have you been served any brownies by less-than-trustworthy individuals? How about recent head injuries? Diagnosed schizophrenia? Perhaps you take antipsychotics and your pharmacy's supply chain has been infiltrated by Chinese counterfeits. These things happen."

Paul shrugged and poured each of them more whiskey. "None of the above. It happened, whether you believe it or not."

"I haven't said I don't believe you, Paul. I just said your story isn't remotely believable. There's a difference. I'm trying to eliminate more likely explanations. I've already eliminated the possibility that you're playing a prank on me. You're not that mean spirited---and it would be mean spirited because of my history and connection with this particular game, which you couldn't possibly have known about anyway. So..."

"So, I don't know, Min-woo. I suppose I can't be a reliable judge of my own sanity, but I don't feel crazy. How about you tell me about the game?" Paul said. "I wouldn't have taken you to be a computer gamer."

Min-woo gave him a long, cold stare like he was deciding whether or not to be offended, and then he smirked. "I'm not, nor have I ever been what I would consider a gamer. I liked computer games before they had pictures. In the 90s, when I was first on my own, coming of age and all that, I couldn't make sense of the world around me and how I fit into it. I needed an escape, where the world looked the way I wanted it to. In the computer lab one night when most students were out drinking or fucking or whatever normal kids did, I saw a student, a boy, and the screen in front of him was an interactive novel with maps of ascii characters.

"He didn't see me looking over his shoulders. I must've stood there for, oh, half an hour, wondering what he was doing before I finally asked. His name was Trevor, and like me, he was born outside of the U.S. but adopted so young that he never knew what it was like to truly be the person he saw in the mirror. Trevor wasn't his real name. His birth name, I should say. His real name was Rezső, Hungarian. My adoptive name was Luke, incidentally. Before I changed it back. Did I ever tell you that? Luke Beasley. Do I look like a Luke Beasley to you?"

"I'm not sure what a Luke Beasley looks like," Paul said. "But the name doesn't conjure up images of a five-foot Korean guy with an impeccable wardrobe."

"Half-Korean. And I'm five-two, *dongsaeng*. Five-two. As I was saying, Trevor brought up a telnet session on a neighboring computer and connected me to a server halfway across the world. He ran a script that translated everything to English, more or less, then told me just enough to get me started and ignored my many requests for help. *Learning how to play the game is the game*, I remember him saying." Min-woo flipped through the pages in the binder, running a finger along a printed sentence here and a scribbled note there, nodding. "I played it off and on for the remainder of undergrad. I would've gotten my degree at least a year sooner had I never touched it, but the trade-off was worth it. And what did I care? My birth father, who I'd never met, had died and left me enough guilt-money that I didn't need to worry about graduating and getting a job. He was a US Army officer of some kind at the garrison near Pyeongtaek, where he met and impregnated my mother, but that's a story for another time.

"Back to the matter at hand. Yes, like I said, the Between is a computer game. Do you have a laptop? I still remember the IP address of the original server. It's probably been down for two decades, but it's worth a shot."

Paul grabbed his black laptop bag from the shelf next to the back door. In the minute or so it took to boot up, neither man spoke, as if they had begun a peculiar game of chicken where the loser had to question his sanity. Finally, Paul looked up from the computer and said, "Open the browser?"

Min-woo shooed Paul away from the computer's driver's seat. "Nothing so fancy as a browser," he said and opened a terminal window, which he expanded to take up the entire screen. A white cursor flashed on a black background. "What are the odds the original server still works?" he said as he typed:

```
>TELNET SIMULATO.INTERLA.HU:4444
```

For several seconds after Min-woo hit enter, nothing happened besides the cursor's slow blink, like an impatient finger tapping on a table. Then text began to scroll up the screen in a flurry.

"Well, what do you know? It's still there after all these years."

Even with Min-woo's head turned toward the screen, Paul could hear the smile in Min-woo's voice. The screen went all black for a second, and then a login screen appeared in a language Paul couldn't read. "Looks kind of like Spanish but it isn't," he said. "Is that Esperanto?"

"Right you are," Min-woo replied. He hit a combination of keys, and, like magic, the words became English.

Welcome to the Between

I can't let the others know about the opening until I understand it myself. It may be the biggest discovery of mankind. I've compiled all of my notes into this simulation. I'm leaving nothing to chance. One wrong move and I could end up dead. But if I make it to the bottom, past the black river and the bell tower, something great is waiting for me. I know it. Eternal life?

Name or [Enter] to Start New Descent:

"Now here's the real test," Min-woo said. He typed in the letters B E L I T and then entered a password. When the next screen appeared, he jumped out of the chair and did a little dance. "This is like Christmas in, what is it, June? Christmas in June! My character is still here! After all this time. Poor girl, she probably thought I'd left her for good."

"Bêlit?" Paul said. "Like as in the pirate woman from Robert Howard's *Conan* novels?"

Min-woo turned and gave an impressed head nod.

Paul pointed to the bookshelf against the far wall of the living room. "That garish pink hardback over there is the 1953 edition of *The Coming of Conan*. Did you know Howard lived not too far from Abilene? As a kid, I loved those books. I wanted to be a barbarian like Conan."

"And I always wanted to be the Pirate Queen, Bêlit." He pointed at the screen. "Looks like we've re-entered in a very familiar place: the sitting room maze. There's an FAQ entry with the sequences we'll need. Sometimes they change, which can be maddening, and then you just have to guess and hope you get lucky."

Paul leaned in and read the description on the screen.

[1]SITTING ROOM

YOU FIND YOURSELF IN A SMALL, ORNATE ROOM, FILLED WITH ANTIQUE FURNITURE. IN THE CENTER OF THE ROOM IS A SOFA ATOP A FINELY WOVEN RUG. DOORS LEAD IN ALL FOUR DIRECTIONS.

"That's it?" he said. "That's all the description there is? What about the velvet wallpaper?"

Min-woo typed:

>LOOK WALLPAPER

YOU SEE NO "WALLPAPER".

"There was some goddamn velvet wallpaper," Paul said. "And a lamp. It doesn't even say anything about a lamp. Ask about the lamp."

>LOOK LAMP

YOU SEE NO "LAMP".

Min-woo shrugged. "No lamp either. Want me to check for a missing coffee table? How about a footstool?"

"I'm amazed at how little description there is."

"The description is all in your head, *dongsaeng*, as you just demonstrated. Now look in the notebook and tell me the sequence to get to the ladder, and I'll show you where Jay and Supriya claim to be headed."

Paul started flipping through the pages, looking for the entry on the sitting room maze. Then he remembered that he already knew the sequence Min-woo had asked for. Corinne had told him.

"Really rotten cantaloupe breeds creepy bugs."

"What is that?"

"It's the mnemonic device I made up when Corinne gave me the sequence. Corinne. The woman with the skull makeup who I used to date in high school, but not in her past, only in mine. Remember? She told me it was right, right, center, back, center, back."

Min-woo rubbed his chin. "Yes, the Skull Girl. There's no Skull Girl role in the Between. And the navigation options aren't right-left-center-back. They're north-south-east-west. But let's assume right is east, center is north, et cetera, et cetera..." Each time Min-woo entered in a direction, the same room description appeared on the terminal window. Until the last.

[1]LADDER ROOM

IN THE CENTER OF THE ANCIENT STONE ROOM IS A LADDER STRETCHING UP TO A HATCH IN THE CEILING. IT SMELLS DAMP, AND THE AIR IS HEAVY AND WET. THE EXITS ARE UP AND NORTH.

"It appears your sequence was correct. Hmm. Anyway, let's continue."

>UP

THE HATCH IS CLOSED.

>OPEN HATCH

WITH ALL YOUR MIGHT, YOU MANAGE TO GET IT OPEN. ABOVE, THE AIR IS AS DARK AS A MOONLESS NIGHT.

Min-woo pulled his hands away from the keyboard as if it had suddenly become scalding. "Hang on," he said. "You either have to be extremely tough to survive up there, or you need to know a few secrets. Let's see what our little Bêlit has under the hood."

>ROLE

YOU ARE THE NENIO, A LESSER SERVANT OF CHAOS.

>INVENTORY

YOU CARRY:

- A BLOODRED SCEPTER (HELD)
- A BLOODRED ROBE (WORN)
- A PAIR OF SANDALS (WORN)
- A CANTEEN (EMPTY)
- A BOX OF CRACKERS
- A LOCK OF RED HAIR
- A CHILD'S DOLL
- 2 GOLD OBOLS

"Ah... My darling Bêlit is the *nenio*, the Priestess of the Coming Oblivion, mistress of the *Katedralo Kaoso*—the chaos cathedral in the third world!" Min-woo exclaimed. "I remember this game. I had never been the *nenio* before. It took me weeks of playing, and then I became terrified of dying and losing it all. My last character ever, waiting all these years for me to return." He clapped with glee. "The *nenio* is supposed to be one of the most powerful roles in the Between. Watch this."

>LOOK SCEPTER
  YOU RECOGNIZE THE SCEPTER AS THE TWILIGHT SCEPTER.
  USES:
  [IGNITE SCEPTER] CREATE ILLUMINATION
  [FLASH SCEPTER AT <TARGET>] DIRECT A BLINDING FLASH OF LIGHT
AT AN OBJECT OR ENEMY
  [NEGATE <TARGET>] WEAKEN CREATURES OF ORDER
  [SMASH <TARGET>] PERFORM A MELEE ATTACK
  >IGNITE SCEPTER
  THE SCEPTER BLAZES WITH LIGHT.

"The Twilight Scepter is the *nenio*'s artifact. I always imagined it like a lightning bolt grabbed out of the air."

>UP

    [1]Cavern Graveyard - Center

You climb out of a tomb in the middle of a graveyard inside a great cavern. Streetlamps lead to a mansion on a hill to the east. Another path leads into darkness to the west. The graveyard continues to the north and south.

>EAST

    [1]East Graveyard - Path to the Mansion

You are at the edge of the graves. The path to the mansion continues up a grass-covered hill to the east.

A scrap metal skeleton has followed you.

Min-woo cracked his knuckles and did a little wiggle with his shoulders. "The scrap metal skeletons are the minions of the *masinisto*, who lives in that mansion. The *masinisto* is the Keeper of the World Lens, a lesser servant of Order. I could fight the skeletons, but they'll keep coming. In the Between, it's better to know the tricks than to try to smash through everything. Watch."

>FLASH SCEPTER AT SKELETON

    The skeleton freezes.

"Whenever they get near, you just shine the light into their faces. Even a flashlight will work. Simple." Min-woo navigated Bêlit around the graveyard and along the cavern walls, before returning her down the hatch. To Paul, the scenery matched up with the story Jay had told.

Over the next two hours, as the light outside dimmed to twilight,

Paul watched as Min-woo raced Bêlit through game representations of places that had been hauntingly real a day before. Almost everywhere, Min-woo demonstrated some trick or secret. In the field by the broken colossus, he showed how you could see a floating city high in the clouds if you knew to look. He showed Paul how to access a hidden storage chamber under the rug in the sitting room which contained golden coins (obols)—empty now because his character already possessed them. He killed every creature he encountered with ease, and then navigated down a black staircase that led to a colorless world of a desert.

[2]THE GRAY WASTE

BEFORE YOU ARE THE REMAINS OF A LONG-DEAD WORLD. DUNES OF ASH ROLL OFF IN EVERY DIRECTION. THE SKY IS COLORLESS AND THE SUN IS DIM, DYING. THE AIR IS FULL OF GRAY GRIT AND ASH, STINGING YOUR EYES.

A DARKNESS RISES IN THE WEST THAT MAY BE A CRAG OF ROCKS. ALL OTHER DIRECTIONS LEAD DEEPER INTO THE GRAY WASTE.

"See the little 2 in the title?" Min-woo said. "We're now in the second world. Each time you go down the Grand Staircase, you go to another world. Or maybe they're the same worlds at different points in time. The game's not really clear on that. There are at least eight worlds in all, including the Patchwork World at the top and the Underworld at the bottom. Purely from a game standpoint, you can think of the worlds as levels, but the descriptions suggest they're spiritual reflections of each other or something. Like I said, the game isn't clear on this stuff, so you fill in the blanks with your imagination."

Paul was about to ask what exactly Min-woo meant by *spiritual reflections*, but Min-woo had already sped through location after location. Paul had to read the screen quickly to keep up.

"You're always getting turned around in the Gray Waste," Min-woo said. "If you head directly toward the rocks, you'll eventually get to the Ruins. We don't want to go in that direction, so—"

"What's in the Ruins?"

"Death and despair," Min-woo replied ominously. Then he chuckled. "Other than that, it's pretty fun. The ruler of the Ruins is a role called the *malespiro*, which I think means despair in Esperanto. The *malespiro* is a lesser servant of chaos, like the *stelisto*. Tougher, but more subtle to play." Min-woo looked Paul up and down, rubbing his chin like he was evaluating livestock for purchase. "So what would be the right role for my Paulie-boy? The FAQ lists all the known roles at the time I printed it. I added some more. Who knows how many there are."

Paul leafed through the heavy notebook until he found the entry for roles. He read the overview.

Unlike the player classes in Dungeons & Dragons and rogue-like games (e.g., warrior, wizard, cleric), the Between uses roles that include class-like attributes but also personality elements and unique objectives in the overarching story. For example, the stelisto *has many thief and assassin attributes but also is compelled to kill. It is important for players to understand the roles' personality elements and to stay consistent with them, else you may lose control of your character.*

A player becomes a role after taking possession of the role's artifact. Roles are exited when the player assumes a new role, when the role is forcefully taken by another player, or when a player dies. There are no other known ways to exit a role. Only one player may inhabit a role at a time.

So, by picking up that knife, Jay was stuck playing a role, and the only way out was to switch to another role or have someone take the role of the *stelisto* from him? He skimmed down the page until he reached the list of roles. Under the Chaos heading: the *stelisto*, the *malespiro*, the *nenio*, and the *songo*. Under Order: the *masinisto*, the *gardistaro*, the *serĉilo*, and the *klaro*. Min-woo had scribbled an entire paragraph about lesser and greater roles. He had highlighted and circled his final sentences: *Is it possible to play Malluma Sinjoro or even the Koŝmaro? What about the gods: Dio Kaoso and Dio Ordo?*

While Paul shook his head at the unfamiliar names and the

implied scale and complexity (order/chaos? lesser/greater?), Min-woo kept jabbering on. "Not the *malespiro*. Too malevolent and dark for our sweet, innocent Paul. I could see your bride as a nice *klara*, which is also a role here in the second world. One of my favorites. Calm. A Buddha-like figure. But that's not right for you, either." Min-woo craned his neck to look over Paul's shoulder. "I've got it!" he yelled, pointing at a name in the notebook. "The *serĉilo*. The searcher. That's you."

"The searcher? That doesn't sound very exciting. Why would I be the searcher? What am I searching for?"

Min-woo did a terrible Yoda impression, "The first task of the *serĉilo* is to understand why he is the *serĉilo* in the first place." Min-woo laughed and said in his usual, effeminate Texan drawl, "But you can figure that out during your own game. Right here, I've already got a role, so let's keep moving along."

Min-woo navigated through the ash desert, always going the opposite direction of the rocks, which he explained was the secret to getting to the next staircase leading down.

The third world was the City Above, which they had seen from the colossus' field. Min-woo sped Bêlit through the city, fingers fluttering on the keyboard like he was playing an instrument, until he reached a gothic cathedral called *Katedralo Kaoso*. Atop the cathedral, he had Bêlit perform a ritual, and a door opened that led back *home*.

"Home?" Paul said.

Min-woo grabbed the notebook and flipped through until he came to an entry for *Worlds of the Between*.

The Between contains 8 known worlds, or levels, not including the Outworlds. Travel between the worlds occurs via the Grand Staircase. The worlds are also linked via the World Tunnels, but travel there is not recommended due to their frequent use by the Koŝmaro.

The Outworlds

|

The Patchwork World (The First World)

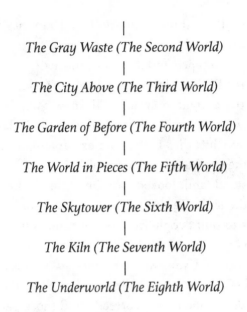

The Gray Waste (The Second World)

|

The City Above (The Third World)

|

The Garden of Before (The Fourth World)

|

The World in Pieces (The Fifth World)

|

The Skytower (The Sixth World)

|

The Kiln (The Seventh World)

|

The Underworld (The Eighth World)

Min-woo said, "One of the quirks of the game is that you can't save your game while in the Between. You have to find an exit that leads home. It fits with the general conceit of the game, that it's a simulation and not really a game at all, that this world—the real world we're in right now—is one of the *outworlds* connected to the Between. In the game, when you're home, in addition to saving, you can resupply. We just exited at the Altar of the Sky in the third world. It's the most accessible exit early in the game."

"Not counting the exit provided by the *gardistaro*," Paul said. "That's how I got out. Jay and Supriya also."

Min-woo narrowed his eyes and studied Paul's face. "Yes, the *gardistaro* can open a door back home if you know how to answer her questions. If you *are* the *gardistaro*, you can escape also, but only from the Patchwork World. I'm assuming you know how the *gardistaro*'s powers work."

"I don't have a clue, Min-woo. I didn't know there was an FAQ, I didn't access a Hungarian server, and I certainly didn't play a text-based computer game. I went to a real place that was exactly like what I'm seeing here on the screen, but I only saw a sliver of it, and it was enough to be terrifying. I never went down any stairs. In fact,

Corinne specifically told me to not do that. I ran into the *gardistaro* and said *no* when she asked if I wanted answers."

"And then you escaped and the door vanished?"

"The door is still there, in the middle of my fucking backyard. We can go back there right now and I'll show you. It doesn't lead anywhere. Like I said earlier, I tried to show Julie last night, and underneath it was just dirt. Is there an explanation in the computer game for why the way back in would vanish?"

Min-woo stood and looked out into the backyard from the window over the sink. He turned to Paul and said, "The *masinisto's* primary role is to pull people from the outworlds into the Between. He or she does that using the World Lens on top of the graveyard mansion. Supriya said she was the *masinisto* before becoming the *gardistaro*. If the *masinisto* role hadn't been refilled, the World Lens may not have been functioning correctly, and those particular paths to and from the real world wouldn't be open. I hate to say it, but you and Jay and Supriya... Your stories line up." He walked to the back door, opened it, and beckoned for Paul to head outside. "I can't believe I'm even entertaining this possibility, but here's your chance to prove your story. It's been almost 24 hours, enough time to refill the *masinisto's* role and realign the World Lens. Let's see if your door has returned and settle this once and for all."

CHAPTER 22
PERMADEATH

Cold air poured out of the hole in the ground, knocking Paul back so that he almost lost his grip on the heavy iron door, and then it rushed back by him, down into the hole like a deep breath trying to pull Paul into the darkness. This time the door did slip from his fingers. He turned away from the plume of dirt he expected it to release when the door hit the ground, but as it fell, it dissolved into nothing. His backyard fence dissolved into nothing, also. Instead of seeing his neighbor's yard, his neighbor's house, Paul saw only rolling hills of scrubland and mangy Mexican juniper trees. He spun around, and Min-woo was gone, as was his house. Just more of the moonlit scrubland. West Texas ranchland.

He turned back toward the hole, knowing what he would see before his eyes took in the circular rings of stone.

The familiar smell of mildew and decay.

The pull of the opening, inviting him—commanding him—to lean over the stones and stare down into the void.

The knowing of a presence there in the void, *Cadejo* waiting for him, calling to him.

You always come back to me, Paul Prentice. It's time to be with me again.

Something had him, grabbed around his waist. He thought it was going to push him into the well, but it tugged him backward, and then he was falling over. When he hit the ground, the stench of decay was replaced by the smell of cut grass, and the world of his backyard snapped back into being.

"I thought you were going to fall in, you clumsy oaf!" Min-woo exclaimed. The orange of the bug zapper traced around his outline and made him look like he glowed with a flame. Min-woo tiptoed to the hole, which had returned to being the concrete-surrounded hole with an iron door, and he peered down into it. "This changes things a bit. I'm not saying I believe you, *dongsaeng*, but..."

Paul stood. His legs felt hollow, and his heart seemed to have pushed its way up his throat so that its beating echoed in his ears. "You know, Min-woo," he said, surprising himself with the casualness of his voice, "I was hoping the hole would be here again, to prove to you and Julie that I'm not crazy, but now that it's right in front of me, being crazy doesn't sound half bad."

Min-woo jittered about with nervous energy and excitement. He gave Paul a quick double flash with his eyebrows and said, "Oh, I still think you're crazy, Paul, but it's healthy to be a little bit crazy, as long as it's the right crazy. A little delusion makes the world bearable and keeps the bad crazy away. Religion inoculates you against nihilism, et cetera, et cetera. I think of it like the little back-burning fires that fire-fighters set to stop big forest fires." He started walking toward the house's back door. "Now let's set our own back-burner and indulge the crazy idea that this is all real. We'll need some items from your house, just to be prepared. I'm still certain I'll be disappointed." He turned back and gave Paul an impatient look. "Come on, now. Don't worry, I know exactly what we'll need."

Paul sat on his kitchen counter watching silently as Min-woo shuffled about the kitchen, laundry room, and garage, gathering items and stuffing them in Paul's old college backpack. Bottles of water, two flashlights, spare batteries, more spare batteries, bandaids,

Neosporin, ibuprofen, more ibuprofen, a box of protein bars, a box of cereal, and a box cutter. Finally, Min-woo stuffed the head of a sledgehammer in the bag so that the handle stuck out about two feet from the top.

"Do you have a crowbar?" Min-woo asked.

"I'm not going down there," Paul said. His heart still hadn't slowed. If he hadn't chewed his fingernails to the quick earlier in the day, he would've been going at them now. He grabbed a rolling pin sitting next to the sink and held onto it for no particular reason he could identify.

"A rolling pin is not a workable substitute for a crowbar, my friend." Min-woo looked around as if he might find a crowbar lying around the kitchen table, and then he gave a little frustrated huff and walked into the garage. He returned a minute later with a crowbar and Paul's old little league baseball bat, neither of which could be crammed into the backpack.

"Did you hear me, Min-woo? I'm not going down there again."

"I heard you, but you're wrong. Of course, you're going down there again. You wouldn't let your neighbor go down there by himself, would you? And I, most certainly, am going down there."

"Don't try to guilt me. You may know the game backward and forward, but what I experienced was no game."

"Your friend was quick to go back."

"That's because Jay's an idiot."

"Jay's not an idiot, and you don't really think that. You shouldn't say things like that about your friends, even in jest."

Paul let out a deep breath and dropped to the floor. "I know. I know. I don't really think that, although he can be juvenile and impulsive. And I'm sure if I went back down there first, he'd be right behind me without a second thought."

Min-woo threw the backpack over his shoulder, and the weight spun him in an off-kilter pirouette. "You better carry this, Mr. Muscles." He shoved the bag into Paul's hands and said, "Wipe the forlorn look off your face. I still find it unlikely that your mysterious bomb shelter will lead to a real-life version of the Between, but on the off chance it does, keep a few things in mind. One, I have spent hundreds if not thousands of hours in the Between of the computer game and of my imagination. As you said, I do know it backward and forward. The earlier levels, anyway. Two, we have my notebook to fill in any gaps in my memory. Three, we are only exploring the Patchwork World, a.k.a. level one. Just enough to prove it's real and to ensure it really is identical to the game. And then we leave. Now come on."

Paul chased Min-woo back outside, the overstuffed backpack on his shoulder. "Like that? No more discussion?"

Min-woo stopped and walked back to Paul. For a split second, Paul thought he might've gotten through to him, but Min-woo only wanted to get a flashlight from the backpack. With the light in hand, he marched back toward the hole, and without hesitation, started climbing the ladder down. "Do you want to spend your whole life avoiding adventure, Paul?" Min-woo said just as he disappeared below.

"I don't avoid adventure," Paul said to the night air, which didn't seem the least bit convinced. He turned away from the hole and tried taking slow, deep breaths, but the pounding in his head wouldn't slow down. Not looking at the hole made it somehow worse. In his imagination it became the well again. Was that a cold breeze that touched his neck? A cold breeze in the Texas summer night?

You know you're coming to join me.

His fingertips started to go numb.

Come join me, Paul.

The ground of his backyard felt like it was rocking, and every step he took to keep his balance felt like a step in the wrong direction.

"Come on, Paul!" That was Min-woo, yelling up from the darkness. "You're supposed to be my pack mule!" Min-woo's twangy voice caused a break in the tide of doom rising within Paul. A break that gave him a moment of clarity.

He wanted to walk back inside and act like none of this had happened. But how could he leave Min-woo all alone and without any of the supplies? How could he leave Jay? Go to work the next day as if closing out May's financials had any real meaning to him now that he knew about the existence of this parallel set of worlds called The Between?

The thought of going back down into the darkness was terrifying, but only a week ago he'd been terrified of giving a presentation to the hospital's executive council. Maybe Min-woo was right about that crazy back-burning fire business. How could he ever fear public speaking again after seeing the giant, reality-warping *Kosmaro*? How could the executive boardroom ever be intimidating after being in a recursive sitting room that seemed to violate the properties of spacetime?

He turned to the hole and stared into the darkness. His body shook so badly that he had to pull the backpack over both shoulders to keep it from slipping off, but he didn't look away.

"I've wanted to control everything about my life, and I've ended up binding myself into a smaller and smaller box," he announced to the night and to himself. Despite the pounding in his head and the jelly feeling of his legs, he walked forward. "If Jay and Min-woo can charge into the void, so can I."

As he put his foot on the ladder's top rung, a voice in the back of his head—the hyper-rational, core-Paul voice—pointed out a problem with Min-woo's fire analogy. What if the back-burning is bigger than the forest fire you're trying to prevent? Does it become the new, even bigger forest fire?

By the time that thought sunk in, he was on the floor of the concrete bunker, and Min-woo was already trying to push aside the bookcase blocking the path onward. Paul nearly tripped on the revolver's suede bag sitting on the floor at the bottom of the ladder. He shoved it in the front pocket of the backpack and went to help Min-woo with the bookshelf, trying not to think about the massive fire they were about to start.

Maybe it was the lack of windows, Paul thought, that gave a malevolent feel to an otherwise plain and simple room. The commingled odors of linseed oil and mildew formed an old-house smell that manifested itself almost like a physical presence, as though the room had kept some part of its former occupants, a part forever unable to escape.

Min-woo didn't seem the least bit concerned with any form of a ghostly presence. "I can't believe I'm in the sitting room maze in the Between," he exclaimed, running his fingers over every part of the room's furnishings as if he had to touch everything to believe it was real. "It doesn't look at all like I thought. I always imagined the sofa covered with those clear plastic protective thingies."

Paul tried to act as if anxiety weren't threatening to tear his insides apart. "Clear plastic?" he asked. "The type that crazy people have?"

"My parents had those on our living room furniture. Sofa, loveseat, and two chairs. All covered with plastic except about three or four times a year. Most notably Christmas—for the pictures."

"What's the point in owning furniture you can't use?"

Min-woo brushed off the seat of his pants before sitting on the antique-looking sofa. "It gets worse. My adoptive father didn't take the television remote out of the plastic sleeve it came in until the batteries ran out and he had no choice. Oh, and he left the plastic on the speakers to the surround-sound system in the family room. Not the formal living room—the family room, where no one went but us. With the volume turned up, the bass made the plastic vibrate like a robot farting. So we had surround-sound robot farts as a major element of every movie I watched at home, starting at about age 15."

"You know what Tolstoy said: All happy families are alike; each unhappy family is unhappy in its own, neurotic, plastic-covered, robot-farting way," Paul said. The hyper pragmatic part of his mind complained that they should be planning: how to find Jay, how to survive, how to get out of the Between alive. But the conversation was calming Paul's nerves, so he kept with it. "What causes that kind of behavior? Owning things that you're afraid to use? Is it some holdover from Depression-era scarcity that they picked up from their parents?"

Min-woo raised an eyebrow. "That's a charitable explanation. If I were being uncharitable, I'd say that the highly religious are often preoccupied with the appearance of things. It's understandable if you think an invisible god is watching and judging your every move. But that's being a little unfair to my parents. They're loving, pleasant people with a peculiar set of behaviors that don't resonate with my genetic predispositions. This is a lovely sofa, incidentally."

"Surprisingly comfortable, isn't it? Jay had this idiot idea of dragging them out and selling them on eBay since we have an endless supply."

Min-woo began to roll his eyes—possibly a conditioned response at the mention of one of Jay's ideas—but mid-roll, he stood from the sofa, as if something had pinched his ass. "Your manchild friend is a genius. I was thinking about all the gold and jewels and other wonderful baubles and trinkets down here, but we don't even have to go beyond this room to cash in. Once we find Supriya, she can use her *gardistaro* abilities to make a doorway back out, and we simply drag out sofa after sofa."

"And push them through that narrow cavern? And up the ladder? And where do we store these hundreds of sofas?"

"Details, details, details. We'll get a warehouse. It doesn't matter. It'll be like printing money."

Paul frowned. "It won't be anything at all like printing money. Who's going to buy a fancy sofa from us? When they ask where it came from, what will we say? A computer game dungeon?"

"Still with the details? Won't you just allow me these seconds of imaginary wealth? We'll start selling them cheap. A hundred dollars. And as positive reviews come in and demand grows, we'll start upping the price."

Paul dropped into the sofa's corner. "It almost sounds like it might not be completely idiotic. But how big is the eBay sofa market for only this one particular sofa? No, don't answer that. We're supposed to be looking for Jay and Supriya, and then getting back out while we're alive, not strategizing how to turn the Between into a sofa-ATM."

"The Between as a sofa-ATM... I love it!"

"You're as bad as Jay. Speaking of... Do you know the route to the *stelisto*'s chamber? That's where Jay said for us to meet. Or do I need to get out the notebook? Min-woo? Min-woo?" Paul looked up from his backpack at Min-woo and followed Min-woo's gaze to a familiar sight.

The ash dog had crept in through a door Paul knew they hadn't left ajar. Its nails scraped against the wood floor leaving creosote trails. Under its char and soot skin came a faint ember's glow, like a radioactive power source at its core.

Paul pulled at the sledgehammer's handle, his hands shaking, but everything else in the backpack had shifted, and it wasn't coming loose. He unzipped the bag and was about to dump the contents onto the floor when Min-woo rested a hand on his forearm.

Min-woo calmly took a water bottle from the bag and untwisted the cap. As the ash dog circled, Min-woo took a slow sip. Then he pointed the bottle at the dog and squeezed.

Little clouds of steam burst from the ash dog wherever the water struck it, and the creature wailed in pain as parts of its torso disintegrated into blackish sludge. Min-woo did the same to another dog, its head just entering the room.

"They come in threes, so hang tight for a second. The *malespiro* sends these creatures up from the Gray Waste, to pick off the newbies. But I'm no newbie."

As the final dog entered, its paw touched a puddle of water, and the paw and leg seemed to sink into the floor. The dog cried and pulled its stump of a leg in close to its body. Paul felt a moment of pity, but Min-woo didn't hesitate, pouring the bottle's remaining contents on the ash dog's head, like pouring salt on a slug. It let out the beginnings of a snarl before its muzzle melted off and its body slumped to the ground.

"Like I said while showing you the game in your kitchen," Min-woo said, "it's better to know the secrets than to try to fight your way through."

"Clearly." Paul's heart was threatening to beat out of his chest, but Min-woo looked cool as a cucumber.

"Now let's catch up to the others and get the hell out of here," Min-woo said.

Following the notebook's direction, they navigated to the *stelisto's* chamber, but Jay and Supriya weren't there. Paul saw a moment of hesitation flash across Min-woo's face.

"What is it?" Paul asked.

"I'm guessing they got impatient and went to the cavern graveyard to find Supriya's exit. We have flashlights, so the scrap metal skeletons shouldn't be a problem, but I'd like to see the Grand Staircase first-hand before we leave, if you'll indulge me. We'll stay safely at the top. It won't be dangerous. I promise."

"And then the cavern, and we're out?"

"Just the stairway, and I'll be satisfied." Min-woo led Paul back into the sitting room but hesitated before continuing through the sequence to the Grand Staircase. "Hang on a sec," he said. He pulled up a corner of the rug and lifted away two loose wooden slats. "Like in the game," he said, reaching his hand into the darkness under the floor. He held up three gold coins.

"Souvenirs?" Paul asked.

"Golden obols. They'll make beautiful souvenirs. And they'll be an insurance policy just in case."

"In case of what, exactly?"

"In case we become revenants. Ghosts doomed to wander the Between until they fade into nothingness."

"Ghosts? You mean, in case we die? These coins are like extra lives or something? I thought you said there were no extra lives in the Between."

"An extra life is like a complete do-over. There are no complete do-overs in the Between. The obols can bring the dead back to life if you have two of them. But it sets some *very bad shit* in motion. So you might be better off dead. If you only have one obol, well, at least your revenant can pay the ferryman at the river to the underworld." Min-woo slid one of the coins into his pants pocket and handed the other two to Paul. "Take these and don't worry your pretty little head. Nobody's becoming a revenant on my watch."

Paul had the sudden urge to pull out the notebook and read everything about death, ghosts, revenants, golden coins, and the underworld—the Between had an underworld with a Charon-like ferryman?!—but more than anything, he wanted it to be over as quickly as possible, to be back home with Julie, with tons of concrete poured over the iron door in his backyard.

"Whatever," he said. "Let's get out of here."

"To the staircase, then," Min-woo said, as he began the next sequence of sitting rooms.

At first, Paul thought they had entered another copy of the sitting room, with the same mahogany floors and damask velvet wallpaper, but this room was much larger. At its center was a massive spiral staircase with a thick iron railing, leading down. The steps looked to be smooth stone, possibly obsidian with little gray snowflakes.

Paul walked to the rail and looked down. The stairs spiraled so deep that it felt like looking into a massive seashell twisting off to a distant, obscure point. Flickering candles on wall sconces lit the curved walls surrounding the staircase, but the dim light wasn't enough to tell how far down the stairs went. They seemed to go down forever.

"The staircases don't look anything like I imagined, but they're magnificent," Min-woo said.

"Cases? Plural?"

"Yes. One connecting each level to the one beneath it. Seven in all, as far as I know. What does my trusty notebook say?"

Paul leafed through the binder until he came upon section describing The Grand Staircase.

The Grand Staircase is one of two links between the worlds of the Between (the other being the Košmaro's Tunnels, also referred to as the World Tunnels). The Grand Staircase should not be thought of as a single physical staircase. The location of the exit on a world (e.g., the desert platform in the Gray Waste) is not the same location as the entrance to the next world.

The game describes the staircase as "an unknown number of obsidian steps", although whether "obsidian" refers to the actual stone or just the black color is unclear.

The Grand Staircase varies in its size, seemingly randomly. Players should use caution and not repeatedly hit "D" or "U", in case a monster or enemy is waiting at the next platform.

"It says something about monsters and enemies. I don't like this at all. If we can't find Jay and Supriya, we have to go down there, don't we?" Paul said. "Didn't you say the first exit is in the third world? The cathedral where you exited in the game?"

"Not so fast," Min-woo said. "If Supriya somehow vacates her role as the *gardistaro*, perhaps another *gardistaro* seeks us out. Then we answer her questions like my trusty notebook tells us to, and voila!"

"Without the *gardistaro*, though..."

Min-woo frowned. "Without the *gardistaro*, down we go. But let's not get ahead of ourselves. *Really rotten cantaloupe breeds creepy bugs.* Isn't that your saying to get us to the cavern's ladder? Lead the way."

From the neighboring sitting room, Paul walked them through the sequence, but as he opened the final door, the room behind them seemed to begin folding up. The dark wooden planks of the floor buckled and then snapped. The lamp overturned, and the room's corners began pinching together, caught for a moment on the sofa, like a mouth with something wedging its jaw open. With a crack, the sofa snapped in half, sending wood and stuffing out like a shotgun blast.

Min-woo shoved Paul through the open door as the sitting room completely folded in on itself, filling the doorway behind them with a two-dimensional, smashed version of the room.

"What the hell happened?" Paul asked, running his hand over the flat surface that blocked the way they came.

Min-woo winced and shifted from one foot to the other. He pointed Paul's attention in the opposite direction. The room they had entered wasn't the stone room with the ladder or another copy of the sitting room. It wasn't a room at all, just dark space full of thousands of semi-translucent gears of all sizes, grinding into each other, like the inside of a giant machine. The gears themselves seemed to be there and not there at the same time. Some of them rusty, others gold, but all ghost-like, as if Paul could put his hand through them.

"Watch it," Min-woo said, knocking Paul's hand back.

Had he been about to touch one of the gears? What came over him?

Min-woo pulled Paul away from the gears. "Let's not get too close. In the game, anyway, getting tangled up in these gears is instant death."

"Why didn't the sequence work?"

"Bad luck, I guess. Maybe the FAQ has an explanation, but sometimes you end up between rooms, in the machinery that connects the patches of the Patchwork World. Maybe if you play the role of the *masinisto* you'll understand. Maybe we're inside the World Lens, in a world of its own. When this happens in the game, you have to time the pattern of the gears and hustle through to the other side."

"Time the pattern of the gears? How do you time the pattern? It's a jumbled mess. Even if the damn gears weren't see-through, I still don't think I could see a pattern."

Min-woo shrugged. "In the game, you type *time gear pattern*. That's it."

"Oh, that's helpful."

"I suppose not. Why don't you check the notebook?"

Paul skimmed through the entry and then shoved the binder into the backpack and threw the whole thing on the ground. "So that's worthless."

"Don't be such a pessimist. Everything we need was in that description. You weren't paying enough attention. Look at the room description again." He pulled the notebook back out.

[1]*Inside the Machine*

The door behind you is blocked. Ahead, and in every direction, the gears of a giant machine turn and turn. Time marches forward. Through a gap visible in the pattern of the gears, you see an exit to the north.

"See that about time marching forward? Forward, as in dead ahead. *A gap visible in the pattern of the gears*? It's telling us to march forward at a steady pace. Can you see how each gear is missing one of the big teeth? We're not supposed to run through or guess. We just start at the first, go when we get an opening, and march through the rest."

"March? How fast is a march?"

"It's a march."

"Yeah, but how fast? Like a fast walk? A marching band march? A military march?"

"Those aren't different speeds. A march is a march."

"Were you in a marching band or something?"

"No, were you?"

"No."

"So then trust me. A march is a march. If we needed to run, it would've said *time runs forward*. Probably. Now watch, and follow my lead." Min-woo gave Paul a wink and then casually walked up to the first set of gears. As the gap appeared, he stepped forward and continued without hesitation.

Paul could see Min-woo through the ghost-gears, becoming more of an obscure shape as the gears came between them.

From somewhere far ahead, beyond so many gears that Paul could no longer see any sign of him, Min-woo yelled, "See! Like that.

Now, your turn. Once you start, keep going no matter what. No matter what!"

"God damnit, Min-woo," Paul muttered under his breath. He exhaled and stepped near the gears. They looked airy and insubstantial, like he could push his hand right through them, but he also had that hackle-raising feeling of standing next to something massive and kinetic. Like a subway car in motion just inches away.

The gap swung down, but by the time Paul recognized it, it had already passed. He waited for it to come around, and when it did, it once again surprised him with its speed.

"What are you waiting for?" Min-woo's voice came over the rumbling hum of the gears.

The gap came again, and this time Paul's leg twitched. But that was it, and the gap was quickly replaced by meshed teeth ready to chew up the indecisive.

In his mind, he could see the insurance forms he never filled out sitting in the top drawer of his desk at work. Age 30. No chronic illnesses. No family history of cancer or heart attacks, except an uncle who smoked four packs a day from his teens until his 60s. He thought of that blank insurance form and Julie unable to pay the mortgage on their house without his help, selling the house, taking a big loss. Everything they'd built together falling apart because he preferred not to think about awful but real circumstances...

Would insurance cover him getting mangled by almost invisible gears inside of a world-between-worlds that was too eerily similar to a computer game to be coincidence? What are the terms and conditions of the policy in circumstances like this?

"Stop stalling, Paul! You're building it up and making it worse! March already! March!"

As Min-woo said these words, the gap swung around again, and Paul took that first step. Then he was committed. A hint of hesitation caused a gear to brush against his back, dispelling any possibility of their insubstantial nature.

He closed his eyes and marched. Until he ran smack into Min-woo.

"Was that so bad?" Min-woo asked.

"I need to get home. I have papers to sign."

They exited the gear room through the door ahead to another sitting room, and this time Paul's mnemonic sequence took them to the stone room with the ladder. They took a break and sat against the cold stone walls. Min-woo complained through every bite of one of Paul's protein bars, and they each drained a bottle of water.

A little brown creature scurried out of a crack between the blocks in the wall opposite them. Paul jumped to his feet and yanked the sledgehammer out of the unzipped backpack, sending their supplies all over the room.

The creature was the size of a large rat but with a shiny, segmented shell, like a flatter, insectile armadillo, a rodent-roach thing.

Min-woo calmly tore a corner off his protein bar and tossed it to an empty space on the floor. The roach-rat pounced on the little clump of chocolate and whey like a predator attacking its unsuspecting prey. Min-woo stood, arched his back in a long stretch, gave an amused chuckle, and stepped on the creature, sending out a jet of mustard-like roach-rat fluid, a condiment packet bursting.

"A *blato-rato*. Also known as a cockrat," Min-woo said. "Nasty little, disease-ridden creatures. They can be problems when you encounter lots of them, but food distracts them. Their armor is absurdly strong, but a good stomp liquifies their entrails. In the game, you can collect the shells and make some decent body armor out of them. Feel free."

Paul grimaced at the oozing carcass. Is that what Corinne was wearing under her robe? But he had no intention of being here long enough to need armor. How would one make armor out of giant roach shells anyway? "I think I'll pass," he said. He picked up both flashlights, tested them, and tossed one to Min-woo. "Jay and I got attacked by a room full of these things last time. Let's get on with this and get back home before it happens again."

They gathered their supplies and Paul led the way up the ladder, flashlight jammed into his jeans pocket.

"I can't wait to see the cavern and the junk skeletons," Min-woo said. "Make sure you stay calm. Remember they can't attack if you shine your light in their face."

Paul looked at the heavy hatch above him and then down at Min-woo. "You're a little too enthusiastic about seeing horror-film creatures that want to maim us."

"Reliving daydreams from my childhood. Quite literally."

Paul pushed at the hatch but it didn't budge. He checked to make sure there wasn't a locking mechanism he had missed. Moving up a step, he pressed his left shoulder and neck into the hatch, and instantly a cold jolt from the metal shot through him down to his toes. When he pushed with his legs against the ladder rung, he felt the hatch budge, a seal breaking above, and the ladder creaking below. He pushed the hatch up until it rested on a little chain, holding it perpendicular with the ground.

The space above was a black void. As Paul continued to climb, every nerve in his body writhed at the notion of going headfirst into the darkness, as if the demarcation of the light below and the dark above were the neck-binding of a guillotine, ready to cleave him apart at any second.

Above, in the dirt, still in one piece, he focused on helping Min-woo get up to join him and then waited a good half minute for his eyes to adjust.

They were, indeed, in a graveyard, having emerged from a tomb themselves. The two-sentence description in the game did nothing to prepare him for the sight of the real cavern.

Impending doom. Bad things happen here.

They both kept their flashlights pointed down, into the room below. The only light, beyond the hole, came from the occasional flickering streetlamp, and the windows of the mansion glaring down at them from the hill beyond the graveyard. Paul could barely make out the walls of the surrounding cavern. Most importantly, he could see no elevator door, no Supriya, no Jay.

"Not here," he whispered to Min-woo. Tried to whisper, anyway. His voice echoed, and somewhere to their left, he heard a slow scrape. A rusty door inching open, a blade sliding against stone, a metal jaw opening in expectation of a fleshy treat.

Min-woo surveyed the room with his flashlight, little clicks and scurries coming from the dark spaces trailing its cyclops gaze.

"You're gonna get us killed," Paul whispered, extra quiet this time.

"They already know we're here." Min-woo stood and began to walk toward the wall to their left. "Come on. Let's see if we can see any sign of the elevator door."

God damnit, Min-woo, Paul thought as he crept along in a half-crouch, following behind Min-woo, who was neither creeping nor crouching. They both swept their flashlights across the graves, but the darkness behind the stones left more hidden in their stretched-out shadows than illuminated.

Min-woo reached the cavern wall as Paul passed the last headstone. Paul swept to the left instead of the right with his flashlight this time and stumbled backward as his beam exposed a rusty, headlamp-faced thing only feet from him, its blade-like arm raised and ready to strike. The room seemed to vibrate, but it was only Paul's arm shaking, causing the light and shadows to jitter like a paused VHS movie with bad tracking.

"Ah, you got one," Min-woo said. "I hate to say it but they aren't nearly as scary looking as I imagined. Gangly and clumsy. Unstable. Like the littlest thing would knock it over." He winked at Paul. "That wasn't so hard, now was it?"

Paul's hand wouldn't go steady, no matter how many deep breaths he took. "I don't like having this thing so close to me. Seeing anything? Can we leave now?"

When Min-woo turned back toward the wall, his light swept past a wall of junk skeletons walking toward them through the graveyard only twenty feet away. As the light passed them by, they vanished again in the darkness.

Paul reflexively turned his flashlight their direction, but the skeleton next to him started moving again the moment its headlamp face was free of the beam. Paul swung the light back, and now it was only a foot away.

"More coming, Min-woo!" he yelled.

"Use your flashlight!" Min-woo yelled back like it was the most elementary thing that could be said. Min-woo's light jumped back and forth between two sets of approaching skeletons. "Oh. I see the problem."

Paul kicked the nearby skeleton in the torso, sending it crashing backward on the ground, and then he turned his beam to the right. Two more coming, now frozen by his beam. But to his left, he could hear the first skeleton moving again. He flicked his light that way, and it stopped, back on its feet.

To his right, the others shuffled closer.

"This isn't working at all!"

He tried flicking the light back and forth rapidly between them, and that seemed to work for a few seconds until he felt as much as heard more coming from his left. No matter how fast he moved the light, he couldn't keep all three groups still. Every instant they left the focus of his light, they came closer. He couldn't see them moving— they just appeared closer and closer each time the light flashed on to them. A noose slowly closing around him in stop-motion.

"Back to the ladder!" he heard Min-woo yell, and then Min-woo's flashlight beam bounced in a crazed path like an out of control roller coaster through the graves.

The skeleton noose constricted tighter as Paul flashed the light between them as fast as he could. Something animal inside him reacted, and without realizing what he was doing, he ran toward the nearest skeleton, light pointed in its face, and bowled through it like a defensive lineman crashing through a tackle dummy. The thing weighed a ton, and Paul felt his shirt and skin tear in contact with its rusty edges, but then he was past it and through, jumping over headstones and running toward the hatch.

Something hit him in the side, but he caught himself before

smashing into a crypt. A blade-like forearm clanged against the stone above his head. He slid toward the open hatch, thinking Min-woo was ahead of him. But as he caught himself on the top rung of the ladder, he saw Min-woo's flashlight bounding off in the wrong direction.

"Min-woo!" he yelled. "Where are you going?! Over here!" At the sound of his voice, the flashlight's beam twisted this way and that, and Paul realized Min-woo had gotten turned around. He shined his light at Min-woo, but between them were more skeletons than gravestones, running with their off-kilter bound, both at Min-woo and toward him.

Something hit his hand, and his flashlight flew from his grasp. And then the heavy hatch door hit him, knocking him clear to the floor below. In the half-second before he blacked out, his mind replayed the last thing it had seen above—metal arms crashing down and Min-woo's flashlight going dark.

Dark.

CHAPTER 23
CLAIMING THE SOUL

Three booms came from the dark passageway, a bell ringing loud enough to wake the dead. The junk metal skeletons retreated to their hiding places behind the tombs and headstones, out of the path of the creature they knew was coming for the corpse on the cavern floor.

The corpse itself hadn't moved for hours after its fluids had stopped leaking and congealed, but something in it, simultaneously in and beyond it, stirred when the bell rang. Not a conscious thing, but more of a lingering echo of emotion. That emotion, now, most closely resembled fear.

The flames in the streetlamps turned a bloody red that steadily grew brown and diseased until the graveyard looked like an old, ruined photograph. The gravestones nearest the passageway lost focus, and the worn script carved into their stone shifted names faster and faster until the letters became blurs.

The *Kosmaro* stepped out of the passageway and walked to the body. With its black fingernail, it scratched a spiraling symbol into the corpse's forehead, and then it pressed on the symbol until its finger sunk through the skin and the skull beneath. It curled its finger and pulled, and out of the body came a faintly glowing human form, the echo of life from within. As the spectral form separated from its lifeless physical husk, a small, golden circle came with it from the coin in the body's pants pocket.

The *Košmaro* held the glowing figure with an outstretched arm, turning it left and right, examining it, while the figure, in turn, writhed and wailed. A lantern appeared in the *Košmaro's* other hand, and the dark creature pushed the glowing soul into it. With the lantern in hand, it turned and walked back through the passageway.

The blurry wake behind it dissipated, solid objects returned to their singular form, and all was as it was before except for the corpse, which had become thin and empty.

CHAPTER 24
KATABASIS IS A LOT TO ASK OF A NEIGHBOR

Paul woke to a burning sensation in his left leg that seemed to be spreading up his side. He tried to sit up and grab his leg, but even the smallest motion sent the room spinning. His mind replayed flashes of the last seconds before he fell through the hatch, when he saw Minwoo's flashlight go dark and the metal arms crashing down. But the burning kept interrupting his thoughts, hotter, now like hundreds of little red-glowing pokers jabbing into his leg. Or like sharp, gnawing teeth.

Teeth.

He sat up suddenly, through the dizziness and the pain, to see several of those cockrat-things feasting on his leg with their rat incisors, little armored muzzles slick with his blood. He swatted at them and in his dizziness missed, the motion causing him to vomit on the stone floor next to him.

He scrambled backward, pushing off the base of the ladder and slipping on his own blood. The cockrats scurried after him. He kicked out at them with his right leg, too weak and too slow to be a threat, but it was enough to keep them back for a second. One discovered his vomit and started lapping at it with a jabbing black tongue. And then they were all crowded in a little circle around their new pool of food.

He pulled himself to the door, dragging his backpack, operating on little more than adrenaline and panic. One of the cockrats saw its meal escaping and started toward him. It bit him twice more, on his good right leg this time, before he got the door open and fell through. The door crunched into the pursuing cockrat when he tried to shut it, stunning the creature. He put all the energy he had into slamming it twice more, splitting the thing's head from its body. With the door finally closed, he crawled to the sitting room sofa and leaned against it, too tired to pull himself up.

A part of his mind wanted to succumb to the exhaustion, the darkness creeping in that promised to push away the pain, and he almost let it take him, until he thought about dozens of more cockrats somehow getting through the closed door and nibbling at his unconscious body until they devoured him whole.

He forced himself up to a sitting position on the sofa and pulled his left leg up. He had to tear open most of his jeans to get a better look at what the cockrats had done to him. He took off his shirt, wet it with some of his remaining water, and wiped the blood from his leg. A hundred little notches in his skin started refilling with blood immediately after his shirt had passed.

He should've brought bandages. He should've brought the bottle of whiskey, to sterilize wounds. He should've brought—

No. He shouldn't have brought anything, including himself. He shouldn't have come back. And now Min-woo was dead.

Had he heard a bell ringing? Or was that part of a concussed dream after falling through the hatch?

The bell had been real, and he knew what the ringing bell meant. He had heard it before, with Corinne. It signaled the arrival of that reality-warping monster, the *Košmaro*, coming to take the soul of the deceased to the statue-prisons in the Between's underworld.

It had taken Min-woo, or whatever was left of Min-woo.

He pulled the notebook from his bag and flipped through its pages until he came to the entry for death. Death was different here, in the Between, where a confirmed hell awaited every soul, sinner or saint alike. But it mentioned a way death could be reversed using *viaticum* (here Min-woo had handwritten *"Charon's Obols"* and circled it three times). Paul pulled the two gold coins from his pocket that matched the one Min-woo had kept for himself. Min-woo had indeed called them *obols* when he found them in the sitting room. Paul found their entry in the FAQ.

He skimmed through paragraphs that read like classical mythology, focusing on the tie-in to *katabasis* and rebirth. Two of his electives in college had been Greek and Roman mythology, and Paul had even translated the *Aeneid* from Latin during senior year of high school. This was familiar territory.

Katabasis was the descent into the underworld. Odysseus, Hercules, Orpheus—all the heroes seemed to have their own version of this adventure. Aeneas went to the Underworld in search of his father, and to get there, he had to pay Charon, the ferryman at the River Styx. *Viaticum* was the payment. In the *Aeneid*, Aeneas had paid Charon with a golden branch, or something like that. Not a coin. But others did use coins, right? That's why burials included coins covering the eyes or in the mouths of the dead.

He took a deep breath and tried to ignore the pain and concentrate. Halfway down the page, Min-woo had highlighted a line:

If the player possesses an obol at the time of death, the player awakens as a revenant on the far side of the Black River and may give the obol to Charon to cross back.

Paul felt like throwing up again. In time, he could accept that Min-woo had died. That would be tragic enough. But now, at least according to the notebook, Min-woo might be a ghost of some kind, down in the Between's underworld.

That meant Paul had to undertake his own *katabasis*, to rescue Min-woo and bring him back from the underworld, back from the Between. Paul's resolve lasted about two seconds before he collapsed back onto the floor. Tragedy almost always struck the mythical heroes when they descended to the underworld in search of lost love ones— and Paul was no mythical hero. His leg was still bleeding, an infection probably already started, and his body was bruised from his fall.

Maybe he had a concussion as well. He couldn't save Min-woo, let alone save himself, no matter what he found in the notebook.

The only hope, then, was to make it back to the field with the broken colossus and find Corinne. He made a silent apology to Min-woo and added his neighbor's name to the list of people he had let down.

CHAPTER 25
LET JAY DO ALL THE TALKING

Jay scraped his initials into the wall of the *stelisto*'s chamber. It was his room, so the way he saw it, he could deface it any way he pleased. Then, in foot-tall letters, he scratched N - S - E - W - E, the maze pattern that led to this room. The letters had been there when he and Paul found the room, but they had faded away somehow.

Unless, they had seen *these* letters, the ones he just now carved. Was that even possible? This place seemed to have its own hair-brained rules, so who the hell knew. If the letters had been his, did that mean that the dead *stelisto* on the altar was...

A chill ran through his bones, and he didn't let the thought finish. He turned to Supriya and said, "Where the hell is Paul, anyway?"

Supriya was lying on her back on the altar, eyes closed, arms folded, the white fabric of her dress hanging down the altar's stone sides like icing on a block of cake. Her forehead crinkled in thought, and without opening her eyes she said, "I can sense a new *masinisto* in the graveyard manor. My old role has already been filled. The story keeps moving along, doesn't it?"

"Yeah, but what do we care?" Jay said. "Anyway, we're leaving as soon as Paul gets here. Can you sense him at all?"

Supriya clicked her tongue against her teeth. "Your friend isn't coming. Maybe he chose not to, or maybe the door didn't work for him. Remember, the link had gotten so out-of-skew that I had to use a gateway just to be sure we could get through."

Jay half-listened while tracing the impression of his knife through his jacket. On the altar, Supriya looked like a corpse with her eyes closed. He could see her in death, see how beautiful she would be that moment after life left her body. "I told you to get off that thing, Supes."

She smirked without opening her eyes, and in her smooth, *gardistaro* voice said, "Tempted to murder me?"

He could see the tiny twitches in her neck with every beat of her heart. A clean slice just so... "Not tempted in the least," he said. "But it's nasty with all the blood soaked into that stone over the years. Don't want to get your dress dirty."

"It's impossible for this dress to become dirty," she said. She sat up and gave him a pout. "I know you wanted Paul to come, but he's not going to. I feel a trace of him, in the ladder room leading up to the graveyard, but I think that's residue from when he was here before. I'm sorry, Jay."

Jay angrily jabbed the knife into the stone, which gave little more resistance to the blade than flesh. "Fucking Paul. I would've come to support him. Some goddamn friend."

"You shouldn't have told him to come back in the first place. He can't survive here like we can. He's not like us." Her golden eyes seemed to pierce straight through him. "I think we should go. I can feel the crack in the cavern wall where the elevator door opened. If we go there, as the *gardistaro* I can open the path back. Are you sure you want to come back to my world? Won't people miss you in yours?"

"Miss me?" Jay asked, yanking twice at the knife to get it free from the wall. "Honestly, they'll probably be relieved. Especially Paul. I think he hangs out with me out of a sense of historical obligation. I sometimes think when we're together that his heart isn't in it. Then again, I'm not even sure Paul has a heart."

"That's a terrible thing to say." She dropped from the altar onto the floor and glided toward the closed, wooden door leading back to the sitting room maze. "I'll make the doorway to the cavern now, if you're ready. There's a crypt with a nice, tall gate about ten meters away from the wall, at the edge of the graveyard. The junklings will be aggressive, but that won't be a problem for you, will it?"

"Depends on how long you take." He sighed. "If you really want to go back, I mean, I'll go with you, like I said. Of course, that means I'll have to find my your-world doppelgänger and kill him and take his identity. I've got a recent history of remorseless murdering, but I can't honestly tell you how killing my other self is gonna feel."

"We can't have two Jays," Supriya said with a frown, and then her eyes lit up. "I could kill him for you."

"That's what I love about you, Supes. A real commitment to us." He walked up to her and ran the back of his fingers across her cheek and jaw. "Why are we in such a hurry to go back, anyway? Time probably stopped there, like it did for my world. We could go down a couple worlds. Take over that sky city you read about in the *masinisto*'s journal. I'd be the dashing Lord Jay and you'd be the radiant Lordette Supes. When our subjects piss us off, we can toss them over the sides."

"I have a whole life that I've built," Supriya said. "Thousands of followers. The rehab clinic with Frankie. Oh shit." She sat back on the altar. "The Frankie from my outworld is dead."

Jay studied her face, looking for any signs of the sadness that should be fighting to push through the *gardistaro* calm, but he saw none. "Maybe there's no going back, babe," he said. "At least, not back to the lives we had before." As he said the words he felt relief, like a weight had been lifted. "It ain't such a bad thing. Think about it. Right now you can make holes appear in the fucking air, Supes. The real world's gonna be a disappointment after that." He saw the consideration in her eyes, so he pushed forward. "My dream has always been to run my own business. Build an empire. Prove to people like my fucking dad that I'm capable of making something. But here, maybe I can have a literal empire, not just a bank account with imaginary numbers."

"How do I know if I really want this, or if it's the role talking?"

"It's always the role talking, babe. Even back home. Have you ever considered—"

Supriya held up a hand. "That woman is nearby. The one with the painted face. I can feel her. She knows we're here."

Jay moved to the door in a fluid side-glide, knife in hand, forearm itching for a new kill-mark. He nodded to Supriya, who was already preparing a gateway. But right as he was about to swing the door wide and charge through, the door's shimmering perimeter vanished.

"She moved," Supriya said. "It's hard when she's in the maze." She traced the air around the door again, but before Jay could turn the handle, she swept the gateway away with the dismissive wave of her hand. "She keeps moving."

"Can you tell where she's going? We've gotta make her answer some questions. Open a gateway ahead of her, and we'll be waiting when she comes through the door."

"It doesn't work like that. Not in the maze, anyway." Supriya closed her eyes and shook her head. "I have these hazy memories from when I was the *masinisto*, memories of building the sitting room maze. From whoever played the role first, when it wasn't a role." She opened her eyes and stared at Jay. "I can't open a gateway to the room ahead of her. Even if I knew where she was going, the room ahead doesn't exist until it's needed."

"So if we want her, we have to chase her. That's fine by me."

Supriya made the air around the door sizzle. "I don't know the pattern she's using to navigate the maze, but I can keep us one room behind her."

Jay cracked the door and peered in with one eye. Seeing it empty, he swung the door wide open and charged through, vaulting over the sofa. Supriya had another gateway ready before he reached the next door.

This time, he showed even less caution, feeling pulled toward his nearby prey. He held his left hand over the doorknob, ready the instant the door transformed. A second passed. Then five. "Hurry up, Supes. She's getting away." He dropped his hand and turned back toward Supriya.

Supriya glared at him as she limped around the sofa. "I'm moving as fast as I can. My leg still isn't working right. And besides, the skull-faced woman has left the maze. She's in a field."

"What's she doing?"

"I can't tell. It's not like I can see her. I can only sense her presence." Supriya frowned.

"Well, is she moving?"

"I don't think so. It's a big field, but there's nowhere to go. The only door leads back to the maze."

"So she's just standing there?"

"I think she's waiting for us. Maybe she's been trying to get us to follow her."

"How would she know, though? You've got your special *gardistaro* feelings. You think she has some sort of power like that?"

"I have no idea."

Jay paced. He felt like a loaded gun with the hammer pulled back. "Maybe she wants to talk with us, or cut some sort of deal."

Supriya eyed him suspiciously. "I think it's a trap and we're walking right into it."

A trap? Only someone with a deathwish would lure the *stelisto* and the *gardistaro* to them. "It's not a fucking trap. If Skull Girl really is Corinne, like Paul said, then she wouldn't hurt a flea. Trust me. Either she doesn't know we're following her, or she thinks she can talk her way out of getting stabbed. Whichever case it is, she's wrong." He gestured to the door.

After a heavy sigh, Supriya traced a rectangle in the air, and the door became a gateway.

Supriya shielded her eyes from the brightness of the sun pouring in through the door. She walked up next to Jay, but he held her back.

"Now this is my kind of place," Jay said, staring through the open door at the rolling fields of tawny grass. "A sky so big, so bright, it hurts your eyes. Like back home in Texas." He gave Supriya a confident nod. "Let me go first. Last time I encountered this woman, she got a little testy."

"Testy?"

"Yeah. Like, cranky, irritable. You've never heard the word testy?"

"No. It's a gross word. It sounds like testes, like testicles."

"I said she got a little testy, not that she's got little testes! I didn't perform an impromptu gynecological exam on her or anything. But she was waving a wand in my general direction, which maybe was a bit phallic."

"You're an idiot, you know that?"

Jay ignored the insult and poked his head through the gateway and looked around. "Looks like the coast is clear, but stay behind me and let me do all the talking. I'm a natural negotiator."

"Sure you are. Now get on with it," Supriya muttered.

They paused a few feet in, waist-deep in the grass, sunlight brighter than anything they'd seen in weeks. Jay scanned to his right, with his hand cupped over his eyes. Pieces of a giant, broken stone statue lay strewn far out into the distance, making it impossible to tell how large the statue had been when standing.

"My god. The size of that thing," he said.

Supriya half-expected another of Jay's penis jokes to follow, but when her eyes adjusted enough to see the scale of the broken colossus, any unuttered joke in her mind vanished. It must have been as tall as a skyscraper. Or maybe bigger than that. How could such a thing be possible?

About a hundred feet from them was a makeshift shelter made of wood and cloth, leaned into what was once the base of the giant statue. As the wind blew, the flap of the shelter fluttered open, exposing a bed and stacks of supplies, but not the skull-faced woman Jay had described.

Just then, the residue of Paul she had felt earlier became *fuller*— she didn't know how else to describe the feeling. All she knew for certain was that Paul was here, in the Between, first in the room beneath the graveyard and now in the sitting room. He must have been asleep or unconscious the entire time they had been back. But how was that possible if she and Jay had gone through the door first? There was an entry in the *masinisto*'s journal that explained, in detail, how the World Lens affected time for those who used it to travel between worlds. The answer was in that journal, she was sure of it, but those memories had become cloudier ever since she left that role.

She stopped and turned toward Jay, opening her mouth to tell him about Paul, when she got a sudden image of the skull-faced woman in her mind and the feeling, like a pull, that the woman was standing behind them. Between them and the sun.

She turned. Eyes watering, she could see the woman's silhouette, holding something, pointing it toward them.

Jay turned and saw her, too. "Hey. Long time, no see," he said, right before the air between them rippled and Jay went flying backward into the stone base next to the shelter.

"I told you I'd kill you if I saw you again."

CHAPTER 26
A CHOICE IN THE FIELD

The notebook's entry on the sitting room maze listed dozens of sequences, leading to rooms Paul had never seen. About halfway down the list, he found the sequence for the field.

West. North. South. West. North. South.

He struggled to his feet. The entire left side of his body—where he must've landed when he fell through the hatch—competed for bragging rights on what was bruised and battered the worst. His shoulder, cheekbone, hip, knee, ankle, and, currently winning, his ribs. Each normal step of his right foot was followed by wincing, half step with his left. At this rate, it would take him half an hour to make it to the field.

In the first copy of the sitting room, the sofa called out to him, but he pushed on, taking the left-hand door, corresponding to the *west* direction indicated in the FAQ. No matter how many times he walked through the copies of the sitting room, he always felt a wave of dizziness when he stepped from one copy into another. The north/south part of the sequence made the dizziness worse because it looked like going back to where he'd just come from, but it felt like stepping across the world.

He began to wonder how all of this worked. The same door seemingly leading to different places. It had to be magic, didn't it? But "magic" wasn't a satisfying answer. Magic was a throwaway word that sounded like an explanation but didn't add any new information. Maybe the laws of physics were different here, but systems still had to be governed by laws. The FAQ entry on the sitting room—and all of the FAQ entries he had seen so far—told *what* things did but not *how* they did them. Arthur C. Clarke had hit the nail on the head: *Any sufficiently advanced technology is indistinguishable from magic.* Something made it all work. It couldn't just be magic. Thinking about how it all worked kept his mind off the pain of his body. At least somewhat.

He opened the final door in the sequence, and sunlight flooded into the windowless sitting room. The sunlight on his skin sure felt like magic.

A series of pops, like the cracking of a giant whip, came from the field, followed by yelling. He pulled the revolver out of his backpack's front pocket and staggered into the tall grass of the field, expecting to see ash dogs or some of the other monsters Min-woo had encountered in the game version of the Between. Instead, he saw Corinne fighting against Jay and Supriya.

"No, no, no!" he screamed, waving his arms as he limped toward them.

Corinne must have seen him from the corner of her eye. She turned toward him, briefly pointed the silver rod at him, and then recognition appeared on her face. The air next to her crackled, and suddenly Jay was next to her, seeming to move twenty feet in a single step, blue knife flashing out.

At least one of Jay's slashes must've hit, but Paul couldn't tell whether or not it made it through the armor Corinne wore under her black robe. She spun toward Jay with the silver rod, but Jay stepped through another hole in the air and vanished.

Near the stream, about a hundred feet away, Supriya traced the outlines of doorways in the air with her hands.

Corinne pointed the rod at Supriya and a rippling wave of distortion fired out from the device with deafening pops, like the air between them—or the space between them—was tearing. Before the wave reached Supriya, a rectangle of *elsewhere* appeared before her, and the wave reappeared behind Corinne, smashing into her and throwing her to the ground. The silver rod spun in the air with the sunlight flashing off it.

Paul started toward Corinne, to help her up, to physically get between her and Jay and Supriya, but within a second, Jay was already back, stepping out of another of Supriya's gateways. Paul fired the gun in the air, hoping its booming retort would catch their attention, snap them out of it somehow, but Jay attacked without any hesitation.

Corinne rolled onto her back right as Jay stabbed down where she had been. She kicked out at his knee, and as he stepped back out of the way, she threw something she had taken from inside her robe. It was the size of a stone, and when it hit Jay it exploded in a cloud of gray-green. He stumbled backward and fanned his arms in the cloud, trying to clear the air around him.

Another hole appeared in the air next to him, an escape path woven by Supriya, but Jay staggered backward instead of toward it. He wiped at his face and bent over and wretched. All Paul could think of was mustard gas. If he didn't do something, someone else was going to die. He fired the gun into the air again, and again it seemed to have no effect.

Corinne was back on her feet. She had pulled another metal rod out from within her robe—this one red, like anodized aluminum— and pointed it at Jay, who held his hand up as if that could block the coming attack.

Supriya screamed in panic and looked all around her as if searching for ideas. When her eyes found the giant, severed hand of the stone colossus, she began tracing in the air.

Corinne limped toward Jay and straightened her arm, to fire whatever the red weapon was in her hand, but a disc of stone fell out of nowhere right above her, and then another.

Paul could see Supriya's gateways appearing horizontally in the stone statue's hand, severing pieces and dropping them through the gateway's other side right above Corinne. The first caught Corinne in the shoulder, knocking her to the ground, and the second landed with a crushing thud. Supriya's hands danced in the air as she carved off a third slice.

Corinne struggled but there was no way she could escape the weight already on her. The next stone would surely kill her. Before Paul knew what he was doing, he had the revolver pointed at Supriya. Other than the two shots into the air, he'd never fired a pistol before —and never at anything or anyone. Some part of his mind had already made a decision, and he pulled the trigger. That part of his mind envisioned the bullet hitting Supriya in the metal leg, interrupting the fight just enough for him to get everyone's attention. Instead, the shot hit her dead in the chest, and she collapsed, limp to the ground.

CHAPTER 27
IT ALWAYS GETS WORSE

Jay let out a cry, a sound like nothing Paul had ever heard another person make, and he immediately found himself throwing up as well. What had he done? He had killed someone. Not just someone, Jay's girlfriend.

She would've killed Corinne if he hadn't!

He wasn't trying to kill Supriya. At least, he didn't think he was. Just to stop her. To stop them from killing each other.

But the only one who had killed had been him.

Jay looked at him, eyes red with hate.

"You killed her, you motherfucker," Jay said through coughs and wheezes. "I'm killing both of you now."

"I didn't mean to! I swear to you, Jay! I'm so sorry."

Corinne had pulled herself halfway out from under the stones. "You're going to have to shoot him, too, Paul. Like I told you before. Or he'll kill you, and me, and everyone else he meets. They all do it. All of the *stelistos*. Until someone finally kills them or they kill themselves."

With the inhuman look in Jay's eyes, Paul knew Corinne's words were true. "Stay back, Jay," he said and pointed the gun at his friend. "I can't change what's happened, but let's not make it worse."

"You're gonna have to kill me while you still have the chance," Jay said, still trudging forward. "I can feel my strength coming back, and then you won't be able to stop me. Even with that gun."

Paul glanced from Jay to Corinne and back to Jay. It was like he was in the eye of a hurricane. A few seconds of stillness, of relative calm, but destruction was on its way. He kept his gun pointed at Jay, and Corinne had her red wand pointed at him as well. Jay only had the knife, but that unfamiliar, ravenous look in his eyes said he'd never quit. It didn't matter that twenty feet or more separated them, that Jay'd be dead before he made it half that far.

Jay's body twitched. Paul knew he had only a few more seconds.

"Maybe we can still save her," Paul said. With his left hand, he pulled the two gold coins Min-woo had given him from his left pocket. "A lot of things are possible here that aren't back home. We've already seen that, right?" He held up the coins for both Jay and Corinne to see.

"You don't want to use those," Corinne said.

"You know what they are?" Paul shook his head. "It doesn't matter. We have no choice. I think these can save Supriya. I just need to get the notebook out of my backpack to read how to use them." He looked into Jay's red-streaked eyes. "I'm sorry I shot her. I can't take it back now, but if you give me a few minutes, I think we can save her."

Jay's chest heaved and his eyes burned with fury. Instead of answering, he began pacing.

Paul took that as a window of opportunity. "If you remember your Greek mythology," Paul said, digging the notebook out of the bag, "you give the dead a gold coin—an obol—to pay Charon to ferry them across the river Styx. It's kind of like that here, but you can pay for the trip there and back. Two obols and you can cheat death. At least, that's what it says in the notebook." He flipped through the pages, missing the entry for the golden obols, and then missing it again the other way.

Corinne walked over and put a roach-armored boot on the notebook. "It's better not to mess with these. Consider her gone. The coins will make things worse. And we need to leave before the Košmaro comes for her."

"What the hell is the *Koŝmaro*?" Jay growled without turning their direction.

"The creature that takes souls down to the underworld," Paul said.

That made Jay stop. "How the hell do you know this?"

"Because he saw the *Koŝmaro* before," Corinne said. To Paul, "But how do you know about the obols? And what is this notebook? Notes for what?"

"An FAQ for the Between's computer game or simulation or whatever it is. It's a long story. I'll tell it later. For now, think of this notebook as a crib sheet for the Between. Here's the part about the coins. Listen. *When two obols are placed in a corpse's mouth, the player—*the, uh, person*—is restored to life in a very weakened state.* You see? Supriya will come back to life." Under his breath, he added, "It does go on to say that rebirth causes the denizens of the underworld to, um, come looking for the reawakened."

"The what of what?" Jay said.

"Denizens of the underworld," Paul repeated. "Creatures of hell, I guess. It looks like it's mainly talking about the *Koŝmaro*."

Jay rolled his eyes. "Give me the fucking coins. I don't care if Satan himself comes for Supriya, I'll gut him from horns to asshole and mount his head on my living room wall."

Paul looked at Corinne. "Supriya's the *gardistaro*. If we revive her, she can open one of those doorway things back home. Who cares if the *Koŝmaro* is after us. We'll be long gone by the time it gets here."

Jay extended his hand. "Give me the coins, Paul."

Paul looked again at Corinne who merely shrugged.

"Be my guest," she said. "But when it makes things worse, don't look to me to fix it, because I won't be able to."

"How could it make things worse?" Paul said.

"That's what happens here, Paul. Every power has its price. It *always* gets worse."

Paul took the obols out of his pocket and turned them over in his palm. One side had the raised image of a bee, so intricately cast that it looked like a real bee had been pushed through gold foil. The other side looked like an eye, shaped from the hollow imprint of the bee's body. The three-dimensional aspect of the coins made them look like golden eyeballs sitting in the palm of his hand. When he looked up, Jay was walking toward him, hand still outstretched.

Paul pointed the gun at him again. "Stop, Jay."

"I want the coins."

Paul tossed them one at a time, and Jay grabbed them out of the air with his left hand without breaking eye contact.

Jay glared at each of them and then, after a slight hesitation, slipped the knife into its sheath hidden within his black coat. He squatted down next to Supriya's body, took her lifeless hand in his, and closed his eyes.

Paul looked over to Corinne. She had picked up her silver wand and was walking away. Limping, rather, her shoulders slumped, exhausted. Exhaustion hit him as well. He thought about how nice it would be to sit leaned against the broken statue, in its shadow, and close his eyes. But he didn't have the energy to walk there. He didn't even have the energy to keep standing, so he dropped to the ground where he stood.

For a minute or more, none of them moved—Corinne, now sitting on top of the boulder by the stream, Paul using his backpack as a makeshift pillow in the short grass of the field, and Jay holding Supriya's hand while tear after tear rolled down his cheeks.

Then Jay leaned over and whispered something into Supriya's ear, something Paul couldn't hear. He slid first one obol and then the other into Supriya's mouth and then lifted her chin and held her jaw shut.

For several minutes, nothing moved besides the grass swaying in the perpetual noonday breeze and the stream twinkling in the sunlight. Jay let go of Supriya's chin and her jaw relaxed. Paul could see the glint of the sun reflecting off the coins in her mouth.

It hadn't worked.

Jay stood, chest rising and falling in deeper and deeper breaths, as if he was preparing for something. The knife, somehow, was back in his hand. He turned to Paul but before he could do anything more, the bell sounded. Eight hollow, metallic booms, more rapid than Paul had heard the bell before, almost urgent, like it came from a church just over the horizon, a church calling for its flock. Before Paul could contemplate the bell's new sound, Supriya sat up, gasped, and then her eyes rolled back and her body went limp.

Jay dropped back to his knees and caught her as she fell back. "She's breathing!" Jay exclaimed. "She's unconscious, but she's breathing!"

Paul mustered the strength to stand and went to kneel next to Jay and Supriya. Jay shot him a look like he was about to smile, but it soured into a glare. It had worked after all. Somehow, Supriya was back from the dead. Of all the improbable things Paul had seen in the Between so far, this shook his world the most. Supriya's death had been by his hand, but his sin had just been undone. He smiled at Jay. If this wrong could be undone, maybe every wrong could. Maybe...

"I've never heard the bell sound like that," Corinne said after dropping down from her perch atop the stone. She walked up to them and stood so that the sun was at her back, casting them all in her shadow. "We're going to have company soon. Remember your plan about Supriya whisking us all away to safety? How's that looking right now?"

"Supes," Jay whispered, patting Supriya's cheek. "Hey, Supes. Need you to wake up so you can make a gateway for us. Before the hell demon gets here. Supes? Aw, fuck."

Paul looked up at Corinne, but with the sunlight behind her, all he could see was her dark silhouette.

"I know a way to help her," Corinne said. "Jay, I need you to stand up and step back."

"What are you gonna do?" he said, without looking up from Supriya cradled in his arms.

"Nothing until you give me some space."

For several seconds, Jay didn't show any sign he had heard Corinne, still focused on Supriya, and then he gently laid her head on the grass, sighed, and stood. "So, now what?"

A thunderous force struck Jay in the chest and sent him backward, tumbling like a rag doll thrown from a car. When he came to a stop, he didn't move.

Paul jumped to his feet, arms reflexively up to cover his face, expecting a similar blast from the silver wand Corinne held in her hand. But she slipped it under her robe, turned, and began walking toward her tent, without looking back. As if nothing behind her existed anymore.

The *Košmaro* on its way. Supriya unconscious. Jay face down in the grass and maybe dead. Corinne absolving herself of any responsibility in their survival. And Paul, himself, barely able to keep standing, much less run two worlds away to the nearest exit.

Corinne had been right. Things had gotten much worse.

CHAPTER 28
THE REVENANT

Once again the revenant had a body, but this body felt cold and wouldn't respond, wouldn't move. The body just stood there, arms at its side, facing out from the tower, like the others in front of him. He tried to turn his head, tried to scream, but the cold, metal form surrounding him paid no attention to his desires.

Within his statue-prison, the revenant could feel the others, all of them trapped in their own statues, thousands, all trying to scream. All failing. He tried to remember his name, but the statue-prison channeled his thoughts somehow, braided them with the thoughts of the others, and pulled the thoughts back into a great machine somewhere behind him, beyond the bell tower.

Again he tried to scream.

The air remained silent.

An understanding came first, that this prison would be his eternal fate. Then came fear, and finally despair. The great machine devoured the despair and pulled at him for more.

Sometime later, seconds or a millennia, he felt a warmth, or rather a lack of coldness, where the iron skin of his right hand should be. The awareness of this warmth stayed with him, not pulled back into the machine like all other coherent thoughts. The warmth remained his.

He focused on the warmth, became the warmth, and the warmth began to extend out. A golden light flared. His hand—not the iron statue hand, but the soul-form of his revenant hand—had slipped out from its prison, a golden obol shining through spectral fingers wrapped around it. The obol pulled him away from the statue, freeing his whole arm, then tugging out his shoulder and head, and finally the rest of his revenant body.

The revenant stood in front of his now-empty iron statue, and his thoughts stayed with him, free from the machine. His first kept thought was his own name. Min-woo Kim. His second kept thought was: *Being a revenant is going to severely limit my wardrobe options.*

Each statue was different, unique to the revenant within, but they all shared a look of horror on their black iron faces, a captured final realization of their eternal suffering. Thousands of these statues stretched across the shore between the underworld's oily black river and the jagged tooth of the bell tower.

The revenant once called Min-woo drifted among the statues. He could feel a connection to all of those trapped within like they were all knots on a giant astral web. Through this web he could touch them, communicate, but they couldn't respond. Their thoughts, instead, were pulled back into the machine beyond the bell tower, like Min-woo's thoughts had been when he, too, was imprisoned in an iron statue.

He had seen the statue-prisons in the game, of course, and in game-inspired nightmares, but that didn't prepare him for the shared psychic terror of the real thing. If he'd had a body, it would've been shaking.

He glided through the statues toward the tower. At its top was an opening resembling an eye, with the bell at its center. The tower's gray stones looked like scales on a living thing that had grown up, twisted and gnarled from the ground. A finger scratching at the sky.

One statue stood away from the others, next to the tower. A man of plain features, average height. Instead of the captured screams on the other statues' faces, he looked straight ahead, expressionless. If that statue, too, contained a revenant, it was separate from the astral web connecting the others. All Min-woo felt in reaching out to it with his mind was a void.

He drifted past the lone statue and the tower, to the edge of a chasm filled with fog. Barely visible were the outer appendages of a giant machine, arms with countless lenses, twisting and repositioning themselves to channel and focus the agony pulled from the statue prisoners below. The Great World Lens. The city-sized machine used by the Great Order God, *Dio Ordo*, to pull the outworlds together.

Just then, he sensed a new knot forming on the astral web, a knot like his, free from an iron prison. This connection, this shared feeling between the revenants—it wasn't a part of the game as far as he could remember. If the game really had been a simulation of a real place, its author couldn't have made an authentic revenant experience without dying himself. Min-woo reached out to the new knot with his mind, as intuitive an action as reaching out his hand, and found that he knew the form of the human it had once been. This other revenant, worlds away physically, but connected to him in the astral web, was the young woman he had met at Paul's house. Supriya Reddy.

The bell rang, a ripple of dread extending out from the tower, cascading through Min-woo and the statues, across the black water, and beyond. The statue next to the bell tower seemed to lose focus, and then it stepped off its iron pedestal, a cloud of darkness swirling around its form.

The revenant who had been Min-woo slid to the other side of the tower to avoid the *Koŝmaro*'s attention, but its only focus seemed to be in heading toward the river. It was going for Supriya.

Her knot vanished, as suddenly as it had formed, and Min-woo no longer had any sense of her astral form, as if it had been obliterated or if she had somehow returned to flesh. The *Koŝmaro* stopped and looked about as if confused. Paul must have used the two obols Min-woo had given him to bring Supriya back to life! Pride flashed through Min-woo's astral being, like a trainer watching his prizefighter execute a move in the ring they'd prepared for in the gym. But pride was quickly replaced by dread.

The bell rang repeatedly, angry and insistent. The *Košmaro* began moving again, walking among statues which became distorted, out of phase, in its proximity. The *Košmaro* walked past the ferryman's boat at the edge of the water, straight into the river's oily blackness, and it grew bigger and bigger until it was hundreds of feet tall, wading waist-deep out into the fog.

As the *Košmaro* vanished ahead, the revenant of Min-woo frantically searched his memory of the game for what to do next. Paul had the notebook, so they would know to go to *Katedralo Kaoso*, the Chaos Cathedral in the City Above. But even if they survived the journey, the *Košmaro* had a faster way to travel between worlds. It would catch them before they could escape.

Min-woo glided to the water's edge. The Black River would kill any human who touched it, but what about a revenant? Could he glide across the water after the *Košmaro*? Damn, he needed the notebook!

The ferryman turned his shrouded head toward Min-woo and stuck out a bony hand. Min-woo looked at the shining obol in his own ethereal hand. Like in the game, an obol could be used as fare for the journey across. He handed it to the ferryman and glided aboard the boat.

CHAPTER 29
JAY'S MISSION

Jay awoke, bound and gagged, with grass pressed against his face. He tried to move but succeeded only in rolling onto his back. His whole body felt like it had been bludgeoned with a meat tenderizing hammer. He closed his eyes against the brilliant sun overhead and tried, and failed, to bite through his gag. Where was his knife? He could feel it like an itch somewhere behind him, an itch that, going unscratched, was beginning to burn.

A shadow blocked out the sun.

Paul, looming over him, said, "I'm so sorry, Jay, but apologies will have to wait until later. The *Košmaro* is coming for Supriya. If we work together, we can save her. I hope. According to the notebook, there's an exit in the third world at a place called the Altar of the Sky on the top of the big cathedral in the middle of the city. Corinne ... uh, Skull Girl... She knows the way, and she's agreed to help me get Supriya there.

"But here's the thing. You can't come with us. The role of the *stelisto*, the knife, whatever ... it's poisoned you. Corinne wasn't going to... She was going to kill you, okay? But I talked her out of it. We need you. Supriya needs you. We're not gonna make it to the Altar of the Sky before the *Košmaro* reaches us. So ... uh ... that's where you come in. According to Min-woo's notebook, the *Košmaro* travels via something called the World Tunnels. I don't know what those are, but there's an entrance right by the Altar. That's where it should come out." Paul let out a deep sigh. "We need you to go on ahead of us and ... find a way to slow it down."

Jay yelled and cursed at his backstabbing former friend, but the sound that came out from his gagged mouth was, "Muhh-wuhh-hummunnuah!" He wasn't afraid of the *Koŝmaro*, not that he'd ever seen the damn thing. Paul had, but Paul was a worthless prick who ran away from anything remotely scary. While Jay had become the *stelisto*, Paul was still just Paul Prentice the accountant.

"I don't know how," Paul said. "There's nothing in the notebook about fighting the *Koŝmaro*. Nothing about any weaknesses. But if you can't at least slow it down, we're fucked. Supriya's fucked. I've packed a bag of supplies for you, and I tore out the notebook pages you'll need. If we somehow make it to the exit, I'll wait for you. We'll find a way to free you from this role. Somewhere in the notebook there's got to be a way."

Corinne's silhouette joined Paul's in towering over Jay. "You're leaving now," she said. "No discussion. Your knife is on the ground next to the bag Paul packed by the door. If you do anything other than walk straight out, if you say a single word, it will be your last. Got it?" To Paul, she said, "Cut him loose and stand back."

Jay hesitated in the doorway. Every part of his being wanted to spin around and charge toward that skull-faced-bitch-version of Corinne and worthless Paul, to gut them both and put fresh new hash-marks on his forearm—extra-large to make sure they always stood out. He could feel her standing behind him with one of those metal wand things pointed directly at his spine, and he knew that she would make good on her threat.

If he moved fast enough, he could throw his knife right into her chest. The thought of throwing the blue knife, sending it away from him, was sickening, but he knew it would fly true. And while he retrieved it, Paul would stand there weaponless and useless. The blood from one would join the blood from the other, and then...

And then it would be just him and Supriya. Maybe she would regain her strength before the *Kosmaro* arrived, but if not... Paul had given him the directions to the Altar of the Sky, but what was he supposed to do when he got there? And could he carry Supriya the whole way? No fucking chance.

He walked into the sitting room maze and slammed the door behind him. His left forearm itched in the spot where he needed to carve new hash-marks, but that would have to wait. Somehow he'd kill the *Kosmaro*, and then it would be Corinne and Paul's turn.

A cockrat scuttled from the room's corner toward the sofa. Jay kicked it into the wall where it impacted with a satisfying crunch. He unfolded the notebook pages that had been stuffed in his pocket. On the top was the list of sequences for the sitting room maze, with the route to the Grand Staircase circled several times.

He followed the FAQ's sequence (east, north, west, north, east, south), but hesitated before opening the final door. It would be just like those two fuckers to send him to a trap. When he did open the door, it led to the massive, spiraling staircase Paul had described.

The room was decorated much like the sitting room: the same patterned velvet wallpaper, overlapping rugs, deep mahogany floor. The staircase, however, had a very different architectural feel. A black, iron railing encircled the top and led downward, an oscillating sine-wave connecting the floors and stairs to a banister of polished obsidian that matched the stairs.

Looking down, it was impossible to tell where the stairway led, its dark stairs blending with, and eventually being consumed by, the shadows below. According to the FAQ's pages, the second world was some kind of desert. How the hell a staircase could lead from one world to another, Jay had no idea.

He started his descent, taking each smooth stair slowly. As the light from above became a smaller and smaller part of the nautilus spiral overhead, he expected the way to get darker, but it didn't. Candles on wall sconces kept the stairway with enough light to see another ten stairs or so down, but dark enough to make the going treacherous. The impenetrable darkness below seemed to recede with each step downward, so that he had no sense of progress beyond a sinking feeling in his stomach, and maybe a growing pressure against his temples. It could've been a trick of the imagination, but it felt like swimming to the bottom of a deep pool, too deep to swim back up for air.

He should've counted the stairs. By now it had been, what, thirty? Fifty? He started counting, too late to yield an accurate result, but it provided a sense of progress. At least until somewhere around two-hundred, where he lost count and abandoned the effort.

How the hell were the others going to get Supriya down these stairs if she was still unconscious? Everything hinged on them reaching what Paul called the Altar of the Sky on the third world before the *Košmaro* found them. Already, Jay had his doubts.

Minutes passed. Maybe hours. Jay had no way to tell. And then the darkness below became softer, softer until light poured in, light so bright he had to stop and shield his eyes until they adjusted.

Just below, the walls encircling the stairway abruptly ended, and the stairway continued downward into what looked like open daylight. He descended through the strange threshold, and all around him he could see a colorless desert, stretching in undulating dunes as far as the eye could see.

At the bottom of the staircase was a landing, a square platform rising up out of the gray sand. It had the same wood floors and rugs of the room far above, but sand covered much of it, and the sun had burned most of the color away.

Jay looked up and saw where he had come from, a hole in the sky about fifty feet above. The stairs disappeared into darkness within the hole. He needed to get off the landing to have an angle to really see what was above the hole, but he knew it would be open sky. If he hadn't seen Supriya create holes like this, he would've thought himself mad. As it was, this type of thing was becoming a standard phenomenon of the Between.

He took the folded FAQ pages out from his pocket and leafed

through until he found the overview for the second world and the section talking about the staircase.

Gameplay Note

The trick to finding the staircase leading down to the third world (The City Above) is to always move in the opposite direction of the rocks. In other words, keeping the rocks behind you. The location and size of the rocks shifts from turn to turn, a mirage feature of the Gray Waste. Ignore this and continue heading in the opposite direction.

Deep in the Gray Waste, players are likely to encounter ash dogs, scorpions (small and giant), sidewinders, and scoured riders. Be cautious of circling vultures, because they will lead the scoured riders to you.

"Would've been nice to have brought sunglasses," Jay said with a scowl, hands cupped over his eyes as he scanned along the horizon for the rocks described in the FAQ. In the heat-rippled air, every direction looked the same. How was he supposed to walk in the opposite direction of the rocks when he couldn't find the rocks in the first place? "Would be nice to be wearing something other than MOTHERFUCKING BLACK!" He unbuttoned his shirt halfway and tried to fan out some of the heat and sweat that made his clothes cling to him from head to toe. Paul had given him a single, measly water bottle. In two gulps, Jay swallowed its entire contents.

He tried looking at the notebook page again and the glare on the white paper brought tears to his eyes. Wind whipped across the plat-form, but instead of bringing any relief from the heat, it felt more like the exhaust blasting out from a big machine. He crumpled the page and threw it. The little ball of paper fluttered and flew like a living thing, and in a matter of seconds, it vanished in the indistinct distance.

"Probably not the wisest move, there, Jay," he said to himself. The paper had told him one last thing—in the absence of rocks, only one direction made sense: the one that kept the biting wind at his back.

He hitched his bag over his shoulder and set out after the long-gone ball of paper, out into the desert.

———

With each step, his foot sank into the sand, and the sand seemed to push him back. It might've been like walking in fresh snow, but Jay wouldn't know. In his 30 years of life, he'd only seen snow on the rare occasions when it fell in Austin. More common was freezing rain, and ice on the roads and sidewalks.

Walking in sand was nothing like walking on ice.

Ice. His heat-delirious mind grabbed onto the word.

Frozen rain. Frozen water.

Water.

With his bottle now empty, every thought seemed to wind-up focused on water no matter where it began. All his sweat was gone. That couldn't be a good thing. Ahead he saw a grayness in the hazy air, a grayness that looked more substantial when he didn't look directly at it. Could it be the rocks? He looked over his shoulder, wondering where the staircase was, but it had been out of sight for who knows how long. Only the grayness interrupted the uniformity of sand surrounding him. He walked toward it knowing that if it was, in fact, the rocks, he was doing the opposite of what he was supposed to do.

But he had to know.

The grayness seemed to always stay disappointingly off in the distance. Before long, he stopped looking up, and just trudged on. And then he was almost on top of it.

It was the staircase. The grayness in the distance was the same fucking staircase he had come from.

He stepped up onto the platform and collapsed against the iron rail. Above him, the darkness called, where the sun couldn't reach him. Surely Paul and gang were already on their way down, and before long they'd find him here, dead, at the bottom, having accomplished nothing.

The knife in its sheath pressed in against his ribs, reminding him that it was there. The knife offered another way out. Instead of dying of thirst, delirious in the sun, he could wrap both hands around the handle and pull it into his heart. It would be easy. The knife would do most of the work itself.

The knife wanted to give him one last gift.

He didn't remember pulling it out, but here it was, now, in his hands. Did he even have the strength left to lift it? How was it moving?

The point was resting against the flesh of his chest, a little slit cut between the embroidered flowers of his shirt. The warm trickle of blood.

If he let the knife do its work, he'd never have to ask Big Cal for money again. He'd never have to watch his business finally fail like he knew it eventually would. Like everyone knew. He wouldn't have to keep pretending to anyone, most of all to himself.

The littlest effort and the knife would take it from there.

He looked up, wishing he had a single tear left to shed for himself, but he had nothing left. One more deep breath. One more rise of his chest, and then, when it fell...

At the last second, some part of his mind resisted, recognizing what was right before his eyes that the rest of his mind had become blind to. The rocks. Maybe a mile out but there, solid.

He pushed himself to his feet and slid the knife back into its sheath. Where had his sudden energy come from, or had it been there all along? Had the knife wanted him to succumb?

The real question was where the hell the rocks had come from? Had they been this close to the platform before? He looked up into the hole in the air where the stairs spiraled away into darkness. Was this even the same staircase?

It didn't matter. Nothing mattered but pushing on. Wherever the rocks had been, they were right in front of him now. He stepped off the platform, the rocks at his back, and once again set off into the sand.

Ash dogs, like he and Paul had encountered back in the Patchwork World, stared at him from atop a dune near the rocks, but after a chorus of scraping-metal howls, they vanished. The rocks themselves never seemed to get any farther away, and every hundred steps or so, he had to check their position and adjust his course. The FAQ had prepared him for that. The FAQ also said to avoid taking too long, because vultures would begin circling overhead, and those vultures would bring what it called the *scoured riders*.

Jay squinted at the sky above and saw the dark masses of large birds in their languid spirals. And then to his left, atop a dune, a lone figure on horseback.

He looked back at the rocks and then forward into the nothingness ahead. If he had seen a second platform, with stairs leading down, he would've pushed on. He would've done as common sense and the FAQ instructed. Instead, he turned toward the rider, and energy seemed to flow from the knife into him. The energy of coming death.

"That's a nice cloak you have," Jay muttered through his dry, cracked lips, waving his most friendly wave at the figure. "Mind if I take it off your corpse?"

CHAPTER 30
SKULL GIRL AND THE PARKING GARAGE

The tall grass fanned out around Supriya like a nest or a womb, cradling her as she slept. The blood on her *gardistaro* gown had sloughed off, leaving the pristine white of its silk. The skin of her chest, though, was caked with the dark red evidence of the gunshot wound. The blood had run over her collarbones and around both sides of her neck, drying into a necklace.

Paul wanted to wipe it off, to wipe away the damage he'd done. What had happened to the bullet wound? Had it turned to scar, now, or was the dried blood covering only smooth skin?

Her body quivered and she let out a whimper. She turned her head into her shoulder and her eyes pressed tightly closed to lock out whatever nightmare was chasing her. Paul had tried to wake her, softly at first, but even water poured onto her face couldn't pull her out of whatever strange sleep she was in.

"You're wasting time," Corinne said. She started tearing apart her makeshift shelter and stuffing supplies into a bag she'd made with a stretch of canvas and rope. She hadn't looked at Paul when she spoke, hadn't really looked at him since Jay left.

"Sorry." He went back to work constructing a sled he hoped would allow them to drag Supriya and the supplies until she woke up and could either create one of those gateway things or walk herself.

He still didn't understand why Corinne had changed her mind and decided to help. He'd asked but she hadn't responded, which made the question dig into his mind.

In the silence, a ringing in his ears began to grow, a metallic film leftover inside his skull from the ringing of the bell. He worked his jaw left and right, felt the crunch and pops below his ears, but the ringing kept growing. The knot he'd been tying to hold together the framing poles of the sled came undone for the third time. So he began talking, filling the silence with his own voice. Corinne made no indication she was listening, but she didn't tell him to stop, either.

He talked first about the days and nights he had spent at Jay's family ranch when they were young. The good times, nothing about the well. Driving four-wheelers on the dirt paths cutting through the brush. The cougar they saw one night slink from shadow to shadow not more than fifty feet ahead. The staccato barks and howls of the coyotes. The arrowheads they found. The bones. The curved fragment of skull they were certain belonged to a Comanche warrior killed by a tomahawk. The paths that Big Cal had said were carved into the earth by the *travois* made from teepee poles dragged behind the Native Americans as they traveled from place to place. Big Cal was probably full of shit, but it was those stories that had given Paul the idea of making this sled.

"I'm sorry I'm rambling on over here," he said, testing the way he'd tied the corners of the canvas to the poles. It looked like it would hold. Hopefully. He looked up at Corinne. "Why did you decide to help Supriya, anyway?"

"I'm not helping Supriya, I'm helping you," she said. "This place is going to kill her, one way or another, but I don't want that to be your fault. I don't want it to poison you, like so much of my past has poisoned me."

Her words hung in the air. He waited for her to say more, but she continued quietly gathering supplies and putting them into her makeshift bag. When the bag was full, she set it down next to him and started tying another corner of the canvas to the travois frame. For the next several minutes, they worked wordlessly next to each other, until she said, "It would've been, what, trigonometry with Mrs. Blair?"

He looked at her, confused. "Trigonometry? Mrs. Blair? Oh yeah. Sophomore year."

"I do remember you," she said, "but just barely. It could be the power of suggestion, though. You have such a vivid memory of me that maybe I've invented a familiarity--a false familiarity--of you. I'm a pleaser through and through. One of my many fatal flaws. I do recall Jay, even though we weren't friends. How could anyone forget Jay?" She stopped tying for a second and finally made eye contact with Paul. "Do you remember me breaking my nose?"

"No," Paul said. "I would remember that."

"Hmm. Maybe if we'd dated I guess it wouldn't have happened. Shit. If I hadn't broken my nose... My broken nose set everything else in motion." She moved to look down into her bag and began sorting through the supplies, not really accomplishing anything as she continued talking. "It happened in 6 a.m. basketball practice. Good ol' Coach Bernwater. Coach Burns-when-I-make-water. Coach B. I remember her telling me that, maybe, sports involving balls weren't my cup of tea. This was right after missing one of her high-velocity chest passes, while blood from my nose was pooling all over the wooden floor in front of me.

"I hated 6 a.m. basketball practice. And Coach B was right. Now, I'm sure part of her motivation in saying that was passing the blame off on my inadequate reflexes and not her trademark howitzer passes, but that's neither here nor there. Maybe you should try ballet instead, she told me. She didn't know the first thing about ballet, because only a sadist would send a 5'7" girl with weight issues toward ballet. I consider this the single worst advice I've ever received.

"In three years, I went from not knowing how to pronounce *fouetté en tournant* to landing a full scholarship to OU's Marjorie Kovich School of Dance. Yeah, Oklahoma has one of the best dance programs in the country. Who'd have thought, right?

"I knew two things before ever setting foot in Norman, Oklahoma:

1) that I had a natural affinity with dance that couldn't be taught, and 2) my body was not cut out for that shit.

"I grew almost three more inches after committing to Kovich at age 17. Yeah. How many 5'10" ballerinas do you know of? I compensated by controlling the one thing I could---my weight. My lunches consisted of bowls of lettuce sprinkled with water in the place of salad dressing.

"Bulimia: check. Anorexia nervosa: check. Think of my insides like a tangled mess of obsessive-compulsive and competitive tendencies. Imagine it as tangled bramble and brush, and ballet as fire. At no point did I ever enjoy ballet, but my natural talent, and my desire to be good at something--irrespective of what that something was--conspired against my better judgment and health." She paused briefly. "I hope I'm not boring you with this."

"You're not boring me at all," Paul said. "Keep going."

"Where was I? Ah. At my final show, shortly after accepting a position with a relatively prestigious New York dance company, I blew out my Achilles tendon in a *grand jeté*. A move I had done thousands of times. The thousand and first was too much for my body, I guess. The company dropped me, leaving me with a useless degree and an eating disorder that has haunted me every day since.

"At 23, I married a 52-year-old gallery owner who reminded me of my ballet instructor—abusive and condescending but always pushing me to better myself. The marriage lasted a little less than three years, and by the end, you could add painkillers to my list of addictions. Vicodin. Lorcet. Lortab. That's where it started.

"I did get one good thing out of that marriage. My blog. I had started it for the gallery. At first, it was just about us and the upcoming shows and pieces. But then I wrote a few posts on trends and up-and-coming artists. It got kind of popular, for that type of thing, anyway. It probably wouldn't have led to anything, but a stock trader who dabbled in art speculation noticed that artists I highlighted tended to get follow-up profiles on popular general-interest blogs. You know *BoingBoing*, right?"

"Nope."

"No? At the time, it was one of the most popular sites on the internet. I have no idea if it's even still around. Anyway, this stock trader noticed that pieces from my highlighted artists tended to quadruple or more in price when they made the quantum leap to *BoingBoing*. He suggested I publish a premium newsletter that contained my newest finds a couple months before they hit my blog. The stock trader was thinking purely about his own best interests, but I consider the newsletter thing to be the single best piece of advice I've ever received. The money-making scheme eventually fizzled, but I ended up with a print magazine, a staff of eight, and a pretty damn good setup.

"Until it all fell apart. Which of course, it had to. All good things, right? And that's how I ended up here. The hydrocodone wasn't cutting it anymore, so I moved on to Dilaudid, crushing it and snorting it. When I ran out of doctors who'd give me refills, I started buying from quote-unquote friends. I was shooting up with heroin, still convinced it was because of the injuries from dancing.

"The magazine was on life support. Finances were awful. I had already let half of my employees go. One of the artists I highlighted back at the beginning, Carlos White, well, he had become huge, rolling in money, and he was gonna bail me and the magazine out. Actually, he was going to buy it, and just absorb the losses. Carlos had that kind of money. I kept telling him not to. I mean, of course I wanted the magazine to survive, but I didn't want it to be because of pity. He didn't see it that way. It was a karma thing. He was weirdly spiritual. I guess Carlos saw the losses as like a tithe thing. I don't know.

"In the end, I was gonna let him do it. What else was I gonna do? We had this costume party planned. A relaunch of the magazine at his house up on the cliffs overlooking the city. But two days out, he had a heart attack and died. His estate didn't want to continue with the deal. Maybe if I had a lawyer I could've made them, but the party was already canceled, and, anyway, how could I take Carlos's spiritual-karma-thing and force it on his family? No, the magazine died with Carlos.

"I got the call while I was standing at the top of a parking garage, high as a kite, looking over the city. It was probably midnight. All the cars were gone. I had ridden my bicycle to the grocery store to buy costume makeup and champagne for the party. It was around Halloween, and I, of course, had waited until the last minute to figure out my costume, so I was stuck with whatever I could find at the grocery store. I found some white powder and halfway decent costume makeup. Some artificial flowers. I decided to dress in a *Dia de los Muertos* costume. The Mexican Day of the Dead. I guess that makes me *Santa Muerte*, Our Lady of the Holy Death.

"So I get the call, and Carlos is dead, and the party's off, and the magazine is dead, and I've already called my quote-unquote friend, because all this means to me is that I can't get my next fix. And this friend's got it all worked out. Money's no problem, he says. Just come by and he'll hook me up in exchange for a favor. I know exactly what he means, and it doesn't even faze me.

"I look out over the edge. I'm maybe six or seven stories up. I come here often to look out at the city. But this feels like the last time, the last moment of clarity. I think about jumping. Instead I decide to open the bottle of champagne and just sit there drinking it all. A farewell to Carlos, to the magazine, and to whatever my life had been.

"I don't really think about how the champagne is warm and how it had bounced around in the basket of my bicycle. When I open it—yeah, you guessed it. It goes everywhere. The cork hits me right between the eyes—between the fucking eyes—and I drop the bottle. Bang. Shatters right at my feet.

"I'm crying and laughing at the same time. I'm crazier than if I had drank the whole bottle. And so, do you know what I do? I get out the makeup, and I paint my face. Up there at midnight, with a little mirror from my purse, sitting on the concrete edge of the garage. I do a magnificent job. This, see? I couldn't do this with my makeup mirror at home and spending hours, but I do it up there like it's nothing.

"I get on my bike to ride home. I coast down the ramps of the garage, taking the turns wide because there's no one there but me, and the wind feels so strange on my painted face. I keep coasting.

When I get to the ground floor, I don't want to ride out into the night. So I keep going down. The garage has a few floors underground. I don't know how many. I've never gone down there.

"I pick up speed. I'm feeling reckless, like the bike could slip out from under me at any time, and the recklessness and the wind on my painted face make me want to go that much faster. One floor. Two. Three. Four. Five. I'm not even paying attention to how strange it is that it goes this deep. Not until ten, at least. Then it's another several before I finally stop.

"Why would they build so many floors underground? I worry for a second about having to climb back up, but it's not too far down yet, and I see an elevator. More than anything, I'm curious. So I get back on my bicycle again and let gravity take me deeper.

"At fifty floors below I'm convinced I'm insane and imagining this, but I keep going. At a hundred I finally stop again. I should be terrified. Something's wrong, obviously, and I'm aware of it, but somehow I'm distant from the part of me that's afraid. Maybe it's the costume. I don't know.

"I try the elevator, and it doesn't work. Now the scared part of me is screaming, but I don't want to listen to her. I can hear her voice struggle, her throat tearing from all the maniacal, animalistic certainty-of-death screaming, but my painted skull face, my painted bone jaw smiles its bare-teeth smile.

"I can't climb the hundred flights of stairs or ride up the hundred ramps. Not with this malnourished body. So the only way out is down. I get back on and vow not to stop until I reach the bottom.

"And you know what I found at the bottom because you found it also. And Supriya, and the others before us. I found a door that led here."

CHAPTER 31
DOWN THE GRAND STAIRCASE

Paul hated to break the shared silence, but he could feel doom, somewhere off in the distance, drawing closer. "I think we need to get going."

"Shit," Corinne said. "Why'd you let me ramble on like that?" She walked over to Supriya, who was asleep on a folded cloth. "Help me move her." They set Supriya on the rope webbing of the travois, and Paul started to use the loose ends of the rope to tie her down.

"I guess I got lost in your story, also," Paul said. He wanted to say more, something to at least acknowledge what Corinne had just shared, but the words and the feelings were a jumbled mess in his head. And Corinne had regained her steely demeanor. The walls were back up.

He stepped into the open triangle at the top of the travois, squatted and gripped the wooden poles, and then stood, the weight settling into his shoulders. "Better than carrying her, but I don't know how long I can do this. My left leg is a mess, and she's not what I would call a small lady."

"We can take turns. Let's go," Corinne said and then pulled open the door to the sitting room.

Paul dragged the travois, loaded with Supriya's weight, the backpack, and a bag of Corinne's supplies. The travois worked remarkably well across the tall grass, sliding with ease. Years of his own weightlifting and pull-ups had given Paul a strong grip, but that could only last so long. It would've been easier if one of them could've put on Supriya's gown, taken on the role of the *gardistaro*, and made gateways as needed. Assuming the artifact wasn't keyed to Supriya somehow, and cross-dressing aside, the thought of taking on a role, of replacing some part of his identity, made his stomach turn. Since Corinne hadn't volunteered, he wasn't about to ask, to offer a powerful drug to a recovering addict.

The wooden rods rubbed the doorframe, causing Paul to strain to pull the travois through. "I guess we didn't count on the frame spreading because of the weight," he said to Corinne, but she didn't respond, focused instead on moving the sitting room furniture out of the way.

When they reached the staircase leading down, Paul gently lowered the travois and stretched out his fingers. Supriya shifted a bit, her breathing catching for a second before settling back into its slow, unconscious rhythm.

"Now for the fun part," Paul said. He inspected the staircase's rails and glanced down into the darkness of the spiraling center. "How far down did you say it goes?" he asked Corinne.

"Don't know. A long way."

With her white makeup and full costume, he couldn't see any of the familiarity of the young girl he once knew. He stared at her, wanting her to say more, not sure what about, but more than the three-word sentences since she had finished her story.

"Maybe it's better off not to know," he said. "This is going to suck. I need you to help me get her on her feet." He had a vague idea of how he wanted to carry her—across both shoulders, a fireman's carry —but no clue how to get her there. In the end, brute force won out, but he used far more energy than he had wanted. He felt every bit of Supriya's dense, muscular body settle into his shoulders and spine. The metal rod of her prosthetic leg seemed like a good thing for him to hold onto, but at its cold touch, he pulled his hand back. What if he accidentally pulled the whole prosthetic off? So instead he contorted her on his shoulders until he could grab her right ankle. If he wasn't careful, Supriya's *gardistaro* dress would end up covering his face.

Corinne went first and pulled the now-lighter travois behind her, slapping down on each step. Paul walked to the first step and let out a long breath. With both hands holding Supriya behind his head, he wouldn't be able to use the railing. He already felt her weight threatening to pitch him forward. If that happened, he'd have no way to stop the fall without dropping her.

He took the steps one every three seconds or so, ensuring a firm footing and taking a deep breath in between. At least they were going down and not up, he thought. After a few minutes, based on aches that had already begun in his knees and back, he wasn't so sure going down was preferable after all. A few more minutes and fatigue began to set in, lactic acid building in his shoulders, thighs, and back. All the little bites on his left leg screamed in a chorus of pain, but the muscles themselves were fine. He could ignore pain.

Years of weight training had taught him that many of the body's complaints were tied to false limits, probably serving an evolutionary role to protect against injury. The mind, with training and will, could push those complaints aside and continue. It had become second-nature to him to separate himself from his body, to push through the false warnings. He pushed through now, relying on a ritualistic process he created:

> step right down,
> exhale,
> step left even,
> inhale,
> step left down,
> exhale,
> step right even,
> inhale.

The danger with pushing through the body's physical warnings was, of course, spontaneous and spectacular failure.

"Seven-hundred and twelve," Corinne said at the bottom.

Paul laid flat on his back, and Corinne draped her robe across his face to block out the blinding sunlight. The hot, sandy wind buffeted the exposed skin of his torso and chest but he lacked the energy to do anything about it.

"Seven-hundred and twelve what?" came Paul's muffled voice from under the robe.

"Steps. I was counting," Corinne said. "Seven-hundred and twelve is hardly any."

"The fuck it's hardly any."

"Sometimes the stairs go on for days. Sometimes minutes. We got lucky. That was only about half an hour."

"I thought you said you didn't know how far down it went," Paul said.

"I didn't know. Like I said, it isn't consistent." After several seconds, she continued, "No sign of Jay, but I think I see the rocks far off that way. I hope it's not a mirage."

Paul pulled the robe from his face and tried to look out into the desert surrounding the platform, but the light was blinding.

"We need to keep moving," Corinne said. "Sorry, Paul. No rest for the weary."

Corinne took the first turn pulling the travois loaded with Supriya's cloth-covered form and the supplies. Paul kept them heading the right direction, periodically adjusting their trajectory as the rocks seemed to shift position behind them.

Eventually, they came upon a dead horse and rider. Paul knelt by the corpses and brushed away the sand obscuring the rider's features, and then yanked his hand away when he realized that there weren't more features to see. It was as if the sand had worn the rider and horse all smooth and featureless. Across the rider's neck and chest were gaping, dry gashes. The horse-thing had similar gashes on its neck and across its ribs.

"Looks like Jay introduced himself."

"I think that's the other platform," Corinne said, pointing beyond the nearby dune.

"No way can I carry her down another set of stairs," Paul said. "Not without rest." He looked behind them. The rocks somehow seemed closer than ever. "What's wrong with going to the rocks? Maybe there's shelter of some kind."

"Every minute that goes by, the *Koŝmaro* gets closer," Corinne said. "And the rocks are the entrance to the Ruins, home to the *malespiro*, another chaos role. We don't want anything to do with the *malespiro*." She pointed at the vultures circling overhead. "Besides, I know that if we stay here much longer, we'll have more of these riders looking for us."

Paul let out a deep sigh. "Tired or not, I guess it's more stairs for us."

CHAPTER 32
PILGRIMS OF THE KOŜMARO

On the opposite bank of the black river, a crowd of barefoot pilgrims had gathered, awaiting the *Koŝmaro* wading through the water. The *Koŝmaro*'s giant form seemed to shrink as it scaled the riverbank, until it was around three or four times the height of a normal man. The pilgrims surrounded it, kneeling, pressing their foreheads to the earth in its path. Postures, clothing, and faces shifted rapidly as the *Koŝmaro*'s cloud of decoherence swept over the pilgrims. They emerged, changed from its passing, bowing and crying in thankfulness for its blessing.

One persistent pilgrim shuffled alongside the *Koŝmaro*. Something about this pilgrim seemed different. She wore tattered gray robes like the others, and nothing about her features particularly stood out, but a faintly glowing halo surrounded her, visible to Min-woo's revenant. Perhaps he was seeing her soul-form shining through. Perhaps that meant she was from an outworld, like Paul, like Min-woo had been before... If that were the case, how could someone from a world like his become a pilgrim seeking out the *Koŝmaro*?

The *Koŝmaro* swatted at the pilgrim like an insect, but the pilgrim returned, ultimately kneeling directly in the *Koŝmaro*'s path. It stopped and a hush came from the other pilgrims.

The revenant of Min-woo drifted from the ferry's bow onto the shore, watching. Although nothing in the physical world seemed to touch Min-woo in his revenant form, the black river's water, only at ankle level, sent an icy wave through him. Numb and slow, he glided to a hiding spot behind a broken stone pillar.

The *Kośmaro* reached out its black hand and placed it on the pilgrim's head. Its clawed fingers curled around to the base of the skull and sunk through the skin and bone. The pilgrim's gasp lasted only a split second before her jaw hung slack, eyes wide and unfocused. The *Kośmaro's* grip tightened until the pilgrim's head came off. It raised the head and inspected it for a few seconds before it took the index finger of its other hand and scratched a spiral into the forehead. Then it pressed its finger through the center of the spiral and pulled out a writhing, iridescent human form, a form that clearly didn't share the longing for the *Kośmaro's* touch that its living counterpart had.

The *Kośmaro* threw aside the empty, shriveled head, and in its place appeared a lantern. It pressed the soul-form into the lantern, the lantern again vanished, and the *Kośmaro* walked on as if the encounter with the pilgrims had never happened.

During all of this, the pilgrim's headless body remained standing, shifting with different clothes, different bodies, and even different heads appearing while still in the *Kośmaro's* proximity. As it exited the distortion field, it remained with its last form, a woman, head intact and hairless, pilgrim's robes replaced by tattered scraps that covered little of her flesh.

The other pilgrims gathered around her, but she just stood expressionless, staring out at the winding path ahead where the *Kośmaro* walked.

Is this a body without a soul-form? the revenant of Min-woo wondered. Could I slide into it and become real again? He drifted toward it, unseen by the pilgrims. Something about the woman's body looked hollow, unlike those around her. Hollow and inviting, like he could indeed slip inside. As he reached out, the pilgrims took tools from within their robes, knives and hammers and picks, and began beating and stabbing the woman.

She didn't cry, call out in pain, or react in any way. She collapsed, and they kept up their attack until certain that her empty form no longer lived. They threw her bloodied body into the black water.

The revenant of Min-woo slid away from the pilgrims in horror. Had they known she was empty? Were they trying to destroy her before something like me came to inhabit her?

Behind him, the *Košmaro* was winding up a slope to a tall mountain. Either it had shrunk to its normal, human-size or it was much farther away than should've been possible at its current pace.

The revenant of Min-woo followed, gliding fast through rocks and ruins.

CHAPTER 33
LONG ARMS AND LONG LEGS

Jay sailed down the spiraling stairwell, chest on the wide obsidian rail, using the sole of his right boot as a brake. The darkness made it hard to tell how fast he was descending. Judging by the air blowing past him, he guessed his speed at somewhere between breakneck and suicidal. Hopefully he'd hit the bottom before he wore out his boot.

Hit the bottom? Did the rail have one of those decorative ball-things sticking up on the end waiting to eviscerate his nads? He hoped not. But if the rail just ended, at this speed he'd be like a bug hitting a windshield when he reached the third world landing. He twisted his head to get a better look at the stairs spinning up to meet him, but that caused him to almost fall inward down the stairs. He caught himself, but then overcorrected and almost fell off the outside of the rail into the empty space between the stairway and the stone wall.

I need to slow this train down, he thought, but before he pushed his boot harder into the rail, the light vanished. He pressed hard against the rail and hugged it tightly with his thighs and forearms. Everything burned. Above him, he saw the last of the candle wall sconces growing farther and farther above him. Until he was surrounded by darkness.

"This fucking place and its goddamn darkness!"

He had finally stopped. He stretched his right leg down until his foot met the stairs. Then the left. So now, what? A thousand more stairs in the dark? It was a guarantee that sooner or later he'd twist an ankle and tumble to his death.

Three steps later, the railing ended also.

"You've got to be kidding me. Pitch-ass dark, and no mother-fucking railing either? What am I supposed to do, sit on my ass and scoot the rest of the way?" He had the sudden desire to grab the knife and stab something—but the only thing that wasn't made of stone or metal was himself. "Bah!" he screamed as he sat hard on the edge of a stair. "Don't worry, Supriya! Your boy's gonna ass-scoot his way to the *Kośmaro*! Unless I ass-scoot right off the edge!"

He extended his legs toward the stair below, but the stair he was on kept extending out. He stretched and probed with his foot, expecting an edge but not finding one. He reached up to the railing, followed his hand to the banister, and then felt his way down to the stair at the bottom.

Was he at the end of the stairway? He stood and reached out to either side. He slid an inch at a time on the floor—certain there'd be a drop into an abyss waiting for him. There was always a drop into an abyss waiting for him.

After several minutes of inching around, he hadn't found any drop-offs. No walls or anything else, for that matter. He stopped and turned as if to look back at the stairs behind him, but of course, in the darkness, he couldn't see anything. He wasn't even sure he was facing the stairs.

Somewhere down below, the *Kośmaro* thing was headed this way, coming for Supriya. And every second he spent fucking around, it got a little closer.

He could hear what sounded like static coming from his left. "What the hell," he said, and he set out through the darkness toward the sound.

As the sound grew louder, light began to penetrate the darkness, until ahead of him he saw an exit. He emerged in a narrow stone alleyway lined with colorful buildings and balconies overhead adorned with hanging plants and vines. It reminded him of a place in Guanajuato, Mexico, called *El Callejon del Beso*, the Alley of the Kiss. The locals had a bullshit Romeo-and-Juliet-style legend about the place, but Jay didn't remember how it went.

A man walking by stopped and looked at Jay with wide eyes and then turned and ran, checking every few seconds back over his shoulder as if he expected Jay to be chasing after him.

Jay looked down at his black, flower-embroidered shirt and pants. The man must've recognized the outfit of the *stelisto*. *Don't draw attention to yourself*, Corinne had told him when describing the City Above.

"Too fucking late," Jay muttered. In his bag, he had the rough, sand-colored hooded cloak he had taken from the rider in the desert. He pulled it on. A couple inches of his pants showed at the bottom, the colorful flowers seeming to scream for attention. For the thousandth time, he wondered why he had to wear the goddamn costume, anyway. He considered taking his pants off right then and there and throwing them into the dark tunnel. The fucking shirt, too. But then he'd be naked except for a scratchy cloak that didn't even have buttons or a zipper or a tie-thing to hold it together.

Being naked-cloak-guy seemed a bad way to avoid unwanted attention.

He set off in the opposite direction of the man who had run away and exited the alley into a crowded square. The buildings had the teal, mustard, and salmon colors of the old-world Latin cities like Guanajuato, but the architecture was wrong, alien. The structures appeared normal at first glance, but as Jay looked closer, he noticed that they seemed too organic, like they had grown into place rather than being built by human hands, stone by stone. Where the buildings met, they intermeshed, bleeding into each other. Columns stood that supported nothing and looked like they never had. Half-arches extended off the sides of buildings into the air. One building even had a random wall with windows jutting out at an angle from its center.

Unlike the colorful buildings, the people all wore drab grays, tans, and beiges. Their skin looked almost bone white, with colorless eyes and thin lips that lacked any hint of red. Jay pulled his cloak tight and lowered his head, letting the hood cover his face as best he could. He wandered through the crowd toward the fountain at the center of the square where he'd be out of the way and could think.

When he got close enough to the fountain to really see it, vertigo rippled through him and he had to grab onto the fountain's railing to avoid falling. Water poured in streams off what looked like a stone torch at the center of the fountain, but instead of falling into a pool, the water fell into the sky and clouds.

The whole city was high in the air, hanging somehow above the green-brown land visible through pockets of the clouds. A giant figure stared up at him, chest emerging from the clouds, one hand shielding its eyes from the glare of the sun. The figure, a statue of stone by the looks of it, must've been standing on the ground far below, but that would make it a mile tall. Nothing made of stone could be so massive without collapsing under its own weight.

Like the collapsed colossus in that bitch's field. Maybe there were more of these statues all throughout the Between. Or maybe—and he grew dizzier with this thought—it was the same giant statue he had seen before, only now viewing it before it fell.

He backed away from the fountain's railing and bumped into a woman walking by.

"Uh, sorry," he said as their eyes met. The woman gave him a sour smile, and he couldn't help but grimace at her brown, rotten teeth. He tried to recover with a smile of his own. "Might wanna try a little something called a toothbrush, there, pale lady." And then, "Shit, Jay."

He was supposed to be attracting as little attention to himself as possible, and here he was not only bumping into people but speaking to them in what had to be a foreign tongue. Instead of walking on, the woman reached into a pocket and pulled out a little winding, seashell-like device that, when worn, wrapped around her ear and trailed down next to her colorless lips.

She beckoned to him to repeat his words.

"Oh, fuck me," he said before he caught himself. "I was just saying pardon me and how that's a lovely, uh, smock-thing you're wearing. It really accentuates the color of your, uh, shadow."

The woman's eyes went wide, and then she looked him up and down like livestock she was considering purchasing. She reached a hand out as if to squeeze-measure his thigh, and he jumped back. Somehow, she thought this was hilarious.

"*Zhah-zhah, go dinda, jho!*" she said, and a little mechanized voice came from the shell, overlaying her words: "Oh oh, me sexing, yes!"

"What? Me sexing, yes? What the hell does..." Jay started, backing into the railing hard enough that for a moment he thought he was about to tumble into the sky and fall through the clouds. "Oh, yeah, when I said fuck me, I didn't mean literally fuck me, you crazy, bean-toothed lady."

Her smile melted as the shell-thing translated his words.

"Not that you aren't desirable! To someone who isn't me." He tried to recover. "It was a mistranslation. Your ear-mabobber made a MISS-TRANS-LAY-SHUN. Got that? Hey. Don't get all feisty." What was he doing? Accidentally propositioning this crazy woman who looked like she was about to claw his eyes out when he was supposed to be looking for the *Koŝmaro*'s tunnel near the cathedral. That gave him an idea. "Uh, cathedral. How about church? Do you understand the word church?"

"*Gan-tho?*" she said, eyes narrowed, arms now crossed, and the shell-thing said: "Worship-place?"

"Yeah, uh, *gan-tho* I guess. Church. Do you know where the fuck, I mean, where the hell it is?"

She waited, listening to the shell's translation, and then she stepped back and spit at him. "*Dinda, gadanda gan-tho?! Dinda, gadanda gan-tho?!*" she screamed, and then the shell screamed: "Sexing in the worship-place?! Sexing in the worship-place?!"

Until now, the crowd had ignored them, but every time she

screamed, "*Dinda, gadanda gan-tho?!*" more and more stopped and stared until they had formed a little semi-circle around Jay.

The knife seemed to vibrate against his ribs. He could slash his way out of this, take the mob by surprise. He caught himself reaching for the knife. Even knowing it was the wrong decision, it still felt right.

"Nothing to see here," he said and began pushing his way through the crowd. He made his way around the corner of a building, periodically looking back. Their eyes followed, but fortunately, that was all. He kept his head down and took random turns, trying to keep to the more crowded streets and avoid anywhere he might stand out. He looked out for the cathedral, but all the damn structures looked so similar, like colorful variations of the same building.

The clock in the back of his mind kept ticking. The tunnel is in an alley near the cathedral, the FAQ had said. The crazy city was full of alleys. So far, asking for directions only succeeded in drawing attention to himself. He glanced back over his shoulder to make sure he hadn't been followed, and a pair of hats caught his eye. The hats weren't particularly odd, in and of themselves—they were just black top hats bobbing among the heads of the crowd. But none of the others wore hats. A few hoods, like Jay's, but no hats.

He watched as the hats wove their way down one side of the street and then crossed to the other, where he was. In flash openings of the crowd, he saw glimpses of the hats' wearers: both in matching gray overcoats, one considerably taller than the other, taller than everyone in sight, now that Jay noticed.

He picked up his pace and cut through a couple alleys, checking every second or two on the location of the hats. Another few turns and they were gone, assuming they were even following him in the first place. He backed into an arched doorway and tried to look casual and nonchalant, leaning up against the wall. Still no sign of the hats.

Now he was just wasting time. A building much taller than the others stood directly across from him, and it gave him an idea. He could go to the top of that thing and see the entire city.

He crossed the street and took the stairs leading up to the

building two at a time. When he got to the doors, he pulled on the left—locked—and then the right—also locked. Of course, it was fucking locked. He shook the door handles out of frustration and even considered trying to jam his knife into the space between the doors. It looked too sturdy for that, and if he wanted to avoid attracting attention, the worst possible way would be trying to hack through a door up here above the crowded street for all to see.

He put his back to the door and slid down. So much for Paul's idiot plan. For all Jay knew, the *Kośmaro* may have walked right past him while he was getting away from the crowd. Hell, it might even have caught them by now.

What was the point, anyway? Attacking the *Kośmaro* was supposed to be suicide.

Suicide.

The knife seemed to vibrate at the thought. Assuming the *Kośmaro* was still ahead of him, and assuming he could get to it in time, would it even be that bad if the *Kośmaro* killed him? If he could slow it down just enough to let Supriya--fuck the others, who cared about the others--enough to let Supriya escape, it would all be worth it. He'd never have to face her eventual disappointment, or the collapse of his business, or anyone complaining about how much he'd been drinking. He'd never disappoint Big Cal for failing to be the vicarious remedy to all of his dad's own failings.

While taking stock of all the future disappointment that could be avoided by his own death, his eyes followed the two gray splotches making their way toward him. The crowd parted, and two men began walking up the stairs toward Jay. They both wore the shiny black top hats and overcoats, but nothing else about the two of them was similar. The one on the left was tall, maybe even seven feet, with legs that seemed much too long for his otherwise normally-sized body. The one on the right was a full two feet shorter but with arms that almost reached the ground.

Jay jumped to his feet, his knife already in his hand.

"We wouldn't do that if we were you," Long Legs said. They both smiled mouths full of jagged, sharp teeth.

"We've seen boots like these before," Long Arms said.

"We've tasted boots like these before," Long Legs added.

Jay glanced down at his black, flower-stitched boots emerging from the bottom of his cloak. "You've tasted boots like this before? You mean you got kicked in the face? Is that how you got those fucked up teeth?"

A cockrat scurried next to the building, and Long Arms snatched it from what seemed to be a good five or six feet away. He held the writhing creature in front of Long Legs, who licked his lips and then bit it in half.

"We have tasted almost everything," Long Legs said, mouth full of viscera, blood dripping down his chin.

"But we have not tasted you," Long Arms said.

Jay bolted, taking all the steps in a single leap, and rolling hard on the ground. He sprinted toward the crowd, taking a half-second to see how close they were behind him, imaging a giant arm only inches away, about to grab him by the back of his cloak. What he saw instead turned his blood to ice.

Long Arms had jumped onto Long Legs's back, and they were running after him as a single, towering, four-armed thing. Long Arms was reaching out, parting the crowd in front of them, pushing people away, while Long Legs stepped over anything that got in their path. Within a few strides, they had already almost caught up to Jay.

He saw a street market to his left and cut hard toward it, hoping to lose the duo among the stands and densely packed shoppers. But before he made it there, a hand clapped onto his shoulder, spinning him sideways. He tried to slash backward with his knife. It was enough to make Long Arms let go, but it sent Jay tumbling sideways onto the hard cobblestone ground.

A man pushing a wagon full of vegetables happened to step in Long Legs's path, giving Jay a brief second to get back to his feet again. Long Legs kicked at the cart, snapping its wooden side in two and sending vegetables everywhere. The cart owner turned in anger, but when he saw his giant, two-bodied assailant, he backed away and fell into his pile of vegetables.

Another two of Long Legs's strides, and they had caught up to Jay again. A hand grabbed him by the hood, almost sending his feet out from under him. But he leaned forward and the cloak came off in Long Arms's hand.

Jay scrambled behind a cart with slabs of salted meat hanging overhead. The meat merchant took one look at Jay in the *stelisto*'s black garb, screamed in his peculiar guttural language, and dove out of Jay's way. He cut behind a flower stand and accidentally knocked over a pyramid of woven baskets. Every time he looked back, he saw Long Arms towering over the crowd, eyes locked on Jay, an expression of hungry anticipation on his face.

No matter what Jay did, he couldn't lose them. It didn't help to be the only one in black in a sea of tans and beiges, nor the shrieks and panic of the crowd encircling Jay like a halo of terror. And then suddenly he was in the open street. Ahead, at the other end of the thoroughfare, maybe a distance the length of a football field, was a towering building with steeples jutting off it like spikes and buttresses extending out in every direction except the way that made architectural sense. It had to be the cathedral, but without crowds or any obstacles to slow down his pursuers, there was no way to make it there.

He backed away from the market's edge. Long Arms's torso bobbed closer. Carts fell to the left and right, clearing a path until the stacked pair emerged. Jay backed slowly away, knife in hand. Running would be futile—they'd catch him quickly in this open stretch. Every step backward he took was one fewer between him and the cathedral. Another step back, and then another. Nine hundred and ninety-eight to go.

"The time for running is over," Long Legs said. He lifted Long Arms from his shoulders.

"The time for eating is now," Long Arms said, licking his lips with a sharp, reptilian tongue. The two of them separated and began walking toward Jay from opposite sides.

Long Arms reached at Jay, picking and prodding. Jay slashed out with the knife, but Long Arms always pulled back just enough to make Jay miss. All the while Long Legs circled closer from the other side. Their lips were bared, showing clenched spikey teeth dripping with yellow-gray saliva.

Jay couldn't win this. If he turned toward Long Legs, Long Arms would grab him, and it would all be over, but keeping Long Arms at bay let Long Legs get closer and closer. Why the fuck hadn't the FAQ prepared him for this?

The FAQ hadn't, but maybe Min-woo had. After all, how many boxing matches had Jay seen with Min-woo running commentary the whole time? Sure, boxing wasn't two-on-one, but maybe some of the fight strategies could still work. What do you do against a lanky, taller opponent trying to pick you off with jabs from the outside? You get inside.

Jay feinted toward Long Legs and then dashed at Long Arms, knife flashing out at random, to force the snake-like arms to retreat. And then Long Arms reached out and around Jay's slashes, grabbing him from behind, one hand on his neck and fingernails of the other digging into his side. For a split second, Jay thought he had made a terrible mistake, but he pushed with all his might forward and broke free. Now, a foot away from Long Arms, the tentacle-like appendages became a weakness, slow and awkward up close.

Jay cut three slashes into Long Arms's torso, like the mark of a dyslexic Zorro. He would've jabbed the blue blade into Long Arms's heart—assuming this thing had a heart in the usual human place—but a kick from Long Legs sent Jay tumbling.

He rolled defensively on the ground, expecting Long Arms's hands to already be reaching out toward him, but Long Arms was hunched over on his knees. Jay locked eyes with Long Legs and took two deep breaths before standing.

Long Legs tried to kick out at Jay, but he didn't have the same speed or dexterity that Long Arms had with his arms. Instead of attacking, Jay started backing toward the cathedral. They covered about a quarter of the distance in this stalemate. Just when Jay thought he could make it all the way to the cathedral like this, Long Arms stood and began a clumsy, pained run toward them.

Long Legs hissed at Jay and then, in two giant strides, made it back to his companion. As Long Arms climbed back atop Long Legs's shoulders, Jay turned and ran with everything he had left.

Although Jay had a long head start, the stacked pair caught up right as he reached the stairway leading up to the giant double doors of the cathedral. He looked frantically for an alley nearby, and as expected, there were several. Without slowing down, he cut hard to the left and picked an alley at random. He ducked under a steeple extending out diagonally from the cathedral and ran hunched as the alleyway grew tighter and the cathedral seemed to lean in toward the neighboring buildings. He might've felt claustrophobic, but the tight quarters made for even slower going for his pursuers. Behind him, Long Arms had dropped down from Long Legs's shoulders.

Jay rounded a corner, feeling sure he had picked the right alley—if only to escape his pursuers. But then, while checking back over his shoulder, he ran hard into a door at the alley's unexpected dead end, sending him crashing to the dirty ground. He stood up, and staggered against the door, his shoulder and head blazing from the impact. Two thick chains formed an X across the door with a large black lock at the center.

Long Legs rounded the corner, hunched over, hands on the ground in a four-legged, spider-like walk. Long Arms appeared right behind him, also moving on all four limbs.

"We smell your fear," Long Legs said.

"We soon will taste your fear," Long Arms added.

Jay took a step toward them, knife raised like the barb of a scorpion's tail. But something in the insectile way they moved toward him, and their complete lack of fear of him in his black *stelisto* outfit, of the blue knife in his hand—something told him he'd lose this fight. He spun and brought the knife down hard on the chains stretching across the door. The knife cut through one arm of the chain X with a reverberating clang. It fell away, hanging limply from the corner of the door, but the other three arms stayed in place.

Long Legs and Long Arms were scrambling toward him, too close now for Jay to cut through each section of chain, so he jabbed the knife into the lock with all of his energy and he fell into the door trying to duck away from Long Arms's outstretched reach.

The door swung open, and Jay fell in a somersault into the darkness within. He expected Long Arms to pounce on him, on his back, vulnerable on the ground, and for Long Legs to be on him a second afterward, but when he looked up he saw both backing away, heads turned from the door, winces on their faces.

"We do not like the World Tunnels," Long Arms said.

"We do not like the thing that travels in the World Tunnels," Long Legs added.

Jay looked back and saw that the door led to a dark cave extending off into nothingness. It looked like the tunnel by the graveyard mansion.

"Afraid of the dark, guys?" he said.

Long Legs's wince turned to a jagged-toothed sneer. "You will die in there," he said.

"Or you will come out, and we will be waiting for you," Long Arms added, with a matching sneer.

With all the false bravado he could muster, Jay turned his back on the duo and began walking into the darkness.

CHAPTER 34

THE MALESPIRO AND THE SERĈILO

As the revenant of Min-woo followed the *Koŝmaro* up a mountain path, it looked from its vantage point out across the underworld of the Between. It was as if a mountain range back home had been kiln-fired until the dirt and rocks had fused into a singular, brown-black whole. The underworld looked ancient and freshly burned at the same time. A gray fog hung above the Black River, but elsewhere the sky was a cloudless pale yellow.

In life, Min-woo had paid little attention to geography and wouldn't have been able to tell Everest from Kilimanjaro from Hood, but here, now, he had the sense that these mountains were familiar. Were they walking on mountains copied from an Earth like his, or was this the Earth he knew but a million years past or a million years yet to be?

The *Koŝmaro* moved in broad, deceptively quick strides, and Min-woo had to glide through open stretches of the path to keep up. The *Koŝmaro* didn't seem to notice. Its focus was on the cave that had come into view ahead at the top of the winding path.

The caves were how the *Koŝmaro* traveled from world to world. Unless Min-woo could find a way to slow it down, it would soon be in the world of its prey. Min-woo slid along the path's edge, looking for loose rocks to throw, anything he could use to distract the *Koŝmaro*.

But he couldn't find anything, and what would it have mattered, since he didn't seem able to interact with the physical world in his revenant form?

He slowed and drifted to the cliff's edge, away from the cave, letting the *Košmaro* get farther and farther away. If he couldn't slow the *Košmaro* down, following it meant being a helpless witness when the monster finally reached Supriya. Perhaps it was better to let his revenant slip off the cliff and eventually fade into the dead surroundings of the underworld.

Beyond the cliff, he saw the sunlight glinting off something in the canyon below. His revenant eyes seemed to hyper-focus, and then it was as if he was in the canyon himself instead of miles away and high above.

The Grand Staircase descended out of nothing, out of a hole in the sky above the canyon, the polished obsidian stairs and rails shining like mirrors. But some of the glinting reflections Min-woo saw hadn't been from the staircase. The reflections came from dozens of motionless, armored soldiers positioned around the staircase. They seemed to be waiting for something, hiding behind the outcroppings and fused boulders near the staircase. Two ash dogs slinked between the rocks, like lions about to attack an unsuspecting antelope. One of the soldiers had the outworld, halo-like glow that the pilgrim woman had. His armor was covered with spikes, and in place a helmet, he wore the black mask of a face that looked like it was both laughing and in terrible pain.

The *malespiro*. The name came to him from distant echoes of his living memory. One of the chaos roles of the Between. One he dreaded finding when he played the game. What was the *malespiro* doing in the underworld positioned for an ambush around the staircase?

Min-woo's focus shifted back to the *Košmaro*, which had now almost reached the cave's entrance. The *Košmaro* either wasn't aware that the *malespiro* was nearby or it didn't care. It just continued toward the cave.

A cracking sound echoed from the canyon. Min-woo returned his attention there, like jumping miles in a split second. The soldiers were all moving, fighting. Their trap sprung. Within the staircase, a smaller group, all clad in white, fought back, but they were encircled and exposed. The ash dogs snarled and attacked, their growls like grinding metal buzzsaws. The *malespiro*, armor now covered in blue flame, had pushed his way up several stairs. He raised his arms above his head and a shockwave seemed to explode out from him, sending several figures in white over the sides of the staircase's railing, landing in heaps on the pedestal below. The cracking boom made its way to Min-woo's vantage point on the cliff several seconds later.

By then, the fighting had disappeared up the staircase beyond the hole in the air. For what seemed like an eternity, Min-woo shifted his attention back and forth between the *Košmaro* and the staircase.

The *malespiro* re-emerged, dragging another figure behind him down the stairs to the platform at the bottom. The other figure, crumpled on the ground and surrounded, also had the halo-glow of an outworlder. It was a man, with short, fire-red hair, wearing robes or a cloak of white stained with fresh blood. He must be playing one of the roles, also—likely the *serĉilo*, the searcher, from the look of him.

Again Min-woo looked back at the *Košmaro*, still disinterested in the happenings within the canyon. It stepped into the darkness of the cave, and a wave of dread and failure rippled through Min-woo's revenant form.

Surely the encounter between the roles was important, Min-woo thought, but the *Košmaro* didn't care. There's always a fight, and the roles are always dying and being replaced—at least, that's how the game worked, the story seeming to progress from your perspective while playing, but from a broader view, it was the same story, repeated over and over again with only minor differences. Different actors, same plot.

In the canyon, the *malespiro* had removed the mask, revealing the face of a young girl of no more than 15 or 16 years of age. What do we have here, Min-woo wondered, his ghostly lips curving into an amused smile. To Min-woo's eyes, everything about the *malespiro* seemed to have changed, from the shape of her armor to the way she carried herself. How could he have mistaken this poisonous flower for a dull and brutish man? She sneered and lectured the wounded man on the ground before her. Despite himself, Min-woo cheered her on. So what if he was cheering for the villain.

The robed man looked up at her from the ground, slowly shaking his head back and forth. The calm disagreement seemed to enrage the *malespiro*. Her left hand became covered in blue flame, and her soldiers spread out in a circle around the two of them.

The man held a hand up as if to ask for her to wait or for mercy, but his eyes belied a different motive. He slapped his hand down on the platform, and it shook like an earthquake, knocking the *malespiro* and most of her soldiers off their feet.

So it is the *serĉilo*, Min-woo thought. The *serĉilo*, who the game described as *having the strength of many*.

The *serĉilo* jumped to his feet, less injured than he had appeared, but his last surprise was too little, too late. The soldiers surrounded him and stabbed him with their swords, beat him with their clubs, until he was dead.

Dead. Min-woo could feel the man, feel his soul-form separate from the lifeless body on the platform. And that meant...

The bell rang and the mountains shook. The *Koŝmaro* re-emerged from the cave and walked toward Min-woo at the cliff's edge. The soldiers below were pointing up at the cliff. They may not have seen the apparition floating there, but the *Koŝmaro* would be impossible to miss. It stopped at the edge of the cliff and looked at Min-woo. By now, Min-woo had grown accustomed to his revenant form's detachment from the physical world and his seeming invisibility. But the *Koŝmaro* didn't turn toward the canyon and instead continued toward Min-woo.

Min-woo slid backward. Any farther and he'd go straight off the cliff. Would he even fall? And if he couldn't touch the ground now, how could it hurt him, even if he did fall the hundreds of feet to the canyon floor below?

The *Koŝmaro*'s field of distortion seemed to grow as it came nearer. Min-woo had no other choice but to go off the edge. He fell as quickly as if he'd been made of flesh, but there was no sensation of falling, no wind rushing against his skin. He stopped suddenly when he reached the ground. The move from the cliff to the ground had felt no different than gliding two feet ahead.

Above, the *Košmaro* was climbing down the face of the cliff, like a spider climbing down a wall. Min-woo glided to the Grand Staircase. He could see the soul-form writhing within the *serĉilo's* body, still in the state of shock that follows death. He tried to reach out to it, but it was only incoherent flashes of emotion, of fear.

All of the soldiers except one scrambled up the staircase and into the hole in the air. The remaining soldier stood next to the *malespiro* and watched as the *Košmaro* reached the bottom of the cliff wall and began heading toward them.

"I almost want to stay and fight it," the *malespiro* said, her youthful voice thick with a deep south accent of Mississippi or Alabama.

The soldier responded in a strange, guttural language, but a device encircling his ear translated into a mechanized, choppy English. "The nightmare cannot be killed."

"Is that so?" the *malespiro* said.

"Come now, you must. It draws near," the soldier said.

The *malespiro* lingered a few seconds longer, staring at the approaching *Košmaro*, before she turned and began up the stairs. Then she paused and looked at the *serĉilo's* corpse and opened her mouth as if to deliver a final insult. But her face softened, and for a second Min-woo saw the young girl behind the role, not a cold-blooded killer, not the bringer of despair. Then she, too, left up the stairs.

Min-woo slid away from the stairway's platform, behind an outcropping of rocks—not that he expected to hide from the *Košmaro*. If it wanted to catch him, he was sure it could.

The *Košmaro* reached the platform and went through the same ritual Min-woo had seen down by the river's edge. It pulled the soul-form from the *serĉilo's* body and placed it in its lantern. It looked briefly in Min-woo's direction and then headed back toward the cliff and the cave entrance high above.

After it had scaled the cliff wall, Min-woo slid from his spot behind the outcropping. He stopped next to the *serĉilo*, whose corpse had become like a dried-out husk, leaving only the robe and the silver bracelet he wore looking like they had been made for someone much larger.

Min-woo recognized the snakelike bracelet as the *serĉilo*'s artifact, the Silver Spiral. In the game version of the Between, the only objects revenants could touch were the artifacts, because they somehow existed across all worlds, including the astral plane of the revenants. He reached down and picked up the bracelet. It wouldn't be any use to him, but...

The serĉilo. *The searcher. That's you.* The flesh version of Min-woo had said these words to Paul, while they huddled around the laptop in his kitchen. Maybe Min-woo wasn't so useless after all. With the Silver Spiral in his ghostly hand, he glided to the cliff and followed the *Koŝmaro*.

CHAPTER 35
TOWARD THE KATEDRALO KAOSO

Supriya felt like a papier-mâché version of herself. Again she tried to stand, but the alleyway spun and she had to sit back on the cobblestone and push her back into the wall to get the spinning to stop. Her body ached for food, but her stomach had twisted itself into a knot and didn't show any signs of easing up. Her *gardistaro*-worldsense had returned, but like her physical body, it felt paper-thin, untrustworthy. She couldn't make a gateway if her life depended on it. And it probably did.

She could feel Paul and the ghoul-woman nearby, along with the thousands of the inworlders in the City Above. The inworlders felt *lighter*, somehow. She almost thought of them as less real, but seeing them walk by the alley's exit, they looked as real as Paul and Corinne sitting next to her.

She felt another outworlder, an unfamiliar man somewhere to the north-east, high above the city, in a tower, part of the *Katedralo Kaoso*. The man was the *nenio*, a servant of chaos. Corinne said they might have to kill him to get to the Altar of the Sky.

The one outworlder she wanted to feel was, of course, Jay, who had gone ahead of them to slow down the *Koŝmaro*. Her stomach threatened to upend itself at the thought of the creature. Jay, not just as the *stelisto*, but the man of uncanny luck who had been her lover and partner-at-arms throughout the Between—Jay could find a way to conquer any challenge he faced back home or in the Between. But not the *Košmaro*. The *Košmaro* was the thing you faced after you failed.

She couldn't feel the *Košmaro*, either. Both it and Jay must be deeper.

Or Jay is dead, she thought, and this time her stomach did try to expel its contents, the water and chunks of hard, stale bread Corinne had given her.

Corinne held Supriya's hair back and wiped her mouth clean with the corner of her own robe. Supriya was too exhausted to thank her. The hard look in Corinne's eyes said she didn't want to be thanked. Earlier in the day, they had been trying to kill each other.

"We need to get going," the ghoul-woman said. "The *Košmaro* could be here already."

"It's not," Supriya said.

Corinne stared at her and then said, "You're getting your abilities back. Good. The second you can open a gateway to the Altar of the Sky, you need to do it."

Paul put his hand on Corinne's shoulder, and Supriya noticed how Corinne flinched. "She knows," he said. "We're in the home stretch." He tried to hide it, but Supriya could see the pain and exhaustion in his face. He had carried her much of the way, despite the ravaged look of his left leg and the bloodless cast of his skin. If Jay could see this, he'd have to forgive his friend, wouldn't he?

Corinne already had on a drab, sandy-colored robe, and she threw one to Paul and one to Supriya. "We're going to attract attention no matter what, but these should help. Try not to make eye contact with anyone. In fact, only look at the ground right in front of you."

Paul put on his robe, and after Supriya struggled, he helped with hers. "Not much farther, now," he said, tapping on the binder full of paper he'd been studying ever since she woke up. He had explained where the binder had come from, but none of it had made any sense to her.

With his help, she stood. As soon as he let go, she started to collapse. He grabbed her by the waist and tried putting her arm over his shoulder, but the height difference was too great. They linked arms, she leaned into him, and he, just a little, leaned into her.

Corinne looked them up and down and shook her head. "Remember what I said. Keep your heads down." She turned toward the alley's exit and took a deep breath. Another shake of her head. "Let's go."

———

Based on the cobblestone and the painted walls of the alley, Supriya expected the city to look vaguely familiar and not unlike the dense, haphazard crush of New Delhi, full of structures of beiges and teals and pinks. The City Above looked like a mutated version of her home, where the elements had metastasized into forms no person would ever build. Structures grew out of the sides of buildings like cancerous masses. Doorways led nowhere. Buildings intersected with each other, like trees that had grown through their neighbors and become intertwined as a singular mass. But for every alien architectural feature, there was also a decorated porch, an ivy-covered trellis, or a flower basket hanging from a window, giving the city a lived-in and unexpectedly hospitable feel.

At first, Supriya had kept Corinne's legs in view, focusing on putting one foot before the other, and following in the right direction, but now she relied entirely on Paul. Her walking had become more of a slow fall forward, leaning too heavily on her prosthetic leg, so that she needed Paul's grip on her shoulder to keep her balance. But he had stumbled twice already, too. They couldn't make it much farther.

Supriya's powers stayed just out of reach. Using them would be like trying to run right now. Her body would understand what she wanted to do and fail miserably out of exhaustion if she tried.

So she trudged on, focusing on each step like it was its own entire journey. When Corinne stopped unexpectedly, Paul nearly ran into her, and Supriya had to be told to hang on.

A figure in a gray overcoat and shiny top hat had been walking next to them. When they stopped, their counterpart stopped, too. He had his head cocked, trying to look under the hoods of their robes with eyes three times as large as they should've been. He sucked in air with a hiss through jagged teeth clamped tight.

Corinne said something in a language Supriya didn't recognize, voice sounding synthetic somehow.

The man's large eyes narrowed, and he replied in the same nasal, rolling language. He reached a bony hand out trying to pluck at Corinne's hood. She pulled back, but his hand darted even faster a second time, throwing her hood back entirely. He yanked his hand back as if he'd touched something scalding and began backing away, spitting out what sounded like curses, saucer-eyes even wider with fear.

He darted back into the crowd.

"Looks like your reputation precedes you," Paul whispered.

Corinne pulled her hood back in place, covering her painted skull face, and said, "He'll be back with others. We need to hurry."

CHAPTER 36
IN THE WORLD TUNNEL

Jay walked rooster-breasted away from the *ganglions*—that's what he called those assholes wearing the clownishly large top hats, with the too-big mouths and the needle-like teeth. The malformed bastards acted all tough out there when they outnumbered him two-to-one, but would they come into the pitch-black *Koŝmaro* caves? Nope. Fucking poseurs.

This attitude lasted about twenty feet, or the distance for the outside light to dim to effectively nothing within the cave; also the distance for the cave's meat locker chill to penetrate Jay's cloak, his jacket and clothes, his skin, all the way to his bones.

Maybe the *ganglions* were on to something when they wouldn't follow him into the cave... But it was too late, now. Jay took a few more steps and ran into the cold, damp cave wall.

"Ugh."

It was one thing to be brave, perhaps brave to the point of stupidity—he had a deathmarked woman relying on him, after all —bravery was one thing, but pragmatically, there was only so much he could do without his sense of sight. He remembered years back seeing a video or a newscast or something about a blind guy who learned to use echolocation to compensate for his lack of vision. The guy even rode a bicycle while making this clicking noise with his tongue and teeth, navigating successfully around parked cars.

Jay made a few clicking noises. He turned his head and made a few more. He swore he could tell a difference. He tried again, more to the right and then more to the left. Yes! He wasn't imagining it. There was a slight *immediacy* to the echo on his left. Had he echolocated a wall?

He took a few cautious steps to the right and found open space waiting for him. The cave echoed with his laughter. "Ho-hah!" Holy shit. He was a regular goddamn bat-man. Not batman, as in *the* Batman—that dude never clicked his way through darkness. He probably had a flashlight on his utility belt. Come to think of it, the damn skull-lady probably gave him something for the cave, and one of the FAQ pages Paul gave him might've had some advice on what to do at this point, but it was too late now. Echolocation from here on out.

Jay found it a bit hard to make proper clicking noises while grinning so hard at his newfound ability, but he made do. For about three more steps or so, until he ran face-first into another cave wall.

So much for the blind guy on the bicycle.

The knife throbbed against his ribs from its sheath. He put his hand on it through his cloak and told it to quiet down. The last thing he needed was the knife's bloodlust to start polluting his mind. The knife was expecting to execute a couple sacrificial *ganglions*. Jay would've liked that outcome, too, but it wasn't in the cards.

The knife's throbbing intensified, sending vibrations down his side, making his entire pelvis feel electrified. Truth be told, it felt good, deep in his balls, like it was unraveling something that needed unraveling. But it also had an itch quality, where every bit made him need that next bit more. Soon he was thinking about the veins in his forearms, thinking so hard he swore he could see the blood flowing through them despite the darkness. The knife wanted to open those veins up. Just a bit. A taste.

He grabbed the knife by its handle and slid it out of its sheath. He needed it away from his body. He held it out in front of him at an arm's full length. A line of blue hung in the darkness, so faint it was hard to know if he imagined it. Hadn't it done this before? The more he focused on the blue, the brighter it seemed to get.

In the knife's glow, he could make out the cavern wall a foot to his right. He reached out with his other hand, and he could see his fingers as they traced the surface of the rock. It was better than nothing but no substitute for a flashlight. That thought seemed to cause the glow to intensify and the field of vision to expand until the entire area around him revealed itself in a deep, underwater blue. In his hand, the knife looked like the blue-hot heart of an acetylene torch, almost too bright to look directly at.

"Well, that'll work," he muttered, and then he set out deeper into the cave.

Something about the cave looked off, and the more Jay noticed it, the more it bothered him. The rock walls were uneven—so it wasn't like something man-made had cut this tunnel from raw stone. But there was a smooth regularity to the undulations in the rock and a darkness visible even in the blue glow of his knife that suggested something of how they had been made. Had they been burned into place? What was hot enough to burn tunnels into stone?

He wondered about this as he progressed deeper and deeper into the tunnel, in part because he didn't want to think about anything else: not Supriya, still unconscious when he left; not that backstabber Paul, who was acting like he was making things right while sending his best friend to certain death; not that damn skull-lady, even if she was some version of Corinne; and certainly not the distortion monster he was on a collision course with. He really should have a plan for that thing, right? The *Košmaro* could show up at any minute within the cave—it was the *Košmaro*'s cave after all—and Jay's only idea so far was to try to stab it. He was sure that would work. As sure as he was about Skull Girl's motives.

He became so lost in his own thoughts that when he saw the

human-shaped form ahead of him, he didn't stop to wonder what it was. He kept on toward it until it started gliding backward away from him.

It's the goddamn Košmaro! his voice screamed in his head. He lunged forward, jabbing out with his knife. The thing wasn't so scary after all. It was smaller than he was and mostly transparent.

The phantom form didn't flinch away from the knife, but when the blade struck it, the air sizzled and the phantom pulled away, holding its arm to it as if it had been injured.

"Gotcha now, bitch!" Jay exclaimed, and he slashed again.

A jolt of pain coursed through the revenant of Min-woo as Jay's blue knife made contact with his ethereal form. If the phantom-essence of the revenant was an echo of emotion, its essence had been transmuted to pure pain.

The revenant drifted backward, away from the glowing knife, what he recognized as the Knife of Undoing, a thing that existed to destroy and cause chaos, a thing that could tear apart a phantom form as easily as it could cut through flesh and bone.

Min-woo accelerated away from Jay through the tunnel until he flew like a bullet being launched from a gun. The knife's blue glow dimmed and then became darkness.

Min-woo slowed and finally stopped. He had been looking for the others and had found Jay unexpectedly; more unexpectedly, Jay could see him, too, and then Jay had attacked. He was the *stelisto*, after all. He was only playing his role.

Min-woo tried to call out in the darkness toward Jay, but his phantom body couldn't move the air around him. If he couldn't speak, he wouldn't be able to reason with Jay or even to warn him about the *Košmaro*. As he thought of the thing's name, the air around him and even his own form began to shift and flash through permutations of being. As if the *Košmaro's* name was enough to destabilize reality.

He twisted around, and the *Kosmaro* was there, so close that its field of disruption had engulfed Min-woo like it was consuming him. He tried to glide back, but it was like swimming in an undertow dead set on drowning him. The *Kosmaro* hadn't as much as looked at him with its black eyes. If it even knew he was there, it didn't care.

Min-woo slid backward until he reached the edge of the *Kosmaro*'s distortion field. The harder he tried to push his way out, the more it seemed to penetrate and manipulate his form. As it was, his phantom arms flashed through a hundred different versions of themselves a second, different phantom-clothes, different phantom-flesh. He pushed harder, and something in him split apart. He flew away from the *Kosmaro* like he had been launched from a catapult, but half or more of him had been left behind. His phantom form had become so dim that even his phantom eyes could barely see it.

He had been fading away from that first moment he left the statue. And now there was almost nothing left. The bracelet he had taken from the *serĉilo* seemed to hover in the air even though he knew he held it in his spectral fingers.

Somewhere in the darkness, the *Kosmaro* was still coming. Somewhere in the other direction, Jay came as well. At the center was Min-woo, where they would collide.

Jay ran after the little ghost-thing he thought was the *Kosmaro*. Damn, it was fast. But fast meant scared and scared meant he had hurt it. With his best Arnold Schwarzenegger voice, he said, "If it bleeeeds … we can keeeel it!" It sounded more as if John Wayne had been hit in the head, but it was the best he could do while running. His mind searched for another good, Arnold-like utterance for when he plunged his knife into the thing's ghost-heart.

"Time to cut to da chaaaayse!"

"Your floating days ahr ohva, *Kosmaro*!"

He was cracking himself up on that last one as he rounded a corner right into the phantom. It flew right through him in a flash, a real-world bracelet on its arm smacking Jay right below the ear on the way. He skidded to a stop, working his jaw back and forth. One of his molars wiggled when he touched it with his tongue, and his mouth tasted of blood.

The little fucker had circled back and tried to blindside him. He was about to chase back after it when the darkness in the tunnel ahead began to roil and throb. He backed away, trying to reposition the knife and its blue light to see if it was just a trick of the dark.

The center of the darkness grew, pushing the blue light back until Jay could make out the silhouette of a human figure walking toward him. Its head nearly brushed the top of the tunnel. Jay looked up at the eight or nine feet separating his own head from the tunnel's ceiling and felt like he had suddenly shrunk.

Somehow he could see its eyes, darker than the rest of its body, darker than black, like two holes punctured in reality, open windows into space, the vacuum pulling at every inch of him. He couldn't help meeting its gaze and...

...he was outside in a version of the world where the colors had been leached away and the water replaced by thick, black oil. A tower, like a giant finger scratching at the sky, cast its dark shadow over the thousands gathered before it, statues, frozen in their agonized wails, silent but caught in their perpetual screams, each of them adding their own silent cry except the one that stood empty, hollow and ready, the one that looked like Jay, the one where he would spend a thousand eternities...

The cold floor came up to meet him as he fell backward in recoil from the vision. The little phantom hadn't been the *Košmaro*—it was fleeing the *Košmaro*! He scrambled backward, the knife scraping against the stone.

He could feel the knife burning in his hand, pushing its artificial courage up through his arm like a heroin injection. But it couldn't overcome the fear that had knocked him to the ground. In a matter of seconds, the event horizon of that thing would cross over him, extinguish the light of his knife and, and... His mind skittered from thought to thought. What the hell had he seen? Where was that and why did that statue look so much like...

He somehow got to his feet and kept stepping backward quickly enough to keep from crossing that line, the border into madness. This is what he was here for, though. Some part of his mind, in conspiracy with the knife, urged him to step into the dark, to stab at the creature at its center, but his body wouldn't cooperate. It wouldn't run like half of his mind demanded, and it wouldn't fight. So he kept stepping backward, unable to look away, sure that at any second his ankle would twist or his foot would slip on the scorched rock, and he'd never have to make another decision again.

From behind him, he heard a hollow *clank-clank-clank*. And again getting closer, *clank-clank-clank*. He tried to turn toward the sound, but his body wouldn't obey. The edge of darkness was almost upon him. He stumbled and almost tripped, and the darkness seemed to throb out in anticipation.

Again but louder, CLANK-CLANK-CLANK. He turned his head to the side, away from the giant black figure, face contorted in an expectant wince, and in his periphery, saw the phantom banging its metal bracelet against the stone wall of the tunnel. It was cheering on his obliteration.

If he was going to be devoured by the dark, he might as well take the phantom with him. The knife pulled his focus away from the *Košmaro*, arm cocked for a final killing blow, but in the half-second before he attacked, he saw the desperation in the phantom's face—a face he recognized. Paul's neighbor! The little gay, Korean guy who liked boxing and champagne! Some part of his mind recalled the phone call with Paul before he and Supriya had returned to the Between. Paul had said something about Min-woo—that was his name, Min-woo!—something about him knowing the secrets of The Between.

It didn't make sense, but it didn't have to. It was enough to pull Jay out of his lock-trance with the *Košmaro*. The phantom of Min-woo was trying to get him to follow it. He turned, and with everything he had, he sped after the dimming white apparition gliding through the tunnel in front of him. He could feel the edge of the darkness so close he could see it consuming the knife's light to his sides. Ahead he saw the daylight at the tunnel's end and the two *ganglions* with their clownishly large top hats waiting in the alleyway for his eventual return.

"Here we come, motherfuckers!" Jay screamed.

The little phantom flew out of the tunnel like a photon fired in a supercollider. Instead of colliding with the waiting *ganglions*, it zipped through their bodies without slowing down. The *ganglions*—several more had gathered behind Long Arms and Long Legs—didn't notice the phantom at all, but they did see the Viking-charging, crazed-eyed, knife-wielding man in black sprinting toward them as if he expected to rout the entire bunch through the terror of his war cry.

"Our friend is back," Long Arms said, rubbing at the wound in his stomach made by Jay's knife.

"Deep down he must want to be eaten," Long Legs said, licking his lips.

"Yes. Deep down they all do."

The two of them stepped to the middle of the alleyway and smiled with expectant, needle-toothed mouths webbed with yellow-gray saliva. Their fellow *ganglions*, each with their own misshapen elements, gathered behind them to form a *ganglion*-barricade.

"MOO! MOO!" Jay's voice came from the tunnel, arms waving like he was swatting away a swarm of insects.

Long Legs gave Long Arms a bemused look, and then his over-sized eyes went wide as tea saucers when Jay's face became visible and his words became clear.

"MOVE YOU GANGLY MOTHERFUCKERS MOVE!"

A ripple of unease rolled through the crowd of *ganglions* as the *thing* behind Jay came into sight. The darkness of the cave started to wobble, making it look and feel like the floating city itself had begun to shake.

Jay ran out with the distortion cloud at his heels. He ran through the stunned crowd of *ganglions*, still screaming and waving his arms wildly, but their attention was on the giant black figure of the *Košmaro*, which had stopped outside the cave door, looking, searching the outside world with its void-eyes.

The world within its cloud shifted through permutation after permutation. The door became thousands of doors, made of every material in every state of decay and repair. The ground flashed between cobblestone, dirt, asphalt—even open air with the clouds and earth below visible for a split second.

The *Košmaro*'s attention locked onto something beyond the *ganglions* and the buildings lining the alley, and then it was walking again in its long strides. The bell rang out as it began to move, rattling dust off every surface. The *ganglions* held their hands against their ears—one with giant ears curled under its top hat fell to the ground, hands pressed against its head in a futile attempt to keep the ringing out.

With each of the *Košmaro*'s steps, it grew several feet, until its head raised over the buildings. It stepped on two *ganglions* that couldn't get out of the way of its now-massive strides, and then it was in the courtyard by the cathedral looking directly at the woman whose soul it had been sent to claim.

CHAPTER 37

KATEDRALO KAOSO

Supriya, Paul, and Corinne moved faster now, if only because the crowds had backed away from them. Their robes didn't matter. The city knew they were here.

Two jolts struck Supriya's *gardistaro*-sense like being punched on the shoulder, and suddenly she could sense Jay, nothing about him beyond his presence, but his presence was enough. The other jolt was painful, and the second new presence festered in her awareness like an infected wound. The *Košmaro*. Both of them ahead, and close.

The bell rang out, and the city vibrated underneath them. The crowd scattered, and in less than a minute, the whole place looked deserted, abandoned. The inworlders knew what the bell meant.

"It's coming," Corinne said.

"I can feel it. Jay got here, to this world, right before it did," Supriya said. She felt Paul take a deep breath. His hold on her arm tightened.

Corinne pulled down her hood and let the robe fall to the ground. She pointed to the building straight ahead with thorn-like steeples jutting out in all directions. "That's the *Katedralo Kaoso*, but the World Tunnel entrance is nearby, so we only have a matter of seconds. Run!"

Paul and Supriya didn't exactly run, but they moved faster than she would've thought possible. With their bodies' last shot of adrenaline, they cut down a side street full of abandoned food carts that looked like a whirlwind had blown through it, and then they came to a straight thoroughfare to the cathedral.

Only, this street wasn't abandoned, and the crowd on it—with their too-long arms and too-long legs, their too-big eyes and too-big heads—was running right toward them.

Corinne slid to a stop and had her red wand in one hand, the silver in the other. Paul seemed to fall to one knee, taking Supriya down with him. The backpack slid off his shoulder, and from within it, he pulled out the revolver. He tried to get up twice before his legs stayed steady enough to let him rise.

Supriya tried to create a gateway, even a tiny, thin one to place in front of the charging crowd. Creating a gateway away from a real door was hard enough even in the best of circumstances, and now, in her weakened state, it was like she asked her body to leap from here to the top tower of the cathedral.

"I can't do anything," she said.

"It won't matter," the ghoul-woman replied. "There are too many of them."

Paul began to raise the gun and hesitated. Supriya reached out and pushed his arm up. They both had a connection to that gun, both would've liked to see it melted down or thrown into the deepest part of the ocean, but now they needed it.

A great bell rang out, too loud and too deep to be from one of the towers of the cathedral.

Supriya felt Paul's forearm tense and the revolver's hammer began to draw back. Right before the hammer fell, Corinne stepped back and lowered her wands. "Wait," the ghoul-woman said.

Wait? The creatures speeding toward them had teeth that looked like they could pull muscle from bone with the barest effort. The wrongness of their proportions, as they galloped toward them, triggered panic in every part of Supriya's body. And the ghoul-woman wanted to wait? They should've been throwing what little they had at them.

As the creatures grew near—too near now for anything but to be overrun—Supriya saw that they all had fear in their eyes as well. As they ran, they looked back over their shoulders. They pushed each other away in their panicked attempt, not to attack, but to escape.

In a flash, they had run right by.

A figure in black sprinted across the clearing in front of the cathedral. Jay? she thought. Were they all running from Jay?

"Jay!" she screamed, and then Paul was screaming his name as well. It was Jay, but instead of chasing after the crowd, he was headed off to the right of the cathedral leading somewhere in the depths of the city.

"Where the hell is he going?" Paul said.

"He's running," Corinne said. She pointed at the dark mass visible above the buildings to the left of the cathedral. A black figure the height of a four-story building stepped into the clearing. The world around it rippled through alternate versions of reality as its booming steps took it directly toward them, toward Supriya. "He's running from that."

Paul raised the gun toward the giant thing walking toward them, more an involuntary action than a belief that the little bullets could actually hurt it. He fired and it felt like someone slapped his eardrums. If he hit, the *Košmaro* showed no sign of injury. Strangely, it seemed to be getting smaller with every step until it was roughly twice Paul's height, though it was hard to tell from this distance.

Somehow that made it all the more terrifying. It became what it needed to be, and it didn't need to tower over buildings to deal with the three of them.

Corinne ran toward it. When it was about thirty feet away, she fired her silver wand. The air pulsed out in a cone, but the same blast that had sent Jay flying merely interrupted the *Košmaro* mid-stride for a half-second before it continued on like nothing at all had happened.

With her red wand, she let loose a jet of fire. But the fire became smoke, water, air, and a dozen other harmless things as it passed through the *Košmaro*'s distortion field. She jumped out of the way right as it reached her, arms in front of her face to protect against a blow that never came.

Corinne hadn't even gotten its attention.

"It only wants me," Supriya said. She tried to walk forward but Paul held her. "It only wants me! Let me go!"

Paul started dragging her toward a side street. "Sorry, but I promised Jay. Now quit fighting me, damnit, and run!"

They moved at a pace that would've made Paul impatient while walking, but it was all they could do. At this rate, they wouldn't even make it to the side street before it caught them.

Corinne hadn't given up—how many wands did she have in those robes of hers? It didn't matter; none of the blasts slowed it down until she knocked down a stone pillar directly in the *Košmaro*'s path. It stopped and turned its head toward her.

Corinne fell to her knees under its gaze. She pressed her palms against her temples as if she were trying to keep her head from exploding, and she let out an agonized cry. It walked toward her.

Supriya stopped and made as if to go back toward Corinne and the *Košmaro*, but Paul kept pulling her toward the side street. "There's nothing we can do!"

It had Corinne by the hair, had pulled her to her feet. It reached its other hand toward her face, black finger pointed at her forehead.

Something flashed in the *Košmaro*'s distortion cloud, a figure charging at the creature, flickering between appearances until it plunged a knife into the *Košmaro*'s leg. For a split second, the distortion field vanished and Jay stood there, both hands gripping his knife. The *Košmaro*'s scream was like a concussion bomb, knocking Jay to the ground, sending Corinne tumbling away. Paul and Supriya slammed into the cobblestone road, and glass everywhere, from the buildings nearby to the hundreds of stained glass panels on the cathedral, exploded.

Paul's face was on the ground. He saw the *Košmaro*'s field shimmer back into existence, saw it take a step on its wounded leg, and look like it was screaming again, but all Paul could hear was a constant high-pitched ringing in his ears.

Jay had gotten to his feet and, despite stumbling about, looked like he was taunting the *Košmaro*, backing away toward the heart of the city. Somehow he had the blue knife back in his hands. He caught Paul's eyes for a second and then waved the knife at the *Košmaro*. His lips were moving, but Paul couldn't hear what he said.

Whatever it was, it put a smug look on Jay's face and caused the *Košmaro* to walk toward him, favoring the injured leg, but still covering ground with strides twice as big as any human's.

Paul expected Jay to run, but he didn't. He feinted with the knife like he was about to attack, mouth still moving in a stream of taunts and insults. Then Jay fell to his knees, like Corinne had, under the *Košmaro*'s gaze. But there was no one to rush in and save Jay.

Somehow Paul was on his feet again—had Supriya pulled him up?—and they were moving away from the sidestreet and back toward the cathedral. Supriya was pulling him, and now Corinne had joined them too, the white paint on her face smeared with dirt and blood. With the *Košmaro* distracted by Jay, they had a narrow window to get to the cathedral.

Behind them, Paul could only see the *Košmaro* and the chaos swirling around it. Somewhere deep in his heart, something shattered, and with every step he took away from Jay, he felt more and more empty. Every bad thought he'd ever had about his friend seemed to flash through his mind.

They crashed through the gates leading to the cathedral, none of the group looking back. Only a short distance and some stairs left.

Ahead, at the front of the cathedral where the entrance should be, was a large section of overlapping wooden doors, each with their own hinges, but piled atop one another so that none of the hinges could actually work. It looked like a scab had grown on the cathedral. In its middle, an actual set of double doors had been cut, blocked by two guards in dull silver armor with black soot crosses smeared on their faces.

The broken stained glass crunched under Paul's feet as he and Supriya helped each other up the stairs. Corinne led the way. When she reached the top of the stairs, she tucked her wands into her robe and held up empty hands.

"We have to get to the Altar of the Sky," she said. A mechanized voice followed a second later in a language Paul didn't understand.

The guards stepped forward and crossed their spears. The great bell rang again, and even the guards seemed to wilt while its ringing hung in the air.

Behind them, the *Kosmaro* had finished with Jay and was headed their way. It would be there in thirty seconds, maybe less. Paul could see the tension in Corinne's shoulders and knew that at any second, the wands would be back in her hands, and they'd be fighting their way inside. He held his left hand a few inches away from the revolver's grip sticking out of his jeans pocket. It felt like the calm before a Wild West gunslinger's duel.

Behind the guards, the cathedral's double doors swung wide, and a man in a robe the color of dried blood stood in the opening, two dozen more guards behind him. The *nenio*, described by the FAQ as the Acolyte of Chaos, Herald of the Coming Oblivion.

"What have you done, Skull Girl?" the *nenio* said, eyes wide and focused on the *Kosmaro* walking their direction. "You'd turn that *thing* against my cathedral?" Several of the guards had rifles, all of which were pointed at her.

"It's not your cathedral!" Corinne yelled. "You're not the *nenio*— you're Cole Trainor from Hoboken, New Jersey! There's an exit in the Altar of the Sky. An exit, Cole! A way out! Come with us!"

Paul could feel the ground shake with each of the *Kosmaro*'s steps, shaking harder the closer it got. The next ten seconds played out in a flash in his head: There wasn't time for a discussion, Corinne would reach for her wands, but the guards would fill her with bullets before she even had them raised, and then the *Košmaro* would be on them, and the cathedral doors would slam shut.

Before the *nenio*—or Cole Trainor—could respond, a ghost-like thing flew up the stairs, through the guards, through the crimson robed man himself, and into the cathedral. Paul swore the apparition looked like Min-woo.

The *nenio* and the guards all spun to follow the ghost, and Corinne chose that moment to withdraw her silver wand and send a shockwave into the group blocking their way. They tumbled like bowling pins struck by a perfectly placed ball. And then Paul and Supriya were chasing Corinne through the gate, stepping over the *nenio* and the guards into the broad interior expanse of the cathedral.

Inside the *Katedralo Kaoso*, arches overlapped hundreds of feet above the black marble floor in angles no architect could have designed and no masons could have built. Impossible angles that looked like they grew into place, as though the arches were the bones of a giant serpent attempting to swallow itself. A great dome, like an overturned meteor crater, bubbled above the crossing of the transept and the nave, painted with scenes of destruction, death, and the empty void of space. A spiral staircase, like a skinny clone of the Grand Staircase, led from the floor to a narrow platform encircling the dome and ultimately to their destination, the tower.

The apparition was halfway up the spiral staircase and had stopped to wave to them. It was Min-woo! He had used the coin to cross the Black River and had somehow made it here. Did the notebook say anything about a revenant exiting to the outworlds? Could he return home human, as if he'd never died?

Paul looked back and saw that the guards were already back to their feet and giving chase. But then the door of the cathedral exploded inward—not the smaller, usable door, but the whole giant, scab-like thing—and the guards, the *nenio*, and Paul, Supriya, and Corinne were knocked to the ground once again. Whispering voices filled the air.

The *Košmaro* stood in the gaping hole where the door had been, turning its head from outworlder to outworlder until it found

Supriya. Guards stabbed at it with their spears and fired at it with their guns, but nothing that came within its distortion field reached it without turning into something harmless.

It smashed through columns in its way, and the whole cathedral trembled and moaned. Part of the ceiling, high up in the dome, collapsed, burying several soldiers and filling the nave with dust.

Paul slipped on the dust-covered floor, tried to get up, and slipped again. He turned to Corinne and Supriya, to yell at them to go on without him, but they had already made it to the stairs. When he turned back, the *Košmaro*, twenty feet tall, its head smashing through chandeliers, was almost to him.

Little squares of light the size of dinner plates started appearing before it, and each time the *Košmaro's* field touched one, the whole field sizzled, and the creature had to stop for a couple seconds before continuing on.

Paul made it to his feet and saw Supriya, leaned heavily on the stairs' railing, tracing the outlines of tiny gateways with her right hand. Her eyes were half-open like she was on the verge of passing out.

He reached her, and together they followed the revenant of Min-woo and Corinne up the stairs. They had made it to the catwalk at the edge of the cathedral's great dome high above the ground when the *Košmaro* reached the bottom of the stairs.

We're going to make it, Paul thought, but then the *Košmaro* grabbed the column at the center of the stairs and broke it like it was made of chalk. Without the central support, the stairs buckled, and the railing snapped in pieces. From the bottom up, it all began to fall apart. Right as the stairs fell out from under them, they jumped to the catwalk edging the dome. The last of the stairs, which had led up to the tower and the Altar of the Sky, crashed, leaving them stranded.

Min-woo's phantom glided along the catwalk's narrow, two-foot edge toward the other side of the dome where a doorway led to the outside, to the cathedral's rooftop. Maybe an external staircase was out there, a way to still get up to the tower. It was their only chance.

Corinne went first, seemingly unaffected by the open dropoff next to her. Supriya leaned against the wall of the dome, moving slower than Corinne but still making good progress. Paul took a step and made the mistake of looking down. The whole cavernous expanse of the cathedral spun and he felt himself reach for a railing that wasn't there. Every muscle in his body tensed, and he dropped to his knees. His right foot slipped off the catwalk. The rest of him would've followed had he not collapsed to his stomach first. He pulled himself inch by inch toward the wall of the dome.

He crawled forward, his mind racing *don't-look-down-don't-look-down-don't-look-down* but he couldn't help himself, and the cathedral spun once again. With each washing machine rotation, he saw the *Košmaro* far down below on the cathedral's floor, growing bigger and bigger and bigger.

Arches and columns crumbled as the *Košmaro's* night-body expanded. Walls crumbled in its distortion field. It was already half as tall as the height of the catwalk. Before Supriya could make it to the other side, it could simply reach out and grab her.

The cathedral shook, and a chunk of the catwalk behind Paul broke off and fell. The whole building was about to come down. A flash of red light came from below. Once again, Paul couldn't help himself from looking over the side, his right hand gripping the marble edge of the catwalk so tightly his fingers felt like they were going to snap.

A hundred feet below, the *nenio's* Twilight Sceptre was glowing like a tesla coil. The crimson-robed man called out, and a red bolt of light arced from the sceptre to the *Košmaro*. The red lightning struck the distortion field and broke into a thousand snaking bolts that raced around the field's perimeter. Every white surface in the cathedral shone red.

The *Košmaro* howled and spun toward the *nenio*, its shoulder knocking aside yet another of the massive columns. Part of the dome caved in and fell, taking the section of the catwalk behind Paul with it. His feet hung past the jagged end of the marble, over open air.

Ahead, Corinne and Supriya had made it to the other side. A red lightning bolt slammed into the dome right next to them, blasting a hole to the sky, but they were out the door to the rooftop.

Paul stood and tried leaning against the dome like Supriya had, forcing himself to keep moving. The next bolt of lightning he was expecting hadn't come, and neither had the great sweeping hand of the *Košmaro*. The cathedral rumbled around him and the catwalk began to tilt to the right, threatening to send him off its ledge. The building was going to collapse—it was only a question of when.

He reached the doorway to the rooftop and had to brace against its crooked frame as he stepped through to a narrow walkway leading out over a sea of the roof's stone tiles, curved and shaped like the fingernails of a giant. Ahead, Corinne and Supriya had climbed over the walkway's railing and were on all fours making their way up the steep pitch of the roof to another walkway at its spine. At the spine's far end, he could make out the iridescent shape of Min-woo's phantom waving at them from a ringed platform that had to be the Altar of the Sky.

Paul scrambled over the stone tiles. When he reached the top, he could see the entire city, stretching out for miles in every direction, its curved horizon ending in an open sky. From here, the crooked and malformed buildings looked like they had been torn from other places and heaped together.

The cathedral shuddered, and the form of the *Košmaro* exploded out of the remaining dome, growing so large its head was as high as the rooftop's spine. The whole front half of the cathedral dropped away into a plume of dust that spread out as a gray fog into the city.

The dust burned Paul's eyes, and he could no longer see anything in front or behind him. He grabbed the railing next to him and stumbled ahead in the direction of the altar. Behind him he felt a growing earthquake—the *Košmaro* walking through the building as if it were wading in waist-deep water.

The railing vanished from his hand, and if it hadn't been for Corinne, he would have run past the black stone altar and gone straight over the railing at the other end. Corinne was trying to pull the notebook from his backpack, but Paul pushed her hand away. He had the page for the Altar of the Sky in his front pocket along with the pocketknife he'd need, but he had read the FAQ entry's words so many times that he could recite them from memory. Which was fortunate, because in the dust cloud he couldn't even see Corinne and Supriya and the altar right next to him, much less read words on a sheet of paper.

Waves of dust surged toward them as the *Košmaro* neared. The rooftop trembled and crashing sounds came from all around them. He pulled out his pocketknife and cut a slit in the meaty part of his left palm. With his bloody hand, he traced a circle on the top of the altar.

A circle of light appeared next to them, so bright it burned. The dust everywhere shined with it, making it feel like the air itself had become electrified. Corinne pulled Supriya into the light. Paul's water-filled eyes could barely watch. They were there and then they were just after-images, dissolving and then gone.

He started to follow but his body locked up with the terror and certainty that he would be consumed by white-hot oblivion, that Corinne and Supriya hadn't escaped at all and had instead stepped of their own free will into nothingness. A voice, his voice, screamed to move, to dive through, and another voice, animal and sinister, laughed at him for dooming himself with indecision.

He forced his body to move but by then the roof underneath was falling away and it was too late. His hands shot out and grabbed the stone slab of the altar, but with his blood still wet on his left hand and the dust covering the altar's stone, he felt his grip slipping, unable to hold his dangling weight.

The air behind him became clear, replaced by the field of the *Košmaro*. In the distortion surrounding the creature, he could make out a fading silhouette, flickering between a thousand appearances, but every other one seemed to be Min-woo. The silhouette pressed against the edge of the *Košmaro*'s field like it was pushing from the inside surface of a giant balloon. Every flash of Min-woo's face carried determination and pain.

As the *Košmaro* reached for Paul with a hand the size of a house, its distortion field came into contact with the circle of pure light above the altar. The world shuttered and for a brief moment became like the picture on an old television set tuned between two channels.

Flash! The *Košmaro's* darkness bleeding into the light, and the light, in turn, seeping back into the darkness of the towering figure.

Flash! Min-woo's almost invisible revenant form free of the field, flying toward Paul.

Flash! The *Košmaro* with its hand held to block the light from its void eyes.

Flash! Min-woo sliding something onto Paul's arm, something silver and real and cold that makes him want to scream and pull it away but his hands are already slipping off the stone and...

...The world was replaced by a million dreams, a million flashes of another life, other lives, where he searched for answers across time and across space and across the dimension perpendicular to spacetime, the dimension interconnecting worlds, the dimension of the Between. Life after life he spent searching for what destroyed his world and everything he had known, how his world had compressed into its neighbors until what was left was an amalgam, an imitation, a smeared average of its constituents, and he, the serêilo, *was stuck overlapping beyond the mashed-together world, searching ... searching...*

Everything snapped back into place. The *Košmaro* had stepped back from the light and was now looking at Paul with its void eyes, only Paul wasn't just Paul anymore, dangling off the altar stone, grip failing. Through the thing on his arm, the cold spiral Min-woo had placed on him, Paul felt the strength of another Paul, and another and another, ten Pauls, a thousand Pauls, enough so that the *Košmaro's* void-stare couldn't destroy him, enough so that the altar's stone compressed and cracked under his fingertips until he felt his grip tighten into the stone and his body become light as a feather.

The *Košmaro* reached toward him, sweeping its distortion field over him, and he pulled himself up with his many-Paul strength, or maybe he tore the altar down toward him, or the altar fell, and every-thing fell, but his feet were on the altar's edge where his fingers had pressed into the stone like it had been soft clay, and then he was jumping out above the open air, his body shifting sickeningly in the *Košmaro*'s field, shuttering through permutations that destroyed and remade his psyche over and over and over as the black fingers curled to grasp him, air rushing by as he fell headfirst into the light, into oblivion.

CHAPTER 38
HOUSEGUESTS

Paul crashed into the darkness and tripped over something that groaned with the impact. His momentum carried him into what felt like a wall, and then heavy objects started crashing down on his back, his shoulders, his head. Books, piled on him and around him.

As he pushed and dug his way out, he heard moans from nearby, barely audible over the ringing in his ears. He probed around the floor in the dark with his hands. Every movement felt smeared, with overlapping Pauls mimicking his actions. It had something to do with the cold spiral wrapped around his left forearm, that thing from Min-woo...

Min-woo! His ghost—what the game called his revenant form—had escaped the *Košmaro*'s field, but what had happened to him afterward? Had he made it through the light as well?

Paul's hands searched until he felt a body moving on the floor. Someone's shoulder and bare neck, covered in a layer of powder and grit. Long hair tied into a knot.

"Supriya?" he whispered. "Corinne? Who is this?" He tried to find her other shoulder and help her up.

A hand smacked his arm.

"Let go. I'm fine." Corinne.

From a few feet away, a heavily accented and *gardistaro*-smooth voice said, "What the hell is all over me?" Supriya.

"They're books," Paul said. "We're in the false library behind my house. We're home." It wasn't really their home, just his, and he wished he had said something else. "Min-woo? You there, Min-woo? Jay?" Their names hung in the darkness. He had seen the final collapse of the cathedral. The altar falling. He had seen Min-woo's revenant faded to near invisibility. He had seen Jay buy them the few seconds they needed to escape the *Košmaro*.

Somewhere to his right Supriya groaned and stood. "Maybe they're right behind us."

"Maybe," Paul said. Maybe there were other Jays and other Min-woos in worlds like theirs, connected to the Between. But his Jay and his Min-woo wouldn't be coming back. Were he and Supriya and Corinne really back? He made a silent promise to Jay and Min-woo to grieve for them later and began waving his arms around until he found the ladder. "Sit still for a second. I'm going to ... uh..." Make sure there's a door at all? "I'm going to open the door." The door to my backyard, he thought. My backyard.

At the top of the ladder he could feel the rusty, pockmarked metal of the door. It was every bit as heavy as he remembered, and for a brief second, he felt himself smearing again, becoming many Pauls. But he pushed the others away—he couldn't have explained how— until it was only him again, only Paul alone lifting the door.

The orange glow of the bug zapper. The light-polluted, starless night sky. The neighbor's swingset peeking over the fence. The bleeding, fluorescent glow coming from the kitchen window of his house. The smothering heat of the central Texas night.

At the top, knees on the grass of his yard, grass whose smell he knew even though he hadn't known he knew it until now, he held his right hand out and helped Supriya climb to the top and exit. Corinne ignored his outstretched hand.

Together they all stood under the crescent moon covered with dust, gray like statues.

"Leave the door open," Supriya said. "In case they survived and find a way back."

Corinne looked at him, and he met her expressionless gaze. Then she looked at the spiral on his forearm and her lips curled into a snarl. "Where did that come from?" Instead of waiting for him to answer, she walked to him, grabbed his arm, and held it up to see the spiral more clearly in the moonlight. She dropped his arm and tugged at the side of Supriya's dress. "Neither of you will ever be free until you get rid of these artifacts. Maybe we should try burning the dress."

Supriya gave her coldest *gardistaro* stare and said, "Over my dead body."

"That's one way of doing it."

Paul stepped between them. "Don't start this shit again. People we care about are gone"—*Dead! They're fucking dead, Paul!*—"and we barely escaped. This is my goddamn house, and in my house, people aren't allowed to kill each other. Besides, according to Min-woo's journal, we can't exit our roles by taking off the artifacts. We'll have to figure something else out."

"You can do whatever you want," Corinne said. "I'm going back."

"What?!" Paul exclaimed. "After all that, you're going back? Why would anyone in their right mind want to go back into the Between?"

She walked to the back of the house and started pacing its exterior like she was looking for something. "First, I want one night of good sleep in a real bed. In the morning, I'll give you a list of things to pick up for me at the store, starting with a pair of sunglasses. The midday sun is brutal in the field. Then I'm going back. Ah, here we go."

He heard a staticky noise and the sound of something sliding across the grass. It wasn't until the spray of water hit him in the face that he realized she had turned on the garden hose.

"Holy shit that's cold!"

"Yeah, well, we can't go into your house looking like this."

Two minutes later, while it was Paul's turn to hose down Corinne, a thud came from somewhere in front of the house. A car door shutting. The light coming from the kitchen window grew brighter, and then Julie opened the back door, still in her cocktail dress from the fundraiser.

They stood, dripping in silence as Julie looked at each of them in turn, opening her mouth as if about to speak, and then with a little headshake, moving her focus to the next, and repeating the process like she was stuck in a loop of confusion. "What, exactly, am I looking at, Paul?" she finally said.

He eyed Corinne with her skull makeup melting down her face and then Supriya with her wet *gardistaro* dress leaving very little of her muscular body to the imagination. Both women shrugged as if to say, you're on your own, pal. Over Supriya's shoulder, he saw the open iron door. He pointed at it. "We came from down there."

Julie's confused half-smile melted. "Where did the dirt go? Is this a joke?"

Paul winced and said, "The good news is I'm not crazy. The bad news is we really do have a portal to the shadow realm, as you called it before, in our backyard. I hope you're in the mood for houseguests."

CHAPTER 39
YOU CAN'T ALWAYS GET WHAT YOU WANT

In his exhaustion, Paul should've fallen asleep the second his head hit his pillow, but now, in the small hours of the night, he stared at the ceiling while memories of the Between exploded in his mind like fireworks in the night sky. For some reason, the Rolling Stones song "You Can't Always Get What You Want" accompanied the vignettes, but the song was playing at triple speed, looping over and over and over again.

He supposed Corinne and Supriya had finally fallen asleep—in separate rooms of course, so they didn't kill each other in their sleep. Hopefully neither was sneaking into the other's room with a pillow primed for suffocation.

Julie, next to him, was making the little chuckle-snores he had first heard that night back in... After the...

He couldn't string together a coherent thought from one end to the other. Was that a scratching sound he just heard? In his mind, he saw a little bucktoothed cockrat gnawing on the baseboards. His ears strained to hear the little *click-click-clicks* of its rat nails walking on the wooden floor of their bedroom, but the only sound was the high-pitched tinnitus ring from the destruction earlier that day. He tried to ignore the ringing but it seemed to get louder and louder.

He looked at Julie, with her eyes closed and her mouth hanging open, a tiny shudder in her shoulders with every snoring breath. They had spent almost two hours sitting on the bed, with him recounting the events starting at Min-woo's demonstration of the command-line game in the kitchen. He expected his voice to crack and for emotion to overtake him as he explained how he and Min-woo had gotten separated in the graveyard and how the junk metal skeletons swarmed on Min-woo like insects. But the sadness felt removed, or rather locked away where it couldn't come out, and he heard his voice continue unaffected. He had, throughout the story, glanced down at the *serĉilo*'s artifact wrapped around his arm. His voice didn't sound different to his own ears, and the words he used were all his, but his feelings were wrong, somehow. It was as if all of his emotions had been weakened or in part replaced by curiosity. When Julie's own eyes teared up, Paul found himself, instead of consoling her, wondering if the authenticity of her reaction was due to her trust in him or because of all the circumstantial and supporting evidence.

It all, eventually, had been too much for Julie to take in, and she stopped him after he contemplated, at length, whether Supriya's revival absolved him of his crime of killing her. Julie had turned away from him and curled into a fetal position with her head half-buried in the pillow. She didn't pull away when he held her, and she eventually fell asleep.

His mind kept asking question after question.

As he climbed out of bed, the moonlight leaking through the blinds glinted off the *serĉilo*'s artifact on his forearm. Julie had asked about it, and he, truthfully, said he didn't think he could get it back off, not without a lot of work, and she had left it at that. He didn't tell her that he didn't want it off, even knowing that it tied him, somehow, to the Between.

He shuffled toward the kitchen, where he knew he had a supply of antihistamines that, under normal circumstances, could quiet his monkey brain like a tranquilizer dart. Whether any amount of medication could offset the personality-warping effects of an artifact from the Between was anybody's guess. His left leg had gone stiff, and the softer he tried to walk the more noise he made, the decades-old floor slats squeaking as they rubbed together under the weight of his footsteps, the pier-and-beam cavity of his house's foundation acting like an echo chamber.

In the living room, he bumped into *First Mother*, which he mistook for one of the gangly, fang-toothed creatures from the City Above. Adrenaline and the *serĉilo*'s multiplicity filled him with even more unwanted energy. He lifted the statue and carried it through the kitchen to the back porch, where, without a second thought of the thousands of dollars at stake, he threw it toward the open door leading down beneath the ground. The statue missed, the buffalo head snapping off upon impact and rolling under the bug zapper to stare back at him.

Was it laughing at him?

Come back down, Paul Prentice. Come back and be with me.

Nope. Nope. Nope. I'm done with this, he thought. This is all in my head, and I'm shutting it down. He walked through his yard, keeping the hole in sight and as far away as possible until he reached the severed statue head. He rolled it like a soccer ball with his bare feet, avoiding touching it near its carved mouth on the off chance it decided to bite him, and he kicked it down into the hole where it landed with an echoing thud. For good measure he closed the iron door, letting the *serĉilo*'s bracelet add another two or three Pauls worth of strength so that he could set the door softly into its concrete frame.

Back in the kitchen, he shook three pills from the antihistamine bottle into his hand. In the act of tossing them into his mouth, he caught the laptop out of the corner of his eye, and before he knew it, he was spitting the pills into the sink, the chalky, half-dissolved pill coatings leaving little pink swirls in the sink's moisture.

He didn't want to sleep, as much as his body needed it. He wanted answers.

The laptop flashed to life after he lifted the lid, and he brought up the command line terminal. What had Min-woo typed? Simu-inter-something. There was a .hu at the end and a port number. 6's? No, 4's.

After several minutes of failing to reconstruct the URL, he remembered that he could hit the up arrow to recall the last command that had been entered.

>TELNET SIMULATO.INTERLA.HU:4444

He hit enter, and after five cursor blinks that seemed to take a minute a piece, text began to scroll up the screen.

WELCOME TO THE BETWEEN

I CAN'T LET THE OTHERS KNOW ABOUT THE OPENING UNTIL I UNDERSTAND IT MYSELF. IT MAY BE THE BIGGEST DISCOVERY OF MANKIND. I'VE COMPILED ALL OF MY NOTES INTO THIS SIMULATION. I'M LEAVING NOTHING TO CHANCE. ONE WRONG MOVE AND I COULD END UP DEAD. BUT IF I MAKE IT TO THE BOTTOM, PAST THE BLACK RIVER AND THE BELL TOWER, SOMETHING GREAT IS WAITING FOR ME. I KNOW IT. ETERNAL LIFE?

NAME OR [ENTER] TO START NEW DESCENT:

What did it mean by *the opening*? Paul looked out the window at the line in the yard where the iron door reflected the bug zapper's orange glow. Supriya's opening had been a misdirected elevator. Corinne's had been a door at the bottom of an impossibly deep parking garage. He read the description on the screen again. It was infuriatingly short, but every piece of it connected back with his own experience.

...end up dead...
...the black river...
...the bell tower...
...into this simulation...

...this simulation...

...simulation...

He started a new game—a new simulation—using his own name, Paul, for his character. He tried to pull up the FAQ in a browser window, hoping for a more updated version than the tattered notebook that had returned with him in his backpack, but all his web searches of "the Between" turned up were a Canadian television series and a novel from the 90s. Adding search terms like *Hungary*, *alternate worlds*, *Esperanto*, and *multi-user dungeon* didn't help. In frustration, he closed the browser window and tried to ignore the quiet laughter coming from somewhere deep in his mind.

Over the next hour, he barely moved any part of his body besides his hands, typing commands on his laptop keyboard, his eyes dissecting every line of poorly translated text. He started cautiously, but a run-in with the *stelisto* ended his first game before he even crossed the five-minute mark. Had this *stelisto* been another person, like him, sitting behind a computer, or had it been a programmed part of the game?

He pushed back from the kitchen table and stared at his computer like it was an alien artifact. Was there some deeper connection between the computer game and the real, physical worlds of the Between that he had just escaped from? It seemed impossible, but there had to be some connection, right? Did one mirror the other somehow? The more he tried to make sense of a connection, the more his head ached.

Learning how to play the game is the game, Min-woo had said. Maybe the only way to find answers was to keep playing. He leaned over his laptop and started a new character, another Paul, and then set out again into the ascii world. Other than a vague need for answers, he couldn't say what, precisely, he was searching for. He tried to become the *stelisto*--it had been easy enough for Jay to do it accidentally--but without finding the prior player of the role dead, he had to kill the incumbent himself, which proved to be exceedingly difficult. Each time he encountered a role character—the *stelisto*, the *malespiro*, the *masinisto*—they killed him with the barest of efforts.

He dug through the notebook, but there was so much information, so many pages. His delirious mind searched for answers to questions that hadn't fully coalesced into meaning. He speed-read the
descriptions of location after location, looking for anything that
would add sense to the previous days. He died—or, more accurately,
the ascii character version of Paul died—over and over again, but all
the deaths taught him was that the Between could kill you at a
moment's notice.

His eyelids drooped, the green text on the screen starting to float
around and lose focus. He lost track of where he was. Some part of
his mind knew he was in a room that needed the door shut behind
him. Was something chasing him, something laughing? His fingers
tried to type the right command.

>CLSOE DOOR
    Do what to the door?

>CLOSE DOR
    You see no "dor" to close.

>CLOSE DOOR
    The heavy door shuts with a thunderous boom.

The word *boom* snapped into focus so suddenly that he swore he
heard and even felt the door close. His whole body had flinched, and
the physical reaction shook him out of the semi-delirious trance he'd
been in. Had he started falling asleep? Had he slipped into that space
where dreams overlap waking perception?

He looked around his kitchen. Nothing looked different than
when he sat down an hour or more before, but a part of his mind
nagged him that something had changed. He looked through the
window at the bug zapper, illuminating the back corner of his yard
with its Halloween orange glow. Had it flickered? Gone off and then
back on again? He stood, and a queasy wave ran through his body,
causing him to hold onto the table with both hands. He looked below

the bug zapper to the dull reflected line of the iron door. The reflected line seemed to have moved, its angle wrong.

The chair behind him crashed to the floor, and it took a second before he realized that he had backed into it. He looked at the screen and then back out into his yard. The description on the screen hadn't triggered a sound in a dream. The sound had been real.

The iron door was open.

It had to be Jay. Before he knew it, he was outside, running toward the hole. His mind was imagining a scene, some number of years in the future, where they were having beers at a bar, trading stories of their time in the Between, and Paul was buying one for Jay to make up for chasing after Corinne without him, and Jay was buying one for Paul for saving Supriya. Maybe Supriya was there also. And Julie. Who knew. In the flash of the future, the only certain thing was the feeling that this whole episode ended and they somehow moved past it. Paul wanted to fast forward to that moment.

The bug zapper flickered and went out.

The animal laughter in his mind started up again.

Paul stopped about twenty feet from the hole and felt in his pocket for his phone, which he had left plugged in on the table next to his bed. He couldn't see the hole anymore, and if he kept walking forward, he'd risk falling in.

"Jay?" he said. The weakness of his own voice surprised him.

No response. Somewhere among the night-sounds of the wind and the crickets and the highway a mile or so away, he heard a sound that didn't belong. A *creak*.

Another *creak*.

And another.

Someone climbing up the ladder.

He called out Jay's name again and noticed that his own shadow had vanished into the darkness. He looked back over his shoulder, and his house was just a dark area butted against the starless sky. Where was the kitchen light?

Like the bug zapper, it had gone out. The streetlights, too.

creak

creak

He said Jay's name once more, barely a whisper as he backed toward his house. The only light was the pale sliver of moon hanging over the trees like a scythe, and that sliver had turned red, a red edging toward a diseased brown. Whispering voices came from all around him, too quiet to make out anything except his own name repeated over and over. *Paul Prentice. Paul Prentice.* The darkness in front of him seemed to disconnect with the space it should've occupied, as if he now stared into an abyss drawing him in, like forward had become down, like the world around him had become concave, tilting into the darkness.

Despite the dark, he could see its hand reach out of the hole.

Despite the dark, he could see it pulling itself up and out until it stood in the grass, the top of its dark silhouette rising above the trees, whispering voices now filling the night air.

It looked at him and he tried to turn away but...

...he was pulled toward the iron statues, toward the one that wore his own pain-wracked face under the gray sky of the underworld, under the shadow of the bell tower, stretching its clawed peak toward the dimming sun as if its touch would extinguish the light and bring a darkness more complete than the oily black depths at the bottom of the river, and his stat-ue's cold iron pressed against him, crushing him into the thing that was in the hollow statue with him, the laughing thing made of bone and rotten flesh, breath of sulfur, the carcass that he'd carried with him in his mind since the well now with its legs wrapping tighter and tighter around him, humping with animal frenzy, laughing as it shook him, as its bones dug through his flesh and its disease wormed into him, pushing deeper into him until the statue compressed his body fully into it, until nothing physical of him remained separate from Cadejo's *laughing carcass, until he became one with the laughing carcass, and all that was Paul was an endless stream of pain and agony slipping through the iron threshold, the darkness welcoming and devouring his stream of pain for all eternity...*

The vision vanished. Someone or something was dragging him around the side of the house. In a panic, he twisted and pushed away, thinking the *Košmaro* had him, but in the sepia light of the moon, he saw a familiar skull looking down at him. Corinne. Her ghoulish skull mask had returned.

"How did it get through?" he said, scrambling to his feet.

"Same way we did, I guess," Corinne said.

From the front yard, he heard Julie scream his name. He crashed into the air conditioning unit next to his house and almost knocked Corinne over trying to keep his balance. The side gate was open, and he stumbled into the front yard where the light of the moon was so dim that he could barely see Jay's truck parked out by the street.

Julie ran to them and grabbed him by his shirt. "I couldn't get the garage door open. Corinne told me we have to leave, but the car's stuck in the garage."

He took her hand and started pulling her toward Jay's truck. "Everybody in!" he yelled, motioning to Supriya standing on their porch. Jay's Ford truck had a numeric keypad on the side, and Paul knew the code: all 7s. The keys were under the driver's floor mat, as usual. It wasn't until he had them in the ignition and began turning the key that Paul realized the interior lights hadn't come on when he opened the door.

No clicks. No studders. No wheezes. Nothing.

"Shit! Everybody out."

Outside the truck, Corinne stepped between Paul and Julie. "Take Supriya," she commanded to Julie, "and keep moving and don't stop until you fall over. Do you understand? Now, go!"

Julie turned to Paul, but before she could say anything, the side of their house collapsed and a void began making its way through the rubble.

"Go!" Paul screamed. As soon as Julie and Supriya started down the street he turned to Corinne. He held his forearm in front of her, the Silver Spiral shining too brightly to just be reflecting the light from the moon. He could feel other Pauls overlapping, bleeding through from their outworlds, becoming—for a moment—one with him. "We can fight back!" One Paul could do nothing to the *Košmaro*, but what about ten, a hundred, a thousand?

"It won't matter, Paul! We can't stop it!" She pulled her red and silver wands out from her robe. "But maybe we can slow it down!" She pointed the silver wand at the void, and a shockwave rippled through the air, tearing apart half the remaining structure and sending debris into the air.

Paul looked down at his empty hands. Corinne's wands would do little to the *Košmaro*, but at least they were something. He ran to the brick mailbox with a vague notion of tearing it from the ground and hurling it at the *Košmaro*, like a comic book hero. He grabbed its boxlike form by its edges and pulled. The harder he pulled, the more he felt other Pauls converging, until he was five and then ten Pauls. Instead of breaking free as a whole, the mailbox came apart in his hands and he had to jump out of the way to keep the loose bricks from landing on his feet.

He ran to Jay's truck and with the strength of fifty Pauls tore off one of its doors. He hurled it at the darkness where the right half of his house used to be. When the door entered the *Košmaro*'s field, it flickered through a dozen forms before becoming part of the darkness.

The night boomed with each of the *Košmaro*'s steps. The next-door neighbors' windows shattered. A cone of flame erupted from Corinne's red wand, briefly illuminating the night like a little sun, but even the light couldn't pass through the *Košmaro*'s distortion field without being warped and consumed. And then Corinne fell to her knees, wands dropped to the grass.

He started to run toward Corinne, to pull her free of its stare like she had done for him only minutes before. What else could he do? No amount of strength could slow the *Košmaro* down. But maybe strength wasn't the *serĉilo*'s real power. He had an idea, and before doubt could enter his mind, and despite every instinct of his body, he ran straight toward the *Košmaro*. The heat from Corinne's wand still hung in the air, burning his lungs as he ran through its aftermath. He pulled on all the overlapping Pauls, trying to become as many of them at once as possible. When he hit the *Košmaro*'s field it felt like his skin had been torn off and replaced a thousand times in the blink of an eye, like his own skeleton had become a jackhammer rattling away within his body, but still, he kept running. With every step, his overlapping Paul-layers were torn away. He sprinted through the wreckage of the house, still with sufficient many-Paul mass to smash through debris as if it weren't there, past the *Košmaro*, until he reached the other end of the distortion field and he emerged again, stumbling into the open remains of his kitchen.

All of the layers, the overlapping Pauls, had been stripped away, leaving only the exhausted, singular him. He fought through the nausea and grabbed his dust-covered backpack. From its front pouch, he retrieved the revolver. It hadn't hurt the *Košmaro* before, in front of the cathedral. But he had fired from outside of its field. What if he shot it from within? From point-blank, with the muzzle pressed against its black body?

Like Jay had stabbed it from within.

Paul focused on the Silver Spiral and tried to pull more Pauls from their neighboring worlds. He couldn't tell, in his exhaustion, if it was working. Maybe he had destroyed every other Paul in getting here and there were no more Pauls but him. He tried looking in the revolver's cylinder, but it was too dark to see if any bullets remained.

He turned toward the whirlwind of emptiness, took one last deep breath, and...

Run to me, Paul Prentice! the darkness called and filled his head with its bone-scraping laughter. *Come to me and let me embrace the core you, Paul Prentice! Let us become one!*

Julie pulled at Supriya, collapsed on the street still in the *gardistaro* gown. Supriya's prosthetic knee had hyperextended and ruptured, sending them both to the ground. They hadn't even made it fifty feet. Whatever it was that had just torn apart their house, they wouldn't be able to run away from it.

Neighbors had begun opening their doors, calling out from the darkness within their own homes. "Someone call the police! Call the fucking army!" she screamed.

A jet of flame flashed out toward the *thing* coming for them, so hot Julie could feel it from the street. In its brief light, she saw Paul running toward the darkness, and before she knew what she was doing, she was running toward it as well. "Paul!" she screamed.

She reached her yard and the skull-painted woman—Connie? Carol? Corinne!—had fallen to her knees. Julie tried to help her up, but Corinne was staring at the creature as if hypnotized.

Julie looked up at its giant, dark form, walking through the house as if it were made of tissue, and saw Paul sprint past it, his silhouette seeming to blur until he reached the back of the house. And now Paul was running back, something in his hand—was it a gun?

She screamed at him again. What was he doing? He was going to get himself killed! She looked around, frantically searching for something, anything she could use. In the grass near Corinne was the cylinder she had pointed at the creature. The thing that shot flames.

Julie grabbed it and pointed it toward the dark figure, now only twenty or thirty feet away. But the cylinder didn't respond. "SHOOT!" she screamed. "FIRE!" Paul was close, now. If she couldn't get it to work in the next few seconds, she'd lose her chance.

She felt something *in* the cylinder that connected to a part of her she hadn't felt until this second, almost like an astral hand *within her hand* reached through the metal cylinder and touched the crystals within. As she felt the crystals, flames shot from the wand with such a force that she had to grab on with her other hand to keep it from pushing back into her.

Half of the house and a nearby tree burst into flames. Her aim had been true, but the fire seemed to vanish as it reached an invisible sphere of some kind around the creature. She let go of the crystal and the jet of flames stopped, the wand hot in her hand.

Corinne gasped beside her like she had come up from deep underwater.

The dark thing's two void eyes turned to meet Julie's.

It had been Julie—Julie!—who had used the wand this time, and now the *Kosmaro* had her in its gaze! Flame arced around Paul as he ran toward the *Kosmaro*. Even if he had exhausted the Silver Spiral's power, even if he was defenseless against the darkness, even if he was doing exactly what the laughing voice in his head wanted—he had to run into the void. He had to finish this. He hit the *Kosmaro*'s field in cold determination, and instead of fighting to hold onto himself, he let every part of his being be torn away, transformed, disfigured, remade, except the determination, until he *was* the determination, and nothing in the *Kosmaro*'s field could transform him further. The chaos of the *Kosmaro*'s field had vanished. The ground before him had turned into knee-deep water that stunk of algae and death. The slime-covered stones of the well surrounded him. At the center, where the *Kosmaro* should have been, stood the dead dog *Cadejo*, missing eyes trained on Paul, towering before him, front legs held wide offering a welcoming, final embrace. Paul ran toward it until he slammed into its rotten flesh and bone, and every part of it snapped closed around him, pressing, pressing its beating black heart into his.

We are together forever, Paul Prentice! FOREVER!

Dissolving him into it, into nothingness, into oblivion.

What was left of Paul pushed further in, until he felt the cold, black heart against him; until he felt it turning him to black, dead flesh; until there was no Paul, there was no gun, no final bullet, only the determination to drive a hole through the darkness, to rupture the emptiness so that life flooded back in.

A shot rang out, and the world of his burning and demolished home snapped back into existence, only the air was filled with the scream of the *Kosmaro*. Its field had vanished as had its eye-grip on Julie. As it clutched its chest and screamed, they all fell to the ground, wave upon wave of pain flooding from it through them, until they became its pain.

Julie couldn't have said when it ended. A minute? An hour? Corinne, next to her, looked unconscious, maybe dead. Julie stood on legs of jelly and tried to walk toward where she had seen Paul next to the thing, in the wreckage of their house. She glanced over her shoulder, expecting to see neighbors gathered to see just what the hell had happened here, but the street was as bare as a horror movie scene after the world had gone dead. The streetlights had all burst, and the only light continued to be bloody brown-red of the crescent moon.

She saw Paul, crumpled, half-covered with a chunk of what had been their roof. She climbed and crawled her way to him and pushed at the section of roof until it slid off into a pool of water and mud.

He was breathing. Short, jagged breaths, but still alive.

She wiped the dust and dirt from his lips. "Paul. Paul," she said, but he didn't answer. Something pushed against her. She shifted position and then pushed against it, thinking it was the remains of a pillar, but when her hand touched it, it felt so empty that it sucked the breath out of her.

Towering over her, the *Košmaro* stood, clawed hand clutched at its chest, its black silhouette expanding and contracting in deep, ragged breaths. The air sizzled and flickered as its distortion field snapped in and out of existence.

She held onto Paul and tried to drag him away, but the creature reached down and grabbed her, claws tearing through her pajamas and her skin. It cast her aside as if she were a rag doll.

She watched helplessly as it lifted Paul to his feet by his hair and, with the claw of its other hand, a hand dripping with its own color-less blood, scratched a spiral into his forehead. Then it took its claw and started pressing at the center of the spiral.

"Hey motherfucker!" came a voice from the backyard. Jay came strolling into the moonlight, both arms held wide like he had stepped triumphantly onto a stage, wearing some sort of Victorian military suit, with knee-high polished black boots, and a peculiar crown full of circular glass rings upon his head. "I'm back for a rematch!"

The *Košmaro* dropped Paul as metal skeletons poured out of the hatch like angry ants from a mound. A bronze blade jutted out from one of Jay's sleeves, and with a cackle, he waved the blade in the air, commanding his army.

Several of the skeletons started climbing on top of each other, almost like they were forming a pyramid. Their arms and legs began to interlock, and their bodies began to fold until they formed a single, giant metal skeleton twenty feet tall.

"You see that, Supriya?" Jay yelled. "Mega-junkling! Supriya? Where the hell is Supriya?!"

The mega-junkling bounded toward the *Košmaro*, shaking the ground with each of its steps. The *Košmaro* knocked away dozens of junklings at a time with sweeping blows of its arms, but when the mega-junkling hit, they both went crashing to the ground. Junkling after junkling piled on top and smashed down with their license-plate-clad arms. The whole thing looked like an industrial meat grinder, chopping and churning away.

The *Košmaro* cried out in a scream so deep it pulsed through the air in a shockwave. The one remaining wall of their house collapsed like all the mortar had turned to water. Paul pressed his hands against his ears, but the howl shook his skull, threatened to liquefy his brain. Through watery eyes, he could see Jay with his hands pressed against his ears as well. Julie had fallen down. Corinne and Supriya were nowhere to be seen. He tried to step toward Julie but the bones in his legs shook, and the ground kept shaking, and the world started to vibrate apart.

And then, in a flash of the whitest fire Paul had ever seen, the *Košmaro*'s death howl stopped. The white fire consumed the *Košmaro*'s distorted corpse, drops of scalding, white fire spewed out, catching alight everything they touched—a neighbor's tree, the mailbox, even a spot in the middle of the pavement in front of the house. The junklings that had dog-piled atop the *Košmaro* burned as fully as if they'd never existed.

Jay limped toward a patch of the white fire burning on the

ground, raised his foot as if to stomp on it, but then fell back as the bottom of his boot melted. From the ground, he pointed at the fire, and several of the remaining junklings ran to it and began stomping on the flame, which consumed two and a half junkling feet before it finally went out.

With the air full of smoke and the smell of burning tar, they all stood and looked at each other in turn. Mouths started to open, words started to form, but in every case, the words wouldn't come. What can you say in a moment like this, Paul wondered. And then he noticed all the neighbors.

The power came back on, and within seconds, every house on the block was lit up like it was a competition to see who could burn the most energy. Some neighbors stood on their porches. Children looked out of windows. A brave few had wandered close but were backing away. Supriya was sitting on the broken remains of Paul's mailbox, barely able to keep herself from falling over.

Paul looked from the neighbors to the wobbling junklings and then to Jay. "Can you do something about those?"

"Oh, yeah." Jay touched the side of his crown, and the remaining junklings all fell into little piles of automotive junk. "Nothing to see here," Jay said.

Sirens filled the air.

"What are we going to tell the police?" Julie asked.

Jay looked around and shrugged. "Let me do the talking."

"That's usually where the problems start," Paul said with a tired smile. "But under the circumstances..."

Corinne stepped in front of Paul and walked up to Jay. They stood there, eyeing each other like two boxers receiving the final instructions before the opening bell. When Paul started to intervene, Corinne said, "How?" She pointed at the *masinisto*'s crown on Jay's head, at the junkling scrap scattered everywhere, at the small smoking crater where the *Kosmaro* had been, and then at the iron hatch, where Jay had unexpectedly emerged minutes before. Again, "How?"

Jay glared at her, jutting his jaw out, and then broke into a wry grin. "I got rid of the knife, like you always wanted, so now we're BFFs again like in high school... Or not... Still need to work on that Skull Girl sense of humor, don't we?"

"I don't believe you," Corinne said. "You've got the knife somewhere, don't you? You wouldn't just give it up."

Jay's grin soured for a second but enough for all of them to see. He walked across the rubble to what had been Paul and Julie's master bathroom. The white porcelain toilet had survived the battle. Jay dropped the cover down, sat on it, and crossed his legs in front of him.

"So the *Kosmaro* just about had me," he said, "until the bell rang again. That was the only time I ever liked hearing that damn bell. It was calling the big warpy bastard to go after Supriya. I was about to follow it, but what good would that do? I needed a fucking army. As soon as I thought that, I remembered Supriya looking like an army general back when she was the *masinisto*, and it all came together in my head. The World Tunnel was right there. We knew about the Tunnel's exit in the cavern. All I had to do was run back into the mansion, kill another *masinisto*, and take his place." He nodded and pursed his lips. "I'm the tits when it comes to killing *masinistos*.

"When the *Kosmaro* came out of the tunnel in the cavern, I thought it'd followed me. But it went down the hatch to the Patchwork World. That's when I realized what had happened. You all escaped at the altar, but it was still on the chase, you know, headed to Paul's backyard through the phony library under the ground here. Good thing, too, because I wouldn't have known how to get back if we hadn't been able to follow it." He looked at each of them in turn. "You know the rest of the story, especially the part where I kicked that thing's ass with the mega-junkling."

Corinne studied him for a second and then looked at the gathering neighbors. "So what's the next part of your plan, Jay?"

"Easy. We play stupid."

"Good thing it comes naturally," Supriya said.

"I'm gonna pretend I didn't hear that, Supes." Jay flashed her a smile and then tried to lift her off the ground in a giant bear hug.

Instead, he ended up falling into her on the sidewalk. "Ow! My back!" He turned to her with a wink. "Nice to see you alive, by the way." Without letting Supriya go, still sitting on the sidewalk, he turned back toward Paul, Julie, and Corinne. "As for the police, I say we play stupid and say we've just got into the junkyard and propane businesses. Had a little mishap. Resulted in a series of unforeseen explosions. Should we have gotten a permit or something? Is that type of thing frowned upon in a residential neighborhood? Cops aren't gonna believe in magical junk robots or twenty-foot tall distortion monsters. They will believe we're all idiots."

"I'm convinced," Corinne said.

Paul surveyed the wreckage of their house. Blood was running down the spiral in his forehead, over his nose and lips. "So ... bail, court fees, lawyers, fines, I'm sure. What else? Damages to property. That pile of ash over there was our next-door neighbor's new car. Plus, Julie and I are out of a house. Insurance is gonna be a problem. Anyone have a spare fortune sitting around to cover this?"

Jay shot Paul his signature crooked grin. "As a matter of fact, we do. Starting tomorrow, the Sofa-ATM is open for business."

EPILOGUE

Missing Austin Man Likely Perished on Mexico's Most Dangerous Road
   Tuxtepec, Mexico

The wallet of missing Austin resident, Min-woo Kim, 42, was found near tire marks leading off a cliff on Mexico's Highway 182 overlooking the picturesque Sierra Madre Mountains. For Duane and Janey Beasley of Waco, Texas, the wallet provides a clue as to what may have happened to the son they adopted from Korea over 40 years ago. Kim has been missing since June of this year. Friend Jay Lightsey recalls Kim mentioning plans to travel in Mexico. "I tried to talk him out of it," Lightsey said, "on account of how dangerous that area of Mexico can be. But I guess we're fortunate someone found that wallet, or else we would've just thought he disappeared. So that's closure, or something." [...]

Recent Ebay Feedback for StelistoJ (739 ☆)

- *This is the best fucking deal on a sofa ever!!! A+++++ Would buy again!!!*
- *Beautiful sofa but one of the cushions smells like someone wiped their ass with it.*

Paul poured coffee into a thin, white mug that looked like the cheapest possible item that could perform its intended function. Like the $599/month extended-stay, one-bedroom motel room that had been their home for the last few weeks. Stained walls and furniture. Two parallel tears in the linoleum of the kitchen where a prior occupant had dragged something heavy across the floor. Jay had offered to spruce the place up a bit with a fancy French sofa, rug, and the rest of it, but Paul didn't want to be near anything from the Between.

The Between... According to Jay, Supriya had been greeting the new arrivals as the *gardistaro*, and she had begun to talk in riddles. Like Corinne had suspected, Jay had indeed kept the blue knife, reverting back to his role of the *stelisto*. He and Supriya were spending more time there than at home. Was this even home for them anymore? Or was it one of an infinite number of outworlds?

Was this even his and Julie's home after everything that had happened?

Julie's hand touched his shoulder, snapping him back into the present. The coffee had overflowed, and he was still pouring, spilling it down onto the laminate countertop, dribbling onto the linoleum floor. Paul mopped it up with about 50 cents worth of paper towel, mentally deducting the expense from their dwindling supply of funds. He poured a second cup for Julie and was about to pour a third, for Corinne, when Julie said, "Just the cup for me. She went back."

Went back to the Between. Like she said she would. Paul had naively believed that bringing her home would somehow save her. But this world, his world, was another kind of prison for Corinne. She had family here, but it wasn't *her* family. It was another Corinne's family. And the opiates were here. Some of her suppliers, too. And they'd be as happy to sell to alt-Corinne as their usual customer. Compared to the monsters of the real world, she chose the monsters of the Between.

Truth be told, when Paul would see her in the morning these past few weeks, without her skull makeup, looking reminiscent of the girl he once knew, once loved—when he saw her, he thought of the younger version of himself that she should've known, of the dreams he had, the dreams he would give up. It made him want to stop fighting the role given to him by the Silver Spiral still wrapped around his wrist and exit from the overly safe, on-rails life he'd built for himself. But then he'd see Julie, and he'd wonder how he could hate the very choices that had brought them together. It would all become a jumble in his head, and the only thing to do was to put on the same rumpled, cheap suit he'd been wearing every day since he returned and go into work. To work, where he'd respond to a few emails and then find himself opening a terminal window and typing in the URL of the Between. Another day would vanish, leaving more questions than answers.

He drank his coffee in a long, single swallow.

"I'll try not to be late tonight," he said. He kissed Julie's cheek and walked to the door, where he paused, door open, heat pouring in from outside. The world ahead buzzed, cars jammed together on the highway, creeping forward like a caravan of war prisoners, their guards invisible. The green in the trees had been bleached to a diseased brown by the unrelenting sun and the weeks without rain. Where am I going? he asked himself, unconsciously rubbing the scar on his forehead.

He stepped through the door and locked it behind him.

Later that morning, Julie sat in a rented Chrysler, looking at the orange netting-wrapped fence around the perimeter of their lot, their former home. Somehow none of them had gone to jail. Despite the police recognizing immediately that Jay had been full of shit. The insurance adjuster had listened while shaking his head, and they hadn't heard from him since. The only neighbors who would talk to them were suing.

She got out of the car and ignored the movement of the blinds in her next-door neighbor's window. The fence's gate was held shut with chains and a padlock, but with a little effort, she squeezed under the bottom of the fence where it crossed the concrete walkway to the house. What used to be the house.

Her blouse and shorts were covered in ash and dirt, but she didn't care. She hadn't gone to work since the thing Paul called the *Košmaro* came out of the door in their backyard, destroyed their house, and almost killed all of them. How could things go back to normal after something like that?

Paul *had* gone back to work, despite that thing on his arm. But of course Paul had gone back to work. It was the rational thing to do. Or, it was just something to do. She had promised not to come back here without him. It hadn't been her intention to break that promise, but here she was now, standing in the burned and broken wreckage of everything they had built in their lives together so far.

With the toe of her formerly white Nikes, she pushed aside a jagged stretch of stained drywall and then some insulation. A black rectangle dissolved into mush mixed with colorful slivers when she nudged it with her foot. Their wedding album. She got onto her knees and tried to pick up the album's remains, but it fell apart in her hands. The only partially surviving photograph was the one where she and Paul were pushing forks of cake into each other's mouths. The photo paper had bubbled, and the colors had muted. Holes had burned away their heads so that it looked like two headless bodies were jutting their forks into space outside the photograph.

She let the ruined photo fall from her fingers.

As the midday sun burned her bare shoulders, she dug through piles of masonry, scorched roof tiles, and blackened wood from the floors and frame of the house. Somewhere in this mess was her wedding ring. Even knowing the approximate location of their bedroom, and even finding the remains of the nightstand where she kept it, she couldn't find it. The whole while, she tried to ignore the pit of concentric circles where the *Košmaro* had died in a burst of white flame.

As the sun started to descend, with the skin of her shoulders and cheeks an angry red from the sun, she finally found her ring more by accident than anything else. She had picked up a strange clump of white plastic shaped like a bubbled cluster of insect eggs. She turned the egg-thing over in her hands and was about to toss it over her shoulder when she recognized a faint floral design that had almost vanished from the white surface, like an overexposed photograph. It was the melamine tray she had left on the nightstand, and the heat had turned and warped it into this peculiar shape. She cracked it open on the edge of the metal bed frame, and inside were a set of melted headphones, half of a paperback book, and her ring—completely unaffected by the heat and fire.

With tears in her eyes, she put the ring on and began wandering through the debris in a daze. The ground beneath her became smooth and sloped, and then she stepped on something hard with her right foot.

She looked down and found herself at the center of the *Košmaro's* death crater. She moved her foot. The late afternoon sunlight glinted off something black and shiny. A ring of onyx or obsidian.

She picked up the ring and wiped it clean of dirt. The ring was nothing like her platinum and diamond wedding ring. Instead, it looked like little petrified, intertwined vines that had grown into a circle. One of the vines seemed to glow like the filament of an incandescent light bulb, but only when she didn't look directly at it.

Had it come from the *Košmaro*? She almost dropped the ring at the thought. But the *Košmaro* had been huge, with hands like giant spider crabs. Maybe one of the firefighters dropped it, or it had been lost somewhere in the house from a previous owner.

She slid the ring into her pocket and began walking back to the rental car. Once in the car, she sat for a minute with the air conditioner on full blast, eyes closed, feeling the small weight of her wedding ring on her left hand. She moved to grab the shifter and put the car in drive and saw the circular imprint of the twisted black ring pressing through her shorts. On a whim, she took the ring out and found that it fit just perfectly on her right middle finger.

THE END

ACKNOWLEDGMENTS

I would like to thank the following people for helping me turn the mess in my head into the book you have just finished. Lindsay Leslie, my wife and best friend (as well as a brilliant children's author to boot), has encouraged and supported my writing since we first met back in art history class at the University of Texas. I have learned more from her than she will ever know. My two boys, Mars and Levi, cheered me on the entire way. I wish I had half of their creativity.

Emmanuelle Morgen spent countless hours reading versions of The Between and coached me through a much-needed rewrite that resulted in some of my favorite scenes. My Parliament House editors, Celeste Hawkins, Megan Hultberg, and Chantal Gadoury, took their knives to this manuscript and improved it in every possible way. What a team.

Many people read the manuscript and provided feedback, suggestions, emotional support, encouragement, and also whiskey. I am especially thankful for the input from Steve Yarger, Jason Boulette, Jack Conover, Nicole Elmer, Stephen Yoch, Walker Stemple, Ned Levelle, Tom Kim, Stephen Bekanich, Jason Reichenberg, Mike Chabib, Chris Pomajzl, Shawn Morgan, Tobey Forney, and Brian Nahas.

Bethany Hegedus and the Writing Barn in Austin, Texas,

provided a transformative 4-day workshop where I gained invaluable feedback and new writer friendships. After reading an early version of the first chapter, fellow attendee Heather Harwood asked me a pretty brutal question, which I paraphrase: "You've made a lot of heavy promises to the reader here. Can you make good on them, or will this be like that television series that disappointed everyone?" That awesome question haunted and drove me as I revised and revised the manuscript.

Finally, thank you, reader, for giving a new author a shot. If you liked it, send me a note of encouragement and I'll try to keep it up. If you didn't like it, why the fuck are you reading to the end of the acknowledgements anyway? Sheesh.

Did you enjoy The Between?
Reviews keep books alive . . .

Leave your review on either GoodReads or the digital storefront of your choosing.

ABOUT THE AUTHOR

Ryan Leslie oversees research for a large health system, where making stuff up is generally frowned upon. His creative outlet has always been writing fiction. He lives in Austin, Texas, with his wife, children's author Lindsay Leslie, and their two sons.

Printed in the USA
CPSIA information can be obtained
at www.ICGtesting.com
LVHW091727091123
763363LV00024B/61/J

9 781956 136760